A GIRL NAMED COCO

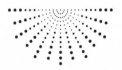

JENNIFER SPURGEON

SIGNET MEDIA LLC

To a December week in New Orleans

Imagine a camera panning over every face, every race,
Dreams, fears, hope, suffering, pain
   Are we not all the same?
   ...Everyone sets at the same table
   ...Do I have your attention?

— FOREST BLAKK -BOTH SIDES

CHAPTER ONE

THE AUGUST DAY was stifling hot and the smell of horse dung hung idle on the thick, humid air. That, however, did not stop the streets from bustling with activity. The St. Louis Hotel had opened its grand doors just two and a half months earlier, and it was there in the French Quarter of New Orleans that you would find the prestigious ladies and gentlemen of Louisiana.

"Ho." The gentleman of fine dress pulled back on his horse's reins.

A black man in a pressed butler uniform quickly approached him. "L'me take da horse here for ya, seh. Ya stayin' at da Saint Louis?"

"I am." The man dismounted and adjusted his coat.

"Den we welcome ya, seh. Ya been here wid us before?"

"Not since the reconstruction after the great fire," he responded, unlatching his small leather suitcase from the back of his horse.

"Well, den ya sure to enjoy ya'self! Yes seh! Ya get in der and get ya some of dat free lunch nah. Chef's got a new dish he calls da gumbo. I recommend it to ya, seh." The butler gave a quick bow at the waist to the gentleman, who nodded and moved to enter the white French doors.

The splendor of the grand hotel was unparalleled. A great chandler hung from the tall ceiling and the carpeted stairs on either side led up to the main lobby. The gentleman removed his hat and ran his hand over his oiled hair as he glanced around, stepping to the side to allow two women to pass.

"Ladies." He nodded. They were splendidly dress in black silks and colored satin and glittering in precious jewels—the perfect portrayals of luxury.

"Dawlin'," one of the women responded with a cheeky beam as they passed.

He watched them with a grin before he moved, light footed, up the stairs to the lobby.

"Checking in, sir?" the man behind the counter asked.

"Yes."

"How many nights, sir?"

"Just one."

The man nodded as his finger ran down the book. "Here's a room. Became available earlier today. Your name, sir?"

"Toussaint. Albert Toussaint."

"Mr. Toussaint, you will be on the third floor, room 310." The desk clerk opened a draw to retrieve a key. "You here for the auction?"

"I am."

"Very good. The auction is held in the rotunda and is from noon to three. Might I recommend finding yourself a good beverage over at our dining hall across the way, on the other side of the staircases? Enjoy your stay, sir."

"Thank ya." Albert took the key and made his way up the impressive staircase to room 310.

Pleased to find a well-furnished, lavish room, he placed his case on the bed before making his way over to the glass door leading to a private balcony. He unlatched the door and stepped out to see wrought iron railing cut in an intricate French design. The humid scent of the city hit him in the face, but the energy there was undeniable, and it made the smells and heat bearable. In the air, the sound of drums and quill pipes could be heard, played on one of the street corners below. It had an unusual but pleasant beat, and many of the white men had started calling the sound Dixieland tunes. Albert reentered his room and latched the balcony door.

After refreshing himself with a splash of water, he changed his shirt and vest before making his way down to the dining hall. The tinkering of plates and flatware created a melody of extravagance as the ladies and gentlemen chattered above the noise. The host interrupted Albert's survey of the room.

"How many in ya party, sir?"

"One."

"Would ya like a seat at da bar?"

"I would prefer a table."

The host nodded. "Right this way, sir." He led Albert to the center of the room, next to a table of four boisterous men and one astute woman.

Albert nodded to his server as he raised the freshly poured cool water to his lips and took a glance at the menu. "I need a minute, thank ya."

"Here, here now. Party must be running late," came the loud voice from the table of five.

Albert raised his water glass again. He hadn't realized how parched he'd become on his ride.

"Table of one, where there are four seats, your party must be running late," the voice from behind him sounded again.

He lowered his head before tipping it in the direction of the voice. "Are ya addressing me?"

"I am," the man said, leaning back in laughter as his vest buttons bulged around his belly. His face was a soft, cream complexion, and an auburn goatee shaped his thin smile.

"Well, ya have my attention now," Albert responded, nearly annoyed.

"No harm meant in interrupting your privacy, sir. Merely made observation of the quantity of chairs at your table and the number of its occupants. Name is Bordelon, William Bordelon. This here is Mr. Rouselle, Mr. Roup, and the young Mr. Harper, who joins us all the way from the great state of Alabama! And, of course, lest we forget to mention the ever-lovely Ms. Elizabeth Treme."

A small gleam crossed the face of the woman, too slight to be noticed by the table but detected by Albert, who nodded in her direction at the introduction.

"I'd venture to say," Mr. Bordelon continued without pausing for breath, "Mr. eh..."

Albert took a deep breath. "Toussaint."

"Mr. Toussaint! That you are here at this fine establishment for...the free lunch." Mr. Bordelon lowered his head and looked at him with a smile. His head, balding in the shape of a horseshoe, was polished so smooth that Albert could nearly see his reflection.

"There is no such thing as a free lunch," he replied flatly.

At this point, the waiter stepped up to the table. "Have you decided what you will be having, sir?"

Albert's eyes shifted under his furrowed brow as he took a deep breath, his lower jaw protruding forward. "I'll take me a plate of the oyster patties," he said handing the menu back to the waiter.

The waiter nodded, but before he could walk away, Mr. Bordelon waved his hand to stop him.

"Here, here. Let me also order a coquetier for my new friend here, Mr. Toussaint." The waiter nodded and walked away. "Now tell me, Mr. Toussaint, how there is no such thing as a free lunch when that is what you just ordered," he said, raising his glass of liquor to his lips.

"There are always strings attached. A person will drink more frequently if free lunch is included."

This drew a hearty laugh from Mr. Bordelon, and his table joined in. Albert pressed his lips together with a nod as their voices mingled in meaningless chatter. The waiter returned with an egg cup.

"Here nah. Let us toast"—Mr. Bordelon raised his cup— "to drinking more and free lunches! Cheers!"

"Cheers!" the others at the table joined as Albert raised his glass with them.

"Now, Mr. Toussaint, you said you was here…"

No sooner had Mr. Bordelon begun speaking again than Albert turned back around in his chair with not so much as a word to excuse himself. He could hear the shock and insult that it gave the man, followed by his hearty laughter and a pleasant excuse as to why "Mr. Toussaint must refrain from further pleasantries."

Albert was glad when the waiter brought the steaming tray of oyster patties. The smell of garlic, oregano, and thyme reminded him of how hungry he was, and he ate his plate with ease before ordering another coquetier. Upon retrieving his pocket watch, he reviewed the time and then paid his waiter for his drink before leaving the dining hall.

It wasn't hard for him to find his way to the rotunda; there was an increasing flow of people going in the same direction. Soon, the hall opened into a vast, majestic room encircled with archways and lined with exquisite designs. The decorative walls reached high, forming a grand dome ceiling where, at its apex, the noonday sun gleamed through the glass skylight. Three podiums, evenly distanced, were elevated on platforms in the center of the room, and that's where the auctioneers began taking their places. This was a high-end social gathering for those watching and participating. This was the auction house.

Albert made his way through the crowd. Women dripping in

jewels gathered in circles of gossip or engaged in flirtatious conversation with the richly dressed gentlemen drinking fine liquors. He stopped at a billiards table for a moment and watched the men play, until the smooth voices of the auctioneers took turns welcoming the people, one in French, one Spanish, and a third in English. Across the room, being led to the center of the auction house and onto the platform, was a strapping young black man. The French auctioneer kicked off the bidding at two hundred dollars, and the energy of the room ignited as the bidding war began. It hung for a minute on three hundred and twenty dollars before the English-speaking auctioneer put his hand up.

"Now, now, now, ladies 'n gentlemen... Only three hundred dollars I understand fa some average Negro but look here at this one. We did not save da best fa last, and I am in the understandin' that this one speaks French! I'll let him say somethin' so you can hear fa yourself. Go on, say somethin' in French fa the crowd."

"Bonjour, mesdames et messieurs." The crowd perked up.

"Go on. Say some more," the auctioneer insisted with a nod. "The more valuable you are, the better owner you'll have."

"Je serai de bon service pour mon nouveau propriétaire," the man said in flawless French as he looked out over the faces of the men and women. The room filled with the hum of shocked and excited chatter.

"See now," the auctioneer continued, "and ladies, just imagine throwin' the social highlight of the year and entertainin' your guests with a Negro that speaks French! Now, can I get five hundred dollars?" The bidding continued in a wave of female excitement as women pulled on their husband's arms to place a bid and chattered among themselves behind their silk folding fans.

One by one, slaves were led to the platform to be auctioned off.

"Sold!"

"Vendu!"

"Vendido!"

"Sold!"

Albert bought two men and had been in a bidding war for one with Mr. Bordelon across the room. William gave a hearty, belly shaking laugh when he gave in to his bid of three hundred and ninety dollars. Albert, annoyed, knew the Mr. Bordelon was only bidding to drive up the price.

"Here now we have ourselves a griffe," the auctioneer called out. "She has been trained to govern household servants very efficiently and can read and do simple mathematics. Don't let her young age fool you—you will get your money's worth with her! Starting the bidding at five hundred dollars."

Albert had turned to get another drink, but when he looked back to the platform and saw the young woman, he took a deep breath and his brow furrowed. There was something in the woman's appearance that demanded the attention of the audience. It was something more than her fine features and beautiful face. She stood with an air that spoke both of assurance and bashfulness. The bidding was at eight hundred dollars in no time. As he sipped his liquor, he couldn't help but overhear the conversation of the people behind him.

"That is Samuel LaLaurie bidding over there."

"What? Where?"

"Yes! Right over there. See? There, he just bid," the man pointed out.

"I thought all the LaLauries left the city?" the woman said, shocked. "I heard they moved back to France."

"Madam Delphine, perhaps, but that's her son, Samuel. I'm certain of it."

Albert's demeanor stiffened. The Madame LaLaurie had escaped to Paris after the discovery of her horrific abuse and mutilation of her slaves. A mob of local citizens, outraged by her illegal cruelty and torture, attacked and destroyed her mansion as she fled undetected from New Orleans. Though it had been a few years, the name LaLaurie still provoked a great rage and indignation to those who knew it.

"The audacity for a LaLaurie to show his face at the auction house—and *bidding* on slaves!" The woman sounded disgusted.

"It was his mother's crime, not his. Should he bear the judgment for her sin?"

"Blood is thick." The woman smirked.

The bidding was hung at nine hundred and thirty dollars. "Do I hear nine-forty? Nine-forty? Nine-thirty going once..."

"That poor woman, a LaLaurie slave," the female voice said quietly.

"Nine-thirty going twice..."

"One thousand!" Albert raised his bidding paddle, his heart racing in shock of his own action.

The surprised auctioneer pointed at him. "One thousand! One thousand going once... One thousand going twice..."

Albert took a sip of his liquor, hoping the man across the room wouldn't counter his bid.

"Sold," the auctioneers called out, "to bidder two-twenty-one!"

Feeling the need to step away for a few minutes, Albert turned to leave. His gaze met the wide eyes of the lady who had spoken behind him, and he pressed his lips together and gave her a nod as he walked past. After stepping to the back of the rotunda, he leaned against one of the many columns woven throughout the building. Taking out his pocket watch, he reviewed the time: 1:52 p.m.

Soon after, the same woman walked up to him. "Excuse me." Her golden-red hair was parted smooth with variations of ringlets covering her ears. A black velvet choker, from which hung a stunning gem, adorned her neck, carrying attention to her perfect collarbones. "I was standin' behind you durin' the auction."

"Yes?" He watched her as she fidgeted nervously with her lacy handkerchief.

"Well, I wanted to say thank you for your last bid."

"Why would ya thank me?"

"I feel like you may have done it outta good will."

"How so?"

"You can't tell me you didn't overhear us behind you. You hadn't bid once on her until the end there."

"My dear madam, whatever conversation you and ya husband was having did not affect my sense of business. I am here to buy slaves. I do not run a charity."

"That is not my husband." The woman gave Albert a half smile with her dreamy auburn eyes before turning, just slow enough for a good tease, and walking away.

Albert grinned as he watched her hourglass figure move across the hall. After taking a few more minutes to himself, he rejoined the bidding and, before 3:00 p.m. ended the auction, had purchased two more slaves.

After retiring to his room, he rested for a couple of hours and then cleaned himself up for a night out on the famous streets of Royal and Bourbon. The hot, humid day made for a warm, sticky evening as Albert began his walk down busy St. Louis Street. When he entered through the grand doorway of the celebrated Antoine's restaurant to a vast, glistening dining room, he was greeted by the host.

"Yes, meeting someone. Have ya seated a Mr. Menken?"

"Toussaint!" came a voice from across the room. "Toussaint, over here!" The man rose from his chair and raised his hand to get his attention. His thick, graying hair was combed smooth near its part but the unyielding curls refused to lay flat.

Albert made his way between the tables of lordly aristocrats to join his fellow bidder. Shiny chandeliers hung low, bouncing their light off the warm, red interior of the room.

"Glad you could join us!" Mr. Menken extended a hearty handshake as he stood to greet him. He pushed his round spectacles up with his forefinger as he repositioned himself onto his seat. "Let me introduce the table. John Grimes, Alex Williams, and Julien Lacroix, meet Mr. Albert Toussaint. Sit; we haven't ordered yet. We were just talking of Mr. Lacroix's vast real estate holdings." Mr. Menken raised his glass with a crooked grin, leaning his head back. "He owns a lot of ground!"

A man in his thirties, Julien Lacroix was an educated free man of color whose success had achieved him great wealth and respect in the city. His hand brushed down the front of his well-tailored, deep blue dress coat and a red neck scarf ruffled around his sharp jawline. He sat with his legs crossed at the knee.

"The Lacroix brothers have made quite the name for themselves," Mr. Menken continued as he poured a glass of Bordeaux DX for the newest guest.

"I've heard the name. Pleasure to make your acquaintance," Albert said. "I hear you are a merchant of exports. Do you deal with any local goods?"

"Only the finest," Julien said in a deep, smooth voice.

"Well then, we should talk."

"Are you local, Mr. Toussaint?" Mr. Grimes cut in raising his cigar to his lips. John was clean shaven and always maintained a relaxed expression except for the single, deep crease between his eyes, favoring his right brow. A black silk scarf printed with small, red fleur-de-lis was held in place by a red pin resembling a sharp arrow pointing upward. It was tucked into his cognac vest. A striking ensemble under his black tailored coat with large gold buttons.

"I'm not. I own a plantation in St. James Parish."

"Sugar, I presume?" Albert nodded in response. "Smart! That white gold is booming right now." John replied.

"I hear that new sugar companies are poppin' up everywhere," Alex put in eagerly. "All over the state and into Texas." His eyes shifted from John to Albert as if looking for validation of his claim.

"It is the hour of the sugarcane," Julien added.

"It's not too bad," Albert said with a smile and a nod. "It makes the wife happy and supports all of her extravagancies." The men laughed at that. "And what is it that you do, Mr. Grimes?"

"Law. I practice Louisiana law." He took another pull from his cigar.

The finest of Creole food was ordered and another bottle of wine opened as the men continued their conversation, ranging from law on subject properties to the launching of the SS *Great Britain*. At the end of dinner, one of the men suggested they go to a nearby ballroom to enjoy a game of craps. The music was lively, and the audience refined. At the back of the ballroom, the raucous gamblers and onlookers gathered to watch the dice roll against the house.

"Hi-Lo," the dealer called as bets were placed. "Hot dice!"

Albert looked up and met eyes with the same woman from the auction. She gave him a nod, and he made his way over to her.

"Do ya play?" he asked.

"Oh no, I just enjoy the banter," she responded without hardly a side glance.

"Your hand is empty. May I offer ya a drink?" Albert suggested.

"Really now, we must be careful, runnin' into each other twice in the same day like this. People will start talkin'," she teased. "White wine," she continued, her attention on the table.

Albert smirked and went to order a glass. When he returned, she said, "Thank you, Mr...."

"Albert Toussaint."

"Mr. Toussaint," she finished before placing the glass to her rosy lips.

"I didn't get the pleasure of your name."

"You can call me Emily."

"Ms. Emily, you look lovely tonight."

"Mr. Toussaint, I believe the liquor has made you bold," she baited.

"Bold and poorer. Do ya live in the city?" His blue eyes, glazed from alcohol, kept looking down to her mouth where a front tooth was slightly forward from the others.

"I do."

"Certainly ya not out alone?" he asked, and Emily gave him a side glance and a smirk. She amused Albert. Her soft demeanor and mischievous responses made for charming conversation. "I'm not saying women shouldn't be entertained with a night out. Surely the opera or theater is a more suitable place."

"I see plenty of other women in here, enjoying the music."

"Not without a party to escort them. I would think a young woman such as yourself would find an evening of dinner and a sewing circle with other ladies more appealing."

"Mr. Toussaint, a lady can find pleasure in a night out, a game of craps, or a glass of fine wine just as much as any man. Besides, I am no stranger to these halls."

"I'm sure a lady like yourself can find pleasure in many things." Emily blushed and her heart raced at his suggestive flirtation. "Would ya join me for a walk down the street a bit?"

"I could use a stroll." She finished her wine in one drink and looked at him with a smile.

Dusk had not yet given way to night when they stepped out onto the sidewalk. They walked through the active city streets in good-natured conversation until suddenly, Emily grabbed hold of his arm.

"Wait, we have to cross the street here," she said with a glint in her eye before making her way across without him.

Albert's brow creased slightly before he joined her. "What was that for?"

She smiled and motioned with her head to the other side of the street. "John Davis's. Never walk in front of that place—someone is sure to be thrown through the doors. It's full of young, rowdy men! Nearly every week there's duel in the back there. They bring pistols for two and coffee for one." She laughed, tossing her head back and making her ringlets bounce.

Soon they found themselves back in front of the doors of the Omni Royal. "Well, Mr. Toussaint, I suppose I'd better let you enjoy the rest of your evening however you see fit. It was a pleasure meetin' you."

"Ya want to come in for a night cap?"

"A generous proposal...but I must decline," Emily said politely.

"Instead of gratefully accepting? Come in," he urged gently, taking her by the hand.

Smiling softly, she allowed him to walk her inside. Albert ordered a bottle of champagne to be brought to the room, and they toasted before stepping out onto the balcony to enjoy the night. She had hardly finished a glass when he leaned in to kiss her.

"Ya want another glass?" he asked in amusement as he took in her flushed and dreamy-eyed state.

Emily shook her head. "I'll take another kiss, though."

Albert stepped up to her and, with firm but gentle hands, took hold of her. For the next few hours, they enveloped each other in human passion, finding pleasure in each other's company.

"Ya can stay the night," he said as Emily redressed in her lace petticoat.

"Thank you, Mr. Toussaint, but I believe we both have our own obligations tomorrow, and mine demands that I be home tonight."

He got out of bed as she pulled her dress up over her shoulders. "Don't," she said sharply as he was reaching for his money pouch. "I am not a paid woman. I wanted that as much as you did...

"Do you mind?" she asked, turning her head over her shoulder to look at him. He walked over to her and slowly began helping her button up the back of her dress. As he finished, Albert stretched his head forward and gave her a gentle kiss on the neck. After turning toward him, she put her arms around his shoulders.

"This was nice. You are a gentle, kind man." She kissed him again on the lips before leaving. "Mr. Toussaint," she said.

"Ms. Emily." He nodded with a smile.

After leaving the room, she paused for a moment outside his door and took a deep breath, touching her neck. Her step was light as she left the hotel.

The next morning, Albert checked out of his room as the sun was rising. He had called for his wagon and trusted slave, Foy, who had made the trip with him. After collecting his five new slaves and loading them into the back of the wagon, he mounted his horse and they began their trip back to the plantation.

It was Sunday morning, and the slaves of the city were starting to gather unsupervised along the streets and the square. The beat of the bamboulas, a native African drum, and strum of the banzas drifted in the air as the men and women gathered in circles of music and dancing.

Albert rode ahead as Foy urged the wagon forward through the streets. The five in the back bounced along without a word as they stared at each other or off in the distance, listening to the African-style music grow more and more distant as they rode toward their new home.

CHAPTER TWO

THE SUN WAS SINKING under the horizon in brilliant orange hues when Albert rode onto his plantation. The old dog the children called Dashy ran up to the trotting horse, tongue hanging out in a thirsty pant and large brown eyes eagerly waiting for a greeting from his owner. Two of the children played beneath the grand, moss-covered oak in the front yard, while Mrs. Toussaint sat on the veranda, holding her youngest and listening to their oldest daughter of age twelve, Marianne, read *The Old Curiosity Shop*. Albert dismounted his horse in front of the house and gave old Dashy a good rub behind the ear.

"Stop there, Marianne. Ya father's home," Justine Toussaint said. She put little Isabelle down from her lap, and the child made her way to the veranda steps and onto the lawn.

Albert crossed the green grass and swooped up the excited two-year-old into his arms. Justine stood at the top of the steps as the wagon of new help came to a stop. Her beige cotton dress, carefully tailored, fit smoothly and closely over the waist creating a V shape over the wide skirt, and was printed with thorn stemmed roses and raspberries. A wide, shallow neckline that was nearly off-the-shoulder revealed her soft, white complexion. Her brown hair was parted down the center and looped smoothly over the ears, drawn back into a chignon.

"How was it?" her gentle voice asked.

"It went well," he replied, propping a foot up on the first step. "I think we'll get some good outta these."

"Are there five faces in that wagon, Albert?"

He looked to the wagon and then back to his wife. "Yes."

"I thought ya said ya was only gonna buy three?"

"Well, I bought ya a gift—someone to help ya in the house... with the children, and to head the other slaves."

"I don't need any more help in the house." Justine's brown eyes looked at him with an air of simplicity and modesty. "How much? How much did ya spend, Albert?"

He took a deep breath and put down his wiggling daughter, who ran after the other two still playing under the oak. "Twenty-three hundred."

Her eyes widened and her thin mouth opened in unbelieving titter. "Over two thousand dollars, Albert! For only five slaves? Ya could've bought over five times the slaves for that, and they'd have been actually working in the cane!" She shook her head in disbelief.

"I need smart help, Justine! As we grow, I can't manage it all by myself. I need slaves we can train as drivers to manage the others in the field." His wife looked out into the distance with a timid expression that suggested that not even once did the faintest of scandals ever cross her fair name. "Will ya please not question me? Trust me, Justine."

"All right." She raised her brows and looked at him. "I'm sure ya tired and hungry. The children have already eaten their dinner. I'll have Nan warm ya up some while ya see the slaves away and clean up." Albert gave her a nod and then walked across the lawn toward his horse. "Children, that's enough for tonight," she called out. "Come on inside. Albert Jr., help ya sister. Stop pushin' her down! Now help her up."

Albert mounted his horse and made his way to the back of the property, Dashy eagerly trotting along behind him to where eight wooden huts housed the slaves. There, three children frolicked around a silver iron tub. Their laughter rang out until the oldest stopped them still in their tracks at the arrival of the wagon. They sat at the entrance to one of the huts and quietly watched. The sun was now below the horizon and the evening bush bugs and frogs began offering their songs to the night like an orchestra. The five new slaves sat quietly and looked around at their new home.

"My name is Albert Toussaint, and ya work for me now," he said in a smooth, commanding voice when he approached the wagon. "I don't know where y'all come from, but I don't need to know. The day starts at four, and I expect diligent work until the day is done. Now, I paid a premium price for y'all Negros, because I have expectations and specific work I need from ya. I expect to get what I paid for outta ya."

Foy got down from the wagon and made his way to where Albert stood. A black hat was pulled low on his brow shading his already dark eyes. The hair on his face was graying around the corners of his mouth suggesting he was a man of middle age, though no one knew or asked, but his stature was as strong as any man in his youth, his hands large and course. His tongue moved the chaw in his cheek before he spit a stream onto the ground. He always chewed tobacco on the trips to purchase new slaves. He stood behind Albert, his arms crossed. Foy was Albert's right hand on the plantation. He ran the land and the help as well as if it were his own property. Albert trusted him unlike he had with any other Negro, and in fact, he trusted him more than he trusted half the white men he knew.

"What's ya name?" Albert asked the griffe, who was staring at her feet. "Griffe, what's your name?"

One of the men in the wagon nudged her foot, and her head snapped up and turned to Albert. Her almond-shaped eyes, dark and curtained by equally dark, thick lashes, found his hazel blue eyes staring at her. His stare was bold and admiring. She quickly averted her gaze as her tongue wet her full lips.

"Dinah," she said quietly. There was something unusually exquisite and beautiful about her. Her hair was like the finest thread silk that fell softly in curls around her face and was gathered in a loose bun at the base of her long neck. She sat straight and with good posture. The loose, black auction dress couldn't hide the fact that her form was as striking as her face. Albert noticed her delicate hands folded on her lap. For a minute he wondered how such a fine creature of natural graces and beauty of the most dazzling kind could have ended up at the auction house. Perhaps she was mad, or slow, time would tell.

"Ya work in the house and will see to Mrs. Toussaint and the children." He studied her sharp profile, pausing before continuing, "the rest of ya, listen to Foy. He will show ya the ropes around here, he's in charge of ya. I'll see ya tomorrow. Foy will show ya where ya be stayin'. Welcome to the Toussaint sugar plantation."

He made his way back to the house, left his horse with a young stable boy, and went inside. The house was quiet. Flickering candles and lanterns let off a warm glow against the colorful walls. The sound of his boots clicked against the wooden floors.

"In here, Albert," a soft voice called from the back of the house, where the kitchen was.

He walked in and saw Justine uncovering a plate and pouring a glass of wine. "Where is Nan?"

"I sent her on her way. Go sit at the table; I'll bring ya plate."

He did so, and after she set the plate down in front of him with the glass of wine, he picked up his fork and started eating. "Children asleep?" He broke the silence.

"Yes." She paused and then said, "I'm sorry about earlier. I shouldn't have spoken to ya like that."

"Don't worry about it."

"I just can't understand why you'd spend so much on just a handful of slaves."

"I don't expect ya to understand, Justine. I expect ya to trust me. This is my plantation—my household! I will take care of it," he said, reaching for his glass and taking a full drink.

After continuing his meal in silence, he reached up and put his hand on hers. "Why don't ya go on upstairs and get ready for bed? I'll be up when I'm finished." He offered her a slight smile as he looked her in the eyes, and she agreed and left the room.

After finishing his dinner in silence, he took his glass in hand and leaned back in the chair to relax. By the time Albert got to the bedroom, Justine was asleep. He undressed himself, turned out the lantern, and crawled into bed.

The next day, the crow of the roosters warmed the morning air well before the sun did. Rolling over, Albert put his arm around his wife and pulled her close. His mouth explored the warm regions of her neck as he caressed her body with his hand.

"Not this mornin', Albert. I'm tired," her hoarse morning voice uttered.

"Justine, I've been away. I want to feel you," he said, continuing to touch her.

"Stop, Albert. Maybe later." She moved closer to the edge of the bed.

Albert frowned as his tongue moved across the sharp edges of his teeth. He got out of bed, dressing himself while his wife rolled over and pulled the sheets up around her chin. He grabbed his brown felt hat and left the room.

Dinah heard stirring in the cabin and slowly opened her eyes. Nan, a woman Dinah learned the night before was the head of the Toussaint household, was a woman of nearly fifty. Dinah fell easy enough into conversation with her the night before but sensed that she was not a woman to be crossed. She hummed sweetly over the pot of grits as she poured molasses into the hot mixture. Her spotted chocolate and white calico dress fit neatly over her hefty curves, and a brightly colored head handkerchief tied back the curls on her head.

"Nathan, come on now and get ya some," she said to the oldest boy, whose hair stood up from his head like puffs of the finest cotton died black and was around the age of thirteen. Nan had a total of eight children, one dying its first week of life on earth. Three were born to her before she had been purchased to work at the Toussaint plantation. One, Dinah later found out, had died at the hand of Nan's previous owner. The boy had been sick with a fever during harvest and was not well enough to work in the fields. The tyrannical master believed him to be faking the sickness and would not have him to stay in bed. The boy fell in the fields dead the next day. Though it was inadvertent, Nan blamed the death of her son on the cruel owner who showed more anger at the loss than remorse. Her other son was sold the following month. Bitterness burned in her bosom at the loss of her two sons. Before the harvest of the next year, Nan was sold as her eagerness to work had greatly declined costing the owner 'more than what she was worth'. Her daughter, however, was kept by the owner, and was used by his wife in the house. Nan was twenty-eight.

The boy jumped up off the dirt floor where he was helping another child and eagerly scooped a ladleful into a bowl. He reached into a basket and took out a piece of cornbread that was bigger than his outstretched hand, chomping out two big bites before wiping his mouth with his forearm.

Nan's hand was quick to slap the back of his head. "Bless dat bread before ya eat it, and don't be actin' like no animal! Sit down at da table and act like a human!" She gave the boy a push in the direction of a wooden stool.

"Girl, ya better get up. I see ya eyes openin' over der," Nan continued as she pulled a plain green cotton dress over the bare chest of a girl no older than five. Miracle, Nan named her, because she had the child when she thought she was passed the age of childbearing.

Dinah was housed with Nan, her husband, an old man Nan

called father, Nathan the oldest and the stable boy, the three other children, and another woman who looked to be in her late twenties who rarely spoke but observed everything. She was described in her sales as "a chronic runaway". A large scar stretched from her temple, across her lips, and to her chin, giving her an eerily callused look. Sitting up on the pallet she slept on, Dinah rubbed the back of her sore neck.

"Da men already ate and are out. We have a ways to walk to get to da house. We'll be leavin' in a few minutes. I suggest ya get yaself some grits before we go."

Dinah made her way to the pot of grits and, without a word, dipped up some into a bowl. She sat on a stool across from Nathan. Glancing up, she caught his curious face staring at her, and her gaze dropped back to her bowl. When she looked up again, his hand was extended toward her with a square piece of cornbread. Dinah took it and gave him a small, crooked smile.

"All right, let's go," Nan said as she urged the children toward the door like little chicks.

Nathan jumped up, grabbing his hat, and dashed barefoot out the door. Dinah looked around at the small, silent cabin. After taking three large mouthfuls of grits, she pushed the piece of cornbread into her dress pocket and rushed out to join the others. It was dark out, and she had to squint in each direction before she finally saw their dark silhouettes. She jogged toward them to catch up.

"How far is the house?" she asked Nan after a few minutes of walking.

"We stay on da backside of da property. Da house is on da front side. Nah Mr. Toussaint is real strict bout da day startin' before da rooster crows, to get a full day of work in. Ya won't see much of him. He's typically in da fields, unless it's meal time or Mrs. Toussaint is throwin' a party."

The wind blew crisp, refreshing air across Dinah's face, and the large blades of grass were soft with dew beneath her bare feet as she moved to keep up with Nan's quick pace. "Where is the other woman?"

"What other woman?" Nan questioned. "The one in our cabin? Oh, ya mean Harriett. She doesn't work in da house. Mr. Toussaint bought her, oh, about two years ago. Harriett was helpin' with da children, but Mrs. Toussaint couldn't stand da sight of dat scarred face of hers and sent her out to work in da fields. She's worked da cane ever since."

"Did she get her scar here?"

"No. Dat was given to her by her owner before Mr. Toussaint, back when she used to run; but she don't run no more." Nan raised her chin a bit as she said that. Soon, a deep melody was hummed softly in her throat as they continued without further conversation.

It wasn't long before Nathan and two of the other children cut across a field toward their day's work with the livestock. The plantation home, even in the darkness of predawn, stood out in its grandeur. Its white columns not only framed the front of the house but also wrapped around its sides. Nan, Dinah, and the young girl in the green dress walked up to the back entrance and quietly entered. Nan took the rag from over her shoulder and knelt to wipe the feet of the girl, who stood and patiently waited in silence as she had done every day since she could remember. Then Nan began wiping her own feet clean.

"I don't like wearin' my shoes on da walk—they get too dirty," Nan whispered. "So I keep dem hidden in da kitchen. It's easier to wipe my feet clean and have a clean pair of shoes waitin' fa me." She handed the rag to Dinah.

Once their feet were dried and cleaned from dirt and grass, Dinah followed Nan through the dark halls of the house until they reached the kitchen. Nan put wood in the stove and started a fire before lighting the lanterns. The glow spread like the warmth of a familiar friend's smile. Soon they were mixing lard and flour to create beautiful biscuits.

"Mornin'." Another black woman entered the kitchen. She walked to where the girl was standing on a box crate, stirring a mixture of batter, and placed a kiss on top of her head.

"Mornin', Franny," Nan replied without skipping a beat. "Franny, dis here is Dinah. She's new to da plantation and will be helpin' out here at da house."

"Nice to meet ya," Franny said with a toothy, decaying smile. The braids on her head stuck out like branches against her thin, straight, tree-like frame.

"Franny stays here in da house."

"Nan could stay in da house too, but she won't, 'cause she wants to stay wid her husband. I guess if I had a man to keep me warm and give me lovin' at night, I wouldn't eitha," Franny teased as she wrapped her arms around herself in a mocking embrace.

"Nah I'll take a switch to ya, Franny," Nan boomed as she pretended to make her way over to the woman. Franny giggled, quick to move across the room. "I don't have da patience fa ya nonsense this mornin', girl. It's too early fa that kind of banterin'!"

The roosters crowed their salutations to the early morning, and Nan turned to Dinah. "Over there you'll find da coffee. Ya know how to make a pot of coffee?"

"Yes."

"Well, get da coffee started," she ordered.

"Mr. Toussaint will be down shortly. He always comes down and gets himself a cup of coffee before da othas wake up," Franny put in as she busied her hands with food prep. She stopped and handed Dinah a kettle. "Always shortly afta da roosters crow. You'll see." She smiled.

Dinah couldn't understand why Franny seemed so cheerful. Nan was right that it was too much for this early in the morning. A few minutes later, just like she said would happen, the owner of the plantation stepped into the kitchen.

"Mornin', Mr. Toussaint," Nan said.

"Mornin', Mr. Toussaint," Franny echoed as she hastened to pour him a cup of coffee.

"Good morning, Nan, Franny." He nodded as he took the cup from her. "Dinah." He blew on the dark liquid before taking a sip, and Franny watched him, eyes wide. "It's good coffee," he said after his second sip.

Franny's mouth spread in that awkward smile, and her eyes beamed like a child. "Oh, dat's fine, Mr. Toussaint. Dat's just fine! It was Dinah here dat made da coffee this mornin'. I was a little worried it wouldn't be to ya likin'."

Dinah stood by the stove, her gaze traveling back and forth from Franny to Mr. Toussaint. Her mouth was agape in disbelief at Franny's comfortable conversation with him.

"No, it's good. Well done," Mr. Toussaint said, looking at her.

"Ya hear dat? Well done, Dinah!" Franny said in excitement.

"Nah Mr. Toussaint, I got ya sittin' room ready fa ya like I always do. I'll be in later to warm ya coffee."

After he left, Nan looked to Dinah and rolled her eyes as she wiped her hands on her apron.

"Dat Mr. Toussaint," Franny continued, her hands on her stomach, "he's a good master. Ya will see, Ms. Dinah. He's kind." She moved over to the cupboard and started taking out the plates. "Nah I've had my share of switchin' since I've been here, but they were fair...I deserved those. And they were nothin' like those switches I got from da master before Mr. Toussaint."

"Ya deserved switchin', like a dog or a horse?" Dinah asked, an edge in her voice.

"I didn't say I was some kind of animal," Franny corrected as she gathered the flatware, no more bothered about the conversation than a dog with an itch.

"But ya deserve switchin'?"

"Nah, when I do wrong..."

"Who decides when ya do wrong? Ya master?" Dinah snapped in mockery.

"Da good book does say to obey ya Earthly masters as though ya was serving da Lord."

"I'll switch da devil out of both ya girls if ya don't stop this bickering right now," Nan chimed in. "Our life is what it is. We cannot change our circumstances. We have only to do da best we can. Nah as it goes with Mr. Toussaint, he is just as good as any master can get. Many of us here can attest to cruelty from masters before comin' here. But Mr. Toussaint, he takes us in. He knows kindness and cares for his slaves."

Franny nodded as she hummed, "Uh huh."

"So ya tellin' me he's a good-will slave owner. Can ya even use those two words in the same sentence?" Dinah said quietly, shaking her head. "Slaves."

"Girl, ya is a slave!" Nan's eyes ignited.

"It's not right."

"But ya is—ya's a slave! Nah stop this fool talk and go set da table before ya help Franny bring da children down."

They took up the dishes and made their way to the dining room. It was another hour before the sun started to shine through the eastern wall of windows in the dining area, illuminating the beautifully dressed table as if it were on fire.

Just as the sun cast its first ribbons of gold, Franny took hold of Dinah. "Now we go wake and dress da children." They made their way up the curving staircase to the second story. "I wake da oldest girls first, seein' how they can tend to themselves more than da younger ones. It sure will be easier getting' them all around nah that ya's here."

Franny slowly opened the door to the first room. She softly walked over to the window and pulled the silky drapes open. "Mornin' nah, girls!" her soft voice sang. "Time to open them pretty eyes of yas." She walked over to where Marianne had pulled the covers over her head. "Miss Marianne, dat blanket isn't gonna save ya from da sun risin'. Come on nah, get yaself up."

On the other side of the room, a messy, golden haired girl sat up in bed. Her cheeks were large and round, and dimpled where she smiled. "Who's that?" She pointed to where Dinah stood.

"Dat is Dinah! She's to help us here in da house."

Franny walked over to the girl's bedside. "She is nice; ya will like her. I just need ya to be good and keep dat little devil inside ya put away." She tickled the girl's ribs, and she burst out in giggles. "Let's get ya dressed nah."

The girl scampered out from under her covers. "I want Dinah to pick out my dress," she said, walking over to her new acquaintance and taking her by the hand.

"All right, Miss Rose. Show her ya dresses." Rose gave her hand a tug and led Dinah to the closet. "Rose is always bright eyed and bushy tailed in da mornin'," Franny continued. "It's Miss *Marianne* who has a hard time gettin' up! Nah come on, breakfast is about ready and I don't want to have to explain to ya father why we was late gettin' down fa breakfast."

The older girl huffed, sluggishly got out of bed, and allowed Franny to start combing out her hair. Dinah, listening to Franny's continuous chatter, undressed the young Rose and helped her put on a yellow dress adorned with stitched pink flowers around the lace neck.

"Da girls share a room, but here in a couple of years Miss Marianne will be havin' her debutante ball. Then she'll get a room of her own! And we'll put little Isabelle in here with Rose. She'll be around four then."

"I'm seven," Rose interjected. "Issy is only two." Dinah offered the child a warm smile.

"Your teeth aren't dark like Franny's."

Dinah pressed her lips together and looked over her shoulder to where the other woman was assisting Marianne. Franny let out a hearty laugh. "White teeth, dark teeth, or no teeth fa that matter, a smile is a smile, child."

Dinah turned back to Rose, who was squinting her fair blue eyes and showing off her own baby teeth.

They finished getting the girls ready for the day and sent them downstairs before they moved to the next room. When they walked in, there was little Albert Toussaint III sitting in front of the window, buck naked and trying to put on his pants.

"What's it ya doin', little Al?" Franny giggled.

His big brown eyes looked up at her. "Goin' to help pawpaw in da fields."

"Well, that's just fine, Albert. Let me help ya so ya can get on out there." Franny looked at Dinah. "Across da hall is Isabelle's room. Why don't ya go ahead and get her ready? I'll help Albert."

Dinah gave a nod. When she stepped back out into the hall, though, she was looking at the three closed doors. "Which door? There's three!" she asked, popping her head back into the room.

"Da one on da end down there."

She rolled her eyes as she turned around. "There's two ends," she mumbled to herself.

Opting to first choose the end opposite from where they had entered the hall, Dinah slowly opened the door just enough to let in some light. Relieved to see toys on the floor, she pushed the door open wider. There against the wall, staring at her though the dark, Isabelle stood in her crib. She mumbled some unknown toddler chatter as Dinah moved forward and opened the curtains. This room was on the west side of the house with less of the morning light, and it only dimly lit the room.

After lifting the child out of the crib, she proceeded to change and dress her. Isabelle reached up and took hold of Dinah's hands with her own little ones.

"Here now, I've got to finish with ya."

Isabelle giggled and reached again for her moving hands. "Miss Isabelle, I need to button ya up."

Dinah moved her hands, followed by Isabelle taking them in her own with a giggle.

"So that's how it is. Ya want to play, I see." Dinah smiled before tickling the child with both hands.

Isabelle fell over in peals of laughter before trying to scamper away, and Dinah sat on the floor and watched her. She took out the cornbread she had taken earlier from her pocket and, after breaking off a piece, put it in her mouth. Isabelle looked at her with wonder before moving to stand in front of Dinah, her intense gaze on the bread.

"What? Ya want some of this here cornbread?"

Isabelle opened her mouth like a little bird expecting a feeding, and Dinah dropped a small piece inside it. Isabelle's eyes widened as the enjoyment of the sweet bread showed on her face. She smacked her lips and reached for more. After handing her a bigger piece, Dinah put the rest back into her pocket and then finished dressing Isabelle as the girl calmly enjoyed her mouthful of cornbread.

"Ya done dressin' da child?" Franny peeked her head into the room. Dinah nodded and picked up Isabelle. "Let's go downstairs then." She stepped to the side as Dinah carried the toddler out of the room. "What's dat child chewin' on?"

"Oh, nothing," Dinah said, reaching up and wiping Isabelle's mouth. "Probably her tongue." She moved quickly ahead of Franny, so she wouldn't examine further.

The Toussaint family gathered at the table for breakfast. The table was spread with sweet breads, pork, and eggs. The children reached across the table for seconds and chugged down gulps of milk between childish chatter, while their parents ate silently. Dinah stood at the back wall of the dining room, watching and waiting to be called upon. There wasn't much exchange between Albert and Justine. Mrs. Toussaint sat straight and proper, occasionally addressing the children's behavior or responding with "Yes, dear," or "That's nice," or "I see," when Mr. Toussaint would say something.

It wasn't long before he excused himself from the table. Little Al scurried from his chair to his father, pleading to go with him to the fields.

"Albert, stop pestering ya father," scolded Justine.

The little boy's lower lip pushed out over his upper, and his eyes filled with tears. Albert picked up his son as they flowed down his round, pink cheeks like water over a broken dam.

"Oh, now this is silly. Dry ya eyes and stop the fussin'," Justine said.

"He can come out with me," Mr. Toussaint said, reaching up to wipe away the warm tears.

"I don't want him out there in the cane, Albert. He'll be in way! He could get hurt, he'll get dirty…"

"Boys are supposed to get dirty," her husband teased, giving his son a squeeze and a bounce on his hip.

"I said no."

"Aw hell, Justine!" he said, aggravated. "The boy can come out with me, and I'll bring him back during lunchtime. He'll get so wore out that he'll sleep the rest of the afternoon and ya won't even know he's around."

"Have it your way then, *husband*." She blinked rapidly and wiped her hands on her napkin.

Albert gave his son a wink and yanked his hat over his head. Franny, who was standing next to Dinah, gave a little smile.

"Ya better keep ya eyes on him, and he'd better not get hurt. I don't like him goin' out there in the cane with the colored," Justine voiced as she slapped her napkin down on the table.

"Don't forget this will be his plantation one day," Albert stated as he left the dining room.

"Yes, well, he'll be older than five and I'll be dead," she countered. Franny let out a little snicker, and Justine whipped her head around to where the women stood.

Dinah's wide eyes shot down to the floor, her mouth open slightly as her breathing quickened. Neither woman moved as they heard the chair slide across the floor. As Mrs. Toussaint told her daughters to finish up and move to the sitting room, Dinah looked up, watching her standing there in her soft cream and light pink dress, her hair gathered low at the base of her neck. Then Justine turned in their direction and caught her looking. Dinah quickly averted her eyes, gripping her hands behind her back as she felt Justine's gaze on her. Then slowly, Mrs. Toussaint turned and walked out of the room.

Dinah turned to Franny, who still stood with her head down. "Good lawd, now I know why ya get switched!"

Her words brought a smile to the other woman's mouth, along with a quiet, chesty laugh. Dinah huffed and shook her head.

CHAPTER THREE

FRANNY TOOK Dinah under her wing, showing her the ways of the Toussaint household. Every day held the same routine. Dinah would wake before 4:00 a.m., eat some grits, and help get the children ready for the day. She would walk with Nan and the four children through the dark, warm mornings, serenaded by the bush crickets and the early morning call of the song birds, to the white silhouette of the house. Franny would join them in the kitchen with her joyful nature, Mr. Toussaint would take his coffee after the roosters crowed, the children would be dressed, and then Dinah and Franny would wait at the back of the dining hall as breakfast was enjoyed. Dinah would then be put to work cleaning the house, tending the garden, or readying lunch and dinner. Rarely was she ever in the same room as Mrs. Toussaint or the children, and for that she was relieved and grateful.

Two weeks had quickly passed, and it was after lunch was served one day when Nan sent Dinah into the sitting room with the afternoon tea for Mrs. Toussaint and the children. She walked carefully as she carried the silver tray holding the fine swan-necked pot embellished with birds, butterflies, and stemmed flowers on a white glossy ground. The creamer and sugar bowl rims were beaded, and a gilded rose topped the lid to the sugar bowl. Cups and saucers, both with gilded scalloped rims and the cup handles also accented with gold, were decorated inside and out with birds, flowers, and butterflies. The cups clinked against each other as the tray was lowered onto an end table.

On the floor, little Albert wrestled with Isabelle. Rose sat next to her mother as she worked on needlework, while Marianne read aloud to whomever would listen.

"Marianne, I don't know why ya like to read that Poe fellow," Justine complained as her oldest daughter raised her voice for theatrical effect.

Dinah set the delicate cups on their saucers and began pouring the tea as she listened to the words from Marianne's lips.

"'And now, as I continued to step cautiously onward, there came thronging upon my recollection a thousand vague rumors of the horrors of…Tol…Toledo. Of the dungeons there had been strange things narrated-fables I had always deemed them-but yet strange, and too ghastly to repeat save in a whisper.'" Her hand came up as her voice lowered for effect. Dinah's lips pressed into a nearly hidden smile as she continued placing the teacups in perfect order.

She continued after her brief pause. "'Was I left to perish of starvation in this sub…subter…'"

"Subterranean," Dinah said, lifting a cup and saucer.

"Subterranean," Marianne repeated. She curiously watched the colored woman walk toward her and set the cup on the end table next to her.

"'World of darkness,'" Dinah continued as she went to distribute tea to the others. "'Or what fate, perhaps even more fearful, awaited me?'"

Mrs. Toussaint watched Dinah with a puzzled look as she walked a cup and saucer over to her.

"Sugar, ma'am?" Dinah asked, handing her the saucer.

"What?" Justine slowly asked, astounded at what she had just heard. "Oh, uh...sugar, yes."

Dinah retrieved the sugar bowl and put a cube in Justine's cup. "Another?"

"No, one is just fine," Justine answered, eyes narrowed. Dinah gave her a nod and lowered her head as she turned. "Now just a minute," Mrs. Toussaint said, stopping her in her tracks. "How is it ya know what Marianne is reading?"

"I'm sorry, ma'am. I overstepped my bounds."

"Answer my question."

"My last owner was an avid reader of Mr. Poe's work," she said, keeping her head down. "I enjoy his dark sentiments, and my master would let me read...read them to me...when Mr. Poe published new stories."

"So, you're a reader," Justine said, surprised, as she took a sip of her tea.

"I understand a few written words, ma'am."

"Well," Mrs. Toussaint chuckled, "if you're readin' Edgar Allan Poe, I'd venture to say ya understand more than just a few." She didn't respond, so Justine asked, "What is it they call you?"

"Dinah, ma'am."

The slurping sound of Justine taking a long drink made Dinah's heart race as she quickly glanced up in her direction several times before leaving her gaze on the sugar bowl in her shaking hand. Justine took her time swallowing before she spoke. "All right. That is all." The slave gave a small curtsy and turned to walk away. "And Dinah?" Justine's stern voice stopped her again. "Don't correct my children with their readin' unless I ask ya for it."

Dinah swallowed hard and gave a nod. "Yes, ma'am."

After returning to the kitchen, she put her hands on the countertop. "Sometimes it takes all I have to harness the frustration inside me." She said, head lowered between her shoulders.

Nan was sitting on a bench, snapping a bowl of green beans in her lap. "It's best just to swallow ya frustration, knowin' it's not goin' to do ya a licka good."

She raised her head and looked up to the ceiling, "All I did was help the girl with a word she didn't know in her readin'."

"Lucky ya didn't get a switch. A colored slave ain't supposed to know more than da white folk, even if it is a child. Nah ya should know to only do da work ya been asked to do. Don't do nothin' more, don't do nothin' less. Ya only be askin' fa trouble that way," Nan warned. Dinah shook her head in response. "Get ya a handful of these beans and start snappin'—and hum ya a song. Music is healin' fa da soul. It clears da mind and strengthens da heart."

A warm wind blew in through the kitchen window, rippling the soft yellow curtains as Nan's strong, deep voice began humming a tune. Dinah went to where she sat and took a handful of the long green stems. After sitting on the bench, she put them in her apron and began helping. Soon, she found a rhythm with her snapping. Between the mindless task, Nan's soothing hum, and the sweet croaking of the frogs blended with the call of a distant owl, the sound of the summer evening hypnotized her into relaxation.

The days passed and Dinah was thankful that Nan set her to do the chores outside the house and left Franny to tending to Justine and the children. It was on a hot day after the Toussaints' breakfast, Dinah began filling buckets with water and carrying them to the garden. Slowly, she poured it at the base of the vegetables, and the soil drank it up like a thirsty traveler. The sun beat down like fire, soaking into her black dress, which held the heat relentlessly. Thankfully, Nan had given her a wide-brimmed hat to wear to shade her face from the beating rays. Beads of sweat dripped from her dark skin, even though the morning hour had not yet hit 10:00 a.m.

Kneeling next to the bucket after her seventh trip, Dinah dipped her hand into the refreshing water and raised it to her lips. She lifted her gaze to the rows of remaining plants that needed watering. It was as if they cried to her for a drink themselves after a long span of hot summer days. They stood up out of the dry, dusty earth, their branches like worshiping arms reaching hungrily for the sun god. The tips of their leaves were a brittle brown, showing the betrayal of the sky to water their thirsty roots. Dinah raised another handful to her mouth before enjoying cool drops on the back of her neck and chest.

After emptying the bucket, she took it by the handle and started her way back to the well. There, walking across the lawn toward her, was Mr. Toussaint, his sleeves halfway rolled up his sunned arms and his brimmed hat shading his face. Although not tight fitting, his brown trousers formed around his thighs, revealing his riding muscles.

"Not much left in the summer harvest, is there?" he asked when she approached.

"Mr. Toussaint," she replied with her head down. "No sir, not much." After a pause, she asked, "Do ya need somethin', sir?"

"No," he said with a squint as he looked around himself. "It's hot out today. I told Nan to make a pitcher of lemonade for ya all."

Dinah's hesitant eyes looked up from under the brim of her straw hat, and she caught his blue stare. His eyes, full of fire and softness, looked at her with undeniable admiration. Beads of sweat glistened on his temples and cheekbones. "Thank ya, sir," she replied softly, her cheeks blushing under his regard.

As he gave her a slight nod, his steady eyes surveyed her person. "All right then. Get those plants watered." She couldn't help but watch him as he walked back toward the house. He was a fine structure of a man, and there was something captivating to Dinah in his self-respecting and dignified stride. She let out a sigh through her puckered lips and whiped her brow before she gave her head a shake and a bashful grin crossed her mouth.

It took Dinah the better part of the morning to finish watering the gardens, and even at that she had not yet given the flowers around the house a good drink. After stepping into the house, she wiped at her dusty feet, cut from dry grass, rocks, and branches. She walked softly down the hall, sweat still expelling from her pores and once in a while dropping from her dark skin onto the polished wooden floor, leaving a salty trail from the back door. As she entered the kitchen, there on the counter next to the wash sink was a pitcher of lemonade, glistening like yellow stained glass in the light. Her tongue ran across her lips, gathering the salty flavor of the sweat.

Before reaching for a glass, Dinah took off her hat and placed it on the counter. She wiped her brow with the back of her hand before using both hands to wipe down her temples. As she took the pitcher by the handle, her hand nearly shook from excitement at the thought of the tart liquid. The swishing it made as it filled the glass made her mouth water, and when she raised it to her lips, the first hit to her tongue was as tangy and as sweet as it smelled. Dinah couldn't help but close her eyes in enjoyment. She had served lemonade more times in her life than she could remember, but never once had the golden drink hit her own tongue.

Just then, Nan walked into the kitchen. "Gawd, ya just soakin' wet!"

Her loud voice gave Dinah a start, and she nearly jerked hard enough to drop her precious glass of refreshing lemonade. "Ah, sweet Lawd Jesus!" Her free hand came up to her chest. "Ya nearly scared me to death."

"Well, just standin' around, sippin' on sweet lemonade, ya should be scared," Nan scolded with a tinge of teasing.

"It's hot as Hell out there! I swear to Gawd da devil must be walkin' around Louisiana today, laughin' at us poor fools, in our cursed human state!" Dinah gave her brow another stroke with the back of her hand.

This gave Nan a good chuckle. "Ya done waterin'?" she asked.

"No, I still need to water the flowers on the front side of the house."

"Ya better get after it! Da sun will be blisterin' before too long now," Nan said as she set out glasses to take lemonade to Mrs. Toussaint and the children.

She walked over to the pantry on the north side of the kitchen, her large frame swaying from side to side, a white pressed turban tied around her head, folded and tucked so precisely that God Himself would've charged her to all the turbans in heaven. There, a door and stone stairwell led down into the small icehouse. It wasn't long before Nan returned, both hands gripping large chunks of ice as it melted against her warm black skin. After placing them on the counter, she proceeded to break them into smaller chunks and put them in the cups. Then, from across the kitchen, she retrieved a different pitcher—different but full of the same tart, yellow liquid.

"Ya forgot a piece," Dinah pointed out. Nan looked at her with a blank, dumbfounded look. Dinah raised her eyebrows and added, "Of ice! Ya forgot a piece on the counter."

Nan's mouth turned down and, in an ornery gesture, she picked up the piece of ice between her forefinger and thumb. She looked at it, holding it up in such a way as it was between her eye and the light gleaming in through the window. Her eyes rose to Dinah's. Then, with a crooked smile, she dropped it in Dinah's cup. "What piece?"

A smile spread across Dinah's face as her eyes glinted.

"Nah, ya better finish up dat drink and get on outside. Ya have been in here more than long enough. Look see? Ya sweat's already dried up, leavin' ya skin lookin' all ashy. Finish dat and get on outside," Nan ordered as she gathered her tray loaded with cups and exited the kitchen with her renowned sway.

Dinah smiled to herself at the harsh mask Nan put on as she took another drink and swallowed the sweet nectar. Looking down into her glass, she watched the chunk of ice, like a clear weightless stone, float around in her cup. Tipping the cup upward, she finished the lemonade, but before putting the cup in the sink basin, she reached inside and took out the chunk of ice. She popped it in her mouth with joy, letting the cold melt down the sides of her hot tongue and wet the back of her throat.

The sun was relentless. Dinah had farther to walk with each bucket this time, as the well pump was on the backside of the house. As the sun climbed higher in the cloudless sky, the face of the earth grew hotter. The heat from the ground scorched her feet, quickening her steps. One bucket at a time, Dinah watered the flowers growing along the front veranda. The pink and red butterfly pentas seemed to thrive in the late summer heat. Where other plants were starting to burn up, the pentas shone radiantly, attracting every pollen-loving insect on the plantation.

During one of her trips to the well, Dinah cautiously looked around as she shifted her weight from one foot to the other. Certain that no one was watching, she poured some of the cool water from her bucket onto her blistering feet. The sensation was not enough. After setting the bucket down, Dinah raised one foot at a time and placed it into the water. She took a deep inhale as she raised her head to the angry sun. Her whole body seemed to thank her for the cool, though short, foot bath.

Hastily she made her way back around the south side of the house to the front. Mrs. Toussaint and Marianne were still sitting on the white-washed veranda; the other children, weary from the heat, had moved indoors with Franny. Their colorful fans opened wide, moving as fast as a hummingbird's wing, stirred the ringlets framing their fair faces.

"I'd be thankful for this breeze if it wasn't so stifling hot!" Justine said.

"Mother, can we go visit the Thompsons? I'm bored and I want to see Elizabeth. We haven't been there for a visit in weeks!" Marianne pleaded with her mother.

The Thompsons were a neighboring plantation family, who, fortunate for Marianne, had a daughter only two years older than herself. Elizabeth was the youngest of the three Thompson children, and Marianne enjoyed escaping her younger siblings and engaging in more mature gossip with her. The girls would often hide around the corner and listen to Elizabeth's two older brothers, Gabe and Byron of sixteen and seventeen, curse and talk about the most attractive ladies in the county. When the boys would catch the girls listening, Byron would grab his sister and threaten to give her "a good lickin'" for spying, to which she would counter that she would tell their mother they were hiding a bottle of whiskey and a stash of smokes if he laid a hand on her. The brothers would swish the girls away with threats of consequences if they came back around. About that time, Marianne would talk Elizabeth into going and playing dolls, something the older girl still enjoyed, but only for a short period of time before she would get bored and crave some kind of mischief.

"I don't know, Marianne. Why don't we plan to go over there another day this week?" Justine said.

"Mother, please!" the girl persisted.

Dinah was watering the flowers by the veranda steps near to where they were sitting. She stood and looked around herself at the flowers still left to be watered, unbothered or concerned about their conversation.

"Marianne, I said perhaps another day." Suddenly, Justine frowned. "Ugh. What is that?" There was a pause, and Marianne looked at her mother. "Do ya smell that? Marianne, is that you?" Mrs. Toussaint's nose crinkled as she looked at her daughter, who put her finger under her nose and shook her head. "Ah Gawd, what is that?"

She looked around before her eyes rested on Dinah with bucket in hand, and her face flushed with half-embarrassment and half-disgust. "Dinah, come up here a minute." Dinah jolted, put down her bucket and mounted the steps. As she stood in front of Justine, the hot wind gusted against her back, and Mrs. Toussaint turned her head in disgust. "Ugh, it's you! When was the last time ya bathed?"

Dinah began stammering apologies. "I'm sorry, ma'am. I've been sweatin' all mornin'—it's so hot out. I know there's no excuse. I'll do better."

"I've had pigs that smell better than you! Nan!" Justine cried out. "Nan!"

"So sorry, ma'am," Dinah continued in an embarrassed plea, and the two women's voices mingled in what sounded like chattering chickens.

"Nan! Get out here!"

Soon, Nan's large frame filled the doorway, her breathing coming in nervous pants. "Yes'm, yes'm," she exhaled as her gaze went from Mrs. Toussaint to the humiliated face of Dinah, with her eyes cast downward.

"Nan, I cannot stand the smell of this woman! When was the last time she bathed? We are sittin' here, tryin' to enjoy the day, and suddenly I get the waft of pig shit!"

Marianne giggled. Very rarely did she hear her mother use curse words, and she always found the instances in which she did to be comical.

"Ya know I hold my house Negros to a higher standard than the field Negros. I expect ya to be clean and proper! That's not much to ask!"

"Na, ma'am," Nan responded with a shake of the head.

"I'm embarrassed," Justine continued. "What if someone had paid us a call and they find out my house Negros smell like the ass of a pig?"

There it was again. Marianne's hand went over her mouth to hide her snickering. Dinah's head sunk low toward her chest.

"Dinah, run to the barn and have Nathan prepare our buggy. Marianne and I *are* goin' to the Thompsons' for a visit."

Dinah wasted no time in fleeing down the steps and running to the barn. She wanted to run far away.

Justine looked back to Nan. "I want ya to take her to the back after she's done watering and scrub her down. Use soap on every inch of her!" She rose from her seat. "I will not have nasty Negros workin' in my house," she said as she walked past Nan. "Marianne, get yourself ready."

The girl popped up excitedly and rushed past Nan.

It wasn't long after that Justine walked into the kitchen where Nan was readying a bucket, soap, and a sponge. Draped over her arm were two dresses, one a pale yellow with green flowers on the upper portion, sleeves, and lining the bottom hem, and the other a deep blue with white ruffles collaring the neckline and running down the front on either side of a line of pearly buttons.

"Here are a couple of old dresses I don't wear anymore. Give these to her, and ya can throw away that black gunny sack she wears," Justine said, handing the dresses to Nan. "Marianne and I will take lunch over at the Thompsons'. I'm leaving the other children here. We will be back for dinner."

Nan gave a nod, still in disbelief at the beautiful fabric draped over her arm that was to be given to Dinah. Mrs. Toussaint didn't wait for a response before she turned and walked out of the kitchen. Shortly after, she and Marianne were climbing into the buggy and making their way to the neighboring plantation. Dinah made sure to stay hidden around the corner of the house until the horses were pulling them down the drive.

She picked up her bucket, mechanically filled it, and began her watering again. Her tears mingled with the sweat rolling down the side of her face, but her expression never betrayed her by claiming them as tears. After three trips, Nan stepped out onto the veranda with her hands on her wide, muffin-like hips.

"How much more waterin' do ya got nah?" she barked.

"Two more buckets," Dinah answered.

"Hurry up nah and get it done! Then come meet me in da back! I got other things to get done, so hurry it up!"

Dinah was ready to be out of the blistering rays of the sun, so she did just that. When she was finished, there in the back, Nan stood by a small trough she had filled with water.

"What is this?" Dinah asked.

"I'm givin' ya a bath!" the woman responded matter-of-factly.

"Out here, in the middle of the day?" Dinah asked.

"There ain't no one around. Da missus is gone and it's just da younger children in da house. Only ones to see ya in ya nakedness will be Gawd and myself. Nah come on and get that dress off," Nan ordered.

Bashfully, Dinah pulled the black dress up over her head. "As if I ain't been humiliated enough," she mumbled to herself as she stepped into the trough, whose walls were nearly knee high.

"There nah, sit down in it if ya can. Gawd child, ya do stink! Whew! Good Lawd," Nan teased as she rubbed the soap against the sponge to get a nice lather.

Dinah rolled her eyes as she lowered her head. Nan started scrubbing, first on her shoulders and back, down her arms and under her pits, and then to the front of her neck and around her breast.

"There nah," she said. "Nah don't this feel good? Gettin' da treatment of Esther." She picked up a bucket of water and poured it over her shoulders. "And after bein' in da hot sun, dis water sure feels good, don't it?"

She appreciated Nan for being so nonchalant about the awkward bath, but Dinah's pride was hurt. She didn't want to smell like the "ass of a pig," as Mrs. Toussaint put it. Her words kept repeating in her head.

"Stand up nah," Nan said, interrupting her thoughts, as she pulled her up by the arm. "I've got to get da bottom side of ya."

"I can wash myself, Nan."

"Missus charged me with scrubbin' ya down, and that's exactly what I'm goin' to do!"

Dinah just shook her head.

Suddenly, Albert Toussaint's strong stride appeared from around the corner at a swift pace. When he saw the naked Dinah standing in a trough and large Nan scrubbing up her leg, he abruptly stopped, his head jerking in shock. Dinah sucked in a gasp of air as one arm flew up to cover her breast and the other down to cover where her legs met.

"Ah, sweet Lawd," she breathed as her head dropped instantly.

Nan turned, the soapy water running down her hands and dipping from her elbows.

"Seh, Mrs. Toussaint told me to scrub her up. That's what I'm doin'."

"I see that Nan," he said, looking at Dinah's dark, glistening skin. Her thick hips shaped a round bottom and met a rather small waist. A stream of soapy water dripped off the arm that covered her small but perfect breast and trailed down her stomach.

"Missus said she couldn't stand da way da girl was stinkin' and wanted me to bathe her," Nan continued.

Dinah squeezed her eyes shut tighter. "Sweet Jesus... Tell me when it's over," she mumbled.

Albert nodded as he slowly moved ahead. "All right." He had nothing else to say about what he'd just walked upon. Nan started her scrubbing again as Mr. Toussaint made for the house door. He took a couple of side-glances as he passed and one more over his shoulder before he stepped inside.

"Here nah, he's gone. Move ya hands."

"I have no pride left," Dinah said lowly.

"Aw, hush nah. Seein' ya naked and bein' washed up means no more to him than seein' his horse get a good brushin'!"

Dinah didn't care what Nan thought. At this point, she felt utterly humiliated. After Nan finished washing her, she put her in the dark blue dress from Mrs. Toussaint, which hugged her small waist and shaped her full curves. Dinah was speechless at the nice cotton garments bestowed upon her. Her pride was hurt even more at having to accept them. They sat under the shade of the small back porch as Nan combed through Dinah's long, wet hair.

It fell in length to the small of her back, but as it began to dry the curls tightened, shortening it.

"I ain't ever seen hair as long as ya's is," Nan said as she continued combing.

"My mother's tribe believed the hair to be sacred. We don't cut it. She said we keep it long as a way to stay close to our ancestors."

Nan hummed in her throat as she turned to the dresses. "Ya will wear da blue one every day and da yellow one fa when they throw parties or have guests. Nah, missus said to throw away ya black one, but I think if we give it a good wash, ya can wear it on days when ya workin' outside, so as not to get da nice ones soiled," Nan babbled as she combed Dinah's hair back with her fingers and gathered it at the base of her neck. She started twisting the hair around Dinah's forehead into ringlets.

"We may be slaves, but we still take pride in how we look," Nan said as she twisted one curl at a time. "And, Lawd, if I may say, I'm takin' pride in how ya look, child." She gave out a hearty laugh that shook her chest and put a hum in her throat.

Dinah couldn't help but to humor her with a small smile.

Franny walked out the back door. First, she frowned, but it was quickly replaced by her big, goofy smile and a burst of excitement.

"Ahh!" She rushed over to them. "I didn't even recognize dat was you! Oh, ain't ya lookin' so pretty! What's da occasion fa? Did Mr. Toussaint sell ya off to a rich suitor?" she teased.

"Hush that foolishness!" Nan barked.

"I was stinkin'," Dinah said with a cock of the head.

"Well, I just can't stop lookin' at ya," Franny continued. "Ya sure don't stink now. Ya smellin' like fresh lye!" Her gummy smile was wider than ever.

That evening, the women readied the dinner table for the Toussaint family. As usual, Franny and Dinah stood at the wall, waiting to be called upon. When Justine walked in, she was taken back at the transformation a little soapy water and a new dress made for her slave. She walked up to Dinah before taking her place at the table.

"Well now, don't that dress look nice on ya?"

"Thank ya, ma'am," Dinah said bashfully. "I'm indebted to ya kindness."

Justine sat with her back to the women, and Mr. Toussaint took his place across from her. As the family ate, Dinah noticed quick glances in her direction from Mr. Toussaint. Instead of feeling tense, though, she felt at ease in her new look. Her shoulders pulled back and she stood a little straighter as a small bit of her pride returned.

CHAPTER FOUR

LATE SUMMER TURNED into early fall, providing relief from the sweltering sun. The days were mildly temperate, and the evening winds held a cool bite that warned that winter, too, would demand Albert's time. It seemed that the cooler days brought a new energy to the entire plantation. The slaves were chattier and broke out in laughter and song in the evenings. The Toussaint children played more freely outdoors, the animals had more spirit, and even Mrs. Toussaint herself seemed more at ease.

But as the cooler weather came and the vegetables to reap changed from corn and beans to sweet potatoes and cabbage, the unspoken dread among the plantation was the fast-approaching harvest of the cane crop—all four hundred and fifty acres of it. It was a labor-intensive time, when the mills were open around the clock and the slaves worked beyond daylight hours and into the night during the grinding season. It wasn't uncommon for older slaves or those who were sickly to die before the harvest ended, so in order to cut back on slave losses, Albert provided extra food during the harvest and alcohol on Sundays to boost their spirits.

The plantation wasn't more than a week into the harvest when Albert addressed Dinah one morning after she handed him his cup of coffee. "Starting today, after breakfast, I want ya in the fields, helpin' with the cane, until the harvest is over."

Her eyes grew wide. She had been told stories during the evenings in the hut of the dreaded harvest. She swallowed hard her surprise. "Yes, sir."

"Ya can go with me when I head that way this mornin'. I'll show ya where I need ya to work," he said before moving to his sitting room.

Franny's face wasn't one to hide emotion well, and as she sliced and peeled potatoes, her lower lip pushed out. She squinted like she was peeling onions as tears spilled down her cheeks until she couldn't bear her emotions quietly any longer and began to softly wail.

"Nah, Franny, what are ya makin' all that fuss fa?" Nan snapped.

"Da cane… Dinah is bein' sent out into da cane," she said, her voice quivering.

Dinah gathered the dishes to set the breakfast table, her mouth pressed thin and her eyes blank.

"Aw nah, she'll be fine!" Nan said, loud and confident. "Labor is more tiresome—long hours—but da girl is strong both in body and will. Nah stop with da tears. Ya scarin' da poor girl."

Dinah lifted her chin. "I ain't scared." She walked past Franny with poise, hands full of plates and silverware. "Besides, it'll be nice to get away from the noise of children. I swear the sass of that Miss Marianne will be the end of me. One of these days, I'm just goin' to smack that child across her backside," she said with wide eyes, shaking her head. "And that'll be it, the end of Dinah!" Even with doubt inside herself, a bright, teasing smile spread across her face as she gave Franny a reassuring wink, rousing a hopeful grin from the woman.

The morning passed all too quickly and, before she knew it, Dinah was walking behind Mr. Toussaint as he rode his horse toward the cane fields. An idea came to her then, and as she started thinking, her pace quickened until she was boldly walking beside him. Albert looked down from his stead and frowned slightly in curiosity.

"Sir?"

"What is it?" he asked.

"If it's not too much to ask…"

"What?"

"Might I run by the cabin and change into my black dress? I'd hate to soil this beautiful fabric Mrs. Toussaint was so kind to give me." She spoke quickly, hoping to convince him by showing her overwhelming gratitude toward his wife. "I'm afraid I'd just ruin it out here, workin'. And I'm so grateful to the missus—I ain't ever had such a nice dress before."

Albert waved his hand in the air. "That's fine. The cabins are on the way to where we're goin'."

Squinting against the bright, rising sun, Dinah looked up at the grand figure on horseback. His brimmed hat shadowed his bearded face, but he seemed unbothered at the request. The sound of the leather saddle squeaked under his weight. One arm hung loosely at his side while the other held the reins, his hands gloved in leather. Dinah regarded him and took a deep breath to steady her heartbeat. Not another word was exchanged between the two as Albert waited for her to change and then led her to the first field to harvest.

The tall, strong stalks of cane stood two to four meters high. Even the shortest stalk was taller than any man, their green leaves waving in the cool breeze and creating rustling along the rows. Dinah watched the first gang of men and women, hunched over at the waist, swinging their billhooks against the thick sugarcane, hacking away six inches above the soil. As the cane dropped, they cut off the top of the stalk and stripped it of its leaves. They moved steadily, bodies bent like the arched back of a cat and rarely if ever straightening upright, always pressing forward swing after swing. Behind them, another gang of slaves, including children, worked at gathering the cane into bundles that they then bound with field twine and loaded onto wagons.

Dinah continued following Albert as they moved through the workers, not one of them concerned enough at their presence to look up from their work, nor to wipe the sweat from their brow. Albert stopped his horse beside a half-loaded wagon; it was here that he dismounted from his horse.

"Foy." He nodded, resting his arm on the side of the wagon where the black man sat, holding the mule's reins.

"Mornin', seh." Foy chewed on a small stalk. "Already got a wagon loaded and on its way to da mill," he said between swallows of the sweet nectar he had extracted from the bagasse. His hat was propped back, making his dark forehead look higher than normal. Giving a tug at his brown suspenders, he spit a piece of bark out and then wiped his chin with the back of his hand.

"Good," Albert replied.

Dinah stood, picking at her thumbnail beds and looking around herself at the people working. Her attention turned back toward Albert when she heard her name.

"Use Dinah out here through the harvest time. She can gather cane and help bundle it."

"Yes, seh. An extra set of hands in da cane will help more than ya know. Nathan!" he cried out. "Come here, boy." Nathan jogged up to the wagon. "Show Dinah how to bundle da cane," Foy ordered, gesturing to Dinah with his morning treat as if jabbing a stick at a dog.

"Yes, seh." A broad smile spread across the boy's lips showing a gap between his two front teeth that were as white as fresh pearls. "Well hi, Miss Dinah."

"Hi, Nathan."

"Come on nah, I'll show ya how it's done."

Dinah gave Mr. Toussaint a side-glance. His blue eyes nearly seemed gray under the shade of his brim. He gave her a nod before she turned and followed the bare-footed Nathan to where the tall stalks were falling like a defeated enemy. She quickly caught on to the work, though she was not nearly as fast as the others.

Glancing up occasionally, she watched Albert move among the workers. He would take the bundles of cane from the younger children and toss them up on the wagons for them. It wasn't long before Foy's wagon was full again. He clicked at the mule and gave him a swift pop of the rein to move him forward. The beast stirred from his idleness, as if awakened from a dream, and began pulling, contributing his part to the dreaded cane harvest.

The sun climbed higher in the wide sky. Dinah stood from her kneeling position when she finished tying a bundle of cane and raised her eyes, expecting to find the strong frame of Albert moving among the workers. A frown creased her brow when she didn't see him. She raised her hand to shield her eyes from the bright sun as she looked around for his white, bearded face. Bending down, Dinah picked up the cane she had just bundled. It was heavy and awkward as she threw it over her shoulders to carry on her back to the wagon, and a man reached in to take it from her shoulders.

"Here, I'll help ya with that," he said in a kind voice. "Ya Dinah, ain't ya?"

Her eyes narrowed. "Maybe. Who are you?"

"Abraham," he said, tossing the bundle of cane like it was nothing onto the bed of the wagon before turning to her with a smile.

He was tall and built like a bull: broad in the shoulders and thick in the arms; a powerfully made man whose face offered a shy-like expression; seemed almost contradictory. A rag was tied around his head to keep the sweat from dripping down into his eyes, his pant legs were rolled up to just below his knees, and his shirt was mostly unbuttoned, exposing his dark, muscular chest.

He chuckled at Dinah's crinkled nose and curled lip as she pulled her head back in a questioning expression, her eyes narrowed. "I've been noticin' ya on Sundays. Just haven't gotten da nerve up to say hi. And with ya in da house through da week and all…" He looked down at his feet and kicked at a loose cane leaves, his full lips pressed into a whistling shape, before he looked back up at her with a coy half-grin.

Dinah squeezed her lips together to keep from smiling as she looked him up and down. "Mmhmm," she hummed. Slowly, she turned and walked back to where she had been binding, and a smile forced its way onto her face.

Not long after, when the sun was overhead, one of the drivers called out as he moved along the row, "All right nah, lunch time! Lunch time nah, everyone, lunch time!"

Dinah looked at Nathan, who she had gratefully stayed near all morning, listening to him tell stories he claimed to be all truth. It seemed to make the time go by more quickly.

He gave his head a wipe of the hand and stood up. "My favorite time of day. Come on, ya can sit with me."

The slaves jumped in the back of some empty wagons and were towed to the huts. There, food was spread out on long, flat tables, served by the elderly slaves. Dinah had never seen how the field slaves ate their midday meal. She followed Nathan to the line that had formed and took up a tin; then she was served brown beans, sweet potato hash, collard greens, and a slice of cornbread.

"Workin' out in the fields durin' the harvest, ya get real hungry," Nathan said. "That's why Mr. Toussaint says two dips of beans, and he gives us extra cornmeal so we can have cornbread at noontime. And he gives us chicken on Saturdays." He gave his head a shake. "It sure does make a person long for a Saturday."

Dinah didn't say much, but the boy usually wasn't quiet long enough for someone else to speak. She sat quietly with him as they ate. Across the way, she noticed Abraham watching her as he finished his lunch.

"What do ya know about that Abraham fella?" she interrupted Nathan.

"Oh, Abraham? Well I know he's got a hankerin' for ya." The boy snickered.

"A hankerin' for me, huh?" Dinah repeated. She slowly put a piece of cornbread in her mouth as she made eye contact with the staring man. In response, Abraham smiled and dropped his head.

"He's hard workin'," Nathan continued without skipping a beat. "He's been workin' for Mr. Toussaint since he was near around my age. They be sayin he wants to be a driver. He keeps tellin the boss to give him more to do, to let him prove himself I guess."

The boy chattered on until it was time to load onto the wagons and head back out into the fields. The workers were allowed one more break in the evening time and worked by lantern light when the sun set until late in the evening.

Albert moved among the fallen cane, lantern in hand, until he came upon Dinah. Her dark face was camouflaged by the night, and when he raised his lantern toward her, it highlighted the curve of her full lips and high cheekbones.

"I still want ya workin' in the house in the mornin', helpin' with the children. We will head to the field together after breakfast."

She nodded. "Yes, sir."

The fall nights were cool. Dinah rubbed her hand up her bare arm. The slaves were gathering quietly into the wagons to head back to the huts, exhausted from the day's work. Mr. Toussaint and Dinah stood in silence looking at each other for a moment before he spoke again. "How did ya do out here today?"

Dinah was shocked that he would even ask a question that resembled concern or care, as if she would voice any discomfort or pain. No, a slave knew to only voice gratitude and praise, otherwise he would be met with the switch, or worse, by his master or driver for being an "ungrateful coon".

"Just fine," she replied flatly.

He gave a slight nod. "All right. See ya in the mornin' then."

"Yes sir. Thank ya, sir." She dropped her gaze, unable to look at him for the discomfort of the familiarity brewing with every stare.

Albert mounted his steed and rode back to the house while the few workers left continued bundling the last of that night's stock at the direction of the black drivers. Dinah was exhausted when she laid her head down that night. She couldn't recall the moment she drifted off; she only knew that it was a short and heavy sleep.

The next morning, along with every morning that week, Dinah woke with the typical routine, only with a sore back and aching arms. She was released from the house duties the moment Albert stood to go outside, and she walked behind him as they headed to the cane fields. Saturday finally came, and just like Nathan had said, chicken was served. The sweet, tender flavor had never been as celebrated as it was on Saturdays. It was just what was needed to push the workers through the last hours before their day of rest and beer.

On a typical Sunday morning, Dinah would meet with the others in the center of the huts for a Sunday "word from da Lawd" and song. She enjoyed the singing and tunes played on the quills more than the preaching of how the "Lawd saved da Israelites," how "Jonah stayed in da belly of da whale," and to "be submissive and trust in da Lawd, for He will deliver ya, fa surely His eye is on da sparra." The words seemed to bring comfort to those listening. The rhythm of the Sunday songs lifted the soul and brought life back; it made a person want to dance.

After the word was given, the music would continue as everyone dispersed to do as they willed. Some would work on repairing their huts while others made pots and pans. Some would work in the plot Mr. Toussaint allowed them in order to grow things to supplement their diets. During the cane harvest, though, many chose to relax and sip on what little beer was supplied.

This Sunday, Dinah did not sit around and continue listening to the music. Instead, she decided to take a stroll around the grounds in hopes of bumping into a certain bashful man. As she wandered languidly, she listened to the music resonate behind her and began to lose herself in the sound.

"What are ya doing, wanderin' around here for?" A male voice startled her, and her head snapped around to see Abraham sitting in the shade with a couple of other men. "I ain't ever seen ya take to strollin' before," he continued with a bold smile.

"I see ya make it ya business what I do with my Sundays."

"Not my business. I just take notice of ya like ya would a flower in the field." Dinah blushed but kept her face straight with no emotion. "Ya want to sit with us?" he asked.

"I'd rather stroll."

"Can I walk with ya?"

"I can't stop ya," Dinah said flatly as she picked up her pace. Abraham fumbled up from his seated position at the urging of the other men, and his step was quick until he caught up with her. They walked in silence for a minute.

"I never see ya at the Sunday service," Dinah finally said.

"The Lawd made Sundays for restin', so I figure He's fine with me doin' just that."

"Nathan said ya's been here since ya was a boy."

"Yeah." His voice was distant with the memory. "Mr. Toussaint was just getting started with his plantation when I was brought to him."

"Ya been here a while then?"

"Most of us here have been here a long while. Massa doesn't like to part with any of his own. Has been bringin on a lot of new faces lately though."

"I see," Dinah responded automatically.

"How ya like workin' in da house?" Abraham asked.

"It's all right. I've had worse."

"How did ya get put up on da auction stand anyways? Ain't no man in his right mind sell a pretty one like you."

"My last master died, leavin' me for his daughter. She was a mean woman, she was. Spoiled... Hateful... I swear seein' someone in pain was the only joy that woman ever had." She swooped down and pulled up a dried blade of grass before beginning to strip its fibers.

"Why she sale ya?"

"Her father just wanted somebody to keep him company in his old age. His children would hardly come around to visit him. So, when he was lonely, he would read and I would listen."

"What kind of stuff would he read ya?"

Dinah smiled. "My favorite was when he read Poe." Abraham shook his head, and she realized he didn't know whom she was referring to. "Edgar Allan Poe is a storyteller. Most of his stories hold a dark sentiment. I suppose that's why I like him so much. His words hold meanin' I can relate to."

"Well," she went on, "when he died and his daughter took me, I played right dumb with her, even though her father taught me. It took some time and some beatings, but I finally wore her down until it just wasn't worth her keepin' me around."

"Weren't ya scared da next would be worse?"

She turned, eyebrows raised, to look at Abraham. "When I say she was mean, I'm sayin' the sister of Lucifer!"

Abraham laughed. "Did she have horns?"

"Not on her head. But I never saw her naked. I'm sure they were somewhere."

Abraham's hearty laughter made her chuckle.

"Well all right then," he said with a smile. "I'm glad Mr. Toussaint found ya before anyone else did." He looked down at her with a gentle smile. "I think ya'll like it here."

"It's not too bad I guess..."

"Hey," he said, giving her arm a playful nudge. "Ya want to drink some beer with me?"

She smiled from the corner of her mouth and answered, "Yeah," with a glint in her eyes.

Abraham gave her a nod and led her back toward the huts, where he supplied her with a cup of beer before getting himself one. There, on the steps of a cabin, Dinah sat with him and some of the others, telling stories, laughing, and playing a tune or two. It had been a hard week of work, but it ended up being a good day off. If there were ever a Sunday that was the Lord's day, this was it.

CHAPTER FIVE

BY THE MIDDLE of the week, the previous Sunday seemed like a distant, sweet dream. There was no laughing and no telling of stories, and the songs that were sung held lament that the cane seemed to absorb. Dinah was bent over, counting and collecting the cane stalks. The counting kept her in rhythm and distracted her from pain shooting down her back.

It was the second half of the day and Albert had just returned to the field. His heavy steps pressed the loose cane leaves into the dirt. As he approached Dinah, he heard her faint voice saying, "Eight, nine, ten," as she added each stalk to her arms.

"You countin'?" His strong voice startled her, and she jumped and dropped her bundle.

"Aw Lawd," she said, grabbing her stomach from the sudden jolt and lowering herself to kneel. "Yes sir, I'm sorry, sir."

"I didn't mean to scare ya," he chuckled.

"No, sir, it's me, sir—"

"I just heard ya countin'."

Their voices mingled as Dinah apologized and Albert chuckled. She left her dropped cane where it fell and stood up slowly, her hand on her lower back. He watched her in her loose-fitting black dress, a blue rag tight around her head, as she struggled. He inhaled deeply through his nose.

"What can I do for ya, sir?" she asked with her head lowered.

"Why don't you come with me for a minute?"

Her eyes grew wide. "Yes, sir. I'll just pick up." She moved to kneel again when he stopped her.

"Leave it," he said. "Just leave it."

He started walking and motioned for her to follow. The others gathering nearby noticed and raised an eye toward Dinah but didn't stop their working. Hesitantly, but without a choice, she followed him.

Albert stepped up to a wagon that was near fully loaded and instructed the man sitting at the reins to get down. As Albert climbed up into the seat, Dinah stood next to the wheel, anxious to find out what Mr. Toussaint wanted.

He looked down at her. "Would ya like to see the mill?"

Dinah's eyes shifted back and forth. "Ya askin' me if I'd like to see the mill?"

"That's what I'm askin' ya," he confirmed. She rightly didn't know how to respond. "Come on." Albert took up the reins and readjusted himself on the box bench as he looked forward. "I may need ya to work the mill sometime anyway."

"All right," Dinah said quietly as she started climbing the wagon wheel to get in the back with the cane.

"Just sit up here." He motioned for her to sit in the box with him. She blinked quickly as she swallowed hard, but she did as she was told. "I'm takin' her to work in the mill today," Albert hollered at the driver, who gave him a nod.

Dinah's eyes stayed cast downward, but she felt the strong glares from the field pinning her in her seat, as if pointing at her with judgment. Albert gave the reins a switch and he uttered a command for the idle mule to pull forward. They rode in silence with only the sound of hooves and wheels meeting the hard ground and the whine of the wagon as it carried its heavy load.

"Ya will get an idea of how the sugar is processed. It'll give ya a break from the field labor."

"Why do I need a break? What about a break for the others?" Her words came out with more sass than she had intended, and she shrank down the moment she asked.

"They are used to the field labor. Ya are not," he said, unbothered by her tone. After a minute, he asked, "Ya ever taste the raw cane?"

"No, sir," Dinah replied.

He pulled the mule to a halt and removed a knife from the leather sheath strapped to his thigh. Turning around, he reached for a stalk from one of the bundles and cut off a piece from the end. After whittling off the outer bark, he handed it to Dinah like one would hand a peppermint stick to a child.

She looked at him inquisitively before reaching up and taking it. "Really?" she asked.

"Yeah. Enjoy it."

"Thank ya," she said with a timid smile.

He smiled at her as she slowly raised the cane to her lips. "You'll have to chew on it to get the sugar out," he said, motioning with his hand in an instructing fashion and clicking to the mule to move him forward.

Dinah began chewing the stalk, and the sweet flavor of pure cane juice flowed into her mouth. Instantly she salivated.

"Ya like it?" Albert asked with a smile.

"Yes, sir! I've never had anythin' like it."

As they rode along, she glanced up at him from the corner of her eye every now and then, but once Albert caught her stare, she bit her lower lip and kept her gaze forward until they got to their destination.

The mill was a well-run operation. Albert had built it a couple of years prior in the hopes of saving money. Dinah hopped down from the wagon and pushed her cane stick deep into her pocket before she followed him into one of the mill's buildings. It was hot inside from multiple fire pits below large copper vats full of boiling sugar juice. At the edge of each vat, men and women stirred the juice as it boiled and then skimmed off the top. Dinah's eyes remained wide as she looked around.

"What do ya think?" Albert asked.

"It's amazing," she replied.

"That man right there"—Albert pointed to a black man in suspenders with a red rag on his head walking from vat to vat—"is the boiler. He's highly skilled. He decides when the juice has been sufficiently reduced and purified." She watched Albert's profile as he spoke. When he looked down at her, she smiled.

"How does the juice get to the vats?" she asked.

Albert raised his finger with a smile. "Good question. Come, I'll show ya." Dinah followed him across the vast floor of the boiling house to the back end, where they followed large pipes to a separate room. There, men were feeding the cane back and forth between massive rollers powered by mules to crush them. Below the rollers, the juice was collected into pans and, from there, poured into the pipes leading back to the nearby boiling house. Dinah listened as Albert explained the process and showed her each step.

"And that's it. Now, what happens after the juice is boiled? I'm glad ya asked." He smiled and she warmly returned it before he led her to yet another building full of barrels and clay pots. "Once the boiler decides the juice is about to crystalize, he tempers it with lime juice and transfers it to a coolin' vat. Once it's cooled, they put it in these clay pots and wheel them here. They sit for a few days before we extract the molasses from the bottom." Albert showed her where the plug was located on one of the pots before walking Dinah over to watch a couple of women work.

"We barrel the molasses and sell it to a distillery to make rum. Now, see this?" He tipped one of the empty clay pots toward her and motioned for her to look. "That is sugar! We scrape it out and let it dry in the sun. Then we pack it up into the hogsheads and ship them off." He spoke proudly, and Dinah couldn't help but feel a bit of pride herself. It was contagious.

"So?" Albert asked, and she looked at him, waiting for the words to follow. "Where do ya want to work?"

"Ya askin' me where I want to work?" Her voice carried a friendly rise.

"I'm askin' ya."

Dinah pressed her lips together and looked around herself before her gaze traced back to his face. "In the dryin' and barrelin'."

Albert nodded. "All right then. Ya can finish up the day here, trainin', and can work in here the rest of the harvest."

She tried to keep the smile from spreading across her face but couldn't. "Thank ya, sir. Thank ya."

He gave her a nod and walked away, leaving her with the others.

Dinah picked up the process of drying and barreling sugar quickly. It was heavy and strenuous work on the upper body but much more pleasant than the hunched over gathering she was doing in the fields. Dinnertime came and the workers hopped on the wagons for their second break of the day.

After Dinah went through the food line, she saw the eager face of Nathan as he motioned to her from where he sat. She went over to him and sat down with her plate of food.

"Where ya been, Dinah? I seen Mr. Toussaint havin' a talk with ya and then ya was gone! Ya didn't get into trouble with the boss man, did ya?" he chattered loudly, never skipping a beat with putting hand to mouth.

"No, I didn't get into trouble."

"Then what happened?"

At that time, Abraham moved from where he was sitting and joined Dinah and Nathan. She hesitated with her response in front of him. "He took me to da mill to work," she said, her head dropping as she ate.

"Took ya to work in da mill?" Abraham repeated, and she nodded.

"What were ya thinkin', getting' up in da box seat with Mr. Toussaint?"

"What?"

"Ya heard me. I seen ya climb up there like ya belonged sittin' where he sat."

"What's it to ya? Ya don't own me," Dinah snapped, fire coming alive in her eyes.

"What's it to me? Everybody in da whole Gawd damn field seen ya ridin' off"—he raised his shoulders in a mocking motion —"sittin' there, next to da boss." She didn't respond. "Watch yaself, Dinah. I'm merely lookin' out for ya because I care. And I hope one day ya see how much I care and consent to be my wife," Abraham finished in a softer tone.

"Ya talkin' foolishness! And I don't need no one lookin' out for me."

"I'm just sayin', that kind of flirtin' with da boss...it'll bring trouble on ya."

"And I'm just sayin' to ya"—Dinah raised her voice— "if ya don't mind ya own damn business, it'll bring trouble on you." She gave him a stern look, her eyes wide and brows pulled upward into high arches.

She finished her dinner quickly without another word and then joined the others heading back to the mills to finish the day's work. It was a different sort of a day—an exciting but still exhausting day—and Dinah was thankful when it was over. Her mind kept repeating what Abraham had said and, with every thought, she fumed on the inside.

The next morning, she had put the conversation out of her mind and set about the morning duties like normal. After setting the morning pot of coffee on the fire, she put her hands into her pockets. There she felt the cane stalk, and a smile crossed her face that she tried to prevent by biting her lower lip. She pulled it out and, with a cock of the head, put it in her mouth and started chewing on it with glee.

When Nan looked up, she took a double take at Dinah. After walking over, she snatched it out of her mouth. "What is this?" Her eyes were wide and her round cheeks puffed out farther than normal. "Nah girl, I know ya ain't been taken bits of cane to be chewin' on! One of them drivers sees ya take a piece of da cane and do that and ya will be gettin' a beatin' fa sure!" She threw the bagasse down on the counter.

"The drivers chew on the cane. I've seen them," Dinah rebutted as she picked up her sweet treat.

"Well"—Nan extended the word long and low—"they be da drivers, and ya ain't!" Her eyes were wide as she stared at her.

"No matter," Dinah said nonchalantly. "I won't be in the fields no more."

"What ya talkin' about?"

"Mr. Toussaint moved me to the mill. I'll be dryin' and barrelin' the sugar," she said with a smile.

Nan's mouth dropped open. "Well, nah how—" Albert walked into the room then, quickly stopping the conversation. "Mornin', sir," she boomed.

"Mornin', Nan. Mornin', Dinah," he added when she handed him a cup of coffee.

"Good mornin', sir," she said softly, her heart jumping causing her to bat her eyelids as she looked up at him, surprised at her body's liberated response.

After he took his coffee and left the room, Dinah was able to tell Nan the events of the day before, omitting only a few details.

As she left that morning with Albert and he pulled his horse back to walk beside her, Dinah's step was a little lighter.

"How did ya find workin' in the mill yesterday?" he asked as they walked.

"It's alright. I learned a lot. My arms are sure sore, though," she said with a laugh as her hands came up to hug her biceps. "Not that I'm complaining," she quickly corrected herself. "I enjoy workin' the mill. I find it so fascinating, the process and all."

"That's good," Albert said, chuckling.

As the weeks passed, Dinah began noticing the ease with which she found herself exchanging with Albert. Every morning, their walk to the mill was like a refreshing wind on a hot day, and she looked forward to it more and more. It even made her respond more gently to Abraham, and it affected her Sunday plans too. She had begun taking extra care with her appearance and gave herself a sponge bath every once in a while, between bathing days. When her change in behavior was addressed by the others in the hut, she merely shrugged and rolled her eyes. They suspected Dinah was growing feelings for Abraham and teased her as such.

One morning, when the sun had just capped the horizon and the birds called out in cheerful song, Dinah was instructed to help unload a large wagon of cane into the pressing room. She lifted the bundles onto her back and took them in to be stacked in a ready pile for the men at the wheel.

"Start a new pile over there!" a man told her.

Dinah took her load and dropped it where he ordered as the men at the roller ran the stalk back and forth until there was nothing left but dry pulp. A frown of puzzlement crossed her face as she noticed one of those men seemed out of sorts, but when they started talking, she turned to get another bundle.

As she walked past the men, a cry stopped her in her tracks, startling her so badly that she jerked around. A man was crumpled next to the rollers, his arm trapped between the two, as blood curdling cries escaped his mouth. The other man was by his side quickly, fighting against the roller. Dinah's heart jumped to her throat as she processed what was happening.

"Somebody get those mules stopped!" the second man yelled out.

Dinah jumped into action and ran behind the rollers to grab

hold of one of the mules in the gin gang. The man's chilling cries continued as he screamed for help. Workers from the other roller had rushed over to help back the wheel up, and they were finally able to release his arm. It fell out, completely crushed from the elbow down. Dinah had to turn her head to control her stomach as they laid the man on the ground.

"Give him some room!"

"Bring water!"

Men shouted orders as they fanned him and tried to calm him down. Dinah joined them where they hovered over him, her breathing heavy. Though she wanted to turn away, she was frozen in place. Someone handed a leather strap to one of the kneeling men, and as he tied it to the man's bicep, Dinah wondered what it belonged to. A rein, perhaps.

"Fire up da axe!" The man yelled out. "Get it red hot!"

Dinah's mouth gaped open. "What?" she whispered to herself.

Before the axe was brought, Albert rushed into the mill and pushed his way to the man. "What happened?"

"His arm got caught in da roller."

"Aw shit," Albert replied angrily. "Here now, calm down if ya can," he tried to comfort the crying man. "Is the axe bein' fired?"

"Yes, seh," the one who tied off his arm replied.

"Ya know what to do."

"Yes, seh." The man shook his head as he pressed his lips into a hard line.

"Make it swift and clean," Albert added, putting his hand on the shoulder of the axe wielder as he stood.

He paused for a minute before moving toward Dinah, who was shaking, her gaze transfixed on the scene before her.

"Come on," he said, taking her by the arm. "Ya don't need to see this."

"They're cuttin' it off, aren't they?" Her eyes were steady on the suffering man.

"Yes." His grip became a little tighter, and she yielded to him as he guided her out of the mill.

"Ya goin' to sell him, aren't ya? A one-armed man ain't much good at the mill." Her eyes watered, but not a tear fell as she resisted his guiding hand forcing him to stop and look at her. "Ya have to sell him, right?" Something in her voice held desperation resembling pain. Albert's eyes shifted between her watery stare, and she felt his hand on her bicep lighten its grip.

Without the answer she was so desperately looking for, Albert led her to a wagon waiting to be driven back to the field for another load. "Get up there," he ordered.

Dinah gathered the long skirt in her unsteady hand as she stepped up to the box, followed by Albert, who had barely sat down before he had the mule moving. The sky was gray and the wind that blew against her face had a refreshing, cool bite. She took in a deep breath as she closed her eyes, not giving much thought to where they were headed; she figured he was taking her back to the fields to gather. When she collected her attention, though, she realized they were not heading in the direction of the cane field. Her heart raced with uncertainty.

Albert stopped the wagon abruptly after a short spell, leaving them alone in the middle of a field. "Ya all right?" he finally asked as he looked at her.

"Yes," she replied, staring into his eyes, which steadily stared back. Without power to control it, tears slowly rolled down her soft, flushed cheeks.

Albert reached up and gently swiped at one with his thumb, letting his touch linger. She didn't move as her eyes fixed on his gaze. Leaning forward, he placed a kiss on her cheek before, slowly, his mouth trailed to her lips. Dinah didn't kiss back, and her eyes didn't shut. She blinked twice, wondering if this was another one of her sinful dreams of Mr. Toussaint that had woken her up in sweat and longing a few times.

"Sir," she whispered.

"Shh."

Closing her eyes, she thought about the way his lips felt: gentle and soft under the bristle of his beard that brought to life the most sensitive parts of her lips. Slowly, she started returning the motion. She felt his tongue in her mouth as his hands took both sides of her face as her reaction brought out more of his desire. He let out a low growl like a hungry dog before stopping abruptly and leading her by the hand to the back of the empty wagon. The wood squeaked on its wheels as they stepped over the box seat. The hay field smelled sweet as Dinah fill her lungs anxiously, her senses heightened as passion stirred in her stomach. She knew what was to follow—she was no virgin. There had been two black men before, and one of them had her at an early stage in her life.

Her dress came off. Gently, Albert guided her to lie down, her back against the rawness of the cool wood, as she looked up into his longing eyes. His weight pressed down on her as he kissed her with tenderness and felt her curves. Desire built in her body, and she reached up and started unbuttoning his shirt. As his lips found hers again, he took it off and then suddenly rolled off of her to yank off his boots and undo his pants. She watched his muscular back as his arms moved feverishly to undress himself. He moved to roll back over her, and she looked at him as a luring grin pulled at the corners of her mouth. She wanted him.

Albert moved into her and her breathing quickened, but it wasn't harsh and fast like she had experienced before. He was steady, and as she concentrated on his movement, a mounting flow of pleasure spread through her body. Dinah reached up and took hold of his upper arms, she arched her back, and feeling his muscles flex as he held himself over her made her pleasure increase more. She vocalized it with a throaty moan. The rough wood of the wagon rubbed against her skin and would leave raw wounds, but the pain was welcomed. His movement quickened, before he reached the fullness of his satisfaction. Lingering over her with heavy breath, he gave her breast attention before resting fully on her. She felt the warm perspiration of his brow and chest against her skin, and her hand came up and gently traced his spine as she forgot for a moment the difference between them.

The peaceful moment didn't last long before they were both dressed again and bouncing back in the wagon toward the mill. He urged the mule slower than he had when they'd left it. The cool wind dried their sweat and replaced it with chill bumps. Albert didn't say anything to Dinah and hardly made eye contact until they pulled up in front of the mill. He looked at her then through eyes like those of an animal with a broken leg, glassy and sad. He gave her a quick nod as he pressed his lips together. Dinah climbed down from the wagon, heart full of dread at the thought that perhaps he regretted making love to her. She knew she would want him again but didn't have the liberty of going to him.

She moved into the drying and barreling house. Her body felt light and energized as she moved through the work mechanically, images of his body and the sounds of his breathing occupied her mind.

CHAPTER SIX

THE LONG DAYS of the harvest continued to pass with its unforgiving labor. Dinah feared what would become of the tension between her and Mr. Toussaint, but her fears were put to rest when nothing between them changed. Albert regarded her in his normal fashion until he desired her, which was more and more frequently, and then he would woo her body to his command and satisfy both of them. Dinah always smiled to herself the moment he pulled her away. She enjoyed the part of him that seemed to release her from the prison of her circumstances, and for some of those minutes, she actually felt he may have some kind of love for her.

It was the end of the year. Christmas had come and gone, though the house still smelled of pine and cinnamon—a lingering reminder, as Franny would say, that Christmas "ain't just fa one day. Da Lawd is fa every day of da year." Mrs. Toussaint was having a New Year's Eve party at the plantation and had demanded that Dinah stay working in the house during the past week to help with the preparations.

The morning of the party came. Dinah rushed to put on the yellow dress the missus had given her when she first arrived at the plantation. She scurried around the hut, getting the children ready while trying to undo the braids she had been wearing for the last week to provide the perfect curl for the event.

"Nah we ain't got no more time waitin' on ya to pretty yaself!" Nan urged as she pushed the mischievous children around. "I got lots to get done before da guests start arrivin'. So, come on nah! Ready or not, we goin'!"

Nan urged Dinah out with her squabbling, and she rushed along, half-braided and half-curled, behind her as they headed out into the cold dark toward the house. Once inside, Nan was quick to put Dinah to work well before Franny joined them. Soon enough, though, Franny's high-pitched laughter was trailing after Dinah as she asked what had happened to her head.

"Don't just laugh at me! Help me get the braids out," Dinah snapped, knowing the hour was coming when Mr. Toussaint would be down for his coffee.

Franny's fingers moved like magic through her hair, separating the braids into spirals that fell around her face. Nan mumbled something, but Dinah continued hurrying Franny as she moved around the kitchen and readied the coffee, the other woman nearly attached to her while she thumbed through her hair.

"Good mornin'." The strong, familiar voice made Dinah jump.

Her head snapped up as Franny quickly pulled her hands down, and their greetings were soft and low. Dinah poured a cup of coffee and bashfully walked it over to him, her hair still not fully unbraided.

Albert seemed intrigued at what he just walked in on. His brow creased a bit as the corners of his mouth tightened in an inquisitive smirk. Dinah, too embarrassed to look at his face, kept her head bowed, revealing the remaining two braids at the back of her head. Without a word more, he took his coffee and exited the kitchen. The women continued their busy morning, and Franny removed the remaining braids at Dinah's pleading before they gathered the children for breakfast.

The children would not be part of the evening's celebration, which Marianne continued to argue with her mother about throughout the afternoon.

The Toussaint family was having their afternoon tea in the sitting room like usual, except this time, Albert joined them. He sat across the room from Justine on a lounge, reading Charles Mackay while the children played at his feet and Marianne debated with her mother.

"Elizabeth is attendin'! All she can talk about is her dress. Why can't I, Mother? At least for dinner?" she pleaded.

"Now Marianne, I've told you no a thousand times!" Justine put down her teacup harder than she meant to, breaking it in two. Albert looked up from his reading at the commotion. "Now look what ya made me do," she continued frustratedly as she gathered the cloth napkin in her hand.

Dinah was quick to take the extra napkin she carried with her —something she had learned from taking care of the younger children—and caught the spreading liquid before it flowed off the end table it was sitting on. She fumbled, picking up the broken pieces into tense hands, as though she was the one under Justine's rebuke. Turning awkwardly to head to the kitchen and throw away the pieces, she looked up over her lowered brow at Albert, who was watching her. She blinked rapidly and swallowed hard as she hastily walked past his following gaze.

"Elizabeth is goin'," Marianne mumbled under her breath.

"And Elizabeth has already had her debutante! Now I don't want to hear another word from ya about this, Marianne, or ya will be in ya room the rest of the day and without dinner!"

"It's not fair," she huffed, crossing her arms.

"Marianne!" Albert's strong voice quieted her, and for the rest of the afternoon she said nothing, even though her body language clearly revealed she was nowhere near over her frustration.

Dinah returned with a different cup and saucer and poured Justine a fresh cup of tea before cleaning up the mess. As she turned, Albert raised his cup toward her. She walked over to fill his cup, the sound of Justine's irritated voice seemingly distant. As she tried to take the saucer from his grip, Albert's hand maintained its hold, his fingers lightly cupping hers. Dinah tried not to look at him, but his blue eyes allured her gaze. She pulled her lower lip in and sucked on it as she refilled his cup. After giving him another quick glance, she pulled her hand back and returned to her place next to the wall.

The guests had arrived by 6:30 p.m. Dinah was told by Nan that they would arrive thirty minutes before the five-course dinner, which would be served at 7:00 p.m., followed by dancing and gayety until well into the dawning hours. It was not uncommon for guests to be leaving as the first light of the morning hit the winter dew on the ground.

Soon, the halls of the plantation house were being swept with the full, colorful skirts of the women. Their pin curled hair was perfectly in place, and jewels and satin ribbons garnished their necks. The older men gathered in groups to gossip on politics, and the stock exchange and market while the young men moved through the crowds, choosing their seatmates for dinner.

Right as the second hand reached 7:00 p.m., Albert walked over to where the most senior lady sat and extended his hand to her. After she put her arm through his, he led her to the dining hall before sitting at the end of the table. Shortly after, Justine entered the hall, followed by a procession of the guests, and she took her seat at the head of the table. The hum of voices and laughter filled the hall. Dinah, along with Franny, Foy, and a dashingly suited Nathan moved among the guests, serving the different courses of the evening. At the conclusion of dinner, which lasted two hours and was as flawless as a waltz, wine was poured for the guests: Burmester, a tawny port, for the gentlemen, and the sweet Chenin blanc for the ladies. After drinking the wine, Justine stood and invited the guests to join her in the ballroom to continue the evening's festivities with music and dancing.

People filled the ballroom and filtered into the sitting room and halls of the house. Dinah moved through the crowd with fresh wine and brandy. As she walked by the wide entry to the ballroom, where both its French doors were wide open, she looked in to see the colorful fabrics move in rhythm to the music and spotted the decorated frame of Mr. Toussaint. Her expression didn't change, but she lingered for a minute to watch him.

Dinah turned with her empty tray to head back into the kitchen. It was nearing midnight and the bantering of the party was growing louder and rowdier. As she turned, she saw a face peering from the top balcony of the second floor, watching intensely. She smiled to herself and then slowly climbed the stairs, going unnoticed by the observer. When Marianne saw Dinah, she shrunk down where she sat.

"Seems like torture to have to sit up here and just watch," Dinah said as she stood over the girl. Marianne didn't respond. Her face was sullen as she looked back down into the hall. "Now why aren't ya in bed?" Dinah asked as she sat down next to the girl. "Ya know, if ya mother catches ya, ya will get switched."

"It's not fair," Marianne finally spoke.

"Well...I know."

"How do ya know how I feel?" the girl grumbled.

Dinah laughed in her throat. "I know that ya feel left out because ya up here and the party's down there. Ya best friend, Elizabeth, will have all these stories to tell about all the good food she ate and the wine she drank, not to mention the music and the dancin'! Oh, the dancin'!"

Her voice rose and fell as she watched the brooding expression on Marianne's face. Suddenly, the girl tucked back and her eyes grew wide. The sudden change in her expression didn't go unnoticed, and Dinah turned to look down at what had caught Marianne's attention: a sharply dressed young man not quite old enough to darken his face with a beard. His dark blond hair was combed back smooth, and she could see the strength of his young body filling out his coat and trousers.

"Oh, I see!" Dinah said.

Marianne shrunk back again. "What?"

"Do ya know that young man?"

"I don't know who ya mean." She frowned guiltily.

"Oh, I think ya see him too. Blond hair, strong frame, talkin' there to Miss Elizabeth."

"That's just Gabe," Marianne said, avoiding her gaze. "Elizabeth's brother."

"Oh," Dinah hummed lowly, "I see. Well, Gabe is a very handsome young man." Marianne shrugged but watched him intensely. "Does he know ya like him?" That got her attention as she jerked her head to look at Dinah.

"I'm not blind, Miss Marianne. I know that look and those feelins. When the sight of him makes ya quiver, and a knot rises from the pit of ya stomach into ya throat." Marianne looked at her with softer eyes as she spoke. "When the palm of ya hands get all sweaty, and there's this warmness that spreads through ya whole body." She closed her eyes and moved her hands with emotion. "And all ya want is for him to take ya in his arms, hold ya tight, and kiss ya." Dinah opened her eyes and looked at the blushing Marianne. "Ya just want to feel his skin, 'cause that's the closest to Gawd ya've ever been." Marianne swallowed hard. Her cheeks were red and lips a rosy pink.

"I bet there are other girls tonight who will not hide how they feel about him. If I were ya, I'd let him know I see him and how good he looks." Dinah pressed her lips together and gave a nod. "All right then." She moved to stand. "Don't let ya mother catch ya out here spyin' on the party."

Marianne smiled mischievously, knowing she would keep her secret. Dinah moved with a light heart back to the kitchen. She felt as if she had, for a minute, connected with the girl on a human level and had been seen as more than just a slave.

The hour was nearing midnight as Dinah busied herself alone in the kitchen. She turned and was startled to see Albert leaning against the back wall.

She gasped. "Mr. Toussaint, sir, I didn't realize ya was standin' there. Do ya need somethin'?"

He didn't say a word as his eyes penetrated through her and he took a steady step closer. Dinah swallowed hard. He stood in front of her before reaching up under her long, curly mane and taking hold of her head in his hand. Pulling her forward, he pressed her lips against his and fervently kissed her. Dinah returned the affection and, before she knew it, her hands were gripping his back, pulling him closer. His kisses intensified and moved to her neck as his hands started pulling up her skirt. Lowering her hand, she felt his eagerness to have her.

His hand moved freely under her dress, and her head tipped back in pleasure as he felt her. The moan in her throat encouraged him to continue. After unbuttoning the top of his trousers and reaching down into them, Dinah took hold of his erection and pulled him toward herself. Albert pushed her back against the wall with force before unbuttoning the remaining buttons of his pants while Dinah drew up the hem of her dress. After pulling himself out, they moved frantically against each other. They released simultaneous sounds of pleasure as he pushed into her. Dinah's grip tightened around him as she felt his muscles squeeze and release while he moved in and out.

"I want to please you," he spoke softly against her neck as his breathing deepened. Strengthening his grip and moving deeper into her, he growled, as her pleasure mounted, and he felt her quim tighten around his erection. He spoke, between gritted teeth, into her ear, "I want to please you…"

As the pleasure built inside Dinah, so did her moaning, and Albert covered her mouth with his hand as he pushed her to the point of orgasm. Then, taking her weak and relaxed body in his arms, he released his own pleasure.

As she let her skirt down, Dinah looked up into his eyes. Albert's strong face glistened with small beads of perspiration. Then he did what she longed for him to do: he wrapped his arms around her and kissed her gently, yearningly.

"Ehem." A throat cleared at the entrance of the kitchen. Albert pulled away harshly. "There ya are, Albert." Justine's voice held an edge sharper than a knife's. "It's nearly midnight, and the guests have been wondering where my husband is. It wouldn't be proper to bring in the new year without the host, now would it?"

Albert kept his head down as he moved away from Dinah. Justine extended her hand, motioning him in her direction, as her angry eyes remained on her. Dinah stood stiff as a statue as the fiery stare burned a hole through her. Albert walked past his wife with a sure, heavy stride. As they exited the kitchen, Dinah exhaled. Her breath came in short, quick bursts as tears began to flow down her cheeks.

It was minutes before midnight, and Marianne breathed out in nervous anxiety before she stepped around the corner from where she had been hiding in the shadows. After talking to Dinah, she had gone back into her room quietly and put on a dress, determined to let Gabe see her. The dress was a soft pink with ash rose satin ribbons trimming its edges. Though it was getting a little tight on her, Marianne loved the dress and the sweetheart neckline, which revealed her breasts starting to form. She didn't take the time to pin up her hair and instead let her long tassels fall on her shoulders. After biting her lips and pinching her cheeks, she stepped forward.

Gabe was in the middle of a hearty laugh with the young ladies he stood beside when he noticed one of them looking over his shoulder with an odd expression. He turned to see Marianne standing with shoulders back and stiff, her hands gripping tightly to one another. "Marianne!" he exclaimed with an embarrassed chuckle.

She offered him a nervous smile. "Hi, Gabe."

"What are ya doing? I didn't think ya were able to join the party."

"Oh, nothing." She stumbled with her words. The girls behind Gabe gave a small laugh, which he acknowledged with a side grin in their direction. "Can I see ya a minute?"

"Yeah sure, kid." Marianne nodded and started walking away, expecting that he would follow. "She's like my li'l sister," she heard Gabe say to the other girls before he followed her into the hall. "I'll be right back."

"Do hurry—we don't want ya to miss da midnight toast," one of the girls said sweetly.

Marianne led him to another sitting room off of the hall, and as he entered, he asked, "What's goin' on? Is something wrong?"

She turned to look at him. "No, I just wanted to say hello and Happy New Year," she said softly, beginning to feel silly.

"Okay!" Gabe chuckled. "Well, happy New Year, Marianne." He noticed she shifted her weight from one foot to the other and twisted her fingers around each other. "Is that it?" he questioned, and she nodded.

"Ya look nice," she managed to say.

Gabe cocked his head to the side slightly, offering her a grin. "Thank you." His eyes surveyed her. "Ya look nice as well." As he looked at her, though, his face changed, as if he were seeing her for the first time.

Marianne heaved her chest slightly as she noticed the change in his expression and his lingering eyes. "May I have a New Year's kiss?" she heard herself asking as he began to turn away. He stopped and looked at her. "It is midnight...and New Year's Eve," she fumbled.

"Sure, kid." He chuckled as he walked up to stand in front of her. "Have ya ever been kissed before?"

"No," Marianne said nervously.

Gabe smiled at her and gently reached up to touch her cheek as he bent his face down toward hers. Slowly, he pressed his lips against hers and then held them there softly. After pulling back, he kept his face close to hers and looked into her dreamy eyes. "How was that?" he asked.

"Perfect," she said, trying not to smile.

He grinned. "Happy New Year."

"Happy New Year, Gabe."

He left her standing there, but before he exited the room, he turned and looked at her. Soft light highlighted her dress. Gabe gave her a wink before walking back to his party of friends.

Albert stayed quiet the rest of the night under the loathsome watch of Justine. He stood with her as she toasted the guests in a speech to bring in the new year and continued pouring glass after glass of scotch when he finished each tumbler.

He stood among a group of men, their voices a bass-like hum as the brandy was poured in abundance. Cigar smoke lingered in circles around their heads. Faces began to blur, and words began to smear into one as Albert leaned heavily on the back of a lounge chair. Before he could catch himself, he stumbled over and was caught by another man. He spoke, but Albert couldn't make out what he said. The man tried to sit him down in a chair, but Albert pulled away and complained about the unnecessary attention. His voice rose in slurred frustration.

"I don't need to sit down! Tell me what to do in my house..."

He jerked back and attempted to walk away until he stumbled again, but this time he fell, sprawled on the ground. Justine was quick to the scene. She took him by the forearm and got him to his feet with the help of the men standing by.

"It appears the new year got the best of him," she attempted a joke with a forced smile. "Ya gentlemen know how to celebrate, and now my husband will be of no use to me tonight." The men let out hearty laughter at her suggestive comment. "Come along, Albert," she said, struggling to get him moving.

A man offered to help her get him to his room, which she gracefully declined with a smile before encouraging him to stay and continue enjoying himself. Justine struggled to get her husband up the stairs and to their bed. She laid him down without bothering to undress him. He reached out to her, but she denied him. Instead, she stood over Albert, staring at his intoxicated state. Her face revealed no emotion as his eyes closed and his hand fell to the mattress.

"Ya insult me and embarrass yaself," Justine whispered under her breath, her tongue pressing against her clenched teeth. After turning her back on him, she walked out of the room and closed the door behind her before returning to the halls full of celebrating guests.

CHAPTER SEVEN

THE NEXT MORNING was hell for Dinah. She woke and attended to her morning routine of readying the children and prepping breakfast along with the morning coffee, but Albert did not come down like usual. Franny, in a worrisome state, continued fretting all through the morning about Mr. Toussaint's absence and how, all through her days with the family, he had never missed his morning coffee, except for that one time when he was ill with the fever and nearly died. Dinah's head pounded. She longed to shut Franny up.

The morning came with the laughter and arguing of children, unaware of the tension in the air. Marianne gave Dinah a sheepish grin with a spark in her eye as she lingered back and waited until Franny had pushed the other children along to the breakfast table.

"I did what ya told me," she said quietly, her cheeks flushed from nervous remembrance.

Dinah's gaze was distant in thought as she tried to bring her attention to the girl. "What?" she asked.

"Last night, I did what ya said." Marianne smiled.

Dinah gave her a look of confusion. "What did I tell ya?"

"To make sure Gabe saw me... To make sure he knew I saw

him!" she spoke eagerly. Dinah wished she could join in the girl's excitement, but her stomach turned with anxiety and her head spun until she thought she may faint. "He kissed me!" Marianne continued, not noticing the grave look on Dinah's face. The girl's hand came up to her mouth as her eyes danced. "I wouldn't have gone down there if ya wouldn't have said that to me."

"I don't think I'd listen to me if I was you, child."

"What are ya talkin' about? That was the best advice I've ever gotten." She took hold of Dinah's arm. "Thank ya. He kissed me!" she said again before letting out a soft squeal of excitement, her face beaming with the glow of a first love. She skipped away like a young fawn, but from then on out, she held her head high, feeling more like a woman.

Dinah and Franny served the children and were standing at the wall when Justine walked in. She looked at the children at the table, eating like hungry hogs, before her gaze went to the two women.

"Mornin', Mrs. Toussaint," Franny offered in a chipper tone. "I hope Mr. Toussaint ain't down with an illness," she continued as Justine slowly walked toward the women, her eyes pinned on the bowed head of Dinah, "and dat it's just da effects of too much fun in da liquor cabinet." Franny chuckled.

Justine stood in front of Dinah. Her eyes burned like embers without a flame, and her jaw clenched as she stood in silence. "Ya get yaself out of my house," she said, monotone. Her lips hardly moved from the words. "Get ya whore ass out to the mill, where it belongs." Dinah remained frozen. "Go!" Justine yelled with unexpected venom, causing everyone in the room, including the children, to jump in alarm.

Dinah nearly ran out of the house. Franny stood with her mouth agape, and the children stared at their mother, eyes wide, as the two youngest burst into tears. Justine's cold face showed no other emotion when she turned and looked at everyone's questioning eyes. She moved to take a seat as Franny rushed over to

Isabelle and took her in her arms, removing her wailing from the table.

"Stop cryin', Albert," Justine said, but the boy continued to whimper. "I said stop cryin'!" she yelled. The boy's hands went up to his eyes and rubbed at his chubby cheeks. "Eat ya breakfast," she said to her children as she reached for a biscuit.

Not another word was spoken at the table that morning; there was only an occasional whimpering breath from Albert.

Mr. Toussaint wasn't seen that day. Franny put a tray of food outside the bedroom door that morning and gave it a knock. She fretted as she took it away, untouched, and left a tray with some lunch.

"Mr. Toussaint must be in some kind of way," she said as she entered the kitchen where Nan was stirring a boiling pot of stew. She set the tray of untouched food on the countertop and continued, "And I can't stop thinkin' bout Dinah. Da way da missus turned her out...she was mighty angry. Can't figure what she's done to make her so mad, but missus near scared da spirit out of all of us, da way she yelled at her."

"Nah I ain't ever seen Mrs. Toussaint act dat way. And it seemed dat everything at da party went all right." Franny was puzzled. "There are only two things I can think of that would upset Mrs. Toussaint so fiercely: messin' with her children, or messin' with her man. And I don't think it has to do with da children. Ya think Dinah upset Mr. Toussaint?"

"Good Lawd, Franny, ya is as stupid as a dog chasin' an imaginary stick! If ya ain't noticed da change between Mr. Toussaint and Dinah, ya is blind." Nan put the lid back on the boiling pot, where the smell of beef broth, carrots, potatoes, and cabbage escaped in clouds of steam. "Da way he looks at her when he takes his coffee in da mornins," Nan continued as she cracked an egg in a bowl and began whipping it. "Da way Dinah is frettin' about da way she's lookin'. I warned da girl! I said 'ya playin' with fire and ya's goin' to get burned.' There ain't no way around it. Ain't no good that can come of it!" Nan's voice rose in passion as she shook her head. "But did she listen to me? No, she too hardheaded, listenin' to her feelins instead of bein' smart in da head."

"Ya not sayin' dat Dinah and Mr. Toussaint..."

"Mmhmm, that's what I'm sayin'."

Franny let out a deep breath of disbelief, followed by a teasing giggle. "Well nah, Mr. Toussaint is fine lookin' fa a white man. I wouldn't blame Dinah fa gettin' herself a piece of that."

"Ya hush now!" Nan lifted the whisk she had been using to mix the batter. "That's no way to talk!"

"I'm just sayin', when ya in da desert and ya find a nice, tall glass of water, ya drink it," Franny bellowed out with laughter as she leaned her body over the counter. "Whew! Nah Lawd, is it gettin' hot in here? My knees are gettin' weak!" She continued, raising her hand to give her face a good fanning.

Nan gave in to a chuckle at Franny's dramatics before chasing her out of the kitchen with threats of taking a wooden spoon to her backside if she didn't get back to work.

Though the winter days were short, the harvesting days were still long. Dinah continued going to the house in the mornings to help set up the table and ready the children, but before anyone came down for breakfast, she would be on her way through the cold morning back to the mill. A week had passed without her seeing Albert. Every morning, she prepared his coffee, but he stopped coming down to take it. A second week passed, and Dinah became a little more settled in the thought that she might have avoided expected punishment.

The morning was the coldest it had been all year. After entering the house, Dinah removed the rags she had tied around her feet and rubbed them vigorously. Her skin felt like prickling needles as her blood began to warm her back up. It was a lazy morning and seemed like everything in the body moved extra slowly. The fire began to spread its warmth through the kitchen, and Nan's deep, slow hum filled the void.

The rooster crowed, and soon the shadow of Albert filled the doorway. Franny gasped. Dinah looked up and could not take her eyes off of him. Her breathing quickened, but her body stayed frozen in place.

"Mr. Toussaint! Da coffee ain't ready yet, sir." Franny scurried around to get him a cup and saucer.

"It's all right," he replied.

"Haven't had ya down fa ya coffee in too long," she continued as she checked to see if the pot had boiled yet. "I'm glad to see ya back at ya old habits again!"

His gaze stayed on Dinah as Franny fumbled with the pot and finally poured him some. "I've got ya fabrics for the year," Albert said to the ladies as he took the cup. "I'll bring them in to ya."

Franny smiled and cupped her hands like a child as he gave a nod and then exited the room. "I love it when we get da new fabrics," Franny said. "Every year about this time."

Albert had no sooner left the kitchen than he returned carrying bundles of fabric. One bundle was of wool flannel. The other two were of worsted calamanco with a glossy finish, one a light blue fabric patterned with red poppy flowers and the other an ash rose with cream strips. On the top of his bundle were three pairs of black shoes. Franny squealed, and even Nan came around the island counter with a smile to touch the new, beautiful fabric.

"I trust these will do for making some nice dresses," he said.

"Oh, sir." Nan's and Franny's voices mingled in admiration of the prints. "These will more than just do!"

"Oh, I do love me some poppy flowers!"

"Pink. I ain't ever had pink before!"

Albert smiled as he handed the fabric to Nan. He looked up to where Dinah still stood, frozen in place, and saw the nervousness in her eyes. "Dinah, come sit with me for a minute," he said, tilting his head.

The two women stopped talking and looked at each other then in Dinah's direction. Franny's eyes were wide as she gently twisted at the material's edge. Dinah glanced at them and then back to Albert. She swallowed hard before following him out of the kitchen.

Albert took his coffee to his regular sitting room. He set the cup down on the desk before turning to look at her. The sun was still below the horizon, but the lanterns lit the room with a warm glow. "How are ya?" he asked.

"Just fine," Dinah lied.

"Sit with me for a bit." He motioned for her to take a seat in a lounge chair adjacent to the desk. Her heart pounded. She didn't know what to expect from this encounter. "Would ya like some coffee? I can have Franny bring ya a cup, if you'd like."

"No," Dinah was quick to interject, "I don't need any coffee. If I may, I'm just a little confused. I…I don't know why I'm here. And I feel like ya have somethin' to say to me. Am I in trouble?"

"No." Albert frowned. "You've done nothing wrong. It was I who was in the wrong."

Dinah's chin raised a little as her eyes narrowed. She observed his face in the warm glow of the lantern's light, his blue eyes shadowed from his furrowed brow. The lines in his stare gave him a stern appearance. The peach color of his lower lip could be seen peering out from the curtain of his beard. Dinah's eyes settled on that lip, as it moved slightly from being pressed to its mate.

He took a breath before speaking again. "I got ya something else." He walked around the desk and took something wrapped in coarse brown paper from where it lay on the chair. He handed it to her. "Go ahead, open it," he said with a nervous twitch in his brow.

Dinah sat, shocked, holding the package. Slowly she tore at its folds, the tearing sound breaking through the quiet room. Her heart raced. Pulling back the paper revealed a red plaid flannel. She looked up to Albert, who stood over her.

"Take it out. It's already made. It's a shawl," he said, helping her take it out of the paper that still tried to cling to the beautiful fabric.

Holding it up, Dinah admired the color of deep red with thick cross lines of royal blue. Along the edge, the shawl was trimmed with a royal blue silk ribbon. "I can't accept this," she choked out. Albert frowned, his eyes squinting before widening again. "I can't," she repeated, shaking her head and standing. She laid the shawl down gently on the lounge.

"Why?"

"It's too fine. When and where could I ever possibly wear it?"

"Wear it when ya walk here every mornin'. It's cold outside. Wear it when ya walk back to the mill."

She continued shaking her head. "No." Dinah looked at him, his body standing so close to hers. He took her by the shoulders. "Please, no," she said.

"Why will ya not accept it?" he asked, his grip tightening.

Her expression hardened. "I am just like the other slaves. I sleep in the same hut; I work in the same mill. As long as they walk through the cold of night without a shawl, then I will." Dinah set her jaw tight.

Albert pulled her to himself forcefully and pressed his lips to hers. She allowed him to overcome her for a minute before resisting.

"No. I'm sorry." She shook her head and started to leave the room.

"Wait." His words stopped her in her tracks. "Surely ya know… I feel different about ya."

She turned and looked at him. "And what does that do for me but make my life more difficult? I can't do nothing with the feelins but bury them and be tormented by them every time I see ya. Ya own me, just like an animal."

"I don't treat ya like an animal!" His voice rose in agitation.

"But I'm owned like one. All my people are owned like one."

"That is how ya run a plantation." His hand rose to express his case. "Without the workers, how would ya operate one? How would the mill run?" Dinah pressed her lips together, her eyes like dancing flames. "Ya speak as if I'm cruel," he spat, insulted. "I treat my slaves kindly, with human decency!"

A huff escaped Dinah's lips as they spread into a questioning smirk. "Kindly?"

Albert's blue eyes flashed like lightning over the seas. He took a stride toward her and grabbed her tightly by the wrist. Her eyes widened and her jaw flinched, expecting a strike across the face for her backtalk. Instead, he just held her wrist forcefully, breath coming heavily through his nostrils as eyes glowered and he stared at her.

"I guess I should've let the LaLaurie buy ya. I could sell ya to him now—then you'd really see how kind I am," he said in a low growl as he gave her wrist a jerk. His grip was painful, but Dinah clenched her teeth, refusing to voice her pain. Their eyes clashed like the blue and red of a hot fire. "What do ya want from me? This is how it's been for centuries."

"Because it is doesn't mean it ought to be," she said boldly. His grip softened, as did his eyes. Knowing he was about to lean in for a kiss, Dinah shook her head.

"Yes," he softly murmured, leaning forward. "Yes," his lips whispered again against hers, the stiff hair of his mustache tickling her sensitive mouth. She kissed him with yearning, and the sharp words between them washed away beneath a stream of gentle passion.

A bruise on her wrist began appearing the next day and lingered for the following week. It was sore, and Dinah gently rubbed it through the day as her thoughts went back to that moment with Albert. He hadn't come around her since the morning of their quarrel, nor even made eye contact with her when he came down for his morning coffee. She thought nervously about him, hoping she hadn't made him too disgruntled toward her.

It was that week that Dinah was making her way through the mill when she saw young Albert in the boiler room with his father. When the boy recognized Dinah, he started running toward her.

"Albert!" Mr. Toussaint yelled.

Little Albert started talking to Dinah in excited chatter. She knelt and took the boy by the shoulders with a smile. He chatted away as Mr. Toussaint walked up behind him, and Dinah looked up at Albert. Her smile slowly faded as she stood. Young Albert reached up and took her hand.

"Good," his father said when Dinah stood. "Watch him for me. He insisted on coming with me today, but there is a problem I need to attend to." She gave him a nod, and he knelt to his son. "Stay with Dinah and do what she says. Don't go runnin' around— it's dangerous in here. I'll be back in a little bit." He rubbed the top of the smiling boy's head and then stood and walked away.

Dinah looked down at the boy, who gazed up at her with a beaming smile. She returned the grin. "Ya want to go taste the molasses?" she asked him, and his smile broadened. She laughed. "All right, let's go."

She led young Albert to the barreling room, where she let him dip his fingers into the dark, sweet gold. The other workers watched her as she made her way, with the boss's son, in and out of the mill, laughing and playing with him.

After some time had passed, the driver caught hold of Dinah. "Need ya help loadin' up da hogsheads into da wagon."

She glanced over at young Albert as he looked out from the railing at the busy workers. "Mr. Toussaint is busy with some problem and told me to watch Albert."

"He can stand off to da side and play like children do. I need an extra set of arms. Ya ain't been workin' all day today and I'm feelin' da lack of help. He can stay close, and ya can just keep ya eye on him." Dinah exhaled in uneasiness. "Come on, let's go," the driver pushed.

"All right. Albert," she called, extending her hand to the child. "Come on now. I've got to do a little work, and you've got to stay close by, okay?" Albert took Dinah's hand and followed her through the mill.

As she worked on rolling the barrels with the others, she kept a close eye on the boy. He sat on barrels or folded himself over the tops of them before he found a cane stick and tapped the tops and sides of the barrels, finding the different sounds he could make.

Dinah breathed easy, as he seemed to be entertaining himself without a problem, until one moment she looked over and he wasn't there. Panic set in as she looked around without spotting him. She stumbled around the barrels quickly, looking for him.

"Albert!" she called out. "Where did he go?" she asked the other workers.

"He was right ova der. I didn't see where he went," one of the men said.

No one had noticed the boy slip away, and there was no sight of him outside. Dinah ran toward the mill, calling out his name. She entered the boiling room at a frantic pace. As she looked around, she saw his small frame standing close to one of the steaming copper vats of cane juice.

"Albert!" she called out, getting his attention.

He spun around in a startled jerk and lost his balance. Tumbling backward, he fell against the vat. His forearm caught the hot metal, melting the flesh from his arm. A scream from the boy filled the air as Dinah ran to him. The boiler, along with some of the stirrers, stopped their work as they hurried to where the child writhed on the ground.

Dinah reached him and threw herself on the ground next to him. "Where's Mr. Toussaint?" she screamed at the other workers.

"I think he took his horse out to da field," a man answered.

Young Albert twisted in pain on the ground, holding on at the elbow of his burned arm. His flesh black and charred, burned into the muscle, releasing a metallic, meaty smell. Dinah swept him up into her arms and rushed out of the hot boiling room.

"Find Mr. Toussaint!" she ordered. "I'm takin' him to the house!"

She ran up to an empty wagon, and after passing the boy over to one of the men who had followed her out, she climbed up into the seat before reaching down and taking him back into her arms. Another man quickly climbed up with her, and after taking hold of the reins, drove the team toward the house at a full run.

Dinah tried to soothe little Albert as she held him in her arms. She stroked his sweating brow and held him tightly, speaking comforting words to him. The boy whimpered and cried from the excruciating pain.

The wagon pulled to a skidding halt in front of the house, and the man jumped down and took the child from Dinah. Together they rushed him inside. The commotion and crying brought Justine and all the children into the sitting quarters, where they laid him on the lounge. Young Albert's cry and raw arm set the two younger children crying along with him.

"Marianne, get the children out of here!" Justine ordered firmly. "What happened?" she demanded. "And where is my husband?"

"He fell against a boiling vat. Mr. Toussaint went to the field," Dinah said breathlessly. "A rider went after him."

Justine looked the arm over. It was burned black and showed the meat from his elbow down his hand. "This should've never happened... My poor baby. Quickly, go get some wet clothes and a chunk of ice," she ordered, and Franny jumped to it.

Mr. Toussaint burst into the room and rushed to where the boy lay. "Let me see him." He knelt beside him and placed a hand on his wet head as he looked at the boy's arm. "Shhh. There, son, you'll be all right," he soothed as he examined the damage.

"Papa," the boy whimpered.

Franny returned with two damp towels and a chunk of ice. As

she handed him the towels, Albert said, "There should be a little bottle of iodine down in the cellar. Bring that to me."

"Shouldn't we send for the doctor?" Justine asked, worried.

"I already have. I sent Foy." He gathered his son into his arms. "Let's take him up to his bed. He'll be more comfortable."

After carrying him up to his room, followed closely by Justine, Albert laid him down. Dinah hesitantly trailed behind, making sure to keep a fair distance between herself and the missus. She stopped at the door frame and peeked in. The room began to spin on Dinah as she watched Albert situate his son on the bed. Franny returned with the iodine and rushed past Dinah and into the room, mumbling words of fret.

"Now, son, this is going to sting. I need ya to be strong," Albert said, looking the boy in the face. "Grit ya teeth, okay? It won't last very long, but I need to do it." He exhaled heavily before slowly pouring the iodine on the wound.

Dinah couldn't turn her eyes away from the dark liquid as the boy cried. The pungent odor filled the room, irritating the senses, and her stomach started to churn as beads of sweat formed on her forehead. Suddenly she knew she couldn't stay in the room, and she rushed out and ran down the stairs. Hardly no sooner was the door to the outside open than she buckled over the rail and vomited. It took her a couple of minutes and some heaving before she could stop. After sinking down next to the railing on the porch, she ran her hand across her face and tried to steady her breathing.

The air was a crisp thirty-nine degrees out, but Dinah remained sitting outside on the porch steps. The cool air seemed to calm her stomach. The doctor had arrived and rushed inside, and a few hours later, he left. Dinah didn't move. She sat there until Albert, with a heavy step, walked out onto the porch. She looked up at him, and the sight of blood on his shirt sent her stomach swirling again.

"How is he?" she asked.

"Doc took his little finger—said it would be of no use to him. Have to watch for infection. He could lose his arm...or his life." He spoke slowly, his words thoughtful and precise. "How did this happen?"

Dinah hesitated and reached up to brush at a tear that fell down her face. "I was watchin' him, but then the driver told me he needed me to help load up the wagons. I told him I was carin' for little Albert, but he insisted. Albert stayed close and just played around the hogsheads. I looked up and he was there, then I looked up again and he was gone. He went back into the boiler house. When I found him, I called to him... That's when he fell against the vat..."

"The driver ordered ya to work after I told ya to watch the boy?"

"I shouldn't have listened to him," Dinah said wiping at the freely falling tears.

Albert was furious. He went down the steps in a quick bound and started walking toward the wagon Dinah had used to bring young Albert to the house. He abruptly turned and went back to where she sat. After grabbing her forcefully by the arm, he led her to the wagon.

"Get up there," he ordered.

Dinah did as she was told. Her head spun and her heartbeat quickened with anxiety. Albert drove the team of mules hard toward the mill. Once he pulled to a halt, he leaned forward with elbows on his knees and head down. Dinah felt his strange behavior and quivered.

"Point him out," Albert said quietly.

Her breathing quickened. "I don't see him."

He climbed out of the wagon. "Come on," he ordered.

She looked at his hard face, jaw set like flint, nostrils flaring, and brow furrowed and darkening his eyes. After climbing down, she walked sheepishly ahead of him at his demanding hand gesture.

"That one," she said quietly when she saw the driver.

When the man looked up and saw Albert marching toward him like an angry bull, his face washed over with fear. Albert grabbed him by the front of his shirt and whipped him around.

"When I give orders, they are to be followed and not over-ridden by what you think needs to be done!" he growled between gritted teeth, his face so close to the man's that the driver felt the heat from his breath.

Albert threw the man down onto the dirt. He turned in fury, looking around himself, and his eyes fell on a pile of cane stalks. After grabbing hold of one, his knuckles turned white as he brought the stalk over his head. It came down in a violent blow across the driver's forearm and shoulders. The man wrenched and hunkered down with his face toward the dirt. Another strike was rendered across his back, followed by another.

"My boy...could lose...his arm!" he bellowed.

Dinah jumped with every blow as she watched Mr. Toussaint's anger unleashed on his slave. Tears involuntarily rolled down her face at the scene before her. The others had stopped working as well and watched from where they stood.

Albert finally stopped. His chest heaved as he looked down at the beaten man. Flinging the cane stalk across the ground, he turned on his heel and stormed from the scene. Dinah quivered down her spine as he walked past her.

Foy took the driver aside, away from the others, to address his wounded back. The others began their work again, and Dinah, numb, found herself stumbling back to the barreling house to work the rest of the day.

The next morning felt eerie. Dinah went up before the sun rose to look in on the boy. As she cracked the door to the room, she saw Albert's silhouette in the low, flickering candlelight. The room still smelled of iodine and gauze, making her stomach churn. She gave him a sorrowful look before backing out of the room and closing the door.

Back in the kitchen, Nan asked, "What's da matter with ya?"

"Oh, the smell of that iodine just sets my stomach to swirlin,'" Dinah said, holding her stomach. The room began spinning as her brow began to sweat.

"Ya gettin' sick?"

Dinah couldn't answer. Her eyes stayed shut as she reached up and wiped her face. She took in a deep breath to try to settle the shaking in her stomach. The smells of the kitchen were too much for her. Shaking her head, she rushed to hug the trash bin. Dinah bent over and vomited until she heaved. After sitting on the ground when she had finished, she looked up at Nan's shocked stare.

"I must be sick," she said, wiping at her watering eyes.

"Ya ain't sick, woman, ya with child!"

CHAPTER EIGHT

THE DAY PASSED IN A DAZE. Dinah couldn't believe what Nan had claimed. They argued for days about her condition, but the symptoms all pointed to her being with child. She couldn't believe it; her heart raced with excitement and fear. As she thought about how to tell Albert that she carried his child, she feared his response.

Days passed. The mornings were the hardest for Dinah with her sickness. Young Albert was finally out of danger of having an infection that would threaten the loss of his arm, even though the healing process was far from over. February came with the approaching end of harvest and the hope of spring.

Nan was good about keeping Dinah's secret, even though Franny was taking notice of the repetitive morning sickness.

"Ya better tell Mr. Toussaint before da baby does," Nan would say, giving her a stern look and a shake of the head.

It was the third week of February and there was no denying now that she was with child. Dinah made the morning coffee and took a deep breath to slow her racing heart. The kitchen was quiet that morning, as if the other two women felt the anxiety that was weighing down on Dinah's shoulders. She woke, like many days before, determined that it would be the day she would tell Albert. Unlike many days before, however, she put on her blue dress and loosely braided her curly hair, letting it fall down her back and leaving her curls to sit freely on top of her head.

The rooster crowed, and like usual, Albert was down shortly after to take his cup of coffee. He noted that Dinah was in the dress she hadn't worn since harvest began, and her appearance was glowing. Without commenting, other than a nod, he took his coffee and went to the sitting room.

Nan looked at Dinah, her eyes wide and nearly bulging from their sockets. "Nah what was that?" she boomed with sass.

Dinah went to the island counter and put her hands on the top. Her head hung. "It's just…"

"It's just what? Ya going to keep puttin' it off until he finds out on his own?"

"There's a baby, isn't there?" Franny chimed in.

"Yes, there's a baby!" Nan replied, throwing her hand in the air. "And I'm fixin' to tell him myself, because ya too chicken to tell him what's goin' on. Ya ain't been shy around him before. That's how ya got in this mess!"

Franny's eyes widened, and her hands went to cover her mouth. "This Mr. Toussaint's baby?"

"Yes, it's Mr. Toussaint's baby," Nan sang, slamming her bowl down on the countertop as Dinah's cheeks grew hot.

"Well, Ms. Dinah, ya just got to tell him," Franny said, going to her side and placing a hand on her shoulder. "Do ya even want da baby?"

Dinah's head jerked up and her eyes snapped to Franny's. "Well yes. I mean, how much choice do I have in the matter?"

"Well now." Franny cocked her head to the side. "I could fix ya up a strong cup of special herbal tea. Ya got to drink it every day until da flow starts again. I've seen some mighty painful cramps in some girls when it happens, but it always works." To that, Dinah was speechless.

"Ya hush up nah about that Voodoo!" Nan barked.

"Ain't no Voodoo. Just a tea to make da flow start again. Can't be no baby if there's a flow."

Dinah began shaking her head. "No... No," she said as she walked out of the kitchen into the darkened hallway.

She stood with her back against the wall, exhaling and trying to calm her racing heartbeat. After turning her head to the warm lantern light washing in from the sitting room, she took a step toward it. As she hesitantly looked in, she knew that, the moment he saw her, it would be too late for her to retract, and for a split moment she wished to pull back into the shielding darkness of the hall. She stood frozen in place.

Albert's eyes gently rose to look in her direction. When he saw her, a trifling grin pulled at the corner of his mouth. He didn't trouble himself to move his head in her direction but kept his eyes pinned on her. "Yes, come in."

His low voice resonated in Dinah's ear like a distant roll of thunder, soothing yet terrifying. She took slow steps toward him and stopped a few feet away. Albert leaned forward from his reclined position and extended his hand to her. Stepping forward, she took hold of his warm, sturdy hand and was gently pulled closer. She stood over him, looking down on his oiled hair, as he placed a light kiss on her fingers. Albert looked up at her, his blue eyes holding a happy glint she had not seen before.

"I'm glad you're here. I've missed you," he said, brushing over her fingers with his thumb.

Dinah couldn't smile at him but returned his steady gaze as he stood. He leaned in and kissed her lips tenderly, but before Albert could put his arms around her, she pulled away and took a step back. She grabbed her waist as she turned her back to him to take a breath. When she turned back around, she looked at his curious face.

"I have to tell ya something," Dinah stammered, rocking her weight from one foot to the other under his strong stare. "Sit down." A frown crossed his brow. "Please," she quickly added, and Albert sat back down in his chair. Dinah took in a lungful of air as her fingers fidgeted with each other in front of her racing heart. "I am with child," she finally let out. She waited for his response, eyes wide and lips pressed together.

Albert's blank expression didn't change. He blinked rapidly before his head turned and looked to his boots.

Feeling the need to fill the cold void of silence, Dinah was the first to speak again. "It's yours." Her voice held a quiver she wished it did not.

"Are you certain?" he asked flatly.

"Yes. Absolutely certain." Her dry tongue went over her bottom lip and drew it in to bite. The few moments of silence seemed like eternity. "It's yours I swear it," she whispered, "Please say somethin'." Her voice finally broke the quiet as her body began trembling.

Quietly, he mumbled, "New Year's," before his hand went up to shield his eyes and rub his temple.

"Yes," she whispered. "What's to happen to me and my child?"

Albert looked at her. "You must be terrified." Dinah raised her chin but said nothing. "How long have ya known?"

"A few weeks."

His eyes narrowed as his thoughts retracted to count the weeks passed. "You're about seven weeks."

Dinah just nodded. The glow from the morning light was starting to touch the horizon and filled the room with a dusky hue. Albert rose from where he sat and moved to stand in front of Dinah. He lifted her chin with his fingers, but her eyes still cast downward. Tears rolled from the corners of her eyes and framed her face.

"Look at me." She did as she was told and found his eyes were pools of solace. "Don't be afraid. Ya not goin' anywhere. I'll take care of you and the child. Okay?"

Dinah sniffled as the tears fell. She gave a nod and licked her lips. After putting his hands on her shoulders, Albert brought her to his chest and held her as he continued speaking.

"Now listen." His voice was resolute, offering her comfort. "Harvest is at its closure, so ya don't need to be out at the mill anymore. Ya can work in the house again."

"What about the missus?" Dinah mumbled against his chest as it rose.

"Let me worry about that." Silence followed. The room was brightening as the radiance of the sun peeked over the skyline. He rubbed her back as he cradled her; she longed for the moment to never end. "Ya carryin' my child. If ya need anything, I want ya to come to me, okay?" She nodded and his arms slowly loosened their grip. "Ya will stay in the house startin' today."

He looked down and watched her reach up and dry her eyes with both her hands. Her gaze went back and forth between his steady stare and finding another object to look at as she composed herself.

"Dry ya eyes, and then go get the children ready for breakfast."

She nodded and, looking at him, offered a small smile. "Yes, sir," she said before she turned and left the room.

Franny and Nan kept steady gazes on Dinah the rest of the morning. Neither spoke of the situation but rather supported her in their silence. As she began working in the house again, Justine ordered that Dinah was not to attend to her, to which Dinah was more than happy to comply.

A few days had passed, and the family had gathered at the table for dinner. The children were chatty as usual as Dinah and Franny brought out the side dishes and rolls. Nan followed, carrying a steaming platter of roast beef, tender and juicy. She carried it as if it were her greatest accomplishment and presented it proudly at the center of the table. The steam rolled off the top, transporting the delicious smell of roast into the air. Dinah placed the rolls next to Isabelle, who playfully tried to reach for one.

Suddenly, Dinah's stomach began to swirl. She frowned as she stepped around to take the pitcher of tea and began filling the glasses. The family began passing the food and tearing at the meat, and the sound of the fidgeting silverware added a mocking clap to the sudden spinning in her gut. Dinah's hand started shaking when she abruptly put the pitcher down and tried to rush out of the dining room. Before she could leave, she crumpled before the large, decorative vase next to the window and started vomiting into it.

The children were all aghast, making faces and noises among themselves. Albert pushed his chair back and began to get up from the table when Franny rushed over to Dinah, taking her by the shoulders.

"Come on," she whispered in her ear. "Stop if ya can and I'll get ya out of here."

"I can't," Dinah whimpered, head hanging over the opening of the vase. "That smell…the meat." After dropping her head back down, she vomited again.

Franny grew nervous as the noise at the table continued with Justine adding comments of disgust. "Come on now, Dinah. Let's just get ya into da kitchen!" she urged, tugging at her shoulders.

Nan was soon in the dining hall to see what all the commotion was about. Her powerful frame marched across the floor when she saw what was happening. "All right nah, get yaself up," she said, taking hold of Dinah by the shoulders. Dinah let Nan guide her away from the embarrassment and into the kitchen, Franny following with the vase.

"Well, that just about ruined my dinner," Justine said after the women were out of the hall.

"Here, quiet down," Albert corrected his children. "Eat ya food."

"Well, Albert, maybe their appetites are ruined too."

"I don't want this food to go to waste, so they're going to eat it!" he boomed. The children quieted down as Justine watched him lift his fork. "She's not in here anymore, so go on, eat!" he ordered, looking at his two oldest daughters.

The children slowly and quietly started eating. Justine didn't move.

After a moment, she spoke. "Why is the color drained from ya face, Albert?" He slowly chewed the bite he had just put in his mouth. He swallowed and looked up at Justine. "Ya face..." Her voice was flat. "Ya eyes..." Albert looked back down at his plate. The children hunkered down in their seats and looked back and forth from each other to their parents. "Say it's not so..." The table was silent. "Say it's not so!" Justine yelled.

The children jumped from the sudden fury, and Isabelle started crying. Albert's gaze jerked up to look at his wife's demanding presence. Suddenly, she pushed her chair back fiercely and stormed out of the hall.

"Marianne, quiet ya sister," Albert ordered calmly. "You children, eat ya dinner."

They ate slowly and quietly before being excused from the table. Then they hid in their rooms the rest of the evening as Albert went to find Justine. The whole house heard her rage that night behind the closed door to their bedroom. Hours passed before Albert swung the door open and stormed out.

"I've had enough!" he yelled as he made his way to the staircase.

Justine stood in the doorway. "Don't ya dare come back to sleep in this bed!" she yelled after him. "Ya do and I swear to God I'll set ya on fire!"

The door to the bedroom slammed; Albert didn't turn around. He went down the stairs and through the house until he was outside. Then he wandered the grounds back and forth. The air was crisp and the sky was clear, showing what seemed like every star in the heavens. The air had not yet warmed enough for the frog or the bush bugs to make music, so silence held the night. Albert stopped pacing, raised his face to the sky, and breathed in deeply. He stayed outside for hours. No one knew when he made his way back into the house or when he lay down on the sofa.

The hum of gossip overtook the huts and soon everyone knew that Dinah was pregnant with Mr. Toussaint's child. It was Sundays that bothered Dinah the most. She received some stares from the corner of eyes while others would look straight on with contempt and judgment. The good brother would preach on Sunday mornings about the Lord's forgiveness on humanity's shortcoming and how a house divided against itself cannot stand. Dinah could never tell if he was chastising her on her Magdalene state or the gossipers who looked down their noses at her.

Only Nan and Franny, along with a handful of others, treated Dinah without disdain. They encouraged her that it would get easier as time passed and that people would no longer care, but as time went by and Dinah's belly grew, it seemed that was the furthest from the truth. Abraham's disappointment was the hardest for Dinah to consider. Over the months, their Sunday chats, walks, and arguments had festered feelings of attachment in her. Now he kept his distance.

"Ya treat me like I have disease," she confronted him one day.

"Worse! Ya got da boss's baby inside ya!"

"Yes, and I can't change it."

"Dat's right. It's what it is," he argued.

There was a pause between them before he continued. "I just can't imagine why ya would do this when I made clear da feelins I had for ya." He pounded the front of his chest with his clenched fist as he paced like a beast in a cage.

"Ya talk like I was already your woman." His dark eyes looked at her, glazed over with hurt. "Was I to tell him no? Ya the boss, Mr. Toussaint, but no... Is that what I was to say to him?"

Abraham's breathing was heavy. "Did ya want him?" Dinah remained silent, so he asked again, "Did ya want him?" He stared at her with wide eyes. "That's what I thought," he said when she offered no response.

"Abraham…"

His hand came up as he shook his head. "No. No more."

Dinah watched him walk away, her shoulders stooped. It was that Sunday that she last visited her people in the community.

Albert offered Dinah a room in the house when he found out the difficulty she was having among the others. She declined, but with him it was non-negotiable. He set her up in a room down from Franny. It was small but had a mattress bed and feather pillow. A nightstand made of polished hickory big enough to hold a candelabrum that had three arms, yet one candle was at the head of the bed next to the door. A single window faced out the back of the house, toward the grove and the southwest sky. Albert had a rocking chair placed in the corner, next to the small closet. It was a humble room, but never had Dinah so much as laid her head on a feather pillow before, let alone have her own room.

She found it a place of solace, a retreat into her own thoughts away from all painful stares and gossiping tongues. One Sunday, Dinah walked in and found a book entitled *Two Years Before the Mast* lying on the nightstand next to the candelabrum. She took it up and thumbed carefully through the pages. The smell of fresh paper wafted through the air, and she breathed in deeply, filling her lungs with the perfume of the written word.

She went to the rocking chair and lowered herself carefully into its trusty hold. The wood crackled as it bore her weight and she began to rock. A cool, shaded breeze from the open window moved the sheer white curtains like an elegant dancer. Dinah looked out the window onto the lawn. The early summer grass was a fresh green and not yet burned from the sun. Right now, the earth was in full bloom for her warm lover, giving all her beauty in vulnerability like she didn't know of the impending heat that would scorch her as it did every year.

As the months passed and the child grew within her, Albert called for the doctor to visit and exam her. Dinah had never been seen before by the white man's doctor, but she recognized him from the dreadful winter when young Albert fell against the vat. His eyes were void of any kind of emotion as he conducted his examination. She sat, gripping the skirt that covered her knees, as he pressed around her belly where the child pressed back. Albert stood in the doorway as he waited with arms crossed.

"The pregnancy seems to be healthy," the doctor said flatly as he latched up his medical bag. "Heavy work will more than likely induce the labor process."

"That's surely not something ya recommend then?" Albert asked.

"Well, it will certainly put the mother and child more at risk of complications. It is the hottest time of the year; she needs to stay hydrated."

"Thank ya, doc," Albert said as he shook the man's hand and stepped out of the room. "I'll send for ya when it's close to time."

The doctor stopped and blinked rapidly at Mr. Toussaint. "Send for me? I figured you had Negro women who could help birth her child. Is this your first slave birth?" He mocked.

"No, it isn't," he said matter-of-factly, "but I will send for ya nonetheless."

The doctor scoffed under his smile. "Well, I can't guarantee that I will be available for ya, Albert. I can't just leave my obligations of care to help birth a slave."

Albert's nose flared as he touched the doctor's shoulder and walked with him toward the door. "Well, we'll see," was all he said.

The doctor's tall, lanky stature looked nearly odd as he climbed into his buggy. He clicked to his bay mare, who jerked her head up and down, as if saying yes, before pulling forward into a trot.

Albert made his way back to Dinah's room to find her still sitting on the edge of the bed, head bowed and hands moving gently over her protruding belly. "Doctor says everything seems healthy."

"I don't want him to come back for the birth," Dinah said.

"What are ya talkin' about?"

"I'm sure I'll do just fine with Nan and Franny."

"Stop with the foolish talk. Of course I'll bring him back. It's my child."

"It's your property." Her words came boldly as she raised her head to look at him. She had become more comfortable in her conversations with Albert after she was given a room in the house and he more frequently visited her. "It's still a slave," she continued.

Albert became offended. "Do I treat ya like a slave? Huh?" His words were more forceful then he had meant for them to be, and her head lowered again and gave a small shake. "When I touch ya"—his hand came up and gently touched her cheek—"is that how I touch my slaves?"

Dinah looked up at him with questioning eyes that watered over like the gentle spring rains. His gaze seemed reassuring to her, and the child stirred in her womb.

Justine had turned the children against Dinah with disdainful talk about her, though she wouldn't mention to them that the child Dinah carried was their father's and their half-sibling. Marianne stayed quiet and observant, figuring out what she assumed was the truth though never asking for confirmation. Rose shied away in confusion from her mother's biting words. Her sister whispered assumptions she couldn't understand, yet she knew the gravity of the situation because Marianne had made her swear, with a firm pinch on the arm, not to say a word to their mother. Her eyes were kind when she looked at Dinah, but she remained submissive to Justine's orders to stay away "from that dirty nigga." Young Albert no longer wanted Dinah close to him and would often scowl at her or run up and hit at her stomach while making an awful, savage noise. Though Isabelle was too little for any knowledge of what was happening, Dinah was no longer permitted to ready her in the mornings. So, she kept her head down as she worked, finding comfort only when Albert called to her or pulled her aside for a short conversation on her well-being and comfort.

The day of birth came on a mild morning on September 23rd, the same day in fact as young Albert's sixth birthday. The family was out on the front lawn with the blindfolded boy. Albert had purchased him a pony, against the advice of Justine, who argued that he was still too young to ride alone. Albert had Nathan, the stable boy, walk the pony out to present to his son. Nathan had taken pride all morning in grooming the speckled pony as if it were his own and oiling down his back, mane, and tail. He had shined the saddle until his face nearly reflected in its mahogany leather. Now he was in front of the family, standing tall with pride, as he held the reins close to the pony's bridle.

The girls were giggling with excitement after being ordered by Justine to hold their tongues. Young Albert, eagerly stomping his feet, begged to take off the blindfold.

Albert knelt behind his son with his hands placed on both of his shoulders. "All right, ya can take it off," he said close to his ear.

The boy reached up and pulled the blindfold off, and a squeal of delight filled the air. He spun around and threw himself into his father's arms. "Really? Really? Is he really mine?" he kept asking as tears of joy ran down his face.

"He's really yours." Albert laughed as he returned the embrace. "Now, don't ya want to go take a look at him?"

Young Albert pulled away and wiped at his eyes, his smile reaching from ear to ear. After letting go of his father, he made his way to the pony. His small hand reached up and stroked at his neck.

"Ya like him?" Albert asked as he smiled down at his son with a hand on the horse's mane.

"Like him? I love him!"

Suddenly, Franny stumbled out onto the front veranda, the screen door slamming behind her. She grabbed hold of the pillar at the top of the stairs. "Masta, Masta!" she called breathlessly. "Baby's comin'!"

Albert's eyes flashed. "Play with your pony, son," he said as he touched his wispy hair. Justine's eyes followed her husband as he walked past her and the children and mounted the steps to the house. Young Albert's lips pressed into a thin line.

"How close is she?" he asked Nan as he stepped into the room. Dinah was lying on the bed, knees bent up toward the ceiling and covered with a tan sheet.

"She'll be pushing this child soon. She's been having contractions since early this mornin', and nah her water's been spilled," Nan said, pushing the heavy weight of her body up from where she sat on the low stool toward the foot of the bed.

"Franny, run and tell Nathan to find Foy and send him to fetch the doctor."

"Yes, seh," Franny responded with a nod before she ran out of the room.

"Nan, step out for a minute, please," Albert ordered. Nan quietly obeyed. He took the stool and put it at the head of the bed before sitting down on it. "How are ya?"

Dinah was breathing deeply through her nose and pushing the air back out through her lips. "Scared," she responded quietly.

Albert took her hand in his. "Ya goin' to be just fine." She found comfort in the look in his eyes. They were warm and inviting as they stared into her soul.

Hours began to pass and the time between contractions shortened until Dinah began to bear down with each one. Foy had not returned with the doctor yet when the baby's head crowned. The room was filled with the sound of labor pains and words of encouragement and direction from Nan, who was waiting at the foot of the bed to catch the child.

Franny stood, nervously shifting her weight from one foot to the other, at the head of the bed, occasionally giving Dinah's brow a wipe. Albert paced the room. Dinah's fingers dug into the bed as she leaned up and gave another hard push. Her mouth opened to let out a scream before she let herself back down. A new cry filled the air—a cry of despair at the cold, wide space the child now faced away from the warm embrace of mother's womb.

"It's a girl!" Nan said, beaming, as she snipped the cord and wrapped the child in a blanket. Her mouth formed an O as she cooed in understanding of the child's cry.

Franny was beside herself as tears fell down her cheeks and she took up Dinah's hand. Her lips pressed together. "It's a girl," she kept repeating in soft tones as her head slowly shook from side to side.

Nan turned and presented the child to Albert, and he took her in his arms. Her dark hair wisped against her milky skin, which had not yet darkened to its true tone. Albert cupped the side of her head in his hand. Her cheeks were large and round, and her lips pursed together as if she were looking for something. Albert looked over to Dinah, who steadily watched him hold her daughter. Tears streaked her face. He took a step to her and lowered the baby into her arms.

Dinah's breath quivered as she took the child to her breast and kissed her head. "My girl," she whispered. "Hello, my beautiful girl." Albert touched Dinah's head and leaned forward to give it a kiss. She smiled up at him. "She's beautiful."

"What's her name?" Albert asked.

"I'm going to call her...Caroline." She looked up at him.

He gave her a nod. "I like it. Miss Caroline Toussaint."

CHAPTER NINE

THE BIRTH of Caroline was the joy of Dinah. She spent the early weeks cradling the child and doting over her big cheeks, pursed lips, and button nose. Her skin had deepened into a smooth dark brown. It was only a few days after her birth, in the arms of her father, when he had recognized her as the color of rich, sweet cocoa. Cradling her in his arms, he called her his Coco in a voice he used only when the two of them were alone or in the presence of her mother. Since that day, the name stuck for those who loved her, even up to the day it was lovingly inscribed in elegant letters on her tomb above the name Caroline Toussaint.

Albert gave orders to let Dinah have her time near the child with no other worry than to care for herself and the baby. She stayed in the room he had given her to avoid the gaze of his white family until the weather began to cool and she longed to take Coco out onto the plantation. She brought a blanket and a book, or sometimes a bucket of beans that Nan declared needed to be snapped, and after spreading the blanket out far enough away from the house that she would not be spied upon, she lay out under the wide-open sky with contentment. It was nearly a daily ritual until the air began to crystalize.

He prized his daughter. Where he had used to spend his mornings taking his coffee in solitude, he now carried her with him to sit in the dimly lit room until the sun rose. Dinah never interrupted his mornings alone with his daughter. It warmed her heart to watch him hold her and speak softly in her ear. Coco's little hand quickly learned which of Albert's strong fingers it preferred to grip while she looked up at him with the dark, almond eyes she inherited from her mother.

Coco was registered at birth as Albert's property, no different from Dinah or the other slaves. It would be nearly six months and after the harvest of 1845 before Albert completed the process of registering Caroline Toussaint as a free person of color. He would pay the licensing fee of $1000, an amount he always said had padded Governor Alexandre Mouton's fat pocket. Governor Mouton would later become an active supporter of the Confederacy during the war of the states, though not in office during the time, and offered his support by devoting large sums of money to the cause.

Albert folded Coco's pass and kept it in his wallet, carrying it with him always until the day in 1857 when he handed it over to Coco. As a free person of color, she would be required to carry it on her person at all times as the tension between the states increased and the Southern states began fearing an uprising of the blacks. Coco obeyed her father and kept the folded paper, which had absorbed the smell of tobacco from its years spent in Albert's wallet. Over time, it finally lost its scent, but she would still often take it out and place it near her nose for a long inhale and the memory of the cherished smell.

The certificate that Coco carried would never show the date September 23rd but rather the 24th. It was a change Albert would never feel the need to reveal to his daughter. Justine refused for Albert's son to share the same date of birth as the "dark child." Bitter hate grew within her and was filtered down to her children as she whispered into their ears. Though she hardly ever saw

Dinah and stayed in the wing of the plantation closest to her room, Justine soon became enslaved by her jealous thoughts. Even the other black slaves felt her hate.

When Franny displeased her, a hand was often raised to strike her, along with severe words. Nathan, the stable boy, heard the brunt of her words as she always rebuked him for not having the saddle shiny enough or the horse ready in a timely manner. She would refer to him as "the stupid boy who might have had a chance in this world if he hadn't been born a slave nigger." Her words began to wear on Nathan until the day Mr. Toussaint saw her treatment of him and stood up to her.

"Don't speak to him like that, Justine!" Albert had ordered.

"I'll speak to him however I chose to."

"No ya won't. He does a fine job, and ya puttin' him down all the time will start to make him doubt his ability. And when that happens, he will stop carin', and then he won't be worth the salt."

"What are ya now, a nigger lover?" Justine accused her husband, and his hand came up and struck against her cheek. The sting from his hand wasn't enough to draw tears—in fact, it could hardly even be considered a strike—but the surprise was, and the tears brought with them a look of hatred.

Nathan jumped with surprise and his eyes widened enough to show the whites. He would never forget his master standing up for him, and because of it, kept his loyalty to Albert until the day the Southern soldiers would take him away. It had been ordered by the South to take all slaves and use them for the hard manual labor the war demanded. The slave owners would be thanked by the officer of the unit for their part in ensuring the victory of the South.

Justine started sipping from the laudanum bottle after the day Albert struck her. Mrs. Thompson had suggested it to her after a visit, when Justine broke down in tears for what she said was for no understandable reason at all. "It must just be the stresses of the household. I've been more and more emotional these days," she told Mrs. Thompson, never revealing the infidelity of her husband.

Mrs. Thompson brought out the bottle she kept safely in a locked cupboard in the study. God knew that if she didn't keep it locked away, her boys, and for that matter her ever-wilding daughter, would find it. "Take a small drink of it in the mornin' until you're feelin' better," she told Justine. "It will calm your nerves." She put her finger to the opening of the bottle, wetting it with the liquid before putting it in her mouth, screwing the lid back on, and handing it to Justine.

"I don't want to take your bottle," Justine objected.

"Oh, don't worry about it." She waved her hand in the air.

"Are you sure?"

"Honey, I have other bottles. God knows, with these children of mine, it's the only way I get through the day. And Mr. Thompson's of no help. 'Boys will be boys,' he says, and he just turns a blind eye to all the mischief that daughter of his gets into."

Mr. Thompson lived freely and without care until the day he took to heavy drinking after the death of his two sons and the crippling of a grandson during the war. Ashley Thompson would lose both of his legs at the knee by a cannon ball in Tennessee at the age of fifteen during the Battle of Hatchie Bridge. They would tell him he was lucky to have survived such an incident, to which he would spit in the dirt and say he would have rather died and damned the Yankees. Though he would still be married to a woman nearly twice his age who had lost her husband during the war, he would complain the day through under her hardworking and caring hands. Ashley loved her for the care and sympathy she offered, mothering over him and tending to his every need until the day of her departure from this world.

Mr. Thompson joined the Knights of the White Camelia in 1867, founded by Democrat-Confederate Army Colonel Alcibiades DeBlanc, a man Mr. Thompson met once and referred to as a friend in political conversations. He was never part of the raids of terror among the black population of Louisiana, but he was talked into joining the militia heading to Thibodaux to protect the strikebreakers during a three-week strike against sugarcane plantations. The tensions broke out in violence and the militia attacked the black workers and their families. Lynching ensued. Mr. Thompson went back home, never speaking of the incident even at the encouragement of Ashley, who eagerly wanted details. Two months later, Mr. Thompson shut himself in his familiar study. He prayed for forgiveness of his sins but doubted God would listen or forgive. Then, after drinking a tumbler of whiskey, Mr. Thompson shot himself in the head with his pistol.

Justine took a small sip of the laudanum the next morning, hoping for the promised escape. It did what Mrs. Thompson said and numbed her pain, and soon Justine wouldn't just be taking a sip in the mornings but adding it to her afternoon tea, as well as sometimes having a few sips before bed to help her sleep. Albert would worry about Justine as her persona began to drastically change. Though he was no longer in love with her, he cared for her well-being as his once-cherished wife and mother of his children.

It was dinnertime on an evening one week before New Year's Eve. The table was the usual, uncomfortably quiet during dinner. This was the only time the children would see their parents together. Marianne had started in about the New Year's party they hosted every year and wondered why none of the arrangements had been made yet. She admitted she knew she wasn't part of it but reminded them it would be the last year of that, since she was to have her debutante in March when she would turn fourteen.

She straightened herself in her chair, and Albert looked at his daughter. She had also changed drastically, in his mind, in the last few months since she began her flow in the fall. Her appetite had increased, and the extra food had added roundness to her cheeks and growing breasts.

"I don't see why ya can't join the dinner this year," Albert said before taking a mouthful of Nan's famous roast and gravy.

Marianne's face lit up with enthusiasm. "Really?"

"Now just the dinner, not the dancin'," he said, pointing his fork at her and raising his eyebrows.

"Oh, papa, that's fine! Dinner? Really?"

"If it's all right with ya mother, I'm okay with it."

A chuckle came from Justine sitting across the table. She raised her napkin to her mouth as the eyes at the table raised to look at her.

"May I, Mother?" Marianne asked eagerly.

The woman laughed again behind her napkin. "What makes ya think we are havin' a New Year's party this year?"

A surprised look spread across Marianne's face, and Albert looked over to his wife. "What?" the girl asked.

"After what happened last year, ya think we will *ever* have a New Year's party again?"

Tears began falling down Marianne's face. "What do ya mean what happened last year?"

"Ask ya father." Justine shot a vile look in her husband's direction and half smiled at his demise.

Marianne's eyes shot back and forth between her parents. "What happened last year, Father?"

"Nothin', Marianne."

"Nothin'?" Mrs. Toussaint laughed out loud. "Nothin'?"

"That's enough, Justine," Albert said.

"So, what then? I am never to enjoy a New Year's party?"

"We will have a New Year's party, Marianne." Albert's hand came up in a cutting motion. "Now, Justine, stop it." His firm voice and Marianne's tears invoked the other children to begin crying. Albert's head dropped as he leaned his elbows on the table. "Can we no longer have a decent dinner conversation?"

"So, this is my fault?" Justine snorted and shook her head.

After pushing her chair away from the table, she said, "Well, then I will just excuse myself."

"Justine, will ya just please…"

"No," she said, shaking her head as she stood. "No," she said again as she walked out of the dining room and to her room, where she took an extra sip of laudanum.

Albert tried to comfort his children before excusing them to retreat to their bedrooms for the evening with assurance to Marianne that there would, in fact, be a New Year's Eve party. He lingered by candlelight in the sitting room with a cigar and tumbler of Taylor port. The tawny liquid rested warmly on his tongue with its delicious nuttiness, and by the second glass, Albert's uneasy heartbeat has settled and his body relaxed.

Through the shadows of the room, Dinah's dark figure moved toward where Albert slumped in his chair. Her long, white cotton nightdress gave away her position, and he watched her move smoothly across the floor until she stood over him. Her dark breast, full from nursing, could be made out under the white veil. Albert set his glass on the end table next to his chair. After putting an arm around her buttocks, he rested his head against her stomach, enjoying the gentle stroke of her fingers through his hair.

As his arms tightened around her and squeezed at her frame, his breaths deepened with arousal. He stood. Dinah's alluring eyes followed his face and held steady his gaze. The aromas of butterscotch and fine oak wood fell from his lips as his breath caressed her cheek and mouth. Soon the gentle embrace turned passionate, and the two entangled themselves in satisfaction.

Albert woke in Dinah's bed with her naked in his arms, hours before the sun dared to be seen. Winter had a way of seeping its cold fingers into the room, and Dinah had used the extra blanket to cover Coco in the crib Albert had provided months ago. His hand moved across Dinah's cool skin, and then he quietly got up and walked, naked, to the sitting room where they had made love the night before. He put on his clothes before picking up her night dress, grabbing a blanket, and heading back down the hall to Dinah's room.

As he spread the blanket over her body, his heart felt love for her, but it was something he would never express to her in words. Then, after moving to the crib, he took up his sleeping daughter and held her until morning, when he placed her in the arms of her mother for her warm milk.

CHAPTER TEN

THE NEW YEAR'S party came to the Toussaint plantation just as Albert had promised Marianne. Even though Justine vowed never to have it again, saving face in the community and keeping the rumors from spreading among the neighbors compelled her to continue the Toussaint's New Year's tradition. The house was in frantic chaos a week before the party, but Marianne was eager to lend a helping hand in all of the preparations. As the halls of the house were decorated and the smell of pine and cinnamon filtered through the air, Justine began to lose herself in the ambiance of the event.

Marianne planned out her dinner attire, trying on every fine dress in her wardrobe, and finally settling on a white and green print she had gotten new at the end of summer. It was too plain for a winter party, and she would have gladly tossed it aside, had she a winter one that displayed her chest and hourglass figure as well as the plain dress. On the night of the party, Marianne put on as many petticoats as she could fit under her skirt to give it fullness and then tied dark green ribbons around her wrist and in her hair.

Her blushing face didn't go unnoticed by the young men of the event, but to her dismay, Gabe Thompson had chosen Mary Lynn Henry, whose hair was as gold as the morning rays, to spend his pre-dinner conversations with and invited her to sit next to him during dinner. Marianne made sure she sat on the opposite side of the table from the couple, so she could keep a watchful eye on Mary Lynn to figure out just what may have caught the attention of Gabe. The end of dinner came, and she was no closer to discovering Mary Lynn's secret, though she would admit that her laugh held both the traits of feminine class and flirtation. It was addicting, and even Marianne found herself bound by its spell. She would practice mimicking it in front of her mirror for months, until the day came that she was sure she had mastered its charm.

The weather started to warm as the weeks passed following the party. The grass began to sprout, and the air smelled of the stirring of dirt as the plantation was at the end of its planting season. It was March 3rd, Marianne's fourteenth birthday and the night of her debutante. The sky was thundering as it threatened the earth with a coming storm. Albert knocked on her door and waited until he heard her soft voice tell him to enter. A week before, they had given Marianne her own room, moving Rose and Isabelle into the same room together. She began to feel more like a woman, and as she stood at the window wearing her gown of white, Albert began to feel it too.

"Father," she said, casting him a smile.

Albert put his hand over his heart. "You look stunning." Her fair cheeks blushed, and he walked up to her, taking her hands in his as he kissed her on the forehead. "I cannot believe the beautiful woman my daughter has become. You are a vision, inside and out, Marianne.

"The guests have been here for a while now and are eager to see the woman of the hour. Are you ready to join them?"

Marianne nodded. Albert enfolded his daughter's arm with his own and led her down the hall to the top of the stairs, where they stopped and waited for the attention and all eyes to rest upon them. Marianne anticipated her jitters would be worse as she entered the party, but instead, as she slowly walked down the staircase escorted by her father, she felt confidence, as if entering a contest she knew she would win.

Albert walked her into the dance hall, where the band started a Dixie tune and they began to dance. Justine, who stood in front of the other observers, smiled as father spun daughter around for all to view. At the end of the dance, he handed his blushing daughter's hand over to the first young man who asked for the next waltz. Albert then stepped to the side of the room, where he poured himself refreshment before turning to watch as the dance hall filled with swaying bodies. After a couple of songs, he took his glass and made his way to the front of the room to stop the band.

"Good evening. Thank you everyone for coming," he began. "Tonight, we celebrate my daughter, Marianne. She has become a young woman no father could be prouder of. The moment your mother gave ya life and you were placed in my arms, I knew no greater love as I cradled ya in those white linens. And here ya are, being introduced to society…I watched ya grow from that bashful, curious little girl to now a beautiful, smart, elegant young lady. In a blink of my eye ya went from my little Mary to a vibrant young woman. Sweetie, I want ya to know that we love ya so much, and are so proud of ya, and the person ya are. Here is to you, Marianne." He raised his glass, followed by everyone in the room. "May your life be as rich as ya have made mine. Happy Birthday, daughter."

The chiming of glasses and some handclaps followed the toast as the band picked up the music again. Marianne went to her father and gave him a kiss before whisking off with Elizabeth to continue enjoying her party, purposefully avoiding Gabe but making sure he was always within earshot of the charming laugh she had mastered. Albert stood by the window and quietly watched.

"That was a kind toast." He turned to see Justine next to him. He gave her a nod, but said nothing, and she remained in silence beside him. "Well we did something right," she finally said, referring to Marianne. "She looks beautiful."

"She has your charm," Albert said quietly as he watched his daughter flirt with a toss of her head and a bashful smile.

Justine looked at her husband's profile. "Do you miss it?"

"Miss what?" he asked.

"The charm I once had."

He looked at her steadily before speaking. "Would you like to dance?"

"No," she said with a melancholy and glassy eye.

"Have a dance with me," he insisted, pulling her onto the floor.

With a forced smile to avoid a scene among neighbors, she allowed him to lead her. Her stiff composure wrenched an awkward feeling in Albert, and he was glad when the dance was over. Through the rest of the evening, the two spent their time in separate circles.

As the night ended and they bid the last of the guests goodnight, Albert kissed the chatty, excited Marianne goodnight and then retreated to the sitting room. As her voice faded to the upstairs, he sat on the couch and stretched out. He breathed deeply and closed his eyes.

"Albert." A soft voice soon stirred him. His eyes snapped open and his head turned.

"Come sleep in your own bed."

"No, I'm fine here," he said, closing his eyes again.

"I want you to."

Opening his eyes, he looked at Justine. Slowly he moved to a sitting position. "You sure?" he asked.

"Yes."

Albert got up and followed her upstairs to their room. She

shut the door behind him before setting the lantern she carried on the nightstand. Albert sat on the edge of the bed as he took off his boots and began undressing. Justine stood before him and slowly slipped her nightdress off of her shoulders, letting it fall to the floor. Her thin hourglass frame looked like fresh cream under the warm light of the flame, soft and flawless. Alberts eyes rested on her pink nipples before regarding the rest of her feminine structure. He didn't move toward her or beckoned her. He sighed. "You are beautiful," he said softly, looking into her sorrowful eyes. She blinked rapidly as she looked away and wet her lips with her tongue. Kneeling down, she took back up her cotton nightdress to cover her body and moved to the other side of the bed.

"Can we fix this?" his wife asked as she lay down in bed.

Albert frowned and lay on his back. "I don't know, Justine."

"Can we try? After watching you with Marianne tonight, I want to try."

"We can try, but I don't know that we can fix it."

Justine rolled over in bed and Albert reached to extinguish the lantern. She wiped at her eyes in the darkness before falling asleep.

As the days passed, she held to her promise of trying, and even forced herself to perform her wifely duties. She kept her snide remarks to herself, and though the bitterness in her chest was like a monster eating at her, whenever she felt she couldn't handle it, she would step outside and turn her head to the sky until the feelings had passed. One day, she screamed as loud as she could as she looked up, and to her surprise, it seemed to release the demon she had been holding so close to her chest. Every day since, she screamed when she went outside. The rumor moved among the Negros that the missus had lost her mind and was struggling with a dark spirit trying to possess her.

Justine was able to talk Albert into staying in the bedroom with her every night, even when he insisted on staying up in the study for a few extra minutes. As her suspicions grew, one evening after Albert fell asleep in his bed, Justine went downstairs and lit a lantern in the study before sitting in the darkness of the dining room facing the same hall. The time passed slowly, and just as she began to feel silly for her assumptions, a figure moved down the hall and entered the study. The woman stayed in the empty study for a time before putting out the lantern and walking back down the dark hall.

Justine held her breath as she made her way to the back of the house and out the door. She walked aimlessly through the foggy late spring night, not caring about the wet ground against her bare feet. She walked until she felt numb and the voices in her mind were silenced by a solution that she was determined would carry her through.

Weeks made months and, to her displeasure, Justine missed her flow. She revealed this news to Albert nonchalantly one afternoon by walking into the room where he was sitting, reading the paper. "I'm pregnant," she said coolly. He looked up from his paper, and before an expression could cross his face or lips, she turned and walked out of the room. Nothing more was said between the two of them.

Justine stopped asking him to share her bed of night. He continued to stay in their room a week or two without her bidding until one night he did not and began sleeping in the study and Dinah's bed again.

The summer came and the days brought with them a severe drought. The dry earth scorched the soles of the feet of the slaves, leaving blisters they would patch with a giant, black glob of chewed tobacco to lessen the sting. The wet rags tied to their heads and necks did little to cool them from the heat waves, and several fell from stroking in the sun, leaving death to claim a handful of both young and old. The songs in the field held a dark, melancholy cry that seemed not to rise above the height of the stalk.

Albert made a trip to Baton Rouge in August, where steamboat *Issac Franklin*, owned by slave dealer George Kephart, was transporting new slaves from St. Louis to be sold down river. It would be making a stop for an auction before continuing to New Orleans. This route was run every two weeks by boat, something Kephart continued after purchasing the domestic slave business from the firm Franklin and Armfield in 1836. Kephart would not be on the boat that transported the slaves; instead, he remained in Fredrick, Maryland through the entirety of owning the business as well as after selling it. In his stead was a man named Ethan Stanson, known as Grizzly, a white man with a face etched by too much sun. He stood at a towering six-foot-two and was known to wear a long, black coat with white pants. Though he was a man of fine personal appearance and engaging manner, he had overpoweringly bad breath because of his love for onions.

Albert took two wagons, driven by Foy and Abraham, who had been promoted by Albert to a driver, with the intent of purchasing twelve new slaves—fifteen, if he could fetch them at a good price. It was Abraham's first time away from the plantation since he had been purchased by Albert, and he was eager to make the trip where he'd "see da great Miss." As the hills came into view, the town of Baton Rouge was delightfully nestled in their midst. It was later described by Abraham to the other Negros that he was sure he must have "rode upon da promised land." His attention was at its height as he looked upon the spectacular Spanish and French architecture.

Suddenly, a gleam of sunlight reflected, as off of a mirror, from the surface of the great Mississippi as they crossed 2nd street off of Main on their way to River Road. The deep billow of the steamers and ferryboats filled the air, as flatboats packed with whisky, tobacco, cotton, and hogs floated downriver. Men, finely dressed, stood in clusters along the levee, laughing and smoking cigars, as the black slaves were pushed by white men, whips in hand, across the ramps connecting the boats to the banks of Baton Rouge. Black men were manacled and chained to each other with iron staples and bolts on chains one hundred feet long. Some even had chain running through the links of iron collars. Abraham's eyes burned as the beauty of the "promised land" opened to "da portals of Hell."

Though he had been a slave the entirety of his life, he had been lucky to escape the severity of slavery that most had endured. Abraham had been sold to the Toussaint plantation at the age of nine, ten, or eleven—no one really new the exact age of the boy. Young Mrs. Ball had rid herself of the five slaves she and her husband owned after he had died, leaving her a widow with hardly money enough to care for herself. Mr. Ball had worked in mercantile and struggled to give his wife the life she so longed for and deserved. After he died in a sudden accident, Mrs. Ball contacted distant family in Virginia and, within a few months, was selling everything she had left to get herself a one-way ticket.

She had promised Abraham's mother she would not separate the two of them, but when the time came, Mrs. Ball sold Abraham's mother with the other three adult Negros to an interstate tradesman purchasing slaves for a gentleman in Alabama. Mrs. Ball knew she had sold her slaves for less than what they were worth at auction, but in her desperate situation, she felt forced. She had stood with her arms around Abraham's young, lanky shoulders as they watched the others walk away at the urging of the man on the buckskin horse. Abraham's mother kept looking over her shoulder at her son with wails of sorrow as their silhouettes became smaller and soon unseen. She wouldn't stop looking behind her, to where they had come and where her son still was, until the white man on the horse turned them onto a road heading east three days later.

Mrs. Ball had let Abraham stay in the house with her and cared for him like her own kin, allowing him to eat with her and even sleep in her bed. It would be another three weeks before she heard of the Toussaint man, a man rumored of outstanding character, planting cane fields. She packed what belongings she had in a leather case and dressed in her finest travel clothes and bonnet. After introducing herself to the Toussaint gentleman, she had a long conversation with him before pulling young Abraham out of the carriage.

Dabbing at her eyes, she'd gripped the boy by his shoulders. "Now be good," she had ordered him. "Mr. Toussaint is ya new master. Do as he tells ya."

The tears fell more readily that day for Abraham than the day the white man had taken his mother, not because he cared more but because it was the end of all he knew and was familiar with. She kissed the boy on his cheek, got back into the carriage, and headed straight to the train station.

Albert yelled over his shoulder to Foy, and with a wave of the hand, gave direction for him and Abraham to stop the wagons. The *Issac Franklin* had not yet disembarked. Abraham's attention kept going to the men who could not shake off their chains and dared not move a yard without the consent of their masters. Soon, the sound of chained men grew closer to the wagons; the *Issac Franklin* was moving its cargo to the levee. The men were unloaded first, followed by the women, who were not chained but tied together by rope, leaving their arms free to guide the children or carry the ones too young to walk.

Abraham looked into the faces of the tired men and women, but his gaze fell on the face of a child no older than two, being carried by a woman. A chubby hand reached straight out to him, as if to show him all five fingers. Abraham looked to Foy, who spit a stream of brown juice from the chaw in his cheek to the ground. His face showed zero emotion.

Mr. Toussaint walked through the first few lines of men and women before walking up to the tall man in white trousers and shaking his hand. Albert leaned in to the conversation, despite the man's odorous breath. Grizzly looked around himself before motioning with his head for Albert to walk aboard the boat with him. The men were onboard for what seemed like hours, though it wasn't longer than thirty or forty minutes. Sweat dripped down the faces of the bound men and women, yet no one dared reach a hand up to wipe their brow. Instead, they stood still with heads bowed, so the sweat would drip to the earth before running down into their eyes.

Abraham swatted at a fly on his neck. He shifted uneasily in his seat as the time seemed to hardly pass. Finally, Albert reappeared, to his relief, and began his walkthrough of the gang of slaves. He would hardly give a nod of the head, and a white man would unlatch the bolt holding the slave to the chain. Each slave had a red flag with a number attached to the loop in the chain, and the white man would untie it and hold it in his hand as he motioned for the slave to go stand by the wagons.

After he had seven or eight flags in hand, the man signaled for another driver to take his place, and he took the flags to Grizzly. Grizzly held a large, leather-bound book that held the names, ages, and heights of the Negros. As the man brought him the flags, he would look up the information and write it into a bill of sale for Mr. Toussaint. Albert didn't stop until he had gone through each line carefully, even taking a second look at some. He selected fourteen slaves, both men and women.

Abraham followed Foy's lead when he got off the wagon to look at the purchase for himself. Foy's hard eyes looked them up and down with nary a look of pity. No one knew the man's history; they only knew he was a hard man who took no slack or laziness from his workers. He was no fool when it came to running a plantation. There were rumors around the black huts that he had bargained a deal with Masta Toussaint to one day be able to purchase his own freedom. No one could otherwise figure his diligence in acting just like the white man when it came to how he treated his own kind, nor why he would be favored by Masta unless he was the favorite, and favorites always got special treatment.

Grizzly walked over to Albert as the slaves were being loaded into the wagons. As he said a few words to him, he handed him his bill of sale. Albert gave it a quick glance before folding it up and tucking it away in his vest pocket. He reached out and shook Grizzly's hand, then tugged at his hat, pulling it down over his brow, and mounted his horse.

A driver was quickly at Grizzly's side. "Here are the last six flags."

He took them in hand and gave the man a nod. "Get the rest of these Negros washed up before they put their auction clothes on." The driver gave a nod and walked away, and Grizzly pushed the red flags into his pocket before pulling out a cigar and lighting it up. The transaction of sale was never logged for the remaining flags and never recorded in the state that those slaves were ever a part of the Toussaint plantation. Albert's private dealings with Grizzly remained a secret, benefiting the profits of both men. Those six flags in Grizzly's pocket would later be floating down the Mississippi, never reaching New Orleans.

As Albert was leading his wagons through the streets bustling with mercantile, he moved his horse around to Foy's side, who pulled back to hear his master. "Find a spot to pull the wagons," he said. "Just make sure ya stay on this street. There's somethin' I want to find before we leave." Foy asked no questions, just offered a nod and a stream of brown juice onto the ground before giving his horse a click of the reins.

Albert took his time going through the streets of Baton Rouge until he came across a merchant store with ladies' articles in the windows. He had his mind set on buying a pair of earrings, which the woman behind the counter was eager to sell him. She pulled out all the fashionable dangle earrings full of colorful stones but gave him a curious look when he said he wanted a small simple set. She tried to convince him of the current women's fashion, even going so far as pulling out a subscription of *The World of Fashion and Continental Feuilletons*. As the woman flipped through its hand-painted pages of elaborate, jewel-like colors of multiple figures wearing the latest fashions, it was evident by the corners of the pages that the magazine had experienced multiple gentle openings. Her hand moved across the page with a silk-like touch, displaying with pride the elegant fashions, though the magazine was dated more than a year ago.

He humored the woman's elaborate pitch before he insisted that all he wanted was something small and elegant. She clicked her tongue at him before reaching behind the counter and pulling out three sets of small earrings. Albert eyed them all before selecting the small gold hoops. "Those are perfect," he proceeded to say as the woman wrapped them and took his payment. Afterward, Albert went down the street and enjoyed some bourbon before calling it a successful day.

The slaves in the wagon soon became chatty as they waited on their new master. "It sure is hot," one said.

"Bout as hot as my ol' missus's temper," another responded.

"I knew a woman once hot o' temper...but that ain't all that was hot 'bout her. She was as crazy as a blind cat, she was. But Lawd, she had that fiery spirit in an' out of the bedroom." The first man chuckled. "Think a man crazy, the way she kept 'em comin' back fa more."

"Ya lucky she didn't take a skillet to that dumb head of yas," one of the women chimed in.

"Ain't no one said she didn't! Why ya think it's shaped funny?" Laugher followed between them.

One would think the slaves were happy with the way they were carrying on, when in fact they carried on in conversation, or song for that matter, to drown their suffering of mind. The conversation died down when Foy reached for the reins again the moment he saw Albert riding toward them. The silence continued for the rest of the day's travel with only humming from one of the women in Abraham's wagon.

CHAPTER ELEVEN

AUGUST PASSED and September came with the first birthday of Coco. Not a single fuss was made over the day by the other members of the Toussaint name, not that anything otherwise was expected. It was the middle of the afternoon, and Dinah was settled in the rocking chair next to the window with her chest bare as she held her nursing child.

The door to the room slowly opened, and Franny's face peered around it. Her face shone with excitement; her smile knew no limits even with less than full occupancy of teeth. "May I come in?" she asked, beaming.

"Yes."

"I come to say Happy Birthday to Miss Coco," she said as she slowly walked into the room with her hands behind her back.

Dinah smiled as she removed the nursing child from her teat and pulled up the shoulders to her dress. "Well, here she is."

"Well." Franny drew out the word as if teaching someone how to say it. "There she is. Happy Birthday, Miss Coco. I got ya a little gift." She brought her arms from behind her back and said, "I made dis for ya," as she handed over the rag doll she had made.

A smooth black cloth stuffed with an old rag for filling was tied off to form a round head. The body of the doll was the loose corners of the cloth. Franny had stitched a red kerchief under the head and tied it there with a piece of twine, and for the eyes, she had sewed on two white buttons. Though different in size, they were as near as any in color, one smooth and the other, bigger one with etches in the button itself. On the top of the head, a blackish and nearly blue puff of cotton was also pinned into the rag head by small thread stitching. The baby's small hand took hold of the doll and gave it a hearty shake.

"Oh, look it there, Coco," Dinah said with a smile as Franny handed the doll over.

The woman gave deep, throaty chuckle. "I dipped da cotton in Massa's ink bowl—dat's how it got its color," she said with a prideful glint in her eye.

"It's a beautiful gift, Franny! Why, I've never seen a better lookin' doll!"

"Let me hold da child before Nan realizes dat I done run off." Franny reached down and took her into her arms. "Ya have to be da most beautiful child I've ever seen," she continued, giving Coco a tight squeeze that made her squirm in her arms. Her large, chocolate eyes looked at Franny, and as she reached up with her free hand and rested it on her face, the baby gave a high-pitched giggle.

Franny bounced her around and then ended up sitting on the floor with her for a few minutes of play before standing decisively. "Let's take a walk to da kitchen," she said. "Let's see if we can get somethin' sweet." Dinah laughed in response, and Franny swooped up Coco and headed with a bounce in her step to the kitchen.

Nan was sitting on the stool next to the island counter, her large chin resting in her hand. "There ya are! What took ya so long?"

Franny paid no attention to her edgy tone. "Here she is! Da

birthday girl herself," she said in a singsong voice, swaying the hip that bounced the baby girl.

"Ya took long enough bringing her in." Nan turned to the counter behind her and brought around a plate with some cake. It was yellow and spongy with a slight hint of honey and lemon.

Dinah's hand moved to her chest as she let out a laugh. "Oh my," she said. "Look there, Coco."

The ladies stood around the excited child as her hands went from cake to mouth. Their laughter rang through the kitchen as they celebrated her first birthday. They cleaned up the kitchen after the cake was gone and moved forward with the day, the Toussaint family none the wiser.

That evening, Albert went to Dinah. He held his daughter and stroked her soft curls. Coco seemed to adore him and, when he appeared, always preferred him to hold her to anyone else who may be in the room.

"I didn't get her anything," he said into the silence.

"She's your daughter and she's got papers to prove that. That's gift enough," Dinah said softly.

Albert blinked quickly before looking up. "I got ya somethin', though." She looked at him as, unnoticed by Albert, her hands gripped tighter the quilt she had been working on. "I've been carryin' it around with me since Baton Rouge." He moved his daughter off his lap and reached into the jetted pocket of his vest. He stood and moved to where she sat on the bed.

Dinah's eyes stayed wide as she watched him pull out a deep purple velvet cloth. She exhaled the breath she had been holding as Albert placed the gift in her lap. She slowly reached forward and opened the cloth, and there, placed in the center, were two gold hoops.

"For ya ears," he said when she didn't respond to the gift.

"Jewelry?"

"I hope ya like them."

"They are beautiful." She lowered her head as tears began to fall, but then she reached up and wiped her eyes. "I'm sorry," she said. "I thought it might be…"

"Ya thought it was ya freedom papers, didn't ya?"

Dinah pressed her lips together and gave a small nod. "Is it wrong to hope for that?"

"Is that all ya want from me?"

Her head snapped up to look at him. "No."

"What would happen if I bought ya freedom? Would ya leave me? Take my daughter and leave?" his voice was harsh for a moment.

"No," she repeated softly.

"What would it change? Ya know this is all there can ever be for us."

"It's just hard with the missus, and I'm scared that somethin' will happen."

"Will it help if I build ya your own cabin?" Dinah looked at him, and he smiled at her soft expression. "Wait until Coco is old enough for her own room upstairs, and I will build ya a cabin."

She looked back down at the jewelry in her lap. "These are so beautiful. I've never been given anythin' so beautiful in all my life." She choked with emotion.

Albert reached up and touched her earlobe between his thumb and forefinger. He gave it a rub and moved his thumb over her ear. "Ya have to get Nan to pierce these for ya." She smiled, and his hand moved to her chin and raised her head to face him. He kissed her tenderly.

The winter came and, with it, the travail of Justine. It was a day in December that brought an uncommon layer of frost over the hardened ground. The doctor was detained and not there after the water broke, and he would not arrive until twenty-six hours after the head of the child crowned. Nan, Franny, and Dinah had all been called upon to help with the delivery.

Mrs. Thompson had come over when news reached her that Justine had gone into labor. She was at the house, giving instructions she assumed the lady of the house would desire, and with that assumption, she ordered Dinah to be upstairs during the birthing process. Justine yelled when she saw her face in the doorway to her room.

Mrs. Thompson turned to look at her after the foul words were yelled. "Go get some more hot water," she ordered. Then she sat, holding the hand of the laboring woman and reassuring her that the slave was out of the room.

Justine was in labor for eighteen hours. When their newborn son, Victor Toussaint, was born, his mother was going in and out of what Mrs. Thompson called hallucinations. "Come in and look!" she yelled at the door, her voice heard all the way down the hall. "Look at my husband holding his son!"

Mrs. Thompson gave her a drink of the laudanum to calm her and put a cold cloth on her head until the doctor could make it to them and suggest something more. Justine finally drifted off into a relaxed state, and Dinah reappeared in the doorway after it quieted down.

Albert was walking back and forth with the small bundle in his arms. Mrs. Thompson was telling him something about how he needed to care for Justine over the next few days and that he shouldn't let her throw the New Year's Eve party, no matter how much she insisted she was well enough to do so. She was in the middle of saying how the Thompson plantation would take up the torch that year when she stopped mid-sentence upon noticing Dinah in the doorway. There she stood, her misty eyes fixed on Albert holding his son.

"Yes?" Mrs. Thompson asked a second time, stirring Dinah out of her trance.

"Um, no ma'am," Dinah stammered. "Just seein' if ya needed anything."

"No, we are fine," she said. When the slave didn't move, she added, "Aren't we, Mr. Toussaint? Do ya need anything?"

"No, I'm fine. Thank you, Dinah," he said, looking her in the eyes. She blinked rapidly before lowering her head and giving it a nod.

"Just a minute," Mrs. Thompson said slowly. "Now ya are a lovely thing—exotic looking, very becoming. Don't ya think so, Mr. Toussaint?"

He looked at his neighbor, questioning her statement's intentions. "She is," he admitted.

"Unusual."

An uncomfortable silence followed in which Dinah felt she was expected to explain her *unusual* and *exotic* look. "My mother was of the Chitimacha tribe, my father African."

Nothing more was said as Mrs. Thompson stared at her and Albert watched her shift on her feet. After giving her lowered head a short nod, Dinah backed out of the room and hurried down the hall and stairs. She had no sooner entered the room Albert had given her in the house and shut the door than the door swung open. Dinah spun around in time to see him striding toward her. Tears spilled down her cheeks as he grabbed hold of her and kissed her aggressively.

She kissed Albert back before pulling away. "No, no, ya were right," she stammered.

"What?"

"What else is there for us? Ya her husband, she has given ya five children, and I am just ya slave."

"I don't love her anymore," he said with passion as he gripped Dinah by the shoulders. "My children, yes, but I don't love her." He looked into her eyes. "You must know how I feel."

"But that doesn't change that there is nothing else for us beyond what we are."

"Isn't it enough?" His eyes searched hers and told all as they gazed at each other. After drying her cheek with his hand, he leaned forward and pressed a kiss to it. Then he left the room, looking back at her before he did.

As the months went on and they entered the spring of 1846,

Albert cared for his wife but spent no more extra time with her. They were like passing shadows. He would visit, however, and spend as much time as he could with Dinah and Coco. He became nearly inseparable from the tiny grip of his daughter. Though he would never admit it, he contemplated how he had never known so great a love as what her small heart had given him.

Justine maintained her distance and focused her attention on her own children. She no longer pined for Albert's affection and approval, replacing those feelings with contempt and vengeful thoughts. Eaten up with envy for Dinah, Justine thought back to the day Albert had first bought her and brought her to the plantation. She went back to the plantation logs one day when he was out overseeing the slaves.

As she fumbled through the leather-bound pages, she ran her eyes down the names of the slaves until, there, she found Dinah's name. Her breathing quickened as her finger traced the line to find the amount Albert had paid. Furious, she threw the book to the ground. Justine paced the room, venting to herself in rage. "He'll pay for this," she repeated to herself. Every day over the next several months, Justine would go into Albert's office when he was out of the house and go through the plantation books. One day, he caught her looking.

"What are ya doin'?" he asked.

"Oh, just reviewin' the books, learnin' the business. What kind of wife would I be if I didn't know how to run the plantation if my husband was gone?"

"Leave the plantation to me," he replied, eyeing her coy expression.

"Ya'd want me to know what was goin' on if somethin' happened to ya…"

Albert shut the book cover with force; Justine jerked back to keep her hand from being slammed between its pages. "Nothin' is goin' to happen to me, so don't ya worry." He gave her a forced smile. "Let me take care of the business."

Justine forced a show of her teeth in a nefarious grin. "It's a time of war, Albert," she said as she rose from where she sat and sauntered across the room. "What if the governor of war calls for more volunteer infantry? Ya know President Polk would've honorably avoided it, but as it is, they've called for Tennessean volunteers. What makes ya think they won't call upon more men? The state of Texas is our neighbor, after all."

"I'm sure ya want nothin' more than to know ya husband died honorably on the banks of the Rio Grande, gloriously fightin' a glorious cause. But I assure ya, my wife, that the farmers of this country serve with due diligence to support the just and liberal policy of the law. It is known that if the farmer prospers, all other pursuits prosper. So, don't ya worry. I'm not goin' anywhere."

"That's a shame," she said coolly.

Albert moved the plantation books after that day and started locking them in the safe where he kept his pistols. Justine looked madly for the key in every drawer and on every shelf, but to no avail.

She spent a lot of her time at the Thompsons' plantation, where she would fall in step in conversation with Mrs. Thompson about the latest gossip. It was summer, hot and sticky—the time of year ladies would fan themselves on the verandas of the plantations, praying that the clouds would bring cooling rain.

The fields were full of colorful rags tied in skillful patterns and knots on the black women's heads. This year, Mrs. Thompson required all her slave women to wear their heads tied with kerchiefs. The news that the Irish fever had made its way to Europe had her in a tizzy. If it could cross the waters to Europe, surely it could cross the waters to America, if it hadn't already, and she was determined in taking extra precautions to ensure that the louse spreading the dreadful typhus would not make their way into her household. Justine followed her example and soon had her own workers covering their heads. Six weeks passed, and not one black woman dared exit their hut without her head tied. In fact, they soon adopted it as a fashion and were comparing the color of cloth and the skill of the wrap design and knots.

Dinah got out of the washtub with Coco. She untied the braids that had held her tresses for the last couple of weeks, and her black hair fell in full curls down her back like a cascade of water flowing down a rocky cliff. She moved about her business with only a folded kerchief tying back the hair from her face. Justine caught word of this from Isabelle, who was still too young to understand what a feud looked like and liked to chatter with Dinah whenever given the opportunity.

Mrs. Toussaint stormed through the house, yelling out Dinah's name. Franny was the first to come upon Justine in her rage. "Where is Dinah?"

"Dunno, missus," Franny said, wringing her hands.

"Is it true that her hair is exposed?"

"I ain't seen her, missus," Franny lied.

"Go find her and bring her to me immediately."

Franny left Justine in a titter and rushed around looking for Dinah to warn her of the angry missus. She found her with two-year-old Coco in the back garden, collecting a basket of ready turnips. Dinah was knelt down, brushing the dirt from one just pulled from the earth, after having just placed a worm in curious Coco's tiny hand. Franny came running up and skidded to the ground next to her, fumbling for words as her hands began twisting and braiding her hair.

Dinah pushed her back with a startled look at the sudden strange behavior. "What are ya doin'? What is wrong with you?"

"Get ya hair up! The missus knows ya hair is down and ya head's not covered. She's fumin' mad."

Dinah's eyes grew wide as she took hold of her longs strands and began twisting and braiding. Franny fumbled with the kerchief as she tried to untie and open it up to cover Dinah's whole head, their hands moving in uncoordinated urgency. Just then, Mrs. Toussaint stormed up behind them. Their movement stopped as both women looked up in panic at their towering overseer. Dinah's kerchief was sloppily tied and her hair only partially hidden, some of it not yet tucked away. Justine's eyes burned holes through the two women hunkered down in the garden. Little Coco still played with the worm in her hand, unmindful of the others around her.

"Missus," Franny uttered lowly when the two finally noticed her presence. Both women shuddered under her glare.

"Ya defy me," she said.

"No, ma'am," Dinah said lowly.

"Ya defy me. Ya hair is down, uncovered."

"No, ma'am. My head is covered. My hair's put away," she said putting her hand up to touch the kerchief.

"Franny, ya traitor. Ya takin' her side, aren't ya?"

"No, missus… I just found her. Seein' her pull the turnips, I plum forgot ya was even lookin' for her. Ya know me, missus," she continued with an airy laugh. "I just dumb sometimes. Things just go and slip my mind."

"Both of ya come with me," Justine ordered. Dinah lifted Coco from the ground and gave Franny a scared glance. Justine led them to the kitchen and ordered Dinah to sit. "Put the child down. Stay here, and don't ya move." Justine left the kitchen but was back before Franny could make her way to find Nan. "We're goin' to take care of this once and for all," she said as she made her way toward Dinah with a pair of shears in hand.

Dinah was quick to get up and move around the center island. "No, missus!" she exclaimed as she backed out of Justine's reach. "Please, ma'am, I'm clean! I washed my hair and everythin' this morning!"

Franny began to panic as she rushed out of the kitchen, yelling for Nan. "She done lost her mind, the missus!" she said in frantic breath behind streams of tears when she found the older woman. "Come quick! She's after Dinah!"

Nan pushed the child with her in the direction of the barn

with orders to find the master, and then she moved as fast as her body allowed. She was panting when she reached the kitchen with Franny. The two women were yelling, Dinah pleading that she let her be and Justine screaming curses and threats. The young Coco sat on the floor near a corner, crying.

"You two!" Justine yelled, pushing back her loosened hair from around her face. "Sit that woman in the chair and hold her still!" she ordered.

"Missus?"

"Ya heard me, Nan!"

"Yes'm." She walked toward the crying Dinah. "Come on nah and sit down. Got to do as ya told."

Dinah's head tipped to the side as her brow furrowed toward Nan. "Please, don't. I'm clean! I ain't got no louse."

"I know. Nah child, ain't none of this matter. Ya come have a seat."

Dinah reluctantly complied, and Franny stood on one side of her and Nan on the other as Justine pulled the kerchief off of her head. She took large handfuls of her black locks as the scissors began forcefully cutting the strands of velvet from Dinah's head. Nan's hand rested heavily on her shoulder, giving a squeeze when a large piece of hair was dropped to the floor. Franny stood, bawling, until she was scolded by Justine to hush up with the threat that she would be dealt with later for her Judas Iscariot behavior. Franny was later tied and whipped.

"There," Justine said breathlessly when she finished bringing the sharp edge of the shears down Dinah's temple, drawing blood. She said nothing else but slammed the shears down on the counter before she stomped out.

The three women remained still, Franny sniffing with a sob. Dinah's trembling hand reached up to her head not heeding the open wound. Some strands were cut next to the scalp; others stood off of her head.

Her hand continued to shake as she looked up to Nan, who stood with her lips pressed together and a look of pity in her eyes.

"Franny," she said softly, "hand me the shears." Franny did as she was told before pressing a terry cloth to the stream of blood that made its way down the side of Dinah's face. "Nah," Nan continued, "I'm goin' to even this out for ya. Don't ya worry—hair grows, Ms. Dinah. It'll be long again before ya know it." She swallowed hard as she trimmed the remaining hair.

By the time Albert reached the kitchen, Franny was sweeping up the black locks from the floor. She had a deep hum in her throat and tears still wetted her cheeks. "What's happened?" he asked. "Where's Dinah?"

"She took Coco and closed herself in her room."

Albert moved with haste down the halls and, without hesitation, entered the room. Dinah sat in the rocking chair next to the window, holding a sleeping Coco.

"Please go," she said quietly.

He slowly walked to her and then knelt. His eyes were wide as he surveyed her head. "Tell me why she did this."

Dinah was slow to speak but told him everything. He lifted a hand and touched her face before leaving the room. The rise and falling of voices could be heard in the upper hall. No one in the house saw Justine or Albert for the rest of the day; the children ate their dinner alone. Dinah didn't see or hear from him for three days, not even to take his daughter. But on the fourth day, she walked into her room to find five colorful scarves, each with a different print, laid out on her bedstead. That night, Albert joined her in her bed—and the next.

CHAPTER TWELVE

THE SEASONS ROSE and fell with the sun. Harvest came, followed by another planting season. The Toussaint plantation continued to grow as Albert purchased more slaves and expanded his crop fields. Shortly after the shaving of her head, Albert built Dinah a small hut on the backside of the property, off the path leading to the mill. There, he allowed her to grow her own vegetables and supplied her with the few items that were necessary for her to support herself and Coco. Every morning, Dinah would gather her daughter and walk to the plantation house before the rooster crowed, so Albert could take his coffee with his daughter as he had done for the past three years. The plantation was getting ready for the harvest of 1848/1849.

A brisk morning, inside her hut, Dinah removed the pan of cornbread from over the fire and took up the poker to stir the flames. Suddenly, Justine appeared in the doorway, her face pale and stern. Dinah's eyes widened as she set down the pan and twisted at the towel in her hand.

"Missus...is there somethin' ya need?"

"Step outside with me," she said without emotion.

Dinah's brow furrowed as she stooped down to pick up Coco.

She held onto her tightly to help with the involuntary quivering of her limbs. She ran her tongue across her lips before she took a deep breath, clenched her jaw, and stepped through the open door. Her eyes met the calloused gaze of three men sitting on horseback, two white and one seedy-looking old negro, with a brick in his hat. One of the white men dismounted, followed by another whose beard was gray and long down his chest.

The first man to dismount took a few steps forward. "Da child too?"

"No," Justine responded.

Dinah's eyes shot back and forth between the men and Justine. "What's goin' on?"

The younger of the two strode toward her. As he got closer, Dinah could see the pitted scars on his face, which would have been covered if the man had been able to grow a full beard. "Put da child down," he ordered when he stood in front of her.

"What?" Dinah exclaimed, fearing the happenings at hand.

"Come on now. I ain't got time to waste," he said, reaching to take Coco from her.

Dinah jerked away and shielded her daughter from his grasp. His leather-gloved hand was quick to rise into the air, its backside striking her across the face. The sudden blow made Coco begin to cry, and Dinah's eyes welled up with tears.

"Put da child down," the man said again with pressed lips.

"No," she said.

His hand came up a second time, this time drawing a stream of blood from her lip. He turned to the black companion, who had dismounted and moved forward. Coco's cries were loud as her arms squeezed around her mother's neck. The old man grabbed Dinah by the arms while the other man yanked at the child.

"Gawd damn it, woman," he growled.

She began to cry out as Coco was finally pulled from her arms. "No, no!" she yelled as the man roughly placed the child down in the dirt.

"Stay put," he growled at her with a frown. Coco sat on the ground, her bare feet curled beneath her long, beige dress. She rubbed at her eyes as she cried.

"Stop! No," Dinah continued to plead. She looked at Justine, who stood like a stone statue. "Please, what are ya doin'?" She struggled against the man maintaining hold of her.

The bearded of the three men, who seemed to be the leader, walked up to Justine and pulled out his money pouch. He placed the bills in her hand with a pause. "How 'bout showin' me a little more of ya merchandise?" he said with a side grin and a chew of his tongue.

"Our business is finished here." Mrs. Toussaint smirked as she drew back her hand. "Now, get off my land and take her far away from here."

His gray eyes narrowed as the man looked at her from under the shade of his hat. "All right, bring her on," he said, turning and mounting his horse.

Dinah dug her heels in to the ground and growled between clenched teeth, "Ya can't do this! No!"

The man with the pitted face put his arms around her fighting torso and lifted her up from behind. Her feet flung through the air, catching the black man on the chin.

His eyes burned with anger. "Bitch!" He lunged forward with a closed fist and struck her in the face.

Dinah went limp for a moment as her eyes tried to refocus from the blow. The man holding her started hauling her toward his horse, where her hands were bound tight with rope. She looked around, dazed.

"No..." she whispered as her tears fell.

Coco stumbled to her feet through her tears and started after her mother before a boot came up and pushed her backward to the ground. She looked up and saw Justine. Somewhat familiar with the woman's white face, Coco made her way to her with arms up. Mrs. Toussaint looked down at her teary, round face and then turned and walked back to the house.

Behind the hut, a fearful dark face hunkered low and peeked around the corner. Nathan held his breath, afraid that they would hear him. He watched as the men mounted their horses and began leading Dinah away. She pulled against the rope as she was led farther and farther from the hut.

"No! My baby! Please, help me! Help me!" Her chest heaved with quick panting. "No!" she finally yelled at the top of her lungs. "Albert! Albert! Help me!" A sudden quick jerk of the rope hurled her to the ground.

Nathan's heart raced. He waited until he couldn't hear Dinah's voice anymore before looking around the corner from where he hid. He moved slowly to make sure no one was waiting for him. The front of the hut was deserted, except for the three-year-old Coco sitting on the doorstep, whimpering. Nathan looked around, confused. After moving toward the crying child, he lifted her into his arms and hurried her into the hut, closing the door behind him. He took up a blanket and wrapped her up in it.

"Shh, stop cryin'. Ya gotta be quiet now. Shh," Nathan whispered. He looked around the hut for a place to hide the child, fearing someone would come back for her. Finally deciding on the dress closet, he opened the bureau and sat the girl inside. "Now, listen to me, Coco," he ordered quietly. "Now listen. Ya stop cryin' now. I need ya to hide in here until I can come back for ya. Understand me? Do ya understand?" He tightened the blanket around her. "I'll be back for ya, I promise," he said as he slowly closed the doors.

After leaving the hut, Nathan began running toward the cane field where he knew Abraham was driving. He ran even though his lungs burned and the ground cut his bare soles. He ran until he fell at the feet of Abraham, panting.

"What da hell, man?" Abraham said, watching the lanky boy's chest heave.

"Some men...men came," he panted. "She sold her... Da missus sold Dinah." He swallowed a large gulp of air.

Abraham's eyes grew large. "What?"

"They took her. I hid da baby." The large man bent the whip in his hand until it snapped. "Think masta knows?" Nathan asked.

"He and Foy still gone."

"What do we do?"

"Dis ain't right," Abraham said angrily as he mounted a nearby wagon.

"What ya doin'?"

"I don't know. I gotta do somethin'."

Nathan climbed onto the wagon just as Abraham gave the reins a hard flick. They rode hard in the direction Nathan said the men had headed. As the four came into view, Abraham slowed the wagon. Their bodies broke into a cold sweat.

"I don't know what ya plan on doin'," Nathan said in a low whisper as they rode closer upon them.

"Just hush and don't say nothin'."

The men noticed the wagon getting closer and led their horses to the side of the road, waiting in place. Abraham pulled to a halt next to them.

"Ya lost, darkie?" the man who seemed to be the leader asked. "What ya doin' out on these roads?"

"There's been a mistake, sir," Abraham said, keeping his eyes straightforward down the road, not turning to look at the man.

"What are ya talkin' bout?" the leader barked.

"This ain't the slave that was to be sold," his deep voice was strong and resolute. He slowly turned his head and boldly looked at the man.

Nathan peered up from where he kept his head bowed and glanced at Dinah. Her bleeding lips quivered.

"Now how do ya figure when her owner was standin' right there as I bought her?" Abraham stayed silent for a moment, and the man moved his horse toward the wagon. "Now ya wouldn't be tryin' to pull a fast one on me, would ya, nigga?"

"No, sir, I'm just here on behalf of my masta."

"And who is that?"

"Mr. Toussaint, sir. He has no intentions of sellin' this slave and will be mighty angry when he gets home."

"What's ya name, nigga?"

"Abraham."

"And ya taken the liberty to speak for ya master? A nigga slave, here on behalf and speakin' for a white man. Are ya sayin' that woman tricked me into buyin' this here slave?" His voice rose as anger began to rise in his chest. Nothing was ever known about the man with gray eyes and a short temper. No one ever knew his story, except those brave enough to stay around when he was drunk. They would hear slurs about his dirt leg mother who always took a beating from the man he was damned to call his father. He would growl in his drunken state that she was a weak bitch and clench his fist as he recalled his own beatings.

"I ain't sayin' that the missus wasn't sellin' ya a good slave. This just ain't the right one."

"Well, my business wasn't with this Toussaint man; my business was with the woman. So if'n this man don't want to sell this here cunt, then he is welcome to come buy her back." Spittle flew from his lips as his white face changed to a shade of red.

"I'm tryin' to tell ya..."

"Now I'm gettin' real tired of ya lip. Ya need to get on back down the road here and go back to where ya came from before I lose my temper."

Abraham didn't say another word. He continued sitting in the wagon, his heavy torso leaning forward on his thick thighs and staring straight at the man.

"Hey!" the man yelled, "I'm tellin' ya, nigga, to get on down the road!" Abraham remained still.

"Did ya hear what I said? Goddamn..." The man grunted

inaudible slurs and reached for his pistol from his holster, his jerking motion causing his horse to side step. He pointed it at Abraham. "Get out of the wagon," he ordered, but the slave stayed fixed. The man's thumb pulled the hammer back as he repositioned the barrel toward Nathan. "I said get out of the wagon, nigga, or I'll spread the brains of this boy where he sits."

Abraham moved slowly from the box seat and set his feet on the ground.

"Get over here!" the man ordered.

He walked around the team of horses and stood before him. The butt of the man's pistol came down across his skull, dropping him to the ground. After dismounting his horse, the man holstered his gun before striking the slave with a series of punches. He was joined in the beating by the other white man as the old black man laughed and pulled another drink from his decanter. Abraham took the beating until he could no longer see and his body lay bleeding in the dirt.

The man with gray eyes mounted his steed. "Fool," he said. Then he turned his horse down the road, followed by the other men leading a bound Dinah.

Nathan stayed where he sat, shaking in the wagon, biting on the inside of his cheeks, until their silhouettes had been gone for an hour. Finally, he moved toward the battered Abraham. Kneeling, he tried to stir him, and after getting a mumble and moan from the beaten man, he worked on getting his large frame onto the wagon to rush him back to the huts. There, the other men helped get him onto a pallet.

As Nathan began telling the story of what happened, he stopped suddenly and his eyes grew wide. "Coco!" he exclaimed.

He rushed out of the hut into the dusky evening with a lantern, moving in a jog toward Dinah's hut. When he reached it, he burst through the door.

"Coco," he called out as he went over to the cabinet where he'd left her tucked in. He peered inside the open door. "Coco!" he yelled, looking around for the child.

Nathan ran out into the yard and called for her as he frantically searched. Finally, he saw a small figure lying in the wooded grove one hundred yards from the cabin.

He crouched. "Coco," he said, touching the toddler by the shoulder. She was startled from her sleep, and her eyes widened in alarm before she started to cry. Nathan took her up into his arms and carried the child back to the others, back to where a woman could comfort her.

The night fell and Nan returned to her hut from her day's labor. She mumbled threats when she walked inside to find it empty and the fireplace nothing but cold ash. Her body swayed in anger as she marched out of the hut and called out for whoever would respond. As she moved across the path between her hut and the next row, she noticed the dim glow of lantern light where gathered both men and women. Nan paused for a minute with narrow eyes before moving forward, toward the humming of a plaintive tune.

"What's goin' on? Someone die today?" she asked as she drew close and pulled at the shawl that was too small to wrap entirely around her large frame.

"Ya best go on in," the woman said, touching her on the shoulder with fingers so light that Nan's bones quivered.

"Best go in then," she repeated in a chant as she pursed her lips in a tight circle, as if she were about to whistle. She mounted the steps and pushed through the bodies filling the doorway. There, inside, she saw the others tending to an unconscious Abraham laid upon a sleeping pallet, his face swollen and discolored. "What in Gawd's name happened here?"

Nathan, who sat with his elbows on his knees and head drooped between them, looked up. His lower lip, pink against his dark upper one, started to tremor when he made eye contact with

Nan. She followed his gaze as it left her stare and moved to where a sleeping Coco was being held in Harriett's arms.

"Why's Coco over here? And where's Dinah?" Nan's voice became raspy as her chest moved up and down. All eyes were on her. "Can someone please tell me what is goin' on?"

"Tell her, boy," one of the men encouraged Nathan.

As he recounted the happenings of the afternoon, Nan's body began to visibly shake and her eyes rolled back. A man standing nearby was quick to brace her, as she could no longer stand on her own.

"No, this can't be... This has got to be a dream..." They made room for Nan to sit down. "The poor child... Did Masta know? Did he do this?" she continued in raspy questions, prayers, and curses. Tears rolled down her round face, something no one in the community had ever seen. No one had ever witnessed Nan cry— not even on Sundays.

Abraham regained consciousness later that night and insisted on being back out in the cane fields after a day of resting in the hut. Nan kept Coco in her own hut, and Harriett was allowed to stay out of the cane fields to watch the child until they could know what to do with her. Nan refused to take her to the plantation for fear of what Justine may do, and Nan didn't tell Franny what had happened either. Franny's sensitive nature would cause a scene she wouldn't know how to handle. Because of that, Nan decided not to tell her until after she had talked to Mr. Toussaint.

It was the fourth day after Dinah was sold before Albert and Foy returned. They had been negotiating and selling barrels of molasses in New Orleans, getting an early start this year and securing a contract before the molasses exports from Havana reached the shore. Boxes of sugar seemed to be less in demand than the previous year, whereas molasses sales had been steadily increasing, primarily in the United States.

Albert rode onto the plantation in good spirits and took his horse straight to Dinah's hut. He was eager to tell her about his plans to implement the steam engine in his mill and his thoughts on distilling rum. The mill was a consistent source of anxiety for him, but he felt a new surge of excitement after getting a hold of essays on the study of sugar chemistry and manufacturing methods sponsored by the U.S. Treasury. Somehow, the inauguration of President Taylor, a man who called the state of Louisiana home, also seemed to ignite in him a feeling of pride, as if he, along with all of Louisiana, now had proper representation, which would somehow make the state and all who lived there prosper. Albert felt good and on the tide of a new beginning.

He dismounted outside the hut and entered with a smile that quickly faded when he saw it was not only empty but cold as well. A frown creased his forehead as he stepped toward the fireplace and felt the ash. A fire hadn't been lit in the hut for days. An eerie feeling washed over him as he exited and mounted his horse. He rode to the plantation house and walked inside, his face showing his confusion. Immediately, Albert made his way to the room Dinah used to stay in, only to find it empty as well. His pace quickened as he walked through the lower level of the house. As he moved through the sitting room, his younger children, happy to see him, came running up to him, full of chatter and stories.

"Just a minute, son," he said to young Albert, who was, in full force, reenacting a scene from his life while his father had been away.

Albert continued through each room until he came upon Nan. "What happened?" he asked her.

She jumped from the unexpected voice behind her and turned. "Yes, sir?"

"Something is wrong... What is it?" he said, and Nan looked down. "Where is Dinah and Coco?" he insisted.

"Coco has been stayin' in my hut. Harriett is watchin' her, sir." Her large limbs began to shake.

"Why? Where's Dinah?"

"She's not here no more, sir."

"What do ya mean not here?" his voice boomed. "Where is she?"

"She's been sold, Masta." The tears began to stream down Nan's face in full force. His eyes grew wide and his face turned ghostly white as she continued, "Four days ago...the missus sold her. Nathan saw it. He saw the whole thing. He and Abraham went after her, and he was nearly killed, Abraham was—nearly beat to death by them men..."

Albert's expressionless face sent chills down Nan's spine. Slowly, he turned and walked out of the room, pausing for a moment in the hall and eyes shifting, before he headed for the stairs. He began mounting them with a heavy boot. "Justine," he called out as he climbed. "Justine!" he yelled louder as his step quickened.

In their room, Justine heard him and quickly moved to the bedroom door to lock it. Albert strode in fury down the upper hall, yelling out her name. He tried the handle before banging on the door.

"Justine! Open this goddamn door!" His fist pounded the door panel. "Who'd ya sell her to, Justine? Justine! Tell me where she's at!" He jiggled the doorknob and pounded again before both hands gripped at the doorframe, turning his knuckles white.

At the top of the stairs, Franny watched with terror. She waved her hand toward the children, who were starting to make the climb up the stairs. "Stay on down there," she ordered. "Rose, get on, take them outside."

But Rose just stood with one hand on her brother's shoulder and the other holding Isabelle by the hand. Nan pushed past the children and mounted the steps to get to Franny.

"What happened? What's he yellin' about?" Franny questioned her as she stood close behind her, one hand twisting at her dress the other on the stair rail, bracing herself.

"Justine, open the door."

"Ya will never get her back," her muffled voice sounded from behind it. "What's done is done. She's gone."

Albert braced himself against both sides of the doorframe as he growled in anger. He stepped away from the door for a moment before turning to face it and thrusting his foot against it just below the doorknob. The lock was no match for his force, and the door busted open. Franny let out a shriek as both women jumped from the sudden, violent force. Mr. Toussaint moved into the room where his wife sat on the bed, wide eyed at his action. Before she could move, he was on top of her, pushing her back onto the bed with one hand gripping her shoulder and the other around the base of her neck.

"Why would you do this?" he asked between gritted teeth. "Tell me who ya sold her to."

"Ya won't find her," Justine answered. "I made sure of that." Albert gave his hand a squeeze and Justine flinched, but the cold stare-down between them remained unmoved. "Go ahead." She said behind her teeth, "Kill me! Go ahead. Do it!" His grip lightened, and she began to laugh spitefully. "Ya can't do it, can ya?" He gave her a push and released his hold, heaving in deep breaths. "Ya think that I was just goin' to let her stay here?"

"She is the mother of my child!"

Justine sat up with defiance. "And I am your wife! You're lucky I didn't sell the child too." Albert shot her a fiery gaze, and his jaw flexed as she sauntered to her sitting table in front of one of the three windows in the room. "No," she continued, "no matter how wicked ya perceive me to be, I am not that evil...even though I hate her." Her hand moved gently over a fragrance bottle on the desk.

"I'll get her back."

"Ya even dare try and I'll ruin ya! Ya will lose everything. The slaves, the plantation, *Coco*—everything. Ya will come to ruin."

Albert mocked her with an airy laugh. "Ya think you're that powerful, to bring me down?"

"Aren't I, though?" She paused before continuing with a saucy lip, "It seems there is a slight error in the bill books. And, given a closer look, one may see there are more slaves on this plantation than the bills of sales reflect. What is it, an eighth or a quarter of actual property ya have not been paying taxes on? And how many years? How many thousands of dollars have ya withheld from the state of Louisiana? I'm sure the governor would love to look into that." Albert's solemn stare didn't even flinch. "Are ya shocked?" Her voice was cold.

"What do ya want?"

She stared at her husband. "For ya to feel the same fury and pain that has been my companion these last five years."

Justine waited a few long moments, letting the cold silence spread between them like a fresh grave. She finally took steps toward the door, letting her shoulder brush against him as she passed, and exited the room. The two women at the top of the stairs watched, wide eyed, as she moved past them. Nan's eyes followed her.

"Don't look at me like that," Mrs. Toussaint said in a conniving nature as she headed down the stairs, "or I'll sell ya too."

Franny blinked quickly to keep the tears from falling down her cheeks. She looked to Nan's round face. "Why didn't ya tell me?"

Nan flushed under her dark skin. "Franny," she said softly.

"Dinah's been sold? Da baby?"

"Harriett's been watchin' Coco out in the community."

Blinking no longer kept the tears back but pushed them in streams down Franny's face. "Dinah's been sold..." she repeated in a distant whisper. She released her hands from holding onto Nan and slowly walked down the stairs.

A loud crash was heard from the inside the bedroom, after which Nan didn't move for several minutes and what felt like hours. Moving slowly, she approached the room and found Albert sitting on the edge of the bed facing the opposite wall.

"Masta," she said gently. Albert didn't respond or turn to face her greeting, so Nan moved forward until she stood next to him. "Masta…"

His hand came up in a stopping gesture. "No, Nan, not now."

"Oh, Masta…" A quiver threatened her steady voice. "What of Coco?"

Albert stirred, as if awakened from a trance. His eyes grew wide. "Where is my daughter?"

"She with Harriett," Nan replied.

He stood rapidly and moved from the room. He went to the community and to his daughter, who reached for him with needy arms.

"Daddy!" she cried when she saw him. She stayed nestled in his arms for the rest of the day, whimpering and crying any time he attempted to put her down.

Albert stayed in the community for the rest of the day and into the night, talking to both Nathan and Abraham. He got all the details of the night Dinah was sold, from the weather and the time of day, what the men looked like, wore, and which way they rode, to what Justine had said and details of Dinah's reactions. "She called my name," he repeated in a whisper as furious tears of sorrow filled his eyes, and his heart ached. Albert returned to the plantation house around midnight and took a bottle of port to the sitting room with him. He drank until the bottle was near empty and he couldn't keep his eyes open. Coco slept on his chest as he stretched out on the settee.

His daughter soon settled back into the house and slept in Franny's room every night, even until the day she turned eight, when Albert gave her a room of her own upstairs, next to the other children. For months after Dinah was sold, Coco had night terrors and would wake up wailing and flailing her arms. Time soon put an end to those nightmares, until they returned in the years she was becoming a woman.

CHAPTER THIRTEEN

"'About five o'clock, three cannons were placed in the street twelve or fifteen rods east of the hotel, and some thirty shots were fired, shattering the wall considerably but proving altogether too slow a method of destruction for these 'law and order' men. They then set fire to the building in different places and put several kegs of powder under it.'"

Albert walked into the sitting room with a glass of iced tea and sat down across the room from Coco, who was reading aloud to whomever was there to listen.

"'The flames and smoke soon burst out at the windows, and the whole building was in a blaze,'" she continued reading, not even skipping a beat at the notice of her father entering the room. "'The walls trembled and fell, and the shouts and yells of the mob proclaimed the triumph of 'law and order' in Lawrence. While the hotel was burning, the house of G.W. Brown was twice set on fire. The floor was burned through. The fire was finally extinguished by some young men of Lawrence. The mob threatened to shoot them, but they were not deterred.'"

Albert had moved to stand over his daughter. He yanked the newspaper out of her hand. "What the hell are ya readin'?"

"An article on Bleeding Kansas." Her father's brow furrowed as he looked the paper over. "It's a piece from the *Louisburg Chronicle*," Coco continued.

"I don't want ya readin' that," he said, slamming the paper down on the low hickory table in front of the settee.

"It's news," Coco countered.

"It's garbage!" His voice rose before becoming gentler. "Why don't ya read a story book or somethin', huh?"

He moved to sit back in his chair where he had left his glass of tea. The June day was hot and Albert had little patience for the shifting politics that were growing more and more unstable every month. Coco waited until he was engrossed in his own literature before slowly reaching over and quietly taking back up the newspaper. The other two in the room, Isabelle and Victor, didn't seem to care what she was reading, that she was scolded by their father, or that she continued reading the article in rebellion.

Most of the time, Coco was invisible to the other children who still lived in the house. Only to Rose did she seem to be another human being capable of emotion or intellect, but Rose had recently moved to Baton Rouge with her new husband of only two years, and though fourteen years her elder, he was remarkably young looking. Albert had only agreed to her marriage of the bachelor with different political views because of his outstanding career in law after graduating from Yale. Edward Mason, or Eddy as Rose called him, had taken an eye for the young beauty when she was only fourteen years of age at the governor's ball, which was, in turn, lucky for Mr. Mason after her debutante. Albert refused the courtship until she turned sixteen and wouldn't give him her hand in marriage until she was eighteen. She married him the day after her eighteenth birthday.

Coco quietly read in excitement the *Chronicle*, her eyes shifting every so often to her father slouched in his chair. The girl smiled mischievously when she saw his head nod as he began to doze off.

"'The spirit of the People of Kansas is not subdued—the blood of the martyrs will enrich the soil of liberty.'" Her loud voice suddenly broke the silence, causing the others to jump and her father's head to snap up. "'From which will rise up a new life and a new power that will overcome the brutal tyranny that now grinds them into the earth.'" She moved from where she sat to dodge her father's grasp as she continued reading with a loud voice and swift step. "'And restore them to the enjoyment of that freedom and independence which was sanctified by the blood of their fathers and is now their own rightful inheritance.'" She finished before her father grasped the paper from her hands and crumpled it in his fists.

"Damn it, Coco," he growled. "Go play with ya dolls."

"But don't ya want to know what's happening? What if that sort of thing starts in Louisiana?"

"Ya don't have to worry about that. Louisiana is a southern state and a long ways from Kansas. Now, will ya please stop with the adult talk of things ya have no intellect for?"

"I know more than ya realize!" she countered, throwing her chin upward as Albert turned and moved toward his chair.

"That's what I'm afraid of," he mumbled under his breath as he took a seat. He looked at his brown-skinned daughter, so different from the cream color of his other two children in the room. Coco was eleven, but already the features of her face whispered of the striking woman she would become. "Victor," Albert said, "ya and Coco go play somewhere."

The boy let out an annoyed sigh as his hands fell limply to his side, dropping the small metal solider figures he was playing with. "I don't want to play with her," he moaned.

"I don't care if ya want to, boy. I said ya two go somewhere and play!" Coco shot a narrow-eyed glare at her father. "Don't make me switch ya both," he threatened.

Coco ran her hands down her lilac colored dress and waited as Victor slowly stood. She turned and walked out of the room, followed by her brother.

"Ya don't have to play with me," she said once they were out of earshot of their father. "We can just say we did but go our own ways." She marched with a firm, determined step a few feet in front of Victor, the hem of her skirts bouncing.

The boy rolled his eyes as he followed her out of doors. "I don't want to be the one gettin' switched." Coco didn't slow down or respond. "Where are ya goin'?" Victor asked in annoyance.

"Nowhere ya want to be!"

He trotted to catch up to her. "Ya goin' out to the huts, ain't ya?"

Coco stopped and shot around to look at him. "Why don't ya follow me and find out?"

"That's a good way of gettin' switched. Ya know we ain't supposed to bother the slaves while they're workin'."

"Well then, don't come…if ya scared."

Victor shifted on his feet. "I ain't scared… I just don't want to go out there."

"Then don't," she said, turning on her heel and continuing toward the community, leaving Victor behind her.

Albert had more than doubled the size of his plantation over the last seven years. The sugar business was booming, and the Toussaint plantation was exporting by sea to Atlantic ports and upriver to western states at an average of $59 per hogshead. By switching his mill from animal powered to the steam driven, Albert began producing four times the amount of sugar and rum with more efficiency than ever before. Planting, growing, cutting, and milling the sugar required more slaves and kept them busy year-round. As the slave community grew, so did the profits of the Toussaint plantation. As it was said through Louisiana, "It took a rich cotton planter to make a poor sugar planter."

When Coco reached the community, she strolled among the huts. It was after the lunch hour but too early for the workday to have come to an end, so the cabins were empty of their occupants. Coco took her time, looking through the garden patches where they grew some of their own food and taking the liberty of pulling some of the wild weeds growing in the vegetable paths. Soon she became distracted with the clearing, one weed leading to another. The fiery sun was merciless with its heat. Coco reached up to wipe her forehead and looked around herself at the rows of huts. She had never been in one before and suddenly wanted to look inside. Standing, she looked down at her soiled hands before brushing them against each other, and then, without hesitation, she moved to the closest hut. She looked around before pulling the door open.

The hut was stifling and dark. Coco left the door open as she scooted her feet over the floor of earth to stand in the middle of the cabin. The whole of the hut was hardly bigger than her bedroom. A stone fireplace towered up one of the walls. There was no furniture, save a bench next to the hearth and a couple of metal pots hanging from wooden pegs. On the other side of the cabin, the ground was covered with hay, rags, and a couple of blankets.

Coco's eyes shifted around when she noticed something peculiar about the cabin walls. She narrowed her eyes and stepped closer to get a better look. Reaching up, she took hold of the maroon rag her eyes had landed on and pulled on it. Light poured through into the cabin, revealing the hole the scrap had successfully filled. Coco leaned hesitantly forward and peered through the opening, as if expecting to see something unusual. Standing back upright, she looked at the whole of the wall and noticed more tatters shoved in the cracks of the wood and other holes. She quickly pressed the rag back into its dutiful spot and hurried out of the cabin.

She ran between the huts and didn't stop until they were behind her. Panting, Coco kept her head down until her eyes shifted and she jerked her head to look at the dark faces that stood only a few feet from her. At first, not a word was spoken as they stared at her.

"Ya ain't supposed to be out here! What ya doin' out here?" the older boy said snidely.

"I'm sorry," was all she could manage.

"Ya think ya better than us? Did ya come out here to gloat? Ya know ya mama was just a nigga slave like the rest of us. Ya ain't no better," the taunting continued. "Just because she was a lickfinger…"

Coco's jaw flexed and her eyes narrowed. "Don't ya say those things."

"What ya goin' to do, go cry to Massa? Ya say a word to him and I'll poison the well." The boy's hand came up and formed a clenched fist.

The other children urged him to get going, as they had stood there long enough and were nervous of his daring taunts. The boy began to follow the others. "Get out of here. Ya don't belong here, cherry," he spat over his shoulder at her.

Coco stayed there, her eyes glazed over with tears, until the children were far from view. After turning on her heel, she began to run, letting the hot, steamy air blast against her face, until she reached a distantly familiar cabin. There were no shreds of cloth shoved into cracks or holes, the floor was wood instead of earth and straw, and the furniture, though ghostly unused, was arranged with care. Coco had been told by Franny that her mother used to live in a cabin on the west side of the plantation, away from the others, where she had cared for Coco until her death. She had found the cabin last year and would often walk there, unbeknownst to her father, to pretend she lived there and was making dinner for her mother, who would be returning with new fabric to make them matching dresses of pink silk.

Coco didn't pretend this time. She lay down on the bed, angry, begrudging her mother for the day she died, until she fell asleep only to dream, once again, of Dinah being ripped from her arms. She jerked up and gathered her wits before she swung her legs to hang over the edge of the bed. She couldn't tell how long she had been asleep, but her sweat left a mark behind and darkened her lilac dress.

She hurried out of the cabin and shut the door behind herself. The sun was low in the sky as Coco began to run toward the plantation, knowing she had been away for too long. As the house came into view, she slowed her pace and tried to walk calmly toward the large, strong figure that appeared to be waiting for her. Albert didn't move as his daughter approached and stood silently in front of him.

He grabbed her by the arm. "I ought to tan ya hide," he said. "Where have ya been? Victor has been in the house for hours. He said ya went to the slave community." Coco didn't say anything as her father shook her by the arm. Albert led her forcefully toward the house as he continued chiding her. "But ya weren't in the community. Ya know how I know that? Because I rode out there! What do ya have to say for yourself?"

"I was just out walkin'."

"Whom were ya walkin' with?"

"No one..."

Albert's grip remained tight as he led her into the house and pushed her into his office before shutting the door. He walked to the windows and rubbed his chin while looking outside. Coco remained standing in the middle of the room.

"Did ya go to the community?" he finally asked after gathering himself.

Coco had learned years ago that it was always easier to be punished for the truth than to suffer for both the lie and the offense, so she answered timidly, "Yes sir."

"Ya know ya not supposed to go out there." His voice rose. "Why were ya there, huh?"

"I don't know."

"Where did ya go afterwards?"

"Nowhere, just there. No one was there. I wasn't hurtin' anything."

"A couple of them said they saw ya there." Coco didn't respond. "Pullin' weeds?" There was a pause before he continued. "What is goin' through ya mind?" He spoke more gently. "I don't understand ya, Coco." Tears spilled over her cheeks, but she remained silent. "I need to think about ya punishment. Go to Franny to get cleaned up and go to ya room. Ya will not have supper tonight."

Coco wiped at her eyes and left the room. She did as she was told, and Franny took her to the washroom, disrobed her, and sat her down in the tub of water. Franny's heavy chatter went unanswered and unheard while Coco was getting washed up. She stood out of the water mechanically as Franny held open a towel to dry her off with. She wrapped it around the girl and began drying her legs.

"The boy called mama a nigga slave…"

Franny stopped abruptly. "What boy?"

"The one at the community. He said mama was a lickfinger," her voice quivered.

The woman started gently drying the girl again as she slowly said, "Oh nah, don't go listenin' to them jealous people. They just be sayin' those hurtful things to ya because they ain't happy…and they ain't goin' to be happy unless they bring someone else down. They just jealous of ya, honey."

"Why, though? I haven't done anything to them."

"Ya don't have to do anythin' to them for them to hate ya."

"But why do they hate me?" she asked, choking on her own voice.

"Because ya is something special," Franny said, taking hold of Coco by both arms and looking into her face. "Ya something that they ain't ever goin' to be, and they can't stand it." Her old smile had lost a few more teeth over the years, but Coco didn't seem bothered by it. Franny stood from her kneeling position to get the girl's nightdress and then pulled it over her bare shoulders.

"Did Daddy love my mother?"

Franny smiled as she pulled Coco's arms through one of the sleeves. "Oh, did he ever love ya mama! He loved her more than anythin'."

Coco looked at the woman's face as she seemed to reminisce. "It was almost like a fairytale. Every time they were together it was like a dry thunderstorm on a summer night, lightin' up the sky." Her eyes lit up. "And Ms. Dinah loved him very much." Her hands unsteadily straightened the girl's dress as she talked. "There now," she said when she was finished.

"Why don't he talk about her then?"

"Too painful, I guess. Sometimes people just bury the past deep inside them, so they don't have to face it. I know one thing is right: I'm sure ya daddy is reminded of her every day he looks at ya. Ya growin' more and more like her," she said tenderly as she touched Coco's cheek, "and not just in that pretty face but in ya sass too." Franny smirked with a hum in her voice.

Coco gave a crooked smile at the lighthearted statement. "I wish I knew her."

"If ya ever missin' her, just look in the mirror and ya will see her lookin' back at ya." Those were words Coco would remember all of her days, and she would often stand in front of a mirror during hard times to pull strength from her mother. There was a pause before Franny said, "Come on nah, let's get ya to ya room."

Coco lay in her bed under the covers the rest of the evening with her lantern lit and reading a book, until a knock came on her door. The door cracked open and Albert looked into her room to where she was reclining. She put the ribbon in her book to mark her spot before closing the cover. When her father walked into the room, he sat on the edge of her bed.

There were minutes of silence before Albert spoke. "Why did ya go out there today?" Coco shrugged in response. "Ya know ya not supposed to go out there, especially by yourself."

"Why? They're my people," she argued.

"They're not ya people, Coco, they're workers!" Albert

snapped. "This family is your people. Now listen to me," he said more calmly, placing a hand on her knee. "Years ago, it wouldn't have been such a big deal. I had a small community of workers, and they were all honest and good. But we've grown so much that I've had to bring on all kinds, and some of them aren't good people. I wouldn't put it past some of them to maybe want to hurt ya, and I would kill a man if he hurt ya. I know ya must be curious, because ya not like the other children…"

"The other children don't like me."

"That's not true, darling."

"It is, though," she countered. "I'm not accepted in here, so I go to the community, but I'm not accepted out there by them neither." Tears filled her eyes as Albert looked at her. "I don't belong anywhere."

He lowered his head. "How long have ya felt like this?" Coco didn't respond. Albert inhaled a long, drawn breath and, after reclining next to her, put his arm around his daughter. "Coco," he said, "ya belong here…with me. Ya not as fair as my other children, but that doesn't mean ya belong any less. Ya not a worker, ya a daughter of the Toussaint plantation. I don't want ya goin' out there where the slaves are anymore, and I never want to see ya hold ya head down again. Never forget who ya are! And never let anyone tell ya otherwise."

He gave her shoulder a squeeze and paused before continuing. "I think it's time I took ya on a little trip," he said, reaching up with his free hand and wiping at the wet streams running down her cheeks. Coco looked up at him. "How about ya go with me next month when I visit your brother in New Orleans? I realize I have not taken ya yet."

She grinned in bashful disbelief. "Really?" she asked.

"Yeah. Ya never been away from the plantation, and I want ya to see where ya belong. There are more people like ya than ya realize, Coco. Ya want to go?"

"Yes," she said in girlish excitement. After a moment of hesitation, she asked, "Is Victor going?"

"No. How about we make it just you and I? He's gone with me before."

Coco gave him a broad smile and a nod. "I would like that very much," she said softly. Albert kissed her forehead and moved to exit the room, until her words stopped him. "Father," she said, "did ya love my mother?"

His hand rested on the doorknob. "Yes," he finally answered. "Goodnight, Coco."

"Goodnight," she responded as the door closed and latched behind him.

Her eyes shifted around the room, as if looking for movement. After taking hold of the lantern, Coco moved to her lowboy and sat down, placing the lantern on its surface. The light from the flame was warm and darkened her complexion in the mirror as she looked at herself, her almond eyes holding the stare of her reflection. Slowly, she reached up and touched the glass where her cheek mirrored her image. After a few minutes, she made her way back to bed and extinguished the lantern, but her eyes stayed open in the darkness until, unwillingly, sleep finally overtook her.

CHAPTER FOURTEEN

THE NEXT MONTH flew by like the wind. Franny and Nan helped Coco pack, Nan stern in her advice to stay close to her father and avoid strangers. Her concern, along with the humming excitement of Franny, set Coco's heart racing. She and her father left just after sunrise, after he had taken his coffee as usual, except this morning Coco joined him in the office. She awoke long before morning and, knowing Albert's tradition, readied herself for the day and went down to sit with him. It was the first time she had ever had coffee, and at his offer to try a cup, with the recommendation of adding cream and sugar, she sat a little taller.

The trip, though long, went by quickly for Coco. She sat across from Albert, who dozed off once before he was awakened by a jolt, followed by a giggle from his daughter. As they approached the city, the journey went from quiet to a sudden bustle of activity, as if the theater curtain had been pulled and the first act had abruptly started. Coco peered out the window of the coach. The streets boomed with movement and the sound of music, a rhythm Coco had never heard before. People went in and out of stores with the purpose of spending extravagant amounts of money while others sat on the side of the street with no other business than to just enjoy the day.

Foy had pulled the horses to a slow walk as they maneuvered through the busy streets on their way to the garden district. It had been more than a year since Coco had seen her older brother, Albert. He had left in the springtime of the previous year to join the University of Louisiana for the study of engineering and architecture when she was only ten years old. He had never spent much time with her, or given her any thought for that matter, and being sent away to boarding school when he was fourteen had given them only eight years together in the same house. He had come home for New Year's and a few months over the summer, but every time he returned, the time away had seemed to add age enough that the boy felt more like a man and ignored the other children.

Notable residences nestled in lush grounds on oak-lined streets soon surrounded the carriage. Coco's gazed followed three properly dressed creole women walking down the sidewalk in gay conversation. She turned to her father with a curious look but didn't say anything at the lack of change in his expression. Soon, the university came into view and the horses were pulled to a stop. The two got out of the carriage and walked toward the main lobby. Coco stayed close to her father and remained silent while he asked where he might find the Toussaint boy and was directed to the library as the best chance of finding him. It wasn't long before Albert was shaking the hand of his son, who he hadn't seen in over a year. He gripped it firmly and held him by the shoulder.

"We missed ya on New Year's."

"I had some making up to do in my studies, since my spell with the fever last fall kept me from it. I'm still paying for it."

"How have ya been feelin', now?"

"Oh, I'm fine now. I've become acclimated. This one, though," he said, flicking the underside of Coco's chin. "I'm surprised you brought her to the city of Necropolis. Do you even know what yellow fever does?" he asked, addressing Coco. After a slight pause, he leaned forward to look at her at eye level. "It starts with nausea and delirium. They start bleeding through their eyes, nose, and ears. Then, before they die, the victims vomit coagulated blood."

"God, son, that's enough. Don't tell her that."

"Well, why didn't ya die?" Coco responded cheekily.

"I'm invincible," her brother said, standing back upright.

She rolled her eyes at Albert Jr.'s attempt to disgust her. This was the most attention she'd received from him in years.

"She'll be okay," their father said, putting his arm around her shoulder. "Where is a good place here for dinner? We haven't eaten since breakfast, save a little bit of bread we brought with us, and I don't know about her, but I'm pretty hungry."

Albert Jr. suggested a restaurant there in the garden district that served superb barbecued shrimp which would pair nicely with a light Riesling. The three dined, avoiding any more talk of the fever as ordered by Albert. Their conversation revolved around Albert Jr.'s studies and his friendly rivalry with Benjamin Harrod, who was in the same field of study but a year ahead of him, as well as how he had become friends with several like him— the university was no stranger to taking in "sons of sugar." Albert stiffened as the conversation shifted to the plantation. His disappointment that his firstborn son didn't want to take over the business was no secret. Their words were edgy toward each other before they moved on to a topic more sensational. Coco continued to crack her shrimp and dip her bread as she listened to the conversation but said nothing. After dining, Albert Jr. insisted he had to finish his week of studying but said he would join them for the weekend. They said their goodbyes for the evening, and then Albert and Coco headed to their hotel. Tired from a long day of travel and the city's excitement, they turned in for the night with hardly a word to each other.

The next few days held renewed excitement for Coco as Albert took her down the main streets of New Orleans. The people amused her, and she tried not to stare at the finely dressed women of color getting in and out of carriages with packages from their day's business. She walked a little straighter and soon relaxed into an easy step as she toured the city. It was the afternoon of the third day that Albert addressed her about business he had to attend while in town.

"Ya sure ya will be all right by yourself? I'll only be gone during the afternoon. I'm leaving Foy with ya with instructions to meet me back at the hotel by four."

"Yes, I'll be fine," she said with more enthusiasm than she meant to show.

"Four o'clock, back here. Ya understand?" he asked firmly.

"Yes," she repeated.

"All right." He gave her a nod and a kiss on the forehead before walking out of their room.

Coco stood still for a minute as she looked around and then smiled to herself. After looking again in the mirror and pinching her cheeks, she picked up her pouch and walked out the door. When she got to the bottom of the staircase that led to the hotel lobby, Foy was waiting, hat in hand, next to the wall, out of the way of the foot traffic.

He approached her and asked, "Want to take the carriage?"

"I think I'd prefer to walk, Foy," she responded gently.

"Yes, ma'am. After ya," he said with a raise of his hand, intent on staying close on her heels.

Coco stepped out onto the sunny, bustling street and took a deep breath. The air felt as full and lively as the music that reverberated through it. As she walked, she looked behind herself every few steps to see Foy only an arm's length away, until soon she walked in the sureness of his presence and didn't have to look. Street led to street as she window-shopped and took in the ambiance of the city.

"Ya want some molasses?" a boy about her age called out, coming up to her. Coco jolted and turned to see who was addressing her. A white boy with a smudged face flashed her a big smile. "Best molasses ya find! Come and see for yaself," he urged.

He started to lead her to the edge of the walk, next to the wall, where a hogshead laid on its side. Another white boy sat in front of it, telling a story to a black boy who lay over its curved back, dipping a stick in a small cup of the black gold and bringing it up to his mouth to suck the sweetness off of it with pure joy.

"Come on, come see for yaself," the boy continued to urge. "Here, I'll give ya a taste." He stepped up next to the barrel and kicked the boy sitting on the ground. "Move over, stupid!" Coco looked at Foy's disapproving face. The neatly trimmed hair on his chin had all but turned fully gray, standing out against his dark skin. He flared his nostrils and narrowed his eyes as he tipped his head to warn her against friendliness. She gave him a crooked smile before she took a step toward the boys. "Dis here is the best ya ever goin' to taste, I swear it," he said, holding one hand in the air and one over his heart.

"He ain't no lie," the boy lying over the top of the barrel added as he took the stick out of his mouth and smacked his lips. "Ya ain't tasted nothin' like it."

"That's right, that's right," the first boy nodded ardently. "Here, put ya fingers under the hole here." Coco leaned over and put two of her fingers where he instructed. "Ya ready now? Now, it will come out when I pull this plug."

The boys watched with delight as it was removed and the molasses spilled onto Coco's fingers. She laughed as the boy struggled to get the cork back in the hole, and then she raised her fingers to her mouth and enjoyed the sticky sweetness.

"Best ever, huh?" he asked.

"Best ever," the other boys agreed.

"It is very good." Coco smiled.

"So, ya want a jar or ya want two? I know ya housemaid will make up some real fine cookies out of this here molasses!"

Foy stepped in and took Coco by the shoulder. "Nah, we don't want no molasses."

"Well, why not now? She likes it."

"We have plenty of molasses—all the girl could ever want," he said, moving her by the shoulder.

"Ya her father?"

"Let's go," Foy ordered as they started to walk away. Coco looked over her shoulder at the boys. She pressed her lips together and raised her eyebrows with a cock of her head as her shoulders raised toward her ears, as if to say she was sorry.

A few moments passed before a voice stopped them. "Hey! Hey now, wait a minute." Foy stopped and looked at the boy hurrying toward them. "Hold on a minute! Here," he said, holding out a small jar.

"I told ya we don't want ya molasses, boy. Now get out of here!" Foy raised his hand, as if swatting at a fly.

"I don't want no money for it, though. I just want to give it to her." The boy held it toward Coco, who took it hesitantly. "It's a gift...fa bein' the prettiest woman I'll see all day." He gave her a coy smile before running off.

Coco blushed when she looked at Foy's confounded expression. He waved her forward with a shake of the head, mumbling his reprimands as he walked a step closer to her. She giggled to herself.

As they continued exploring, they passed a window with women's fine hats. Coco slowed down and looked in. "I want to go inside," she said, turning to Foy.

"All right. Don't be long. I'll be standing right here." He pointed to the ground.

Coco mounted the step and pushed the door open. A bell tinkled, announcing her entry, and the store smelled of burning fragrance. She began looking at the exquisite hats as a woman came through a doorway of beads leading to a back room.

"Well, hello there," the creole woman greeted her with a warm smile. She was tall and slender and dressed in a patterned green dress with a large bow at the collar, held in place with a shiny pendant. She also wore a hat set half back on her head with feathers arrayed in tasteful fashion.

"Hello," Coco said.

The woman moved to stand behind the counter as she watched Coco browse. "Ya want to try it on?" she asked when the girl lingered in front of a cream hat with pale silk flowers and a half veil. Coco pulled her hand back and looked at the shop-keeper. "It's okay," the woman continued. "Ya can try it on."

She stepped around the counter and walked up to Coco. After taking the hat off the rack, she set it on the girl's head and, with a smile, tied the silk ribbon under her chin. "Oh my, now isn't that just beautiful?" she exclaimed as she reached for a hand mirror. Coco looked at her reflection as the woman continued to dote over her and adjust the curls around her face.

"Now ya are just the prettiest thing I've ever seen. I bet ya the light in ya mama's eyes and pride of ya father." Coco's smile faded, and the woman quickly added, "Oh, now what's wrong, child? Was it something I said?"

"I don't have a mother," Coco said flatly. The shopkeeper was quiet as an awkward silence followed. "I never knew my mother. She was a slave and died before I knew her," the girl offered coldly.

"But she knew ya, child, and I just know she loved ya."

"I'm not so sure."

"Well I am," the woman said matter-of-factly. "And ya know how I am?" Coco shook her head. "I speak with spirits." The girl rolled her eyes and gave a crooked smile, and the woman looked around. "Is ya daddy waitin' on ya?"

"No."

"Then come with me a minute. There is somethin' she wants to tell ya."

The woman went through the beaded doorway she had first entered through, and Coco hesitated before slowly following her to a room with colorful stones and a table. "Sit down here," the woman ordered kindly as she lit the candles and took a seat across from her. "What is ya name, child?"

"Caroline, but they call me Coco."

"Coco," she repeated. "Let me see ya hands."

Coco put her right hand toward the woman, who took it in her own and turned it to lift the palm to her. "Oh yes," she said. "Ya mama loved ya very much. She says, 'Don't be sad that I'm gone, 'cause I'm still with ya. Just look in the mirror and ya will see me.'" Tears filled Coco's eyes and spilled down her cheeks. "Oh my, yes, ya have her eyes." The woman smiled, warm and broad, as she looked gently at the girl. "And I'm sensing something else too." She closed her eyes and held her head back. "I see a grand future for ya. Stay humble, but stay strong...and don't let no man—or no woman, for that matter—take ya value from ya."

Coco listened ardently as the woman hummed in her throat. "Ya ever come to the Congo Square on Sundays?"

"No, I'm not from here."

"Well, come this Sunday if ya still in the city. There's someone I want to introduce to ya. Ya ever hear of the Widow Paris?"

Coco shook her head. "Who is she?"

"She is a priestess, a powerful woman gifted with beauty and intelligence. All in New Orleans seek her council! Her mother, a freed slave, was the mistress of her father, Charles Laveau, and when the Widow Paris was born, she was left to be raised by her grandmother. The spirit she has...I see that same spirit in ya. Ya need to meet her. Maybe she'll have some words for ya."

The woman patted Coco's hand. "Come." They slowly left the small room and went back out to the floor. "Now, about that hat." She smiled.

Coco didn't have enough money for the hat, but the woman took what she could afford. She walked out of the store with a smile and a reminder from the woman to find her on Sunday at the Congo Square.

Foy looked at Coco with near frustration. "What took ya so long? Did ya really buy that hat?"

"I did! Isn't it beautiful?"

"Well, is ya daddy goin' to be all right with ya spendin' the money on it?"

"He gave me the money to spend," she countered. "I'm hungry; let's find something to eat." She turned to walk down the street before stopping abruptly and turning toward Foy. "It's pretty, right?"

"Yes," he hesitated with his words, "it pretty. Why, it may be the prettiest hat in all New Orleans." Coco flashed him a smile and spun around with a click of her heels.

The weekend came and Albert Jr. kept his word on meeting them to visit. He seemed different toward Coco—chattier, though not to the point of being too friendly, but he did regard her presence. His glances lingered a little longer, and an occasional smile would render itself across his mouth. He was never one to smile very often, even less so after the war of the states. During that time, he would be two years into a relationship with Evelyn Duminy of French descent, despite the threats of his mother. Justine believed Evelyn was not good enough for her son, even though she was an heiress to her wealthy father's barrel business. He would marry her before the war, in which he would serve as a private in the 8th Louisiana Heavy Artillery Battalion under Colonel Ogden. Later, he would be commissioned as 1st Lieutenant of the 9th Louisiana Cavalry Regiment, participating in marches and engagements in north and central Mississippi until the unit surrendered at Citronelle, Alabama, in 1865. He would lose his wife to complications during the birth of his firstborn but would find love again in the arms of a creole woman. His mother would reject him for his choices, but he remained in a common law marriage with her for the last thirty-two years of his life.

Coco had mentioned to her father her desire to go to church at the Congo Square on Sunday. He was no stranger to the gatherings of both free and enslaved people of color that had been taking place there for decades. The performance of rituals had calmed down after well into the turn of the century, and a large population of the older slaves who knew the traditional dances of the motherland had shrunk significantly. Albert himself had been to the square on an occasional Sunday to observe the jamboree of five to six hundred people as they performed the "wild and savage" native African music and dancing. He also enjoyed the barbecued meats and gingerbread. But now, with tension increasing around the gatherings and the First Division of Louisiana Militia now in place for inspection and review of the crowds, Albert felt an uneasy gnawing at Coco's request to join the parade.

"Why are ya denying me this?" she asked with passion when Albert rejected her request.

"It's not like it used to be, and it was certainly never a place for a young lady," he countered.

"How can this be? It's church!"

"Not church in the sense ya think of it as! It is a traditional gathering of sorts, Coco! Some have even called it savage and barbaric... It's some things that ya are too young for me to explain. It's calmed down significantly over the last few decades, but with the tension of the state, I don't want ya going, and that's the end of it."

By early evening on Sunday, Coco had very little to say. She refused to go to dinner with her father and Albert Jr., instead desiring to be left alone in the hotel room. Albert bent to her will, and the men left for dinner a little before five o'clock, leaving her by herself in the room.

Coco waited until they had been gone about fifteen minutes

before she emerged from her room. She tied on her new bonnet and grabbed her pouch with a shaking hand. Moving swiftly, she looked around herself as she left the hotel. It was too far to walk in a short amount of time, so she waved down a carriage and directed the driver to take her to the Congo Square.

"Ya young to be goin' by yaself. Ya got ya letter of permission?" the driver asked, looking at her with a blank expression and very little amusement or patience.

"I got family there," Coco lied.

"Ya got money to pay?"

"I do."

The driver gave the reins a flick and the horses, manes decorated with red plumes, started pulling. After some time, the driver halted his horse, and Coco looked at the square in anxious amazement. Large sycamore trees were lined up in several rows some twenty feet apart, and an old wrought-iron fence with beautifully framed gates encircled the area. Hundreds of people moved about, hot, sweaty, and nearly naked, singing loudly in different circles of people. The smell of delicious cooked meats filled the air.

"Ya getting out or not?" the driver asked, breaking the hypnosis that had come over Coco.

She reached into her pouch, paid the driver, and then climbed down from the carriage. Clenching at her pouch, she walked toward the activity of the square. There, lined up along the fence, stood a line of militia, and a few men towered on horses at the entrance. Coco made her way in.

"Hold on there a minute," a voice sounded, but it went unheard by Coco. She continued walking into the crowds of moving people. "I say, hold there!" the stern voice said again as its owner grabbed her by the shoulder. Coco stared up at the uniformed man, wide eyed. "I need to see ya papers of permission," he ordered.

She swallowed the lump that quickly rose to her throat. "What?" she stammered.

"Ya papers!"

"I didn't know I needed papers to go to church," she said innocently.

The man let out a bellow of laughter. "Church?" he asked. Nervous tears spilled down Coco's cheeks, but he seemed unmoved by her emotions and just glared at her. "Ya got ya certificate on ya?"

She shook her head. "No, my father has it."

"And where's he at?"

"Dinner with my brother. I'm supposed to meet my aunt here," she lied. "The Widow Paris."

The man's brow creased. "Come stand over here a minute," he ordered and directed her to the gate with the rest of the militia. Coco stood, shifting from one foot to the other, while she waited under watchful eyes. The man who stopped her spoke to another man in uniform, who turned and left the line of militia. "Just stay right there," the first man said when he returned to her.

Minutes passed as Coco stood with shifting eyes and tightly clenched fists. The people continued with their celebration without notice or care about her. A dark woman, nearly naked, rode past them, bareback upon a horse. Coco stared in amazement before looking down at her feet with a flush of her cheeks. Soon, the man approached her again with a creole woman wearing a high headdress of yellow cloth, a black dress, and around her shoulders a sheer peach shawl covered with small white flowers.

"Here, ya know this girl, Madam Laveau?" the man asked in a gruff voice.

The woman looked at Coco, who met her gaze straight on, before looking back at the man. "Yes," she said leisurely. "I wondered when ya was goin' to get here," she addressed the girl.

"She doesn't have her papers," the man continued.

"Well, I will vouch for her," Madam Laveau said.

"Ya know the rules. I'm not to let her in without her papers."

"And there was a day when that rule was not even a thought, Mr. Louis," she said with a glint in her eyes. "How was she to know, comin' in from out of town? No, she's with me, and I'll vouch for her."

"Now, Madam, ya know—"

"Oh yes, and please do tell ya wife I have a special gift for her. I'll be by ya house next week to make sure she gets it." Mr. Louis pressed his lips together, hardly seen under his large mustache. He blinked and then gave the woman a slight nod. "Thank ya, Mr. Louis. Ya have a good evenin', now," she said, reaching out and taking Coco by the shoulder before leading her toward the center of the square.

It wasn't until they were well into the crowd, to what seemed to be a familiar spot for the woman, before she took a seat and looked at Coco. "What's ya name, child, and why did ya say ya knew me?"

"Are ya the Widow Paris?" Coco asked.

"I am," she responded. Her dark eyes penetrated through Coco's being. She just stared at the woman, whose freckles traced the lines of her light-colored, black cheekbones. "And who are you?"

"Coco." She closed her eyes with a quick shake of the head. "I mean Caroline Toussaint."

"And why did ya say ya knew me?"

"I'm here with my father, visiting my brother at the university. I was in a hat shop on Thursday, and the woman said I should come here today and meet ya."

"Ya father know ya here?" Coco shook her head shamefully, and Madam Laveau laughed. "Well, enjoy yaself, Coco. This is a celebration of our ancestry—ya ancestry."

Coco looked around at the tribal circles, which danced to the singing of voices. Earlier that year, the council adopted an ordinance that made it unlawful for drums and trumpets to be played in the square. As it was, the forms being practiced were seen as "immoral and indecent," but they still sang their African vocal chants and the people still danced, though the traditional and pure form was being acculturated as the primitive days slowly faded away. The days of the Congo Square would start to wane gradually as it fell under ever-increasing scrutiny and control. Before the end of the decade, people would cease to attend at all, leaving the remnants of those dances completely behind. For now, Coco watched with nervous anticipation and would later in life recall and tell the story of those events.

CHAPTER FIFTEEN

"Gawd damn it, Coco!" The back of Albert's hand came down against the palm of his other, making a loud slap. "What the hell was ya thinkin'?" His belt had already come across her backside—the only time he had ever taken a strap to her. She stood with a tear streaked face and quivering lip as Albert Jr. slouched in a corner chair, hand over mouth and eyes cast downward. "Ya deliberately disobeyed me! Do ya know how dangerous that was? To go by yaself…to not tell me where ya were?"

Albert and his son had returned from dinner that evening to an empty room. He brought her back a piece of cake from the restaurant, and when he didn't find her in the room, he stepped out onto the balcony. Anxiously, he moved past his son. "She's not here," he said.

"Maybe she went down to the lobby," Albert Jr. replied.

The two made their way through the hotel dining hall and lobby. They called to Foy in hopes that she was with him. The man wasted no time in joining them in the search for her. When Coco could not be found, Albert hastily let the hotel staff know and called for them to notify the authorities. They came to the hotel to gather his statement and a description of his daughter.

"She's about five foot and…ninety, one hundred pounds."

"What was she wearing?" one of the men asked.

"Uh, she had on a green dress with a white ribbon…sash," he motioned with his hand around his midsection. He shifted his weight from one leg to another; his eyes studying the calm demeanor of the authorities with a frown. "She mentioned wanting to go to Congo Square, and I said no. Is it possible she's still there?"

The officer's lips gave a twitch and his right eye narrow ever so slightly. "No. The square is cleared out at six." He crossed his arms over his chest.

Albert rubbed his hand over his head. "Six," he repeated with a growl. "It's nearly eight. Can we get some officers to go out looking for her? She has dark hair and eyes… She's creole."

"I can send a couple of men to the square to ask around. We probably won't get much information around there now. Not much we can do this late."

"I expect ya and ya men to be out there looking for her, knockin' door to door if ya have to." Albert's voice raised.

One of the officers standing behind his chief mumbled under his breath, "Lookin' for some dark girl…"

"What did he say?" Albert frowned, and his eyes shifted between the men as he pointed at the one who'd mumbled. "What did ya say?"

The head officer gently touched Albert's forearm with his gloved hand. "Now, he didn't…"

"No, I want to know what he said!" he boomed.

"I'm sure some foolishness. Now, Mr. Toussaint, I need ya to cooperate if ya want us to do our job."

"He needs to watch what he says before I knock the stupid out of his mouth…"

"I'll send some men down to the square to look around and see if they see a girl matching ya description. That's about all we can do at this point."

"All ya can do?"

"Come now, Mr. Toussaint. Ya know the Congo Square is full of…should we say, rowdy people. If that is indeed where she went, she could be anywhere. The best we can hope for at this point is that maybe she got lost tryin' to find her way back."

Albert flexed his jaw. "I'm riding out with ya. Son, you stay here in case she comes back. Stay in the lobby," he said as he marched out of the hotel.

He and Foy joined the officers, riding up and down the darkening streets to no avail. After an hour of looking, Albert made his way back to the hotel, his lips pressed together.

There, Albert Jr. rushed toward him. "She's here."

His eyes flashed. "What? Where?"

"I sent her to the room."

Albert took a deep breath and turned with his hands on his hips. "Let the authorities know she is safe," he said to his son before moving with a heavy, swift step toward the room. He entered to see his daughter's wide eyes glossed over with tears.

"I only wanted to stay a minute," she started as her father made his way toward her while removing his belt. "Please, I just wanted to see—"

He grabbed her by the arm and turned her around as his other arm came down with the belt across her backside. He struck her several times as she cried, until the door opened and Albert Jr. walked in.

"Father…father!" he shouted, jolting Albert out of his anger.

As Coco stood listening to her father's lecture, her brother now slumped in the chair, she reached into her dress pocket and squeezed a sachet of gris-gris that Madam Laveau had given her. After the square had closed down, the Widow Paris invited Coco to her house for some black tea and "a look into her troubled soul." She kept the child for over an hour, showing all her enchanting ways to the contentment of Coco, until she realized how much time had passed. Madam Laveau didn't let her go empty-handed, however, and put together a mixture of herbs, powder, and stones in a small pouch. After pulling the strings to seal the bag, she had placed it in Coco's hand with a special prayer of guidance and protection against evil spirits.

"What are ya doin?" Albert snapped as his daughter fidgeted in her pocket.

Coco considered telling him, but then finally said, "Nothing."

"What's in ya pocket? Let me see," he ordered. Slowly, she pulled out the pouch and held it up. "Where did ya get that?" He took a step toward her and snatched it from her hand.

"Please..." She moved as if to take it back but stopped. "The Widow Paris—she made it for me."

Albert untied the string and widened the mouth of the pouch. "Do ya know what this is?" His voice rose. "This is goddamn Voodoo!" He clenched the bag in his fist and shook it in the air. "This is what ya went out there for? Damn juju?"

"It's gris-gris... It's just a gift," Coco stammered.

"Gris-gris, juju, whatever the hell ya want to call it, it's the devil's poison! No daughter of mine is going to be walking around with this shit in her pocket." He made his way to the balcony.

"Father, please! It doesn't mean anything. It's just for—"

Albert opened the door and hurled the bag out into the night. Coco stood behind him, speechless. "Ya are to stay in this room unless I tell ya otherwise." After a long breath and a pause, he looked at his son. "Let's go down to the lobby. I need a drink." Albert Jr. got up and exited the room, followed by his father. "Do not leave," he ordered before he shut the door behind them.

They stayed in New Orleans for another day and left on Tuesday. Albert argued with himself about leaving first thing Monday morning after Coco's deliberate act of disobedience, but he decided to stay an extra day to avoid leaving the trip on a sour note. The afternoon was full of beignets and a pleasure ride on the steamboat *Shreve*, which served the finest creole cuisine during sunset on the Mississippi.

The two returned to the plantation and the normality it brought. August came and, with it, a devastating hurricane washed upon the Louisiana shore. Albert Jr. declared himself safe in the letter to his family and went on to describe the disaster.

"All of creation was turned against us. The fiery lightning constantly illuminated the sky. It is a disaster unlike any other, and one can only stand in silent distress, looking around at where once stood homes. Not even the foundations are left. We are surrounded by the dead. I lost my beloved friend and companion, Emma, whom I had hoped to one day coax into marriage. Though my heart is broken, I know I am not the only one touched with the pain of loss. The body count is already up near two hundred, and they are still uncovering the dead from the sand. I will write again soon, my beloved family. Until then, pray for Isle Dernière."

Nature assaulted all of Louisiana that August and wreaked great havoc on the fields as it headed inland after devastating the coast. The eye of the storm swept across the state, leveling the cane in one direction before changing coarse, lifting the stalk, and laying it in the other direction. The loss was unparalleled for the plantation and the Toussaint purse, especially because they had lost the harvest the prior year from the cold, frost, and rain that had devastated the entire sugar region. When harvest came, instead of producing hundreds of hogsheads per week, production averaged only fourteen. Winter passed with the harvest, along with another the next year, like all the ones before it, and just like that it was spring again.

The end of the summer of 1858 brought the preparation for the debutante of Coco's fourteenth birthday. Isabelle was now engaged and boastfully offered her advice and care in prepping Coco for her big night. When Justine found her daughter indulging over Coco, she called Isabelle over to herself and pinched the girl. She lectured her about choosing Coco instead of her own mother, bringing Isabelle to tears. Justine closed herself in her room as the guests started arriving to save herself "the embarrassment". All the children were together again at the plantation for the first time in years, except Rose, who was in the late stages of her pregnancy and had been instructed by her doctor to stay in bed until the child was born. In her place, she sent a kind letter to Coco with her most sorrowful regrets for missing her big day, along with a gift of white silk gloves with pearl buttons up the forearm. Coco pressed the letter to her chest after reading it with care.

The evening was lit up with candlelight and laughter. Coco, the last of the Toussaint daughters, walked down the steps in a scarlet red dress while holding Albert's arm. Long locks of dark curls gathered at the base of her neck. Even at the young age of fourteen, Coco had the full figure of a goddess. Though she already had the genetic endowment, she'd still fretted over padding her bosom and struggled with her corset and bustle until she achieved her desired figure. The appearance of a little girl was long gone, and in her place a glowing woman. Many who attended were not aware of the darker-skinned Toussaint daughter, and others only came to catch a glimpse of the girl they had heard rumors about over the years.

Silence filled the room as her procession down the stairs took place. Gasps and whispers floated through the crowd, primarily among the women in shock that she chose to wear a scarlet dress over the traditional white. As she moved through the crowd with grace and poise, Coco quieted the gossip. She quickly fell into charming conversation with the younger adults attending the ball, while a few of the older generation avoided speaking with her. The party was not as grand as the other debutantes of the Toussaint daughters—Justine still thought Coco unfit to share equal rights with her children—but Coco moved through the crowd with contagious energy, anyway, and insisted the band play more lively music.

"Are ya goin' to dance with me?" Albert Jr. approached her and took her hands in his.

"Dance with my own brother when there are suitors to choose from?" Coco teased as she let him lead her to the floor.

"Half-brother," he corrected as he pulled her into a step of the waltz, "and there is plenty of time for suitors. Consider it your gift for *my* birthday."

"How is the university?" she asked after a few moments of awkward silence.

"Tormenting. I haven't told Father, but I'm thinking about taking a break for a little while."

"Isn't this your last year, though?" Coco asked, shocked.

"It is."

"Well, don't give up now," she chided him. "Not when you're this close."

"I know ya right. I think I'm just lonely."

"It's a city full of people! How could you possibly be lonely?" She laughed. When she noted his straight expression, Coco continued, "Maybe you should come home during your holiday break."

Albert Jr. looked at her smiling up at him and stopped dancing. She frowned at his expression. "Enjoy your suitors," he said before abruptly walking away.

After moving off the dance floor, Coco took a glass of wine. Her father came up beside her and put his arm around her.

"How do ya like ya party, darling?"

"It's wonderful. Thank you, Father," she smiled.

"Is something wrong?" he asked, noting her fallen countenance.

"No... Al is just actin' funny."

"Aw, he's probably fretting over his studies. The boy puts more on himself than he needs to. Don't let that bother ya evenin'." He squeezed her shoulders and looked at her with a smile. "My youngest daughter, drinkin' a glass of wine. God, I...I remember when ya was just a little baby in my arms, smilin' up at me. Yep, just like that."

Coco reached up, took hold of his hand that was wrapped around her, and rested her head on his shoulder.

"I have a surprise for ya," Albert said suddenly, and her head came up in a bounce.

"What is it?" she asked eagerly.

"I brought in a photographer."

Her face lit up. "Really?"

"Shall we go have our picture taken?" Coco bounded into his arms with delight. Albert took her hand in his and led her to where they had set up the camera in front of the settee in the sitting room. "Andrew," her father said as they entered the room, "this is my daughter, Caroline Toussaint, the woman of the hour."

The man was tall and lanky with a shy, nearly shifty demeanor. "Beautiful," he said with a nod. "Congratulations on the day. If you'd like to have a seat here... There you go. Now..." The man arranged Coco and directed her on how to sit and look at the camera. Then he stood behind the camera and took the photo.

"When will I be able to view it?"

"Oh, in thirty minutes or so."

"I want one of us, Father."

Albert consented and stood behind his daughter. Coco always teased him that it captured his personality perfectly—staunch and immoveable. At her suggestion, they gathered the other children and took a family photo with all but Rose and Justine, who claimed her only family was her children. The evening came to an end, and Coco rested in her room, looking at the pictures, when there was a soft knock at her door. Her father entered and sat next to her in bed, as had been their tradition since she was little.

"Did ya have fun tonight?"

"I did! Thank you for everything."

Albert picked up one of the pictures from where they were spread out on top of the blanket. "Look at that," he said, surveying the photograph. He took a deep breath as he looked at Coco's striking image of a memory. "My, you are beautiful." He picked up the photo of them both and asked, "Do ya mind if I keep this one?"

"That's my favorite one…"

"Oh, well, I guess we could just tear it down the middle," he teased as he pretended to make a tearing motion.

"No!" She laughed and snatched it out of his hands. "I love this one."

"Well, how are we going to solve this dilemma? What if I were to give ya something in exchange for the picture?"

She raised her brows with skepticism. "I doubt that will change my mind."

From his shirt pocket, Albert pulled out a silver necklace with a locket. Coco's eyes widened as the silver shone in the glow of the lantern light.

"Oh!" She gasped. "It's beautiful!"

"Open the locket."

She did, and there inside was the picture of Albert on one side and herself on the other. Tears welled up in her eyes. "This is the best gift ever. I love it so much!"

"So you always know where ya belong. Now, may I have this picture?" he teased, giving it a light wave in the air. She gave a nod, holding back the tears threatening to choke her, and Albert reached up, pulled her head toward him, and pressed a kiss on her temple. "Your suitors will be hard-pressed by a jealous father afraid of losing his daughter's affection," he said.

"You'll never lose my affection." Her arms wrapped around his chest as she used his shirt to dry her eyes.

"I love ya so much, Coco."

He and Justine no longer shared a room since the day she had sold Dinah, so Albert framed the picture of himself and his youngest daughter to hang in his bedroom. The months went by and brought them to a harvest that was hardly there. Albert Jr. came home more often, taking three-day weekends to make the trip, and had decided to spend a couple of weeks at home during the semester break.

"I just thought I would feel different after my ball, but I don't. Nothing has changed," Coco said to him over a cup of tea one afternoon.

"Well, ya will get to meet new people now that ya able to go to parties. It'll be different when ya know a man—when ya love him."

"I just don't know if that will happen for me."

"I tell ya what. If it doesn't, I'll marry ya."

Coco chuckled. "Don't be silly—you're my brother."

"Half-brother, and we were hardly even raised together." Silence followed as Coco looked at her cup of tea. "I just don't feel like I'll find love again after…after I lost Emma," he continued.

"You will," she encouraged.

"Would ya have me?"

"No," she huffed. "You're my brother—I don't love you like that. I think your loneliness has made you mad," she added with a smirk as she raised the china to her lips for a drink.

Albert Jr. gave a resentful smile. "Ya look like ya mother," he said. Slowly lowering the cup, Coco pressed her lips together. Never had she heard her brother mention her mother. "I was young, but I remember her… She was beautiful."

Coco swallowed hard, fighting back the urge for tears. "Well, thank you," she finally said.

"I'm sorry for what happened."

"What do you mean?"

"With ya mother."

Her eyes narrowed as her brow furrowed, and she gave a small shake of her head, confused. A knot rose to her throat. "Sorry that she died?"

"Died?" His voice was too fervent, and clear amusement showed on his face. "Is that what they told ya?"

Coco's limbs began to tremble as she choked out her next words. "What do you mean?" He took a drink from his cup and moved to look out the window, as if he didn't hear her question. "What did you mean, 'Is that what they told you?' Tell me!" Her voice grew bold.

Turning to her abruptly, Albert Jr. said, "She didn't die. They sold her."

The news silenced her. She didn't move but sat holding her breath. Finally, after placing her cup and saucer down, she folded her hands in her lap and said, "Sold her?"

"Yes, when ya was three. Father bought ya papers, but she was sold."

"Excuse me," she said suddenly. "I'm not feeling well." Hastily getting up, she moved out of the sitting room and toward the lavatory. Images began to spin into darkness as sweat wet her skin. After closing herself in the bathroom, she leaned against the basin. Her breathing came in quick spurts. With a shaking hand, she poured out water and wet her hands before bringing them up to cool her face. Then a knock came at the door.

"Please go away!" she called.

"I didn't mean to upset ya."

"I'm just not feeling well." The door opened and Albert Jr. stepped in. Coco looked up at his reflection in the mirror. "Please get out. I want my privacy."

He stepped behind her and touched her shoulders, letting his hand move along the skin of her neck. "Let me comfort you," he said quietly.

"Stop it!" She turned around to leave, but he grabbed her harshly by the upper arms.

"Let me help ya," he said with a severe tone as he leaned in toward her.

"You've done enough! Leave me alone." Coco jerked away from him and rushed out of the room.

She stayed in her room for the rest of the day, and the next.

She hardly ate and, when visited by her father, didn't speak a word to him but pretended she was asleep. When she did finally emerge from her room, Coco avoided eye contact or conversation. Albert began to worry about her change in demeanor, but he soon pushed it off as the growing pains of a young woman and nothing more.

CHAPTER SIXTEEN

ALBERT JR. HAD BEEN POURING tumblers out of his father's whiskey cabinet while Justine prepped tirelessly for the New Year's party. "Look at ya," she had said after catching him pouring another. "What has become of ya? A drunk? Ya like ya father, hiding ya failures in whiskey. Shameful!"

"I'm not a failure, Mother," he called back as she exited the room. "I'm graduating with honors in the springtime!" He tipped the glass back and finished his drink.

Moving down the hall, he made his way to the kitchen. "Franny," he said when he came upon her with an armful of fresh garland.

The woman jumped, startled. "Li'l Al, my goodness!" She had never stopped calling him Li'l Al, even though the young man stood over six feet tall now. "Ya know I'm gettin' older and my heart can't take scares like that no more."

"I'm sorry." He put an arm around her shoulder. "Ya was always my favorite, ya know that?"

"And such a sweet boy ya is, but whatever it is that ya tryin' to butter me up for, I ain't got time. The missus is all over me about getting the fresh garland up. She wants it on every banner and every table—"

"Maybe some from the ceilin'," he interrupted, teasing, motioning with his hand in an upward motion.

"Lord…" She drew out the word, as if it were a prayer.

"Well now, can't ya make time to stir me up a little something to eat? I'm hungry and there ain't nobody else that can feed me like ya can."

"Dat liquor makes ya hungry, don't it?" He gave her a crooked smile. "Maybe later I can sneak away, but the missus…she'd take the whip to me if I don't get these put where she said." He made a face like a pouting child, and Franny reached up and gave his cheeks a squeeze. "Such a face, nah."

"Get out of here," he finally said, giving her a wave, "before my mother has your hide."

Franny exited with a chuckle, leaving Albert Jr. in the kitchen and no closer to getting food than when he walked in. He breathed out some low curses before leaving the room with the intent of pouring more bourbon in his father's office. He was mid-pour when Coco walked in.

"Oh," she said, suddenly stopping. "I thought Father was in here." She began to leave.

"Hold on." His words stopped her mid-step. "Come in and keep me company."

"I can't… I'm busy."

"Busy?" He ridiculed her with the air of man who'd had too much to drink. "What are ya busy doin'?"

Coco hesitated before she stumbled over her answer. "I'm writing Rose a letter… I hear she isn't well."

"Ah, our sister, Rose. Well, ya must talk to her more than I do. She's always angry at me…I must be a disappointment to her," he mumbled to himself before clearly speaking up, "Come in and tell me how she is. Ya can write ya letter in here. I won't say anything to ya; I'll be quiet and leave ya alone." As he pulled out the chair behind the desk, Albert Jr. continued persistently, "Come on."

Coco inhaled a deep breath through her nose and, giving in to his pressure, took a seat at the desk. "Do ya have ya letter?"

"I haven't started it yet."

"Oh. Well, here, we need to get ya some paper then." He sloppily fumbled through the drawers and, after finding some, set it on the desk in front of her. "There ya go." He rested a hand on her shoulder. She leaned forward, pulling her shoulder away from his touch.

Albert Jr. walked to the other side of the room and stood in front of the windows. He sipped his bourbon slowly as his eyes went from looking outside to being transfixed on Coco. She glanced over and caught him watching her. After pulling her shoulders back and pressing her lips together in defiance, she continued scripting out the letter. Looking up at him, she glowered, which seemed to do nothing other than amuse him. Finally folding the letter, Coco stood to leave the room.

"Hold on a minute." He stepped in front of her. "Let's have a read." Albert Jr. took the letter from her hand and proceeded to open it. "Well now, this isn't finished. Why didn't ya finish it?"

She clenched her teeth together. "Well, to be honest, Brother"—she emphasized the word as she jerked the letter out of his hand—"you're making me uncomfortable, just standing there, staring at me like some kind of animal."

His eyes flashed like Coco had never seen before. "Uncomfortable?" He grabbed her by the shoulders. "Ya callin' me an animal? Why, what do you know about being an animal?"

She struggled to escape from his grip, but he held her tight. "Stop it, Al, you're drunk."

"Do ya want to know what it feels like to be an animal?" He asked, pulling her closer with his face close to hers. "Ya don't have to be married to experience love... I can show ya."

"Stop it, Al!" She continued fighting against his hold. "You're not in your right mind! Let go of me!" He leaned forward in an attempt to kiss her, but Coco turned her head, trying to free herself. He was steadfast in his hold, though. "Al, stop," she whimpered.

A figure crossed in front of the doorway, and Albert Jr. stopped as he looked at his younger brother. "Go on, Victor," he said harshly. The boy just stood in the doorway with a blank expression.

"No," Coco moaned, "go get Father! Victor, please!" she cried.

"Shut up!" Albert gave her shoulders a tight squeeze and a good shake. "Shut the door, Victor."

"Victor, no." She started to cry. "Go get, Father, please!"

"Victor!" Albert Jr. yelled out.

The boy had stood, unable to move or avert his gaze, until his brother shouted. Slowly, Victor reached for the knob and slowly closed the door.

"No!" Coco yelled. "Stop! Please, Victor please!"

"Shut up!" Albert Jr. ordered with a harsh snap. "Stop crying!"

The door clicked shut, and Albert Jr. jerked Coco over to the settee and shoved her down before moving to crouch on top of her. She resisted him and thrashed her arms through the air, but the weight of his body pinned her down.

"Stop!" she cried, slowly losing the strength to continue the fight. His hands moved over her body, grabbing her with force, as his mouth strained against her neck. She felt his erection as he pressed down against her, and tears streaked down her face. "Al, please stop."

Reaching down, he fought with the hems of her skirts, pulling them up before he felt the warmth of her skin on his hand. He raised himself off of her to adjust his pants, and as soon as Coco felt his weight lift, she pushed against him, moving out from under him and rolling onto the floor. Albert Jr. grabbed for her as he spat out curses. Flinging her arm around, Coco found his face with her hand and struck him as hard as she could. She stumbled to the door, but he reached it first and stood in front of it with a glowering stare.

"Please, leave me alone." His hand came up to touch where she had struck him, and he shook his head. "You're drunk."

"I'm angry now," he responded, taking a step toward her. She moved away from him, putting the desk between them. "So, we're going to make a game of chase of this, are we?" Coco watched his sneering face before she grabbed the letter opener and held it tight. He laughed. "What, ya goin' to stab me with that?"

He moved quickly around the desk as she tried to dodge his movement. Spinning around, she clipped his forearm, leaving a gash followed by a trail of blood. Albert Jr. slapped her across the face, and she fell to her knees. Without hesitation, Coco plunged the letter opener into his thigh. He let out a cry of pain and reached down to where the weapon was lodged two inches deep. Coco scampered to her feet and toward the door as he pulled the letter opener out of his leg and held his hand over the bleeding wound. She looked back at him with tearful eyes as she reached for the door handle before rushing out.

Coco fled to her room, passing Franny at the staircase without stopping when she asked what was wrong. She locked herself in her room before crumbling atop her bed, weeping. Albert Jr. walked slowly with a limp to the kitchen and got a towel to press against his bloody leg. Justine noticed his strange movement but not the blood from another room as he moved down the hall; she finished what she was doing before leaving to find him in the kitchen.

"What happened?" she asked, concerned, as she approached him and noted the bloody towel.

"Nothing."

"What do ya mean nothing? Ya leg is bleeding through that towel! And what happened to ya arm?" Her face was aghast at what she was seeing.

"I said nothing happened!" he growled.

"This is not nothing! Ya will tell me this instant!"

Albert Jr. told his mother that he had been sitting in the office with Coco when she started acting strange. When he tried to console her, he said she went mad and took up the letter opener, cutting his arm before stabbing him in the leg. Justine's face turned red with anger.

"Well, let me see," she said, motioning for him to move the towel. A fresh stream of red oozed from the opened flesh. "My God," she said. "Ya going to need the doctor." As she stood from her kneeling position, Justine said sternly, "She is going to pay for this. Where is she?"

"Don't do anything, Mother. She is obviously troubled."

"Don't do anything? This is not okay behavior! Ya bleeding, for Christ's sake! What if it wasn't ya leg? What if it was ya chest or stomach? No! She is going to pay for this."

His mother's breath was shallow as she argued angrily. She moved out of the kitchen in a hurry, calling out Coco's name as she made her way through the bottom level of the house. Then Justine mounted the steps, quickly moving to Coco's bedroom door.

"Caroline!" she yelled as she tried to open the locked door. "Caroline, ya open this door right this minute!"

Inside her room, Coco scampered to the other side of her bed as Justine banged on the door. She hunkered down on the floor with her back against the door as she tried to hold her breath and stop crying, her chest convulsing in short spasms.

"Open this door, ya devil child!" Justine jiggled the handle. "Ya can't stay in there forever, and when ya come out, we're going to send ya away. Ya stabbed ya brother, Caroline, ya brother!"

"He forced himself on me!" she finally yelled back.

There was silence for a minute before Justine spoke again. "Ya lying! He would never do anything like that! Ya goin' to pay for this!" Her fist hit the door. "Ya goin' to pay!"

Hours passed, and Coco fell asleep on her bed. When she awoke again, the sun was setting. She rubbed at her swollen eyes before moving to look out her window. After a minute, a soft tap came at the door.

"Coco," a voice whispered. "It's me, Franny. Open up and let me in. I brought ya a little something to eat." The tap came again. "Coco…"

She moved hastily and cracked the door to peek out. When she saw Franny's wide eyes, she opened it and let her in, quickly locking the door behind her.

"Here some dinner," Franny spoke slowly as she set the tray on the bed.

"Thank you." Coco's eyes stayed cast downward as she sat next to the tray.

"What happened, child? Why ya do that to Li'l Al for? This is a bad situation, ya know."

"You don't know what he did to me," Coco said, looking up with sorrowful eyes at Franny.

"What ya talkin' about?"

"Doesn't matter—no one will believe me. They will get rid of me like they did my mother."

"Nah, just a minute nah. What ya talkin' about?" Franny asked earnestly and ran her tongue over her large lips.

"Al told me she was sold."

"That why ya stabbed him?"

Coco huffed out, "No! He told me that months ago." Silence followed before Franny encouraged an explanation. "He forced himself on me," she finally choked out.

"What?" The disbelief was tangible in Franny's shocked response.

Coco's lips began to quiver. "See? You don't even believe me."

"Nah, I didn't say I don't believe ya. It's just shockin' is all… He's ya brother. Are ya sure that's what happened?"

"Yes! Victor walked by and saw what was happening, but Al yelled at him to close the door… And then he took me to the settee, laid on top of me…and lifted my skirts…"

"Jesus... Ya tellin' the truth, child?"

"I hope they do send me away..." Coco mumbled to herself.

"Stop that. Nah, ain't no one goin' to send ya away. Ya got to talk to ya daddy."

"I don't want to tell him." Her eyes begged Franny. "Please, I don't want him to know."

"He has to know, child. If ya tellin' me the truth, and I believe ya is, then ya have to tell him too."

"He'll hate me." She began to cry.

"No, no," Franny comforted her as she took Coco's head and held her close while she cried. "He won't hate ya, child. Why, that man could never hate ya! It will hurt him that ya had to go through this, but he won't hate ya."

"But...it's his son." Coco looked up with a tear-streaked face and swelling eyes.

"And ya's his daughter," Franny said with a serious glare. Her words created a fresh stream of emotions from Coco. "Hush, nah. Don't ya cry, darlin' girl, don't ya cry. Shh..."

Franny stayed with her for another twenty minutes before she left the room with a promise from Coco that she wouldn't unlock the door unless it was for herself or Mr. Toussaint. She left the room and marched down the stairs to the study, where Albert had been sitting in shocked silence for the last three hours. He held the bloody letter opener that had been dropped on the floor.

After Franny boldly told Albert what his daughter had said, he sent her away with the instruction not to tell anyone. He went to his daughter's room and stood with his hand on the handle, his eyes shifting quickly, before he took a deep breath and softly knocked on the door. He had been listening to Justine talk all evening about how she wasn't going to tolerate a mentally unstable person in her house. She'd said that, for all they knew, the girl was plotting to kill the entire family, and she demanded they send for the doctor and have him admit her to the Baton Rouge mental hospital.

When no answer came to Albert's first knock, he rapped again and softly said her name against the wood panel. He heard movement within and asked her to open the door. Slowly it opened, and he walked in. Coco went to her bed and sat on the edge.

"I need ya to tell me exactly what happened," he said in a low tone, his face aglow from the warm lantern light.

Silence filled the room for several minutes as Coco sat with her head down, refusing to look at her father. "I don't want to," she finally said quietly.

"Ya need to."

In a soft voice and with much emotion, she told Albert everything, from finding out about the selling of her mother to her brother's attempt at defiling her. As she began to shake and her tears forgot their boundaries, Albert took her in his arms and let her cry. He held her tightly until she couldn't cry anymore. He lay her down in bed and pulled the blankets up over her.

After some time of quiet, Coco said, "Tell me the truth about my mother."

Albert took a deep breath and told his daughter about Dinah. His face became pensive and his eyes distant with tender memories as he talked about her. Coco savored that look on her father's face—a look she only saw one other time, at the end of his life, when he announced complete peace and joy.

"Please don't leave me," she said.

"I won't go anywhere," he replied, raising her hand to his lips and giving it a kiss. He stroked the top of her head as she closed her eyes.

The next morning, Albert went downstairs with an eager step. The sun was well into the morning sky and threatened the afternoon. Albert Jr. was reading a new paper when his father entered the room. He looked up in time to see Albert grab him by the lapel and jerk him to his feet. He practically dragged him to the wall and shoved him up against it.

"What the bloody goddamn hell, Son?" he growled between

gritted teeth. He slammed him against the wall again with a shake. "Why? Why?" As he fumed, his face grew red and the veins in his forehead protruded. "Do ya know what ya've done?"

"I don't know what ya talkin' about," Albert Jr. said with wide eyes and lips pressed together.

"What do ya mean ya don't know what I'm talkin' about?" Spittle flew from Albert's mouth. "I'm talkin' about ya sister, ya son of a bitch. How could ya do that to her?"

"Whatever she said, she's lyin'!"

"Ya expect me to believe that when she can't stop shakin'— can't stop cryin'?"

Albert Jr. gave his father a push back but couldn't escape his hold. Rage showed in Albert's eyes, and his hand rose to strike his son's face. The two began to wrestle as their voices carried through the house, and the sound of furniture breaking could be heard down the hall. Justine, along with the rest of the household, rushed to the commotion. Mrs. Toussaint screamed at them to stop until both men stood out of breath, Albert Jr. bleeding from a busted lip.

"Ya dead to me!" Albert said, breathlessly pointing his finger at his son.

"Ya always loved them more than ya own family!" the young man spat in anger.

"You're mad! I have given ya everything!" Albert's arms were spread wide to display all that was around them. "All that I have was yours, until this day, when you disgraced me. You are a disgrace to the very name Toussaint!"

"Albert, that is enough!" Justine yelled.

"No! On this day, I disown you as my son! You are no longer part of this household, or of me!"

Albert Jr. flexed his jaw as he held back the tears that filled his eyes. "Fuck you, Father," he spat before overturning a nearby end table and leaving the room.

"Albert!" Justine looked at her husband in disbelief. "Why would ya say that to him?"

His chest heaved. "Do ya know what he did?"

"What?" she yelled. "Tell me what he did to make his father disown him!"

Albert turned his face away from her and spoke in a low, forced tone. "He assaulted his sister."

Justine huffed. "Ya think he would do that? Did ya talk to him about it, or did ya just listen to the story of that little tramp?" His eyes snapped up at her. "Well, did ya? Or did ya just come in here, condemnin' him and takin' swings?"

"I don't need to talk to him. I already know."

"Yeah, and how's that?" She paused for a moment. "Even if he had been forthcomin' toward her, he had been drinkin' all day yesterday since noon... But had ya been around, ya would've known that."

"He pressed himself on top of her," Albert said between gritted teeth. "Ya think I want to do this? Ya think I want to disown my own son?" His voice rose in frustrated pain.

"Now that's what she says, but have ya asked him? Maybe she is scared and tellin' lies to justify what she has done. She stabbed ya son! Have ya even reprimanded her for that?" Albert didn't speak, as if thinking about what Justine was saying. "Maybe she was flirtin' with him. Maybe she was angry when he refused her and now she's blaming him. Ya don't even care to find out ya son's side of the story—ya firstborn son!"

"No," Albert said with a shake of his head.

"No what?" She was sure her words were convincing her husband to think more rationally.

"Ya should've seen her cry. No, he did what she said. God, I can't even think about this without feelin' sick."

"So that's it?" Justine's voice was low. "Ya going to renounce ya son for somethin' some half-breed tramp is claiming? Ya going to just blindly believe her and lose ya son?"

"I didn't choose this, Justine."

"Ya are choosing"—her voice began to rise—"this girl over ya own family...over ya own son! He is ya blood!"

"She is my blood!" Albert yelled, his hand flexing with emotion. "She is my daughter!" He paused as a shake threatened in his voice. "Goddamn, Justine, she is my daughter."

"And he is ya son."

"That doesn't vindicate him. His actions are wrong—he shames me."

Mrs. Toussaint began breathing heavily. "Shames you... Shames you? What of your actions and the shame you have brought to the family?"

Albert narrowed his eyes. "What are ya talkin' about?"

"You takin' a slave as a lover," she spat in disgust. "You havin' a half-breed daughter and raising her in the same house as your white children."

"Damn it, Justine, that was a long time ago, and yes, I'm going to raise my daughter! I hold no shame in that decision!"

"I have shame!" Her hand flew up and pounded her chest. "I have shame every day! Shame that my husband had an affair on me! I am bound to that shame every day that girl is in my house. Bound to that shame when I go to an event and the other women whisper of the dark child being raised in my house. It is more than any woman should have to bear, and yet I have to bear it every day!"

"Do I not take care of you? I told you long ago that I was no longer in love with you, but I have not abandoned you. I have stayed true to my obligations."

"I never wanted to be your obligation. I wanted to be your wife."

"What is between you and me has nothing to do with what our son has done, Justine."

"It does, though! It does, Albert, because once again you are choosing her over me. I hate it! It's like I can't get away from her and her hold on you! You are choosing her."

"Enough!" He threw his hands up in the air. "That is enough."

The pause captured tears from Justine's eyes, like a dam preventing a river from flowing. Her lips quivered in a tight line. "You have forsaken me, but do not forsake our son." Albert didn't answer her plea. "If you disown him, I will leave you. I'll take Victor and Isabelle, and I will leave."

He looked up at her from over his brow. "Where would ya go?"

"Alabama," she answered. He raised his eyebrows. "I'd go live with my sister."

"You would separate yourself that far from three of your children?"

"If you disown Al, yes! And as far as I'm concerned, that would not be far enough away from you."

Albert lowered his head and took a deep breath. "I'm sorry you feel so strongly toward me, but I cannot excuse his behavior. I think it would be best if you go. You should write to her." Tears rolled down Justine's red cheeks. "I will send money every month to ensure you have what you need, and I will write to Victor and Isabelle."

"You are really doing this?"

"I am."

Justine reached up and gave her cheeks a quick swipe. "I will make the arrangements," she said with a heavy swallow. "As ya well know, I will require a handful of house slaves." He gave a slight nod. Her voice quivered, but she spoke without emotion. "So, I will take Nan and Franny with me, along with two or three others."

Albert countered, "I think not. Ya can choose one, but ya cannot take them both."

Her lips twitched. He looked down and didn't raise his head as she lingered a moment and then walked out of the room. Around the corner, Franny and Nan were pressed up against the wall, listening with nervous anticipation.

The house was full of closed emotions over the next few months. Justine canceled the New Year's party with apologies to her neighbors and the excuse that an unavoidable crisis had taken place. Albert Jr. had packed and left the day after the fight with his father. He went back to the university without another word to him. Isabelle cried and threw emotional fits. As she was engaged but not yet married, the move forced her to be separated from her fiancé. She threatened to run away with him, but it was met by her mother pulling her ear with a strong reprimand. Albert suggested she stay on the plantation until the wedding, but Justine would have none of it. She remained unyielding, insisting that letters could be written while ignoring Isabelle's tears and asserting to her that love was a folly and a fool's game. Victor kept to himself and stayed immersed in the solitude of his room.

The day came for them to leave—a hazy, early spring day—and Coco walked into the kitchen where Nan and Franny spoke in hushed tones. They turned to see her standing with a quivering lip.

"Aw nah, honey, don't go and start with them tears," Franny said, moving toward the girl. "It's all right."

"It's all my fault."

Franny reached up and wiped at the tears starting to fall down Coco's cheeks. "Oh no, it ain't ya fault. I'll be okay. I'm just goin' a little ways, and I gets to stay with the missus, so it ain't so bad, ya see."

"Do you know how far Alabama is?"

"Well no, I don't. But goin' to another city or another state, there ain't much difference to me. Either way, it's not close enough to ya, and I'm sure goin' to miss ya," she said, fighting back her own emotions. Nan dabbed at the corner of her eyes as she stood by, listening.

Coco rested her head against Franny's shoulder and wrapped

her arms around the woman. "This isn't fair. I don't want you to leave."

"It'll be okay—I'll be okay." It sounded as if she were trying to convince herself as well the girl.

"Here nah," Nan interrupted with a sniff of her nose. "The missus will be waitin' on ya. Ya best be gettin' on."

Franny let go of Coco. Looking her in the eyes, she touched her face. "Ya goin' to grow into a beautiful woman. I just wish I could be here to see it." Coco bit her lower lip as Franny turned to Nan. "Well nah, ya ol' woman, hope ya can get along without me in the kitchen."

Nan raised her chin. "The only thing I'm goin' to miss about ya is ya butter beans. Ain't no one can make them like ya can."

Franny pressed her lips together and gave a short nod. "I'm goin' to miss ya bossy ways."

Nan took hold of her for a strong but brief embrace. "Take care of yaself, woman," she said, letting go.

"Okay then." Franny gave another nod and turned to walk away. The two watched her slowly make her way to the door, and she never turned around or looked back. It would be the last time either of them would ever see Franny.

A solemn cloud rested over the Toussaint plantation that spring day of 1859. The large house was quiet. Albert plunged himself into overseeing the plantation and the mill in a way he had not done since Coco was a baby. She immersed herself in playing the piano and reading everything she could get her hands on. Nan hummed in the kitchen.

CHAPTER SEVENTEEN

June 1, 1861

My Dear Beloved Father,

I hope this letter finds you in good health and spirits. It seems that what I have both longed for and dreaded has now come upon us. Since the seizing of Fort Sumter in South Carolina, the activity and spirit of the South has come into full fruition. Both men and women seem eager for the "glory" of war, which I am afraid will end in a needless bloodbath. Since Louisiana has followed South Carolina's lead back in January, I hear also that Texas has seceded from the Union; Baton Rouge has become a city of men filling the streets with loud voices, proclaiming an early victory for the Confederate States of America. The infantry grows daily, and our production of small-arms ammunition is unlike anything I have ever seen. The entire city has come together to support the cause.

Pliny House is not without its diligent support. The ladies of Pliny have invented a new feature in our fairs. A parcel of us girls have set ourselves up and allowed the fellers to kiss us for twelve and a half cents per kiss. Before you feel the need to reprimand me, Father, know that our fair raised $62 in one evening. One man took $11 worth! We are planning another fair next week. My only sorrow is that my dearest friend

Liza will not participate. She thinks herself too plain. If only she knew how beautiful she really is.

With all the hubbub of activity, I hardly have time to take pen in hand, but I read in the newspaper that on May 26th the Union Navy set a blockade of the Mississippi River, primarily around New Orleans. How will this affect the export of our trades? I am anxious for us. Oft at night my heart sorrows. That is when I have time to reflect on the goings-on around me. That is when I miss you the most, Father. I honestly do not know how much longer I can bear being away from you. And though my services here are well utilized, the daily call for more soldiers and cannon guards sets my heart to beating heavy. Sometimes I feel as if I can not breathe. I wish to come home soon, Father. I long for home. My soul is at unrest. I will write again soon.

Your loving daughter,

Coco

Albert folded the letter and rubbed his fingers down the seams of the paper as he turned his face toward the noon sky and blinked. The days were dusty as July arrived. Looking over the expanse of land, Albert turned on his heel and headed straight toward Nathan, where he made repairs to the roof on the live-stock barn.

"Nathan!" he called out.

"Yes seh," he replied, standing and moving closer to the roof's edge, hammer in hand. Nathan was now a slender, tall man in his thirties.

"Prepare the carriage. We have to go get Coco!" Albert sounded rushed.

"Straight away, seh. Everythin' okay, seh?" he asked with concern in his voice.

"No, Nathan. No, it's not. We are in war, and I'll be damned if she is not by my side at such a time so I can protect her."

Nathan ran his tongue over his salty mouth. He pressed his lips back and forth from a puckering position as he bit on the inside of his cheeks—something he always did when he was anxious or thoughtful. He didn't hesitate any longer than a few moments, only to consider the words his master had said. With haste, he made his way down the ladder and prepared the carriage.

He had always looked over Coco, especially after the loss of her mother. Their friendship became a special bond as he adopted her in his heart as his sister. Some of the most special memories Nathan carried were of when she would meet him in the barn to teach him how to write. She was only eleven years old the day she was playing among the horses in the barn and discovered Nathan could neither read nor write. She was aghast.

Kneeling in the dirt, Coco used a piece of straw and wrote his name in the dusty ground. Nathan looked at the symbols and smiled. Tracing through the dirt again, she said the letters that formed his name before pronouncing his name slowly. The glow of joy on his face was unmistakable and resonated with Coco. Later that week, she hid an alphabet book in the barn where she was sure he would find it, and it was that week that started Nathan's journey of learning how to read. Coco would sneak away for a few minutes a day as often as she could to help him understand the written word. It lasted two summers before the lessons began to wane, but not before Nathan learned how to pronounce even words he didn't know.

He and Albert were on their way to Baton Rouge within the hour. By the time they reached the city, it was in an uproar of commotion. Albert order Nathan to stop the carriage so he could address a boy holding up a newspaper and yelling, "Down with the ironclads!"

"Boy, what has happened?" he ordered.

"CSS *Sumter* broke the Unionist blockade in New Orleans. Ten cents and you can read it for yourself."

Albert reached into his pocket and pulled out the change. After putting it in the boy's hand, he took hold of the paper. The boy held up another, yelling out the victory of the Confederates over the Unionists. Albert read on the front page, "The Pirate *Sumter*" and proceeded to read the article on how the 437-ton bark-rigged screw steam cruiser, commanded by Captain Raphael Semmes, escaped from the Mississippi River past the blockading USS *Brooklyn*.

The streets were filled with the celebration of Baton Rouge's eager population over the Confederate victory. Men shot their pistols into the air with whooping calls as Albert rolled the paper in his hands and climbed back into the carriage, motioning Nathan to drive on toward the boarding house. Coco was sitting at the window on the third floor the moment the carriage pulled up to the front of Pliny House. Her eyes first narrowed at the familiar figure driving the carriage before widening at the sight of Albert stepping down from inside. Jumping up suddenly and not bothering to pick up the books that spilled onto the floor from her lap, Coco ran toward the stairwell and quickly made her way down the steps.

Albert had hardly entered the foyer with hat in hand before Coco called out to him, "Father!" She jumped into his arms, the hoops of her skirts swinging in the air. He lifted her into his arms with a groan of surprise and joy before he set her back down on her feet. The head lady of the house would have chided Coco for such an imprudent action, stating a lady of sixteen should maintain a gentle approach and not be so rash toward the male gender, not even a father. "What are you doing here?" she asked, holding onto his hands.

"I've come to take ya home. Go get your things," he responded without skipping a beat.

"Have you not heard? The barricade of the Union was broken! People all over the city are talking about how the war will be over in a few months." She smiled innocently.

"Then until that day, ya comin' home with me. Do ya think the Union is going to stop because of one cruiser that broke past the barricade? No! The Union won't stop until they gain control of the Mississippi. This war is goin' to go straight up the vein of Louisiana. Ya are sittin' on a live cannon, my dear."

His firm stare and message convinced Coco. After a brief pause, she said in a fretful tone, "I'll ready my things."

She went to pack her belongings into her moving trunk. When she returned, she found her father standing outside next to Nathan and the carriage. She gave the man a shallow smile. "It's good to see you, Nathan. How have you been?" She asked giving him a long, meaningful hug, not caring about the rules on gender or status.

"Miss Coco. Right as rain. Seein' ya is like seein' the sun come out from behind the clouds." Age did not fix the gap in this front teeth as he flashed her a big smile.

Her smile moved into her eyes. "I left my trunk in my room. The girls inside will show you where that is," she said. He gave her a nod before his prompt movements took him inside. Coco took in her father's somber face. "Are you really that concerned?" she finally asked.

"More than I care to express."

"Then you are certainly more fearful than the men around here," she said casually as she looked at the group of soldiers that had gathered on the other side of the street. "They talk about how it will end in a few months. Some even say the casualties will be so few that the bloodshed could be mopped up with a handkerchief."

Albert looked at her in near confusion. "Who's sayin' that?"

"Everybody," she responded with a raise of her eyebrows and shrug of her shoulders.

"They're fools," he scoffed.

"I don't know. I think they may be right... I don't think we will see much of the conflict around here."

"We have the single most important economic highway: the Mississippi. It is a lifeline and avenue of the South." His voice was harsh and loud. "Union leaders know the importance of taking the river. It's as important as the railways. The side that gains control of the Ohio, Missouri, and Mississippi Rivers will control the continent and win the war."

Nathan appeared, struggling to carry the large trunk, and strapped it to the back of the carriage as Albert finished his statement. "There's some more I have to get," he said with a motion of his hand, addressing Mr. Toussaint, before he made his way back into the house.

"Surely the two parties will come to an agreement before it becomes that severe."

"I have my doubts, but I hope ya right."

A pause followed as the two of them watched Nathan reappear with another travel tote under his arm, two hatboxes, and a colorful carpetbag in the other hand.

"Good God, Coco! How much do ya have?" Albert jested.

"More than what he's carrying down! I had to give some of my dresses away because they wouldn't fit in the trunk!" She gave her father a look of defeat, her full lips partially open as she let out a huff.

Albert shook his head and pressed his lips together in a smile. "All right. Are ya ready?"

"Can we spend one more day in the city?" Coco asked. "Maybe take Liza out for dinner?"

"I hadn't planned on it."

"Please, Father. Who knows when I will be able to see her again? Please? I told her I'd ask you."

He looked across the street and took a deep breath. "All right," he finally said, "she can spend the evening with us. But we leave first thing in the morning," he finished, matter-of- fact, shooting her a look that said it was non-negotiable.

Coco squealed and trotted back into the house to get her friend, who waited just inside the doorway.

"She got ya wrapped around her finger," Nathan said good-naturedly to Albert as he climbed into the driver's seat. "Just like her mama."

"Yes, she does," he agreed under his breath as Coco approached with her friend.

"Father, this is Liza."

"How do ya do?" she said softly with a small curtsy. Though her lips hardly moved, she smiled with her gray eyes, looking through them like a shy dove. Albert gave a nod and motioned with his hand for the girls to enter the carriage.

Liza was seventeen. Her soft, golden brown hair was wispy around her temples and would not stay pressed below her center part. Her skin was pale, and she lacked any color in her cheeks. She gathered up the layers of her dark green dress, a color that complemented her fair features, before stepping up into the carriage.

Albert learned that Liza was from a wealthy plantation in southern Mississippi. Her father had sent her to the boarding school when she was ten years old, after her mother died of the typhoid fever, claiming he had no mind on how to raise a young lady properly. He had since remarried a young woman not ten years her elder, but Liza still had not been summoned home. She only went home to visit once a year and then only for a week. Her gaze wandered outside the carriage as she mentioned the infrequency of her visits home. Albert switched the conversation to find out more about her hobbies and interests, which at one point brought a pink hue into her cheeks as he expressed interest in her.

After their evening together, Coco took hold of her father's hand. "Thank you for being so kind to Liza. She is frightened about the war. Her father and brothers have already enlisted, except for the youngest of them." Coco leaned her head against his shoulder. "I'm sad for her, but it seems you made her happy this evening. You are the best father," she said, kissing him on the cheek.

They stayed the night in Baton Rouge and left early the next morning to head back to the plantation. The months of July and August seemed not to change for Coco as she grew bored of the plantation summer and urged her father to send her back to the Pliny boarding house, a request he refused. She argued with him over the topic until, one day, he walked out of the room and then reentered, slapping a newspaper down on the table.

"Ya want to know why I'm not letting ya go back? Here, read for yaself the state of the war. Regardless of how ya friends ya write feel about it, we are at war and it's not just going to go away."

Coco picked up the paper, her brow creasing at her father's severity. There, she read about the Confederate victory at the Battle of Manassas. "Why didn't you tell me about this? This happened near a month ago!"

"I don't want ya frightened and wrought about it."

Coco continued reading. "Do you think that's true?"

"What?"

"How many men died there?"

"Well, yes."

"So sad..." she mumbled to herself as she read on. "I don't know why this has anything to do with me going back to Baton Rouge, though. Father, this is all the way across the country in Virginia."

"The battles won't stay there; they'll spread this way. This is just the beginning. And when they do, I want ya where I can protect ya."

"Will you please not keep news like this from me?" Coco's voice was punitive. "I am not a child anymore! And there is nothing to protect me from." Silence followed. "I just miss my friends... I miss Liza," she said more tenderly.

Albert watched his daughter walk toward the window with a stride of defeat. "If she doesn't get called home soon, she can come stay with us for a little while."

Coco's eyes flashed with excitement. "Really?" He gave a short nod. Skipping over to him, she hugged him. "I'm going to write to her right now," she said as she moved out of the room. "Thank you, Father, thank you," echoed down the hall as she made her way to her bedroom.

She received a letter from Liza the last week of September, but it was not the response she had hoped to get from her friend. Liza wrote that she had entered into a courtship with Thomas Cott, a man Coco was familiar with from social events. She was never overly impressed with the man of hardly twenty and wondered why Liza was intrigued by him. He was not a man of great wealth, and though kind, Coco did not find him a good suitor for her friend.

In Liza's letter, she stated, *"I have made up my mind not to end up an old maid. More and more men are putting on the gray, leaving me to wonder who will be left. Perhaps I would not be so inclined to have such thoughts if you, my dearest, were here. As you know, my father and brothers are soldiers in gray, and although I chide myself for thinking such wicked thoughts, should something happen to them, my father's fortune will be left to my stepmother. Should such happen, I would be left with only a moderate fortune and less beauty. I refuse to go into spinsterhood. Therefore, I am securing a promise of marriage from Mr. Cott before he leaves with the militia..."*

Coco put the letter down, sensing a chill feeling of despair. "Oh Liza," she huffed out loud to herself as she leaned her head against the wall where she sat in the bay window. "Why is there the assumption that every woman should be a wife?"

She waited a few days before deciding to write Liza back. She didn't want her frustration to come through her words and make the letter seem harsh. When she finally wrote to Liza, she reassured her friend that she was far from ending up an old maid and extended another invitation for her to come and stay at the plantation for as long as she wished. Though their correspondence would continue through the war, Liza would never take up the invitation to stay at the Toussaint plantation. It wouldn't be until the winter of 1863 that Coco would see Liza again, and in the unhappiest of circumstances.

CHAPTER EIGHTEEN

NOVEMBER BROUGHT cooler weather and the whisper of harvest. Coco sat on the front veranda, reading, when she saw a cloud of dust coming down the lane toward the house. The pounding of hooves, like distant rolling thunder, was easy to make out. Coco stepped into the house to get her father's attention. As one hundred soldiers approached, Albert stepped out to speak with them. Coco, in her simple plaid dress, stood behind the screen door, the wooden frame hiding half of her person.

"Dis ya plantation?" the officer asked.

"It is. I am Albert Toussaint. And you are, sir?"

"I am Captain O'Leary, a commander in the 13th Louisiana Infantry Regiment, and this is my troop."

"Well, Captain, welcome to the Toussaint plantation. How can I help you?"

"May I have a private word with ya, Mr. Toussaint?"

Albert gave a short nod. "Yes. Please come inside."

The captain dismounted, followed by his first lieutenant, and commanded the second lieutenant to stay with the troop.

Albert led them into the house. "My daughter," he briefly introduced Coco as they entered. She gave a curtsy as the men regarded her. "Have Nan bring some coffee into the office," he told her before they continued farther into the house.

As the time passed, Coco sat in the front family room, looking out through the sheer curtains at the men in gray uniforms sprawled out across the lawn. Nan came into the room, breathless and wringing her hands.

"What is it?" Coco asked, concerned.

"These men takin' us…" Her eyes were wide with fear.

Coco stood immediately. "What?"

"They takin' all of us…fa the war."

"They can't do that." Her tone was severe as she frowned.

"They is. Masta's arguin' with 'em, but he's losin'."

"How is that… No! They can't do that!"

"Long ago, I told myself I was done bein' scared, but I'm scared now."

Coco pressed her lips together as worry filled her eyes. "Nan… Go hide yourself," she pleaded.

"I'm a big woman," Nan let out with a nervous giggle. "How could I hide? And they already seen me."

Coco took the older woman into a strong embrace. After pulling away, she looked Nan in her dark eyes. "I'll be right back," she said, swallowing the lump pressing in her throat. "I'm going to warn Nathan."

Nan nodded. "Go out the back, now!" she urged as she let go of the girl and watched her rush to the back of the house.

Coco crossed the back of the yard that led into the grove. It was the longer way to the barn, but she would remain unseen this way. When she got there, she called out for Nathan as she rushed through, looking in each stall.

"Missus, what is it?" another slave asked.

"Where's Nathan?"

"He headed down to da community."

"When?"

"Aw, not too long ago."

Coco wasted no time and, instead of answering the questioning look on the slave's face, started running toward the community. Soon, she saw his figure mounted on a horse ahead of her. "Nathan!" she called out. "Nathan!"

He heard her voice and turned on the horse to see her running toward him. Without hesitation, he planted his heels into the animal's sides and headed to her. When he reached her, he dismounted before the horse had even fully stopped. "Coco, what is it?" Nathan asked, grabbing her by the shoulders.

She tried to catch her breath. "There's a troop of soldiers here. Nan heard the captain talkin' to Father... She says they are takin' all the slaves."

His lips parted as he looked into her eyes with a heavy gaze. "Can they do that?" he finally asked.

"I don't know," she said, raising her eyebrows and shaking her head.

"Well, what are ya doin' out here?"

"To warn you, so you can hide."

His lips puckered back and forth into a whistling position before he smacked his lips. "Aw, sista, they ain't no hidin' from this." He looked across the sky, as if to find an answer.

Coco's eyes searched his face. "Please hide."

"I ain't hidin'. Here now, get on the horse and I'll ride ya back. Ya shouldn't be out here at a time like this." As he finished his statement, a group of horses appeared, heading toward them. They watched as the riders approached.

"We're gatherin' ya all up. I need ya to come with us," the soldier said, looking down from his mount.

Nathan nodded before looking at Coco. "Get on back to the house now."

"No, she's comin' with us too. We're gatherin' house nigga and field nigga both."

A frown creased Coco's brow as she looked at the man. "I'm

not a slave. I am Caroline Toussaint, daughter of Albert Toussaint, the owner of this plantation."

The two soldiers looked at each other. "Let me see ya papers," one commanded.

"They're in the house."

"Well, be that as it may, I'm goin' to need ya to come with us until we can verify that."

Coco looked at Nathan, who gave her a nod. "Do as he says."

"Well, I'm not walkin'," she said flatly. She looked back and forth between the men before lifting her skirt and mounting the horse Nathan had been riding.

The four made their way to the community, where all the slaves were being gathered. Nathan was sure to stay beside Coco the entire time, and the two soldiers kept a keen eye on her as well. She remained on the horse while she watched them round up the slaves. Thoughts of the last time she was in the community as a young girl ran through her mind, and her stomach knotted from the memory. She looked around as the soldiers brought more slaves from the mill, searching for her father's familiar face, but she did not see him. Coco knew her father's plantation was large, but she had never inquired just how large. As she looked out across the dark, worn faces of nearly three hundred slaves, her heart began to race in her chest. She wasn't familiar with any of these faces.

The only field slave she could remember was Foy, who had purchased his freedom from her father when she was fifteen. She remembered Justine going through the house, arguing that slaves should not be allowed to buy their freedom. The year after she left, Albert granted Foy's request and issued the papers for his freedom. Foy built a cabin on a small piece of land on the corner of the property, continuing to work for Albert to pay him for the value of the ground. Foy was at the mill when the soldiers came to gather everyone, but unlike Coco, he carried his freedom papers with him. Once the soldiers confirmed the description and papers of the free man, he made his way to find Albert.

The captain stood at the front and spoke loudly as he told them the Confederate Army was commissioning them in the aid of the war efforts and that, straightaway, they were to be making their way to Baton Rouge. The slaves were told they could take what they could carry and that they would be marching out within the hour. Coco watched the confusion spread across the faces in the crowd as they slowly began to disperse to their living quarters in a hum of perplexity.

She saw her father speaking with the captain and dismounted her horse. As she made her way to him, the men watched her. A soldier grabbed her by the arm forcefully and asked, "Now where ya think ya goin'? Get to ya hut and get ya things." He gave her a shove in the opposite direction.

Coco's mouth gaped open. "Excuse me? How dare you grab me like that!"

"Don't cause no trouble. Now, go on and get ya things."

"That is my father!"

The soldier chuckled. "Sure it is." She began to walk past him again when he grabbed her by both arms. "Now don't make me tell ya again. I said get on out of here!" He gave her a push.

"Hey!" a strong, commanding voice boomed. "Hey!" Albert strode swiftly toward the soldier. The man turned and saw him bulling toward him. "That's my daughter," he growled, pointing his finger. He put his arm around her. "Are ya okay?" Albert asked tenderly. She nodded, and he led her to where he'd been speaking with the captain and lieutenants, giving the soldier a jolt as he passed him.

"I apologize about that, miss," the captain addressed her when Albert rejoined him. "Mr. Toussiant, ya know I will have to see her papers before we leave."

Albert said gruffly, "That's fine, but ya men better stay away from my daughter! I will not hesitate to have my way with the next one who touches her."

"I understand, sir. These men are just followin' orders."

Albert took his daughter back to the house, followed by the captain and first lieutenant. He chided Coco for being outside and for not carrying her papers on her, which he had ordered her to do every day when he handed them to her. The captain looked over the certificate carefully before handing it back to him.

"So, are we not allowed to keep just two or three slaves?" Coco asked her father when they were alone for a minute.

"No." The anger in Albert's voice was notable.

"It's harvest time. What are we goin' to do?"

"Coco, not now," he said, making his way to the window. A few moments passed before Nan stepped into the room.

"Well, I guess that'll be all I can do for ya, sir." Albert turned and saw her familiar frame standing firmly in place.

"Nan," Coco said softly, getting to her feet.

"Nah my chores aren't done for the day, Masta," her voice quivered, "I was too busy stirrin' up my honey lemon cake batter. It's ready, nah, Coco if ya want to put it in the pan and cook it. Ya know it's done when it doesn't jiggle in the middle." Coco pressed her lips together and struggled to keep the tears from rolling down her cheeks. "So, I guess that'll be it then," Nan continued in an uncertain tone.

Albert approached the woman he had known for years. He rested his hand on her shoulder tenderly. "Nan…"

"Don't got to say nothin', sir." He nodded and gave her shoulder a squeeze before letting go.

Coco took the old woman by the hands and looked her in the eyes. "I'm goin' to miss you," she said.

"No tears, child, and no goodbyes. Ya be a good girl nah." Nan's breathing quickened as she squeezed the girl's hands tight.

"Yes, ma'am," Coco choked out.

Albert and his daughter stepped out onto the front porch to

watch the spectacle. When Coco saw Nathan standing at the base of the steps, she walked down slowly to stand near him.

"This isn't fair," she said quietly, not making eye contact with him.

"It ain't ever been fair."

"Please write to me—let me know how you are."

"They won't let no black man write a letter," he said.

"Find a way, even if it's just your name, so I know you're all right."

Nathan bit at the inside of his cheeks. "Take care of ya father for me," he said.

They stood in silence until the lieutenant called out the order to start them all moving. Nathan took a few steps before turning around and looking back at Albert standing behind Coco, her arms folded over her chest as if she were hugging herself. Albert raised a hand to him that balled into a fist, as he clenched his teeth. Nathan returned the farewell with a nod. He swung his sack over his shoulder and turned to follow the troop. Nan moved along, bringing up the rear, as her frame rocked from side to side like a ship in the sea. Coco raised a hand when the woman turned and looked back at the place she had known for half her life and the young woman she had raised. She didn't drop her head as she turned around and continued with the rest of them.

Captain O'Leary moved his horse to the front of the porch. "Mr. Toussaint, thank ya for ya hospitality. The South thanks ya for ya contribution in aiding the assurance of victory for the Confederate States of America." He tipped his hat toward them and then rode down the path.

Albert and Coco stood on the porch until the last man was nearly out of sight. The day seemed hazy, and the silence that followed echoed in an odd emptiness, like the first moments after waking from a troubling dream. Foy stood near the corner of the house. He looked at his once-master, then back down the path where the troops and slaves could no longer be seen. He didn't say anything; he just turned and headed back to his own home. Albert and Coco hardly spoke the rest of the afternoon for lack of words to express the gravity of emotions they were both feeling. Coco put Nan's honey lemon batter in the oven over quiet tears and an upset stomach, and as the years passed, the sweet scent of lemon would forever be a powerful madeleine, bringing up for Coco strong memories from years ago.

The 13th Louisiana Calvary led the slaves to Baton Rouge, where they were dispersed wherever the army saw fit. Nathan left by steamer to Columbia, Kentucky, along with eight hundred and thirty men of the 13th Louisiana Regiment and Captain O'Leary. There, he and other black men and women were used for labor to aid the army. Afterward, the men went to Corinth, Mississippi, and later, in April of 1862, Nathan found himself in Tennessee, gathered around a small fire with a handful of other black men.

"I got a chill in my bones," one of the men said.

"It's cause ya feet's been wet for five days," another jested.

"Nah, dat ain't it. It's all these men and what we all about to face. Dis battle could be the end of the war," he continued.

"I ain't ever seen so many men in all my life. How many ya reckon there is?"

"I heard a captain say that another regiment joined, takin' the count up to forty-three thousand."

One of the men whistled. "That's an army." The rest of them fell silent.

"I say we escape during the battle." Nathan's comment was met with cold, dark stares.

"You a fool? There's no escaping forty-three thousand men," someone said in a low voice as he leaned over the fire. "And even if we was able to get pass the eyes of the Confederate Army, and the bullets, what's to happen if we get to that side and it loses the battle?" The man's voice was low but stanch. He leaned back to his sitting position and shook his head. "Nah, I ain't havin' no part of that."

"The next sunrise could be our last on this earth. What's the difference between dyin' over there or over here?"

"Exactly!" The arguing man's eyes widened. "What's the difference?"

"Dyin' free, that's the difference." Nathan's face shone with passion, and his eye contact never wavered. The men in the circle shifted their weight anxiously.

"I'm in," the one named Smith said in a solid tone. His nose was thick and his eyes wide-set. The hair on his face grew thick but stayed close to his chin.

"Then ya a fool just like him"—the man motioned with his hand—"and I don't want no part of it." Both of his hands came up in a cutting motion.

Nathan looked at Smith and nodded. They were finished with the conversation at that moment but would later articulate a plan to get them to the other side of the line.

Before dawn, bullets rained down on the unsuspecting Union soldiers. Flashes of fire from the muskets lit up the darkness like red lightning. Nathan and the other black men were far enough behind the line of fire not to see the fight, but it was heard echoing through the ravines without break or rest. After the morning had long given way to the afternoon sun, Smith looked to Nathan eagerly. Nathan gave his head a small shake.

"Why ya shakin' ya head?" Smith spoke quietly and without moving his mouth as he approached the leery Nathan. "This was ya idea and now ya backin' out?" he spat between gritted teeth. "I got three others comin' with us."

"Not now," Nathan said calmly. "It's not a good time."

"When will ever be a good time?"

"I said not now." Nathan's gaze snapped with his command, and he stepped away from where he was moving ammunition.

Soldiers were moving through the camp, bringing in the wounded and gathering more ammunition. "How the battle?" Nathan asked one of them.

"We're pushin' em back. Them Yanks are fallin' right and left like flies."

"Sounds like a hornet's nest out there."

The soldier gargled a laugh in his throat. Suddenly, a captain appeared, shouting orders. "All you here—you...you...you," he shouted, pointing his finger to all black men nearby. "Follow me. We need to bring all the canons we have to the front of the line."

The men jumped at the command of the officer. As they approached Fraley Field, the deafening sound of rifle and cannon fire and falling men silenced the earth. Nathan and the others pushed the cannons into place while the soldiers loaded and fired them. Bullets flew by his head as he tried to hunker low, taking cover where he could. Suddenly, his face was splattered with debris and blood from a soldier near him. Cannon fire had taken his left arm clean off, opening his torso, and he lay on the ground, wincing in pain.

The man, who didn't look over the age of twenty, made eye contact with Nathan, his dirty, graying face contorting as he reached up with his right hand. "Help me," he cried, fear-stricken.

The scenes around Nathan looked unnatural as his senses heightened. The crash of musketry and the men around him was pandemonium and nightmarish as he witnessed what artillery fire could do to the human body, blood spilling in ways he could have never imagined. Nathan dropped to his knees next to the young man, whose words were faltering.

"I'm goin' die, goin' die."

"What's ya name, son?" Nathan asked, gripping the young man's chest.

"Tomas."

"All right, Tomas. Ya goin' to make it. Ya goin' to live." His eyes glazed over as the soldier died in his hands.

Nathan swallowed and pressed his lips together, looking at the wounded and dead all around him. The fighting continued well after sunset but lessened until it nearly stopped, both sides shattered and discouraged from the thirteen hours of firing. The army did not allow sleep to cover their eyes, and a chilliness of gloom crept over the entire camp. Nathan later found out that General Sidney Johnston, the commander leading the Confederates attacks, had died during the battle, leaving the entire Southern Army dispirited. Nathan sat with his back against a tree, the wounded and dead lying in every conceivable shape all around him in a heart sickening sight.

"Let's cross over next engagement," Nathan said to Smith after the two found each other again. Smith's lips moved but made no sound. "I'm goin'. We sure to die in this hell anyway, so why not try? You still in?"

The other man looked wanly at him, "Hell yeah. I'm still in," his deep baritone voice uttered.

They didn't say any more. Nathan rested his head back against the bark of the tree, his face turned toward the heavens. Slowly, drops started to fall from the sky. The first one hit his cheek and rolled down, as if it were a tear, followed by another cool drop. He flinched at first but then relaxed as each drop seemed to ease the strain. The soft, soothing rain quickly turned into a torrential downpour, and the men could do nothing to shield themselves from the pounding torrent.

Soon, shots began ringing out again at sporadic intervals, the rain pouring down with lightning and cannon fire. As the night lit up, the soldiers couldn't tell if it was God or man. Then, to outstrip the most fanciful dream of horror, strange sounds began terrorizing the men in the army. "What the hell is that?" One by one, men could be heard asking the question, until one of the wounded yelled out in pain, crying for help. Chaos and cursing ensued as shots were fired. "Fuckin' hogs! Fuckin' hogs are eatin' the dead! Wild hogs are feedin' on the wounded!" Nathan pressed his eyes closed tighter, trying to drown out the hellish noises around him.

Heavy artillery once again filled a new day. "Run for your

lives!" echoed through the Confederate Army as they were pursued by the howling Federal troops, sprouting from the ground like mushrooms. Nathan looked to Smith, who crawled down into a gully with two other men. No words could be spoken, but the looks exchanged cried that it was now or never. The men, dodging wild bullets and cannon fire, ran toward the Federal line under cover of artillery fog. One of the four was shot and could not be recovered, but Nathan, Smith, and the third man continued.

The rumble of cannon fire became unendurable, and the three lay down on the earth, unable to move forward any father for fear and dread. When they were found, guns were pointed into their backs. The men raised their hands as a sign of surrender. As their eyes cleared, they found, to their relief, blue uniforms surrounding them. The Federal Army took them to their camp and gave them food and water. The men sat, nervously waiting to find out what would become of them. After hours passed, they were ushered into the tent of a man they were told was General Ulysses Grant. None of the men looked up into the face of the general.

"My men tell me they found you three in front of the line of cannons, lying in the mud." Grant poured himself a glass of whiskey and took a drink. "If you believe in a higher power, I would be thanking Him that you weren't blown to shreds." He lit a cigar and took a drag. "Because this is a damn miracle," he said as the smoke left his mouth. He let out a chesty laugh, and then he paused as he surveyed the men in front of him. "What are your names and where are you from?"

"Andrew Turner from Alabama," the younger of the men spoke first.

"Smith, Alabama."

"Nathan, Toussaint plantation in Louisiana."

General Grant moved his cigar with his tongue as he bit down on the end of it. "Don't tell me you three ran away from the Confederate Army."

Nathan raised his head. "We run from slavery, not from fighting. We'd take up rifles right now to march with the Federal Army."

"I have no doubt." There was a lengthy pause. "The problem we face here, gentlemen, is that, under the Fugitive Slave Act, I am obligated by federal law to return you to your owners, seeing how you are still recognized under the law as property." He spoke with nonchalant, quick, and nearly slurred words, as if they were forced by memory and not by belief. The men shifted on their feet. "Here is the problem I have with that…" Taking another long drag, Grant took the cigar out of his mouth and waved it in the air. "See, I believe the South is using the mass slave population in their efforts to win the war. *I* believe the massive loss of life over the last two days would not have been nearly as gruesome if they, in fact, did not have the slaves.

"Therefore"—his voice rose until booming— "I am duty-bound to hold you and any other slave that crosses over to the Federal Army as contrabands of war. Though the law of the land orders otherwise, this war has altered that, and the law don't mean squat! I will not be defeated! Therefore, I will not be returning any persons or things that aid the rebelling states in their efforts. Until there is a law of emancipation or otherwise, all slaved persons that reach my army stay in my army!

"Coot!" he boomed.

"Sir." The sergeant took a step forward.

"Find these men some proper uniforms."

"Yes, sir."

Nathan took in a deep breath and then slowly let it out as his lips pulled back into a grin.

CHAPTER NINETEEN

THE STALKS of cane stood tall and undisturbed as the winter months passed at the Toussaint plantation after the day the Confederate troops took the slaves. Coco had attempted to make meals for herself and her father, but over distraught tears, she threw up her flour and water-covered fingers.

"I don't know what I'm doin'!" she cried to Albert when he followed the sounds of angry words and a breaking dish to find her disheveled in the kitchen. Tears rolled freely down her face. "I don't know how to cook anything! Am I really this useless as a woman that I don't even know how to cook for us?"

"What are ya sayin'? Of course not. Ya been makin' us breakfast."

Coco gave her father a look of annoyance. "That was grits, Daddy," she said in a sharp tone. "You just add hot water and salt."

He offered her a grin. "Best breakfast I've had in a long time." Coco wasn't amused. "What are ya tryin' to make?" he asked.

"I thought some bread would go nice with the rabbit stew you cooked yesterday," she said as she began cleaning up the mess she had made.

"I see." Albert walked closer to her. "Let me show ya how to make cornbread."

"You shouldn't have to make all the meals for us. I should be able to cook for you."

"I'm ya father! Feedin' ya is my responsibility, not the other way around." He began rolling up his shirt sleeves and telling Coco what he needed.

"How do you know so much about cooking?"

"I had to cook a lot for my mother as I was growin' up," he said, clearing his throat. "My father died at the Battle of New Orleans when I was just five," he began as he started mixing up the ingredients. "My mother fell into a state of sadness. We was poor…I was young, but I quickly learned how to pull my share of the burden. The older children were able to get paying jobs, but me and my youngest two sisters…well, we had to help where we could." His voice trailed off before he spoke up again. "Ya payin' attention?" Albert asked.

Coco nodded as she leaned on the kitchen counter, smiling modestly at the thought of her father as a young boy taking on the burden of caring for not only his youngest sisters but also his mother. She didn't know his childhood stories—he never talked about his past—and she knew better than to push a conversation with him. He was a very private man, even with his own daughter.

A knock came at the back door near the kitchen, and Coco stood straight and looked at Albert. His brow creased. "Stay here," he said, wiping his hands and walking past her.

She could hear her father's voice but didn't know whom it was he talked to. The voices slowly became louder as footsteps neared the kitchen and then Foy entered behind Albert. Coco smiled at him. Foy hadn't visited the Toussaint plantation for nearly two months.

"Hi, Foy," she said.

"Hi there, missus."

"Father's trying to teach me how to make bread."

Albert poured him a cup of coffee, and the man thanked him as he took it. "Foy killed a gator. He's goin' to share the meat with us."

"I can teach ya how to make some gumbo," he said, looking at Coco.

"I'd like that," she responded. "I can do nothing in the kitchen."

"Don't be so hard on yaself," Albert interjected.

"No, it's true. I don't know where to begin when it comes to cooking. How could I? I've never had to before now."

"Well, I can teach ya a bit," Foy offered. "I know enough to make a few dishes taste good."

Coco smiled. "Father?"

"It's fine by me," he said, taking a drink from his own cup of coffee.

"I came by, figurin' we could help each other out." He redirected his conversation back to Albert. "It's near spring and time for plantin' soon. I figured we could get more done with six hands than with two—help each other with the plantin' and the huntin' and all."

Albert nodded slowly. "I agree."

Foy licked his lips. "We can work on the sugar field too and get what we can from the harvest to sell."

"We won't make shit from what we can harvest with only two of us." Albert smirked. "Would be a waste of time."

"Two of us?" Coco asked. "I can help with the cane!"

He looked out of the corner of his eyes at his daughter. "No."

She huffed. "Well, why not?"

He squinted and shook his head. "No." She raised her brows, questioning, and he added, "The work is too hard, Coco."

The next few weeks were difficult for her. She had never worked the soil of the earth. Albert and Foy worked rows into the dirt as Coco followed behind, planting the seed and gently covering it, as well as saying a prayer that nature would work its magic under her inexperienced hand. As the spring months warmed into the promise of summer, small sprouts of green thrilled Coco as she rushed to share the good news of growth with the two men as they processed what sugarcane they were able to harvest months before.

Coco's feet sunk in the wet soil as she lifted the hems of her skirts to her knees so she could run. She laughed as she skipped, not caring about the mud spraying up her legs and spoiling her shoes. The sun was warm on the skin, the air crisp, and the sky clear and bright blue. Cutting through the fields, she ran toward the mill. Suddenly, she came upon a child kneeling behind the cane. Coco stopped abruptly, the layers of skirts falling from her hands. Before she could say anything, though, the child stood and ran away.

"Wait!" she called as she started off in the same direction. Then, as if rammed by a bull, Coco was tackled from the side and the air was knocked out of her lungs as she hit the ground. "Stop! Get off of me!" She struggled with the frail man who'd taken her to the ground.

"Hold on, Sam. Hold on a minute," a woman's voice said.

They stopped struggling, and Coco gave a hard shove to get the man away from her as she hurried to her feet. "What is the meaning of this?" she asked breathlessly as she pushed her loosened hair away from her face and looked angrily into the black faces of the man who attacked her and woman who pulled him off. The man clenched his fist, as if he were ready to go after her again.

"Now, stop it, Sam. She one of us," the short woman reprimanded.

He glowered. "She ain't, though."

"What are you doing on my land?" Coco asked without hesitation.

The woman looked at the man and then back to Coco. "Wait a minute, dis ya land?" She frowned in confusion.

"Yes, it is."

"Huh." The woman shrugged her shoulders. "Dis whole field?" She extended her hand around them.

"Yes."

"Ya have slaves?" She leaned forward with raised eyebrows and dark eyes wide.

"The soldiers took them all."

"Ya right, Sam—she ain't like us. She turn on her own kind."

"I didn't turn on anybody," Coco said sharply.

"Ya own slaves, don't ya? Beat 'em…starve 'em…hang 'em up."

"No, of course not!"

The woman spit in the dirt at Coco's feet before turning to walk away. "Ya better not tell anyone ya saw us."

"Let me help you."

"We don't need help from some blame cherry nigga."

The pair made their way through the tall cane stalk. After a pause and despite the insult, Coco slowly followed them to find a circle of five adults, a child, and a baby bundled in a wrap. All dark eyes pierced her with worn stares in the silence.

"You're running away, aren't you?" she asked after surveying the group. "Come with me," she finally offered with a crack in her voice. "You can wash yourselves and rest somewhere dry." They looked at each other cautiously and mumbled their concerns. "You can trust me," Coco urged.

Without another word to her, they nodded and then followed her out of the cane fields. Coco first started leading them to the ghostly community but then switched direction to one of the barns that was empty of animals, taken by the Southern soldiers, but which still had hay and straw.

"You can rest in here; it's dry." The seven runaways slowly walked in behind her and looked around hesitantly as she spoke. "There's a well just outside where you can get water and wash up. I'll leave you all to rest a bit. You don't have to worry—there isn't anyone around here. I'll bring you some bread later."

They watched her leave in silence. Coco walked toward the

mill, turning only once to look at the barn in the distance. Her eyes shifted in nervous thought as she walked at a slow but steady pace. When she reached the mill, she found Albert and Foy working together, sleeves rolled up and shirts unbuttoned.

Her father stopped and wiped his brow with the back of his hand. "What are ya doin' out here?" he asked, taking in her disheveled appearance, when he saw her.

"There's, uh... I came across runaway slaves hiding in the cane."

Albert's eyes grew wide and his jaw set. "They hurt you!" His tone caught Foy's attention. Though now in his late sixties, Foy was still a stout man. He stopped what he was doing to join the conversation.

"No," she was quick to say. Albert's questioning eyes remained on her. "I took them to the barn in the west field. I told them they could wash up and rest there."

"No, Coco! Why would ya do that?"

"They looked exhausted. There was a baby."

"That's against the law, Coco. Ya know how much trouble we could face by housing fugitive slaves?" He looked to Foy, and the men moved to exit the mill.

"Against the law? And what about common decency toward mankind?" she asked as she followed them. "Since when is it okay for the law to deny people water and rest, even if they are fugitives? It's human rights!"

Albert stopped and turned to her. "Yes, it is, and I admire ya for standing up for that. But do ya understand the times we are livin' in? These are volatile times. We need to let the authorities know."

"Father, please, just let them rest and then let them go."

"I can't... I'm sorry, Coco."

"Can I at least take them bread?"

"We don't have much to spare."

"Father."

Albert took a deep breath and looked at Foy's unmoved demeanor. "All right."

The three climbed into the wagon and headed back to the house. Coco prepared a basket of bread, a small amount of left-over gumbo, two boiled eggs, and a jar of molasses. She covered the basket with a plaid cloth and returned outside, where Albert and Foy waited for her.

"Is that necessary?" she asked when she saw the shotgun laid across her father's lap.

"Indeed, it is," he responded as Foy gave the horse a flick of the reins, his own gun propped up beside him.

They rode out to the barn in the west field where Coco said she had left the seven fugitives. Foy pulled the wagon to a halt in front of the barn, where two of the men and the woman Coco had first encountered stared at them, motionless. Albert was the first to climb down from the wagon, shotgun in hand. One of the men, who looked to be in his mid-thirties, stood shirtless beside the well where he washed himself. His meatless shoulders hunched forward, curving his back like a scared cat. The scars across it were thick and protruded from his skin like his ribs. Coco tried not to stare, but her eyes were drawn to the unnatural sight.

"This is my father. I brought some food," she stammered as she removed the towel from the top of the basket she held. "There's not much gumbo, but I brought bread enough for everyone." She walked up to the woman and offered her a piece with a hint of a smile. She then gave a piece to the man sitting on the ground nearby before heading to the scarred man at the well. "Here." With uncertainty, he reached up and took the bread from her. "I have an egg in here for you too." She reached in the basket, pulled it out, and placed it in his hand. Then Coco walked with a sure step into the barn to finish her good deed.

Albert watched the man crack the egg. He didn't bother to pick off the hard outer layer before putting the whole thing in his mouth. The bread was eaten just as quickly before the man shook out his shirt and pulled it back over his head. He looked at Albert with a distant stare before walking to the side of the barn and sitting next to the other two.

"Where are ya all from?" Albert asked. No one answered; they just watched him with emotionless expressions. He turned to Foy, who gave him a nod, as if they understood each other. "Well, wherever ya runnin' from, they're probably out lookin' for ya... Hounds will lead them right to ya." Coco walked back outside, her eyes searching her father's face as she heard the last of his words. "The barn closer to the house has a crawl space ya can stay in for a day to catch ya strength. If ya get in the wagon, I'll take ya there. The dogs won't find ya tracks beyond this point."

Coco's eyes widened. "Well, come on," she said, "get in the wagon!"

They hesitated, but the woman went into the barn and gathered the others. After the seven runaways climbed into the bed of the wagon, Foy gave a flick of the reins. Once in the main barn, he and Albert showed the fugitives the trapdoor to the crawl space.

"I recommend ya go ahead and get down there and rest a few hours. We will come get ya to stretch ya legs." Coco gathered horse blankets and handed them to the men as Albert continued. "Rest now. Come sundown, ya all can get on ya way, under cover of darkness."

"Thank ya, seh," the woman holding the baby said with a quivering lip and tears in her eyes.

Albert nodded. "Keep that baby quiet."

"Yes, seh," she said as she lowered herself beneath the floorboards.

Foy closed the trapdoor and Albert kicked loose hay over the top of it. The squeaking of the boards sent an eerie sensation through the occupants beneath them. Albert avoided making eye contact with Coco as he left the barn.

"Thank you," she said as she walked beside him and Foy.

"Let's not speak of it. Foy, ya best stay in the house tonight...

It's only a matter of time before those hounds track them here, and I want us all together."

"I won't argue with ya."

Coco went into the house and poured water into the bath to wash off the mud from earlier in the day. She lowered herself into the tub and laid her head back as images of the fugitives ran through her mind. Her stomach roiled at the thought of their own workers being treated as less than human. Never before had she given it much thought; it was just a way of life, and she hadn't been to the community or among their field slaves since she was a young girl. The plantation had grown to such a large operation under the command of several drivers... Coco squeezed her eyes tightly closed and dropped the water-soaked cloth over half of her face before exhaling a long breath from her mouth.

As the sun sunk lower, Coco put together another basket of bread she had made just for the fugitives.

"I admire ya for what ya doin'," Albert said as he watched her gather what she could. "Just keep in mind we don't have many provisions or money to buy more."

"We can stand to fast a few days," she countered, not looking up from her diligent hands. No sooner had she filled the basket than dogs could be heard barking outside, and a heavy knock came at the front door.

"Put that away." Albert motioned at the basket. "And stay inside," he ordered as he left the kitchen and made his way to the front of the house. He passed Foy, who stood from where he was sitting in the main room.

Albert grabbed his gun before he pulled opened the door to find a dozen men with rifles and three hounds on his front lawn. "Can I help ya?" he asked, taking a heavy step out onto the veranda and letting the door close behind him. His face remained somber and unfriendly.

"Name's Walsh. I own a plantation just on the border of

Mississippi, and I've got some slaves that run off on me. We've tracked them here, to ya plantation."

"That's some distance."

"Four days we've been trackin' these niggas."

"Well, I ain't seen any slaves since the army took mine. I'm surprised you managed to keep some of yours."

The man gave a mock chortle, "Just the same, if it's all right with ya, I'd like to check ya fields. The dogs kept a scent that led right into ya standin' cane."

"By all means."

The man spit a wad of chew onto the ground. "Appreciate it," he said, wiping his mouth with the back of his hand.

Albert pressed his hands down on the railing. "We're south of the Mississippi line. Why would they head down here instead of heading north?" he asked before the man walked away.

"I guess since the damn Yanks captured New Orleans, they think they can find refuge down there."

"Well, ya can look around, but I want ya off my land by sundown."

"Fair enough," the man said, turning around. "Let's go, boys. Get them dogs up." Albert watched as the men started their search again before he stepped back inside.

"Are they gone?" Coco asked.

"No, they're searching the land."

"Why are you letting them?" she asked, frantic.

"Because, Coco, do ya know the crime it is to harbor fugitive slaves? I don't want to give them any excuse to question whether we're doin' that."

"What if they find them?"

"If they find them, they find them. It's out of my hands."

He ended the discussion on those words, and Coco sat nervously at the window for the rest of the evening. An occasional bark could be heard in the distance until silence fell with the sun.

She anxiously paced the floor. "Can we go out there and check on them?"

"No."

"I want to know if they found them."

"If they did, the man would've come back here."

"And fa all we know, those men could have eyes on us," Foy put in.

"That's right. I don't want any of us leavin' the house until we have daylight to check the property. We will find out then."

The next morning, Albert instructed Coco to stay inside as he and Foy traced the property for any signs of Walsh and his men. Before they made it to the barn, the man rode up to them on his horse, eyeing Foy with a frown.

"Didn't find 'em last night," he said, "but my hounds got some heavy scents comin' from ya barns."

"Is that right?" Albert asked.

"Yeah," the man grunted, low and suspicious. "Ya sure ya ain't seen any other nigga besides that one right there?" Foy kept his eyes down, and Albert didn't answer him. "I figure a slave owner such as yaself would shoot honestly with another plantation owner just tryin' to maintain his rights to his own property. Hiding runaways is a crime I know ya wouldn't commit, but I question ya nigga."

"I can relate." Albert looked Walsh in the eyes. "And ya have my word as a Southerner that, if I come across any slaves, I shall bind them, contact the authorities straight away, and give fair punishment to any who betray me."

Walsh gave him a nod. "I'm glad we understand each other." He tipped his hat to Albert before he turned his horse and rode away.

"Let's get back to the house," Albert said to Foy.

It would be hours before Albert felt it was safe enough to open the trapdoor to the crawl space under the barn. The dark faces of the runaways looked up, wide eyed in fear of who may be opening the door. The woman with the baby let out a cry of relief when she looked into Albert's face, and he helped pull her out.

"I'm sorry," she kept apologizing. "We been down there so long, we had to soil ourselves."

Coco shook her head to say it was all right and tried to quiet the woman, but she continued apologizing in embarrassment as the others were helped out from the crawl space. "We heard the dogs and loud voices, thinkin' for sure we'd been given up. But I knew ya spirit was kind when I first seen ya, and we stayed quiet, we did. Them dogs kept sniffin' around... I was so scared, but I kept prayin' to da Lawd that He would keep us like He did Daniel in da lion den and that He would shut the mouths of them dogs. He did, missus! He did!"

Coco rubbed the woman's arms as tears filled her eyes. "We have to get you going."

The woman nodded. "All right."

"Now listen," Albert said to the fugitives as Foy gathered a few blankets and handed them to the men. "It's not safe for ya to be here anymore—it never was. But ya need to get goin' now. The sun will be setting soon. I wish ya luck."

"Thank ya for ya kindness," one man said as another gave a nod to both Albert and to Foy.

"May da Lawd bless ya."

"Here are some rations," Coco said, handing a gunny sack to the first woman she had met.

"I'm sorry for what I said to ya..."

"Don't," Coco said, pressing her lips together and shaking her head. "There's no need."

"Ya ain't like us..." She puckered her mouth. "Ya's better."

"Godspeed," Coco said, her eyes glistening over as she took the woman's hand. The group of seven left the barn and made their way south with haste. As Coco, her father, and Foy stood outside the barn, their silhouettes standing out against a pastel evening sky, she asked, "Why are they heading south?"

"New Orleans is under Federal control."

Tears spilled down her face. "This ain't right, Daddy... This ain't right." Unable to control her emotions any longer, she broke down and wept as Albert took her in his arms, cradled her head against his shoulder, and let her cry.

Foy slowly walked away, toward the Toussaint house, whistling a low, melancholy note.

CHAPTER TWENTY

COCO HAD MADE it a habit as the months pressed into the hot days of summer to wear her father's trousers while she worked. She claimed her skirts were too cumbersome and got in her way. Though too large for her, the pants were held up with suspenders and rolled up at the ankles. Albert didn't like the idea at first, as it showed off his daughter's round buttocks.

"Trousers aren't meant for women," he said the first morning she came down the stairs in them.

"You try going out and working in those dresses!" she argued. "And who's around to see me? You afraid it's going to excite old Foy here?" she mocked as she put her arm around his shoulders where he sat at the kitchen island. The old man grinned and blushed before raising his coffee cup to his lips. Coco moved to stand next to Albert, cocking her head to the side and looking up at him. Her curls peeked around the edges of the colorful bandana tied around her head, and the corners of her mouth pulled back in a playful smile. "You don't have to tell me—I know I look cute."

Albert rolled his eyes as he gave a chuckle from within his chest. "Ya beat all I ever saw," he said as he tried not to smile.

It was a July day, and this particular summer produced extraordinarily large flies, whose wings buzzed like those of hornets as they moved through the muggy air. Coco filled another bucket of water at the well. She lowered it to the ground before dipping her rag into it and then tying it around her neck. The cool water ran down her skin and quickly absorbed into her sweat-soaked shirt. The drips didn't refresh for long, but the cool rag seemed to make it easier to breathe for the next few minutes.

She lifted the bucket and made her way to the garden, where her produce now stood proud, tall, and green. The snort of a horse and squeaking leather startled Coco, and she stood upright and looked toward the sounds. Two men, one in his early twenties and the other in his thirties, sat on horseback.

"Can I help you?" she asked, half stern.

"Sorry for the start. Might anyone be in the house?"

"In the house? No. As you can see, I'm out here working."

The man gave a cheeky grin. "Let me rephrase that. Is the owner of this plantation—the man of the house—at home?"

Coco cleared her throat and stepped out of the garden patch. "I am she!"

The men looked at each other and chuckled. "You here by yourself?" the younger of the two, the one with the fairer complexion and dark auburn hair, asked.

"No, of course not. My father is here, just in the next field. He should be back any minute." Her eyes shifted from one man to the next. "Can I help you with something?"

"You wouldn't mind if we rested ourselves and our horses under the shade of that grand oak in the front yard, would you?"

"I suppose that would be fine. Have you traveled some distance?"

"Traveled through Baton Rouge... We're on our way to Texas."

"What are your names?"

"I'm Thomas Randall, and this here is Beau Smith."

Coco nodded but offered no smile. "Well, you're welcome to rest a spell."

The men turned their horses and headed to the front of the house. Coco waited until they rounded the corner before she made her way to where her father and Foy worked on a broken wheel on the wagon.

"Father?"

"Yes? What is it?" he asked with a growl as he lifted the wheel to its edge.

"A couple of men rode up to the house."

"What?" he snapped.

"Some men asked if they could rest their horses here for a while."

"Soldiers?"

"No."

"Where are they?"

"The front of the house."

"Well, damn it." He threw down the rag he'd used to wipe his hands and stormed out of the barn. Coco stayed there with Foy.

"Can I help you?" Albert's voice boomed as he approached the two men reclining in the grass. His sudden presence startled them, and they both jerked up. The younger of the two jumped to his feet. "Whoa now," Albert said with his hand up the other on the butt of his pistol, afraid the young man would pull his gun in his panic. "What's goin' on here?" he continued.

"Wait a minute there, Beau," said the older of the two, calming his companion as he stood. "Sir, I'm Thomas, and this rowdy young one is Beau. We've been traveling hard on our way to Texas. We asked your slave gal if we could rest in the shade for a bit, since the sun's at its finest."

Albert took a deep breath and narrowed his eyes. "That's my daughter." Thomas swallowed hard and looked at Beau as he fumbled for words. "And no, you may not stay."

"I-I'm sorry for the confusion… But, sir, we are completely weary of this heat."

"No." Albert shook his head.

"Sir, we'll exchange our labor for rest," Thomas continued after seeing he was losing Albert's attention. "Maybe a couple days of rest and a meal or two, and we'll work for you."

Albert licked his lips as he pondered the offer. "I'll give ya a couple hours of rest here, but then ya start immediately. You'll stay in the barn. And if anything goes missin', I will shoot a thief. I'll be back for ya," he said before walking away.

"Nice save there," Beau said as he struggled to lie down, grimacing as he moved his wounded leg.

Thomas laid back onto the grass. "Yeah," he mumbled. "I ain't ever seen a nigga girl with a white father before. Is this still the god damn South?" He chortled as he put his hands under his head. "The hell is this world come to…"

Albert retrieved the men, as he promised, and worked them in the barn until the sun began to set. Foy took two plates of a humble dinner out to them after the day was completed. "I recommend sleep after ya eat," he said, handing the men their grub. "Mr. Toussaint likes to get started real early."

"We ain't no slaves, nigga," Thomas countered, his greasy black hair falling forward as his head lowered over his plate of food.

Foy clenched his jaw and glared at the men, eating as if they hadn't had a meal in days. He stood without moving until Thomas looked up at him, widening his crazed dark eyes and raising his brow. Foy turned and left.

The next morning, Albert was in the barn with a lantern well before dawn to wake the men, who met the early hour with cursing. "We're burning the old stalk and working new trenches today. I'll give ya breakfast after the sun's up."

The men worked alongside Albert and Foy in the dark of early morning. When strips of pink lightened the horizon, Coco went out to where the men worked and handed each one a square of cornbread and an egg. They stopped just long enough to eat the small ration before Albert had them working again. The heat of the day was quickly upon them, and by noon they left the scorching fields to do light chores in the barn and mill.

The next morning, Beau caught Coco away from the others while they were resting after lunch. "It sure would be nice to sit with y'all one evening," he said. "I'm tired of hearing nothing but Thomas smack his dinner in that old barn. Some new conversation would be nice."

Coco observed his face; she hadn't had any one-on-one conversation with either of the strangers. Beau's hair shared its ruddy color with his complexion, giving his freckles a red hue and his face almost a boyish innocence. His green eyes, however, were hollow and pale. She didn't offer him much conversation, nor did she hope for further interaction, but by the time evening came, Albert had invited the men to partake in dinner with them.

Thomas looked at Beau out of the corner of his eye as they entered the house and looked around. Foy had shot and cooked a rabbit, and Coco had snapped and prepared some green beans. As she brought out the meal, the men sat down at the table. Beau lowered his head and glanced at Thomas when Foy took a seat at the table next to Coco. Albert sat at the head of the table. Thomas leaned back in his seat and cocked his head to the side as he looked across the table at the black man and young woman. He scoffed under his breath, shook his head, and then hunched over his plate of food. He took a few bites before he started laughing. Coco's eyes met Beau's stare.

"Man, oh man," Thomas gurgled. "Times sure have changed, haven't they?" He gave his head a shake again. Everyone at the table chewed their food in silence, but he persisted. "I mean, have they not? Just look at us." He pushed more food into his mouth and smacked it while he talked. "Black and white eatin' at the same table…"

"Ya may want to mind ya next words. I advise ya to stop talkin'," Albert said, his fork hovering over his plate.

"No harm in sayin' what I said. Just an observation. Ya got negroes sittin' with white folks—"

"Shut up, Thomas," Beau said under his breath.

"Eatin' at the same god damn table, workin' in the same god damn fields." Food fell from his mouth.

"Shut up, Thomas!" Beau said again, louder and more forceful this time.

Foy removed his arms from the table and lowered them as he pushed back his chair with a somber face. Coco's eyes shifted around the table.

Thomas paid no attention to Beau's warning but widened his eyes and spoke louder. "Look at this. We have ourselves here a slave nigga, a half nigga girl…"

"I ain't no slave," Foy said quietly.

Thomas's eyes widen as he dropped his fork onto his plate, cupping his hand to his ear and leaning forward. "What? Ya…ya said what?"

"I'm a free man. I ain't no slave."

The dark-haired man rested his elbow on the table and propped his chin in his hand. "Well, I'll be damned. Ya free? Shit. First time I ever met free niggas."

"It's time for ya to go," Albert said forcefully.

"Now, I don't think I'm ready to go just yet," Thomas replied.

Albert pulled a revolver he'd hidden under his napkin and pointed it at the man. "Ya getting off my land right now… Get up."

"Just a minute now! Ya overreacting," Thomas said calmly.

"Get up, slowly."

"Just a minute…"

Foy raised the rifle he'd had at his feet and pointed it at the man.

Thomas began chuckling again as he stood with his hands raised at his waist. "Big mistake," he said as Beau also stood. "Ya shouldn't have pulled a gun on me, nigga." His dark eyes flashed madly as Foy stared him down.

"Get on," Albert said urging the men out of the house.

They followed the men out to the barn to ensure they saddled up and left the property, but not before taking possession of their guns. The men didn't ride very far before they stopped in the road.

"You gator-swamped us out of the plan!" Beau chided.

"Oh, this an't over," Thomas said, jerking his horse around.

"What? You don't think they'll be sleeping with a loaded gun after your little scene? Our plan was to scope out the house! But ya can't keep ya damn mouth shut."

"Yeah, well our plan has changed! I'm going to get that uppity nigga. There ain't no nigga going to point a gun at me and get away with it. We're goin' to teach him a lesson."

"Let's just get on out of here and head for Texas. We've been here too long as it is… You know they be looking for us."

"Not before I get my pound of flesh. Now I've been watching him, and every night you see his little lantern heading down the property a spell. He has his own cabin where he lives by himself." The two lurked in the shadows as the night darkened.

Mr. Toussaint insisted Foy stay at the house that evening and that they take shifts standing guard on the front veranda. "Get some sleep," Albert said, "I'll take the first watch."

He sat in the dark with no lantern lit, keeping his eyes and ears sharp. The night air was warm and humid, bringing out the mosquitos, and he raised his shirt collar and pulled his hat down low on his brow. The time passed swiftly until midnight, when it seemed to slow down and hardly pass at all. Albert checked his pocket watch at a quarter till two and decided it was time to step in to wake Foy for his watch.

The man splashed his face with water before taking the rifle and Albert's place on the veranda. The bush bugs were loud until around 3:00 a.m., when it seemed the whole Earth had quieted into daunting slumber. Foy looked around himself at the eerie witching hour. He slowly moved down the steps of the veranda, squinting with aging eyes into the moon's umbra, trying to make sense of what should have been familiar shadows. His knuckles tightened around the stock and barrel of the rifle; his finger ready at the trigger.

Suddenly, he was struck over the head from behind and knocked unconscious. He was dragged to behind his cabin, where he finally regained consciousness before he was stripped naked.

"We've been waiting for ya to wake up," Thomas gloated in jovial tone. "Didn't want ya to miss what was about to happen."

Foy's hands were bound in front of him as he lay on the dusty, hard earth under an old moss-covered tree. After taking the end of the rope his wrists were bound to, Thomas threw it over a branch before giving it a pull, stretching Foy up by his arms. Beau took hold of the rope and held it taunt as Thomas delivered punch after punch to Foy's face.

"Now ya are going to learn your place... Never, never think that ya are equal to me!" He spat in the man's face, spittle flying from his lips. Foy's bruising face looked even darker in the blackness, and he clenched his jaw as Thomas gave him mocking pats on the cheek.

The dark-haired man loosened the long whip, found in the horse barn, in his hand as he stepped a few feet behind Foy. His arm came back and then lunged forward, releasing the tail of the whip with fury across his exposed back. Foy's arms tightened from the pain, pulling his body upward. Another blow was delivered, releasing a cry from his lips. Thomas spat insults and curses at the man hanging, helpless, before him. He delivered lash after lash, leaving Foy to hang from his wrists with no more strength to hold himself up. His back stretched from his weight and the pull of his arms, opening the fresh wounds further, and he soon lost consciousness.

The birds whistled as the morning light broke through the darkness. Coco was upstairs when she heard Albert yelling out her name. She rushed down the stairs to find her father grabbing his hat and pulling on his boots.

"Take this gun and lock the doors," he said, pushing a rifle into her hand.

"What's happening?" she asked breathlessly.

"Foy isn't here—something must have happened. I'm going to search the property for him. Shoot anyone who isn't me. Just cock this, point it, and pull the trigger, like I taught ya." He moved her hands in the positions necessary to handle the gun. "And shoot to kill!" He gave her a grave look before he rushed out the door.

Albert surveyed the ground out front and found traces of blood and hoof tracks. After saddling his horse, he followed the tracks to Foy's cabin. Everything seemed distant and unnervingly surreal with the cool morning breeze and brilliant sky. Albert entered the cabin, cautious and with gun cocked.

After he cleared the cabin and returned outside, he called out, "Foy!" As Albert circled the corner of the house, his eyes fell on a black heap under the nearby tree. "Foy!" he shouted as he rushed to the man. "My God," he muttered as he knelt beside him, placing his hand near the mouth to check if he was breathing.

He holstered his gun and carefully lifted the man into his arms. After carrying him into the cabin, he laid him face down on his cot. Albert's breaths came in spurts and his jaw clenched at the sight of his friend's damaged body. He hitched the wagon, laid Foy down in it, and transported him back to the house before carrying him into the room next to the kitchen. Albert covered his buttocks with a sheet and then moved to the kitchen for towels and water.

"Coco!" he called out as he filled a bowl. "Coco!" he shouted again with aggravation.

Albert set the bowl down and walked down the hall at a severe pace. As he rounded the corner to the main sitting room, he stopped abruptly. In front of him, Coco was being held by

Thomas, a pistol at her temple. A cold barrel pressed into the back of Albert's head.

"There he is," Thomas mocked.

Coco looked at her father, and tears spilled down her cheeks at the sight of blood staining the front of his shirt.

"What do ya want?"

The dark-haired man laughed diabolically. "What do I want? Restitution!"

"For what?" Albert pressed.

"For all of this bullshit!"

"I gave ya shelter and food..."

"Yeah, for working like a slave, and then ya bring us in and disrespect us! I don't aim to be disrespected now." Thomas spit a stream of brown juice onto the floor. "Tie him up," he ordered Beau. The young man directed Albert, under pistol aim, where to sit. "Ya try anything funny and I swear to God I'll shoot her brains out." Albert didn't struggle and allowed Beau to bind his hands and feet with rope.

"Ya find your nigga out there?" the man continued, letting go of his hold of Coco and looking her up and down. "Was he dead?" He raised his hand and ran his finger down her jawline.

"Let's get this done and get out of here, Tom. We've been lagging long enough." Beau shifted his weight to the other leg but quickly shifted back with a grimace and a grunt.

"Where do ya keep your notes?" Thomas asked Albert.

"My parlor safe in my office. Across the foyer, down the hall."

"Go check it out," he commanded Beau.

His ruddy-haired accomplice was gone for a few minutes before he returned. "It's there. What's the code?"

"09-23-45."

Beau left but returned shortly. "That ain't it," he said.

Thomas walked up to Albert and hit him across the face. "What is the code?" he yelled.

Albert spit a stream of blood out of his mouth. "That is the code," he said as he raised his head from the strike. "Maybe he doesn't know how to open a safe," he mocked.

"Ya put the numbers in right?" Thomas fumed back to Beau.

"Well, yeah, I put the numbers in right!" Beau yelled back.

"Ya ever open a safe before?" Thomas continued over the other man's voice.

"No, but I'm no idiot!"

Albert chuckled, revealing his bloody teeth. "He's not turning the dial right."

"Well, God damn it!" Thomas seethed. "Ya watch them," he ordered as he left the room. Soon, there was yelling from Albert's parlor.

Beau strained to understand what he was saying as he stood, gun pointed at Albert, at the entrance. He cursed as he walked from the sitting room and made his way down the hall to Thomas. Coco looked at Albert, who gave her a nod, and she quickly made her way to him and began fumbling with the rope securing his wrists.

Soon, Beau reentered the room and jerked her forcefully away from her father. "I wouldn't be doing that," he said, repositioning the gun in her direction.

Thomas whooped from down the hall as he skipped back toward the sitting room. "All right, gather all the guns and let's go. You're coming with us," he said, grabbing Coco by the arm.

She jerked away from him. "I'm not," she growled through gritted teeth.

Thomas reached up and struck her across the cheek. Albert stood, feet still bound, but his action was quickly met with the stock of Beau's rifle to the stomach. When he buckled over, he was knocked down with another strike to the head.

"You're coming with us for a ways, to make sure he doesn't do anything stupid!" Thomas grabbed Coco again by the arm and yanked her out of the house.

"Don't do anything rash now," Beau said to the plantation

owner, who remained where he'd been knocked down, looking up through the swelling already taking hold of the left side of his face. Thomas yelled from outside for Beau to hurry up, so he pulled his rifle back and gave Albert a couple more strikes before he ran out of the house.

Coco's hands were bound with a rope held by Thomas, who was already sitting in his saddle when his partner came barging through the front door and down the veranda steps.

"Hurry up! Let's go!" Thomas urged as he kicked his horse and started down the road, Coco jogging to keep up. The two rode at a trot until the plantation house was out of sight before they slowed their horses to a walk.

Coco breathed heavily from the foreign cardiovascular exercise. She stopped for a moment to inhale until the rope pulled taut and she had to move forward again. "Please let me go," she pleaded between pants, but her words went ignored as the men bantered about their victory at the Toussaint plantation.

CHAPTER TWENTY-ONE

THE MEN HAD BEEN on the road about thirty minutes with Coco trailing behind them, occasionally looking over her shoulder for any sign of help. Suddenly, she sneezed, and the men turned on their horses to look at her.

"I almost forgot she was back there," Beau said, smiling sardonically.

"I didn't," Thomas responded with a narrow glare.

"How long are we going to trail her with us? We're not going to be able to keep this slow pace the whole way."

"We could sell her."

"There's no one buying slaves right now! Besides, we would have to double back into a whole different territory just to find someone willing to buy her."

"Just let the bitch go." They stopped their horses and Thomas turned and stared at Coco again. He dismounted and stood next to his horse, his tongue playing with the tobacco in his lip. "Let's have a little fun, shall we?" he said as he began rolling up the rope, drawing Coco closer to him.

Beau dismounted as well and stepped around his horse to

stand next to Thomas. A frown creased his brow. "What do ya mean?"

"I mean let's have us a little *fun*." He pronounced the last word in a slow drawl.

Coco pulled against the rope as he drew her in. "No," she snarled. "Stop!"

"Man, just let her go," Beau said.

"If you don't want to fuck her, that's your choice, but I'm not letting her go until I get my dick wet… Just watching her struggle is exciting me."

She pulled forcefully against the rope, digging her feet into the dusty path as her wrist's grew raw. Then Thomas abruptly let go of the rope, sending Coco backward onto the ground. He laughed garishly as the fall jolted her, and she struggled back to her feet before attempting to run away.

"Now, now," he said, picking up the end again before she could get it out of his reach. He pulled the rope quickly until she stood in front of him.

Coco spit in his face. He wiped it with his leather-gloved hand before its backside came across her cheek. After forcing her to the side of the road, Thomas backed her up against a tree. He ripped her shirt and tore her pants buttons open. She cried for help, but no one was near the wooded road. As she struggled against him, Coco clawed down his face, her nails raking up flesh with the motion.

He yelled out from the sudden, stinging pain. "Bitch!" His fist came down on her face, knocking her to the ground with her head propped up by the trunk of the tree. After pulling her pants down, he climbed on top of her.

Beau stepped up close behind him and watched as Thomas raped her. He couldn't turn his eyes away and slowly became aroused while he watched. A sudden cold sensation, like ice, moved smoothly across his neck, and his eyes grew wide as blood spilled from his body before it crumbled to the ground, lifeless. Albert raised his pistol with a straight, steady arm and, at close range, shot Thomas in the back of the head. Brain and blood splattered through the air, covering Coco's face. Her mouth opened as she gasped in shock and she looked up to see her father, smoke still filtering from the barrel of his raised pistol.

Albert's eye was swollen and his face as cold and soulless as the darkness of Hell. He lowered the gun and holstered it in the waist of his pants. Still bound and under the weight of Thomas, Coco didn't move until her father stepped forward and pushed the body off of her. He gently closed her torn blouse before he untied her wrists and threw the rope to the side. She trembled violently, but tears wouldn't fall. There was a sick feeling in her gut that wrapped tighter with every second like a serpent around its prey, and she could hardly breath. Albert, gently reaching up with the back of his forefinger, touched her cheek where the skin was broken and had reddened from the strike. His chest heaved in anger and his eye glazed. He turned away from her long enough to yell out in a furious growl with his face turned upward toward the sky. He shook with fury. Taking a deep breath through his nostrils, he exhaled through his mouth and tried calming himself before looking back at his beloved daughter.

"Come on," he said softly, his eyes keeping full contact with hers. He stood and helped her weak body up. She clenched her shirt closed as he removed his belt, knelt to raise her pants, and then wrapped the belt around her waist, tightening it to hold the pants in place. "Can you mount the horse?" he asked, resting his hand on her shoulder. She swallowed and gave a nod. Albert helped her over to the horse and held him while she climbed into the saddle.

Coco watched her father as he turned and looked at the two dead men. He grabbed the first and threw him over the back of the second horse before going over to Thomas's body. His face was expressionless, set like flint. He grabbed the knife from its sheath and plunged it in the dead man's torso. One thrust of the blade was not enough to settle the raging beast in Albert's chest. The blade cut through strike after strike. Coco turned away from the bloody scene, but the sound of the violent rage of her father strangely comforted the sickening fear in her chest. Albert took the mangled body and threw it over the horse. After taking the horses by the reins, he led them off the road and into the woods, back to the plantation.

When they reached the front of the house, he helped her off the horse. "Go inside and clean up," he said.

She bit her lower lip. "You going to bury them?"

"No," he said flatly. The blood on his arms and hands had begun to dry and crack, but blood still fell in a fresh stream from the bodies on the back of the horse. "Go inside now. I will be right back—I'll be quick."

She nodded and slowly mounted the steps of the veranda. Inside, Coco poured water into the tub and then slowly lowered herself into it. She splashed water on her face, despite the sting it caused from the cut, over and over until she broke down into tears. Drawing her knees in to her chest, she cried. She sat in the tub until she could no longer bear the cold of the water and began shivering.

After Coco bathed, she dressed herself and headed downstairs. Albert sat at the bottom of the steps, waiting for her, also washed and changed. She paused next to him and then sat on the stairs as well.

"What did you do with them?"

"Took them out into a field and dumped them. They don't deserve even a shallow grave... Let the birds and beasts pick at their bones." Albert swallowed and lowered his head. "I'm sorry," he finally said after a pause. "I should've protected you better."

Quietly, tears rolled down Coco's cheeks. "It wasn't your fault," she said. Without another word, Albert put his arm around his daughter's shoulders and pulled her in to his chest. He sniffled as he struggled to hold back his emotions while he held her.

The evening came, and Albert directed Coco to lie on the settee in the upper parlor. He tucked her in with a blanket and took her tea to sip while he attended to Foy downstairs, who was in and out of sleep.

"What happened to da men that did this to me?" Foy asked, looking up through the corner of his eye as he lay on his stomach on the bed.

"I sent them to Hell."

"Good," he said sucking in air through his gritted teeth as Albert changed the gauze on his back. "Looks like they got a pretty good lick on ya."

Albert huffed in his throat. "I'll be fine."

"How's Coco?" Silence followed. "I said how's Coco?" Foy asked a little louder.

Albert cleared his throat. "She'll be okay."

"She *will* be okay? So she's not okay right now... Those bastards hurt our Coco? I want to see her! Where she at?" Foy growled. He tried to move but was quickly stopped by the pain and grimaced.

"Now be still, old man. She's upstairs," he said, holding Foy down by his arm.

"They touch her? Tell me. They defile her?" Albert didn't respond. His hands kept moving to dress the wounds. A tear fell from Foy's dark eye, now haloed with a faint gray, and streamed down his nose as he lay on his side on the bed. "They should've never got past me..."

"It's not ya fault." Albert finished up and gave the man a drink of water. "Try to sleep. I'll be back to check on ya later."

Coco was outside by dawn the next day, taking buckets of water to the garden. Albert saw her from the kitchen window but didn't bother his daughter. By midmorning, she had stepped back in.

"Good morning," she said as she moved past Albert and poured a cup of water.

"Mornin'," he replied.

"I couldn't sleep last night," she offered up freely as she took a drink.

"Me neither." There was a pause. "Ya can leave the work to me, ya know."

She shook her head. "I need something to occupy me. I can't just sit around and be haunted."

A heavy knock sounded at the door, followed by a man's voice calling out. Coco's eyes widened and her heart raced from fear as Albert laced his fingers around the handle of his pistol and walked to the front of the house, his daughter a few feet behind.

"Who is it?" Albert bellowed deeply.

"Colonel Paine with the Union Army, ordering you and the occupants of the house to step out with your hands in the air!"

He cracked the door and peered out before opening it completely. The colonel stood tall with a full dark beard that contrasted with the gray head of hair that stood up wildly around the part. The blue troop around him had eyes narrowed and guns in place, ready to fire.

"What is this?" Albert demanded.

"Step on out here, sir. Is anyone else in the house?"

"My daughter," he said, moving farther outside onto the veranda.

"Call her out," the man ordered. Albert called to her, and Coco stepped out shyly onto the veranda. Paine's brown eyes looked back and forth from her to her father. "We are looking for two men—two Confederate soldiers being held as prisoners of war and awaiting to be shipped to Gratiot Prison in St. Louis. They escaped a few days back, and we've tracked them here." As he spoke, three Federal troops moved up the veranda and made their way into the house, guns raised.

"It has only been me and my daughter since the war started."

About that time, a soldier stepped out of the house. "Colonel, you'll want to see this."

"Watch them," Paine said as he walked past them. He was gone for a few minutes before he returned. Coco stepped off the veranda and stood close to her father in the front of the house. "The man in the back room... Who is he?"

"His name is Foy. He used to be a slave of mine until he was able to purchase his freedom. He still works with me and has a cabin on the corner of the property."

Paine narrowed his eyes. "He is beaten beyond what I have ever seen. Did you do that to him?"

Albert rubbed his lips together. "No, I found him like that next to his cabin yesterday morning. I put him in the wagon and transported him here, so I could care for him."

The colonel walked closer to them and looked at his face. "That's quite the swelling on your eye," he said. "Looks like you developed quite a mark on the face too," he added as he looked at Coco, whose eyes were cast downward.

"Are you sure you haven't seen two men come around here? One dark headed and mouthy, the other fairer with pale eyes. You wouldn't be hiding them somewhere, would you?" A shadow fell over Albert's face. "Maybe hiding them somewhere in the cane?" Paine raised the hand holding his leather gloves and took a step. "Maybe in the barns?" He slapped the gloves into the palm of his other hand.

"I don't know who ya are talking about, but ya are welcome to search the property and the buildings."

"I have a better idea. We set these fields on fire."

Coco's head snapped up. "Why would you do that?" Albert reached up and touched her arm.

"Do you have something you want to say to change my mind?" the colonel asked, but she said nothing more as she looked him straight in the eyes.

The troop did a thorough search of the house and closest barn before the men took torches to the dry fields. The fire didn't take long to spread, and the red flames reached high into the afternoon, darkening the blue sky with billowing smoke. After the colonel felt he'd conducted a thorough search, he gave a severe word of warning to Albert before leaving with his men.

"We have to wet the ground around the barn and the house… and dig a firewall," Albert said once they were gone. "It's too hot and dry for a fire that large to stay contained." His voice was urgent. "I need your help."

Coco matched his stride as they rushed to the barn. Her father grabbed a shovel and a bucket. "Come on," he ordered, "we'll start over here." He led her to the side of the barn closest to the cane field. "We'll just run a straight line." He motioned with a stiff hand. "I'll start digging a trench. You bring buckets of water and wet the ground on that side"—he motioned to the closest fields—"and then we will wet the ground on the other side. Okay?"

He shoved his tool into the dirt, and Coco ran to the well to fill the bucket. They worked fast and tirelessly but made very slow progress. Coco pushed her body as it felt fatigue, nearly crumbling to the ground. "Make sure it's good and wet," Albert repeated as she poured the water onto the dry ground. She ran back to the well, finally collapsing under draining emotions, out of sight of her father. "Stop," she said to herself in a low, grating voice as the angry tears fell. Hitting her forehead with the palm of her hand before clenching her fist and pounding her chest, she growled and pulled from deep within the strength to continue. An hour of struggling had passed when they looked up and saw Mr. Thompson riding toward them.

"Ya have another shovel?" he yelled out from atop his horse.

"In the barn!" Albert responded as he continued digging.

Soon, Mr. Thompson returned and began digging next to him. "How the hell did this happen?" he asked.

"A Federal troop came by, thinkin' we were hiding Confederate soldiers… They set fire to the fields—make sure no one was hiding in them."

"Damn Yankees!"

262 | JENNIFER SPURGEON

Hours passed and the fire continued edging closer to the dug trench. They finally had to consider that what they had done was the best they could do. Coco's heart raced as she took just one more bucket and poured it on the ground.

"I'll have hell to pay when I get back to the missus," Mr. Thompson was saying when she returned. He regarded her and gave her a nod.

"I sure do thank ya for ya help."

"Yeah, well, we did what we could. All there is to do now is hope to God it doesn't reach the house. What the hell happened to your face?" he asked after a moment.

"Accident fixing the wagon," Albert lied. Mr. Thompson's eyes narrowed as they shifted from Albert to the wound on his daughter cheek.

"They never found the soldiers, huh?"

Albert pushed his lower lips out with a shake of the head, "Wouldn't know."

Mr. Thompson gave a nod and didn't inquire further. Albert offered to give Mr. Thompson something for his help, but their neighbor said it was unnecessary. After he left, Coco and her father sat on the back steps, anxiously watching the fire consume everything in its path.

"Do you think that will work?" she asked sullenly.

"I hope so." After sitting in silence, he finally asked, "How are ya doing?"

"How am I supposed to be? I don't have time to even feel anything... All of this is worse than my most horrid nightmare. I'm just in shock, I guess." Albert remained quiet. Words seemed trivial at this point. Coco continued; her eyes unfocused on the dancing flames in the distance. "As if it wasn't going to be hard enough to find a man who would want me. Now I've been used... defiled... It's been taken from me, and I no longer have it to give. It wasn't his to take. I didn't want him." Her voice lowered into an angry note.

"That's not what defines ya," Albert said, looking down and fidgeting with his fingers. "He violated ya, but his crime does not make ya used up or of less value. Makes me angry to even think ya feel that way."

"Men want virgins for wives."

"No, that doesn't make a damn, Coco. They want a good woman for a wife—someone who will stand with them to fight when life is against them...like you just did. Someone who is faithful and caring. You are all of those things."

"I'm not sure I even want a man to ever touch me again. I'm so disgusted."

"When someone touches ya out of love and not out of hate, you will see the difference. I don't want ya to lose who ya are, Coco. Please don't let this take my beautiful girl away from me." He looked at her, her face set like stone.

The fire burned for hours but did not stretch its consuming arms toward the house. A morose spirit fell over the plantation, and for the next few days, Coco would sit with Foy to keep him company and dress his wounds. Their friendship strengthened as he began to open up and tell her things he had long kept silent. She found comfort in his stories.

As the weeks passed and August took hold of the summer, Albert found himself sitting with Mr. Thompson over a bottle of whiskey. The Battle of Baton Rouge had taken the lives of over eight hundred men, including Mr. Thompson's oldest son and Marianne's husband, Gabe, the first of Mr. Thompson's losses. Albert had received a letter from Marianne telling him about how she planned to bring her children, save Ashley, who was still in uniform, home in their time of need.

Coco was not welcome in Mrs. Thompson's house, so she remained behind with Foy after giving instructions to her father to give Marianne her sympathy. Albert stood, looking out through the window, in Mr. Thompson's office, a tumbler of whiskey in his hand. Mr. Thompson sat in a chair, his head leaning on the hand shielding his eyes. Mrs. Thompson avoided being in the same room as Albert.

"They're here," Albert said quietly when he saw the carriage making its way up the drive.

Marianne stepped out of it, her face covered with a black veil, and was met by the wailing of Mrs. Thompson, who took her immediately into her arms before embracing the children. Marianne thanked her quietly and with solemn emotion. She gripped Mr. Thompson's hand softly before reaching her father.

"Hey, Daddy," she said with a quivering lip. He took her in his arms and held her. Then he released her and looked into her eyes as he gripped her hands.

The family went into the house and sat in somber conversation about the war and Gabe's death before taking a turn to remembering times of joy. Mrs. Thompson insisted with unwavering mind that they stay at the Thompson plantation instead of with Albert. He had no mind to argue and cause more stress for his daughter. When the hours passed and he was leaving, Marianne walked him out.

"I'll come by tomorrow," she said as she hugged him.

"Anytime ya like. Please don't hesitate."

Marianne kept her word and went out to visit Albert the next day. "Where are the children?" he asked when he greeted his daughter.

"Mrs. Thompson didn't think I should bring them over. She put up a howl about it."

"Shouldn't come over? Why the hell not?" Marianne glanced to Coco before looking back at her father. "Ya can't bring them over because of my other daughter?" Albert frowned. "They are my goddamn grandchildren too! Who the hell does she think she is?"

"Father, please." Marianne sighed. "Ya know how that woman is...and I'm just too beside myself to argue with her." Albert consented to bite his tongue and welcomed her into the house.

"My, it sure seems different around here," she said as she paced the sitting room, twisting her hanky.

"It is different everywhere," Albert agreed.

"Yes…" she mumbled. "Caroline, ya sure are quiet these days," she said, inhaling as if she struggled to even breathe in the uncomfortable atmosphere as she looked at Coco on the settee. "Not the fiery, ambitious girl I remember from years ago." She offered a snappy grin that didn't last like the memories did.

"Experience changes things," Coco responded.

Marianne lifted her brow as she blinked in agreement. "Yes, well, I'm sorry that the madness of these times we find ourselves living in has robbed ya of youthful experiences."

"I'm sorry these times have robbed you of your husband," Coco said.

Marianne pressed her lips together and lowered her head. "Ya know…at the beginning of the secession of the states, I had one point of view: Fight for state rights and the honor of the South," she said, lowering her voice and raising a fist. "Long live the heritages of the Confederacy. But I had no idea it would come to this… And for what? That I might be widowed and my children orphans? And still I have a son in the war—my firstborn, pulled from my womb!"

She became emotional as her voice rose. "Will he survive this massacre, or will he be returned to me in an oak box like his father? And again, I say, for what? They can take the pride of the South and shove it up their asses." She reached up and wiped the streams of tears falling involuntarily down her cheeks. She lowered herself onto the settee next to Coco. Dismay flooded the room. "Please, someone else say something...let's talk about something different."

"You haven't said anything about the burned fields. Or did you even notice?"

"Coco," Albert said in a chiding tone.

"Well, I figured she'd want to know what happened," she added, matter-of-fact.

"What?" Marianne asked with a sniff of her nose as she looked back and forth between Albert and Coco. "What happened? What is she talking about?"

"Two men came here last month. They nearly killed Foy by whipping him. They beat our father, and they raped me..." Coco's voice didn't quiver when she spoke. Albert shifted in his seat and took a deep lungful of air.

"What?" Marianne frowned.

"The next morning, Union troops came looking for the men—Confederate escapees—and when they couldn't find them, they burned the fields."

Marianne looked to their father. "Why didn't ya write to me about this?"

"What was I supposed to say?" Albert asked.

"I don't know, how about just tell me what happened?" she said loudly before putting her hand on Coco's shoulder. "I'm so sorry."

"I don't need pity," the young woman said. "I was merely telling you how this war has affected us... All of us."

Marianne broke down into tears. Later, she caught Albert in the kitchen and reproached him again. "Why didn't ya write?"

"How was I supposed to write ya something like that? We survived, and we're fine now."

"Yes, I can see how fine ya are," she said sarcastically. "The girl can't can even show emotion or shed tears about her assault!"

"Well, what am I supposed to do?"

"She needs a woman to talk to."

"So, talk to her."

Marianne blinked rapidly. That evening, as the sun was setting, she approached Coco. "I'm going to take a walk before heading back to the Thompsons'. Would ya like to walk with me?"

Coco put down her book. "Sure."

The two slowly began walking west. The sun was on the horizon, shooting out strips of orange and deep hues of pink, and a warm breeze carried the tangy smell of the late summer soil. They walked in silence for a while, just listening to the evening sounds.

"I'm sorry for what happened," Marianne said softly.

"It doesn't matter."

"It does, though," she countered. "It matters a great deal." She stopped and turned to Coco. "How are ya doin'?"

"How do ya think I'm doing?" Coco scoffed. "My virginity was taken from me and I was beaten." Marianne didn't say anything as she waited for her to add more. "It was awful... It hurt me. I can't sleep at night. I—I feel so...dirty. And...and I don't ever, ever want to be around a man. When I think too much, sometimes I can hardly be around Father without feeling disgusted"—her voice cracked—"and I love Father."

"Listen," Marianne said nearly forcefully, "you'll need time to heal from this, but ya have to let yourself heal. Holding on to the pain forever will rob ya of ya life. And I'm afraid just being here, and by yourself, will just make ya fall deeper into melancholia. There's nothing here, and ya need distraction and people.

"I know we don't know each other that well. I mean"—she chuckled with a smile—"ya was only a tiny thing when Gabe and I married..." She trailed off at the mention of her late husband. "And after what happened with my brother...well I blamed ya and didn't want anything to do with ya. But I was wrong to judge you...

"We're different," she finally continued, taking Coco's hand in her own, "but ya still my half-sister. That makes us part of each other.

"What if ya was to come back to New Orleans with me and the children? We could help each other, me with my heartbreak and you with ya pain. The city has changed a lot. It's been under Union rule now for some time...and I don't even care." She sniffed her running nose and looked back out over the horizon. "I don't care who wins anymore," she said in a soft voice. "I just want this damn war to be over before it claims my son like it did my husband." They stood for some time, watching the sun as it slipped below the skyline. "Will ya at least think about it?" Marianne asked.

"I will," Coco said, still staring off into the distance.

The two returned to the house, and Marianne said goodbye for the evening. Coco didn't say anything about what she and Marianne had talked about during their walk. She retired to her room and settled in her bed with a book. She turned through several pages but couldn't recall the parts she had read. After getting up, she walked over to her window and opened it wide. She looked out into the dark fields lit dimly by the full moon. Hours passed, and soon her mind slipped away from all form of thought as the breeze blew against her cheeks, bringing with it the sweet scent of the promise of rain.

CHAPTER TWENTY-TWO

THE STORM KEPT the sun from shining the next morning as the drops fell heavy against the house. Coco opened her eyes from sleep after ten o'clock, the first time in weeks that she had been able to fall asleep during the night without nightmares or restlessness. She lay there, listening to the raindrops hit her window and the roof. The deep roll of thunder was a welcome comfort. Finally, she urged herself out of bed and, instead of dressing herself, merely tied her wrap around her nightgown before she went downstairs.

"It's a good day for that," Albert remarked as he poured himself another cup of coffee.

"I used to hate storms. But now I find an unusual comfort in them… The darkness when it should be light, the wind howling against the eaves of the house, the rolling thunder and occasional crack of lightning lighting up the sky…"

"Very poetic." Albert smiled as he handed her a cup of coffee. "You should be a writer."

Coco offered him a smile. "I want to go with Marianne when she goes back to New Orleans," she said without hesitation after a pause.

"What?" he asked, shocked.

"She mentioned it when we went for our walk. I've given it some thought, and I think I should." Albert didn't say anything as he pondered what she was saying. "It would give me something new to occupy my mind and help me stop thinking about...things."

"I'm just not sure that would be the right decision right now. It's not safe."

"It's not safe here, Father," she countered. His countenance fell, like a child's when he is told no, and Coco immediately corrected her words. "I meant it's not safe anywhere. New Orleans is under Union hold now, so I can't imagine them behaving poorly just because of the color of my skin."

"Bad men are everywhere, Coco! North, South—it doesn't make a damn bit of difference."

"I'm just saying... I read the article where the president wrote emancipation. If that goes into effect, then the Union doorstep would be the safest place for me to be!" Coco's heart began to race the more she talked about the possibility of her going to live in the city. "I can come back any time," she said softly, noting her father's downcast face. "It would do me some good, and the company would do well for Marianne also."

Albert slowly nodded as his eyes stayed lowered. "If ya insist on going, I'll consent."

Marianne stayed with the family for two weeks before she gathered up her children and Coco and left for New Orleans during the end of the second week in September.

"I'm so glad ya comin' with me," she said, taking Coco's gloved hand in her own. "This will be good for both of us."

The trip was long, and Coco was glad when they reached Marianne's home and she could get out and stretch her legs. The house faced a street in the garden district and was fenced in with beautiful black wrought iron. Coco looked up at the large white three-story house before she stepped through the iron gate and made her way to the front door. The children ran past her and were greeted by the black maidservant, dressed in uniform, as she opened the door.

"I'll have Betsy show ya the guest room. Ya will be very comfortable."

Betsy showed her to her room on the third floor. Once she shut the door, Coco removed her hat and walked over to the window, where there was a view of the street. As she looked out, she noticed Union soldiers coming in and out of a neighboring house. Curiosity creased her brow as she watched the street activity. Coco didn't know how long she stood there, gazing outside, before a knock came at the door.

Marianne entered. "How do ya find ya room?" she asked.

"It's beautiful."

"Once you're settled in, you'll find it quite comfortable. Anything ya need, just let Betsy know."

Coco offered a nod as she looked back out the window. "There are several soldiers, aren't there?" she asked as Marianne strode to stand beside her. "There's a house they keep going in and out of."

"Ah, yes, that house is now used for Federal business and Union strategizing. A lot of these houses were abandoned when the battle started. People grabbed what they could carry and ran, leaving their comfortable houses for soldiers to luxuriate in."

"You're lucky they didn't burn down the houses. My friend Liza lives in Baton Rouge and said the colonel of the Union army ordered the homes destroyed so they wouldn't afford shelter to any potential attackers. She writes that the troops are encamped throughout the entire city."

"As they are here. You will see."

"Was it bad?"

Marianne snorted. "Bad? In terms of war casualties, no, but it was terrifying. The cannon fire was louder than claps of thunder, fire and smoke filled the air, and there was the continuous sound

272 | JENNIFER SPURGEON

of battle cries and gunfire. I don't blame most of them for leaving."

"Why didn't you flee?"

"To where?"

"You could've come back to the plantation."

"No." She shook her head. "It wouldn't have made a bit of difference. I just wanted to maintain life as close to normal as I could for my children." She fidgeted with the drape over the window frame. "Would ya like to take some tea with me? We can sit out on the veranda and chat."

Coco heartily agreed, and the two took some time in each other's company before she expressed a need for a nap. Coco closed herself in her room and lay down in the fresh, white sheets. The rest was sweet, and when she woke, she stretched and took a deep breath in, looking around herself with a new resounding sense of comfort.

She dressed herself and then started making her way down the hall and first flight of stairs, but when she reached the next hall, she heard a noise and stopped where she stood. Against her better judgment, Coco slowly moved toward the grunting. The door to the room was open wide, and she stepped over to the frame to see who was making the noise. There was Marianne, sitting naked on a desk and being taken by a man with only his socks on. Coco watched for a minute as the man pushed himself into her and Marianne's arms came around his shoulders to support the movement, her sounds apparent proof of enjoyment.

Coco turned quickly and headed down to the main level. She pushed through the front door forcefully and went to the railing of the veranda. Gripping it with both hands, she leaned forward and exhaled deeply. Her eyes narrowed as she raised her head and looked out into the bright day. There was a different smell in the city than in the air at the plantation. As she looked around, she noticed a bench on the front lawn under the canopy of an oak.

She took another deep breath and then walked to the bench and sat down.

After a few minutes, Coco looked up to see the blue-uniformed general move down the steps and walk the path to the iron gate, where his horse awaited him. He seemed either to not notice Coco or not care about her presence—his steps were resolute. Shortly after, Marianne walked outside to where Coco sat.

"It's such a beautiful day," she said as she reached down and plucked a clover. There was a pause. "I know ya saw me. I watched ya scamper away."

"I don't understand," Coco said. "You're married. I thought you loved your husband."

"God, Coco." Marianne chortled as she swallowed and looked out across the street. "It's just an act. You can make it out of love, or you can just make it."

"Your husband just died… How could you do that?"

"Don't you dare judge me." Her voice was as sharp as a knife. "I have been alone during this war, surviving and wondering how the hell I will do what is necessary to protect my children." Tears filled her eyes. "If fucking a general is what it takes to ensure their protection until this damn war is over, then I will demoralize myself."

Coco looked at Marianne, her face flushed, and jaw flexed from her clenched teeth and pressed lips. "I don't mean to judge," she said. "I don't know what it's like to be in your shoes." She swallowed the knot rising in her stomach. "The act, the thought of it, it disgusts me. It's just…"

Marianne took a step toward her and asked, "May I sit?" Coco nodded. "You will heal…in time," she said. The two sat for some time, settling in to the comfort of the silent support.

The days began to turn into weeks, and Coco found herself settling in and soon enjoying the distractions of the city. She joined Marianne often in her trips to the market, where the sight of Union soldiers was ever-present. Marianne would whisper into her ear, "You'll get used to it." There was hardly a Southern man in New Orleans, unless he was too old or too young for battle.

Coco slowly became familiar with seeing Union soldiers riding the streets. She wrote to Albert every Sunday of the goings-on of the week and when new ironclads would port in New Orleans or head up the river like "dragons clad in armor." Her fear soon turned to curiosity, and she would keep a notepad with her and sketch out drawings with brief, story-like descriptions of the scenes around her.

One afternoon in mid-October 1962, as Coco sketched out an image of the Union soldiers unloading cargo from the ship Madison, she waited for Marianne to return from the postal office.

"Ya have a letter here," she said as she approached Coco before proceeding to open her own. Coco smiled when she saw it was addressed from Liza. Suddenly, Marianne crumbled where she stood. No sound was made.

Coco's eyes grew wide as she jumped to where her half-sister knelt, holding the letter. "What is it?" she asked breathlessly. The paper Marianne held shook as she stared at it. Coco gripped her shoulders. "Marianne," she said, gently stroking her cheek before taking the letter out of her shaking hands. Her eyes ran over the page quickly. "Son, Ashley…wounded in battle… His—" Her hand came up over her mouth.

"My son…" Marianne's voice cracked as her eyes shifted.

Coco put her arms around her shoulders. "Come on," she said, helping her stand. "Let's get you home quickly."

Once they were back at the house, Coco set Marianne up in the sitting room with pillows and a cup of tea. She sat with her for hours, neither saying a word, until Betsy announced the general. Coco looked at Marianne, whose eyes were beginning to swell from the tears. She nodded and motioned for Coco to leave the room.

The general approached her. "What's wrong?" he asked kindly.

"My son has been terribly wounded. I just received word of it."

"I'm sorry."

"This foolish war... He's only a boy of fifteen!"

"But he lives?"

Marianne looked up at the general with fiery eyes. "Yes, he still lives, but what quality of life will he have now?" Her lower lip quivered.

The general sat next to her and took her hand in his. "But he lives," he said with a soothing smile as he gazed gently at her.

She slowly nodded but waited a moment before she spoke again. "They are not sending him home because New Orleans is under Federal power, for fear of him being placed in a prisoner-of-war camp." The general broke eye contact. "Is there anything that can be done? Can you send a letter? Let my boy come back to me... It's already been a year and a half since I've seen him."

"I don't think you understand the full extent of what you are asking."

"I do, though, and I would be forever grateful and indebted to ya." Marianne placed her head on the general's shoulder and nestled into his embrace, encouraging him to take her.

It was December and the day was overcast and breezy, making it a cool fifty-two degrees out. Coco stood with Marianne and the children on the front patio as the carriage pulled in front of the gate and a man stepped out. After moving to the back of the carriage, he unhitched and lowered an invalid chair, wooden with red padding for the seat and back. He brought it to the side and fastened the wheels in place before reaching into the carriage, lifting Ashley under his arms, and placing him in the chair. He opened the gate and began to wheel the boy toward the house. There Ashley sat, both legs amputated above the knee. He was skinny with the worn face of an old man, yet it was still smooth and too young to grow scruff. His gray eyes were sunken in and lackluster.

When he was halfway to the house, Marianne went down the steps to meet him. "My boy," she said as she touched his face.

Then her head fell upon his shoulder and she began to cry. He embraced her, and they held each other until the other children demanded Ashley's attention as well.

His demeanor had much changed since Marianne kissed him goodbye and watched him march for war. He hardly spoke or ate, and at night he would dream of fire falling from the sky with the blast of cannon fire. One night, his terror jolted him upward so badly that, in confusion of where he was, he moved to the edge of the bed and tried to get up to run away but instead fell with a thud to the floor. Too upset and embarrassed to cry out for help, he instead reached up and struggled to pull what he could off of the bed and slept on the cold floor the rest of the night.

The next day, Ashley ordered Betsy to bring him a pour of Old Crow as the family sat in the living room. Betsy looked at Marianne for approval; she gave a nod. Betsy soon returned and poured him the drink.

"Your grandfathers will be coming down for Christmas. They are excited to see you," Marianne said.

He didn't say anything but offered her a faint smile. "Leave the bottle," he commanded as Betsy began to walk away. Again, she looked at Marianne.

"Ashley, dear, don't you think one glass will be enough?" his mother kindly interjected.

"No, I do not."

"Well I do," she said.

He spoke slowly as he gazed into the fire he sat next to. "I have killed men, and I have stood next to men who have been killed, their bodies blown to bits and scattered over the earth they are made of. Did you know the entrails of man has a distinct odor?" He paused as his voice took on an eerily serene tone. "I have been hungry, I have been cold, I have been thirsty, and I have been scared of death… But I have looked death in his hollow eyes down the barrel of my musket," he continued, raising both his arms as if looking down the barrel of a rifle. "I shot my gun in a manic state, taking as many lives as I could, sending souls to the darkness of the grave, knowing that if I didn't, then they would take mine. I did this until it became natural... I would go into battle as calmly as I would to my meal when hungry."

He stopped and looked down at his lap, the room completely silent except for the sound of the dancing flames. Tears fell down Marianne's cheeks. "I have earned my stripes for manhood," he began again in a harsher tone, "and I come home to a mother who wants to treat me like I'm still a boy. If I want more than one glass, I can drink more than one glass. And if I want to drink the whole damn bottle until I fall out of this goddamn chair, then I shall, because I have earned that right!" As Betsy presented the bottle again, Ashley snatched it out of her hand. His chest heaved as he put the bottle on the floor next to his chair.

Coco left the house every day for time alone. She felt the need to escape the ever-increasing gloom that hovered over the house. She tried to befriend her nephew, but he would hardly speak to her, and she would often catch him glaring at her, though he would quickly avert his eyes once caught. It was four days until Christmas, and her father and the Thompsons would be arriving in a day. She left the house in the late morning and made her way down the cobbled street. She didn't think about where she was walking but more on enjoying the temperate day and letting her skin soak up the sun's rays.

She walked for hours before she realized she was in downtown New Orleans. Looking around, Coco blinked rapidly before exhaling deeply in frustration that she had wandered farther than she had intended. As she began walking again, she took note of the businesses and people on the streets. Now a blossoming woman of eighteen, the heart of the city looked different to her than it did as a child, five years ago. The structures still stood in their splendid French architecture, but the people who walked the streets were not dressed in the same grandeur as she remembered. Union soldiers were in abundance as they moved through the city.

After crossing the street, she found herself in front of the St. Louis hotel in the midst of a cluster of soldiers unloading a wagon of wounded soldiers. A large group of men and women moved with urgency to get the soldiers out of the wagon and inside the hotel.

"Miss, miss!" A woman grabbed Coco by the arm. "Can you help?"

She shook her head. "Oh no, I'm no nurse."

"Just let him lean on you for a minute—help him stand."

Coco did as the woman instructed and helped the bandaged man. His left leg was tied off with a leather strap and hung lifelessly below it. He leaned heavily upon her, his arm over her shoulder, as she braced him. The commotion continued as Coco tried to make sense of all that was happening around her before the woman spoke to her again.

"Come," she said, "bring him this way."

Coco helped the man into the building, where she passed him off to another woman. Movement was all around her like organized chaos. She looked at the cots lining the large hotel corridor and the bandaged men lying in them.

"We don't have a bed to put him," she heard a woman say in frustration. "We'll just have to make a spot for him on the floor," she continued with a huff.

"Is there something I can do to help?" Coco found herself turning to the woman.

"Are you a nurse?" she asked as she took the bandage off the soldier lying in front of her.

"No."

"Not that it matters," the woman continued, seemingly not even hearing Coco's response. "I can teach you what you need to know. Jesus," she said, looking at the uncovered wound on the man's arm. "John," she called, "take him to the back room for surgery! The arm's got to go."

Coco's eyes moved back and forth between the woman and the soldier. Neither supported an expression of distress or surprise but rather one of a common proceeding, as if they were doing no more than removing a splinter. There was no sympathy and no floral engagement, just the cold, hard truth.

The woman wiped her hands on a terry cloth tucked in her dress belt. "So, you want to help?"

"Well, if you could use help."

"Oh, we can use it! Are you looking to get paid?"

"I mean, being paid would be nice, but I'm just volunteering."

"Good, because we can't afford to pay you. But we could certainly use you." The white woman was larger boned and had hair the color of dull copper. "Name is Mrs. Hughes. I'm the lead nurse during the day shift. I come from Virginia. Traveled down here with the army after the siege ."

"Caroline Toussaint."

"Ms. Toussaint, are you able to start today?"

"I have a few hours today I can help."

"Good. Do you know how to change bandages?" Coco shook her head. "Do you know anything about nursing?" Mrs. Hughes asked.

"No, ma'am."

"Follow me today, and pay close attention. You can learn the basic set of skills you'll need to know should you decide to come back tomorrow."

"I feel so sorry for these men," Coco choked out as she looked around the makeshift hospital.

"Don't. There'll be no tears in here, Ms. Toussaint. These men don't want sympathy. They know what it is. Should you feel the need to cry, excuse yourself and do it where no one can see or hear you. Do not shed one tear in front of these men. Do you hear me?"

"Yes."

"Good. This is not a job for the faint of heart. These men have been in the brunt of battle. Most of the ones we see here will lose a limb or two, and many of them die. It is our job to make them as comfortable as possible. Feel free to flirt with them—God knows these men need some kind of distraction and joy in their lives. Your pretty face may do just that."

She followed Mrs. Hughes around for the next four hours, watching as she changed bandages and made the men as comfortable as she could. When it was time for Coco to go, she thanked the lead nurse and promised to return the next day around the same time.

CHAPTER TWENTY-THREE

COCO KEPT her word to return the next day and the following. She was not at home when Albert and the Thompsons arrived at the house, but when she returned in the evening hours and saw her father on the patio, she ran to him and embraced him tightly. "Oh, how I've missed you," she said in his ear as she struggled to keep tears from falling.

The sun set early in December, but the New Orleans evenings offered nights of tolerable warmth. Albert and Coco took a blanket after dinner and went out to the patio, away from the others. They sat together, wrapped up in the warmth of the flannel blanket, with the crisp, cool air on their faces.

"Tell me how ya have been. How have ya been occupying ya time?" Albert asked.

"I've been all right. I've been sketching a lot."

"Very good. And you've been treated well?"

"Yes, though I'm a bit of an outcast. Good Lord, could Mrs. Thompson have made any more evident her gall toward me?" Coco made a twisted face and chuckled as she mimicked the woman.

Albert chuckled as well. "It's not you. That woman has hated me for years—not to say that I think any more highly of her."

"I hate how Marianne changes for her on a whim."

"That's her mother-in-law. Ya have to give Marianne a bit of a pass on that." Coco pulled the corner of her mouth back, giving him a skeptical look before rolling her eyes and shrugging. "So, where were you this afternoon?" her father asked.

"I began volunteering."

"That's great! At a church or a girl's school?"

"No," Coco said, looking down and then back up to the street. "A military hospital."

"What?"

"The St. Louis—the hotel."

"Yes, I'm familiar with it."

"It's a Federal hospital now. I'm volunteering as a nurse there." Albert didn't say anything. "It's heartbreaking. There are so many wounded men in there, and I know it's not even a fraction of wounded from the war."

"The irony," he mumbled with a distant look and a memory of purchasing Coco's mother at that very hotel. "Does Marianne know ya workin' at a Union hospital?" he asked after a pause for reflection.

"No, I only started a few days ago."

"Well, try and keep it that way. I know your heart and that you're just helping mankind, but others may view it as you aiding the war effort in favor of the Union."

Coco scoffed under her breath. "I'm sure Marianne wouldn't mind."

"She lost her husband and her son lost his legs because of the Union troops."

"As well as each of those men at the hospital!" Coco countered. "They're all someone's father, husband, or brother whose lives are forever changed by the blast of musketry or cannon fire. It's the foolishness of war."

"I know what ya sayin', Coco, and I'm not arguing with ya. All I'm sayin' is be mindful of those around ya."

Christmas came and Coco spent a good amount of the day at the hospital, sitting on the sides of cots and singing to the wounded soldiers or sketching pictures for them. Albert gave Coco a gift that evening: a small revolver he instructed her to carry at all times someplace out of sight but easy to get to. She began carrying the gun tucked in the top of her right boot, and no one—not even her sister—knew she had it.

As the weeks passed and the emancipation took effect, Ashley became more and more at unrest. He snapped the day Betsy dared approach Marianne about her service to the household.

"Ma'am, if I may…"

"What is it, Betsy?"

"I was wonderin' what ya plan on doin'."

"What do ya mean?"

"With the emancipation and all…" Betsy nervously wet her large lips and twisted her fingers.

"Ya think you're right smart now, sayin' such big words."

"No, ma'am, I ain't thinkin' I'm smart. I was just hopin' for a few cents a day."

Marianne turned red in the face. "I tell you what," she began with a harsh edge. "I'll pay ya fifty cents a day, and I'll hang onto it until you can pay me back what I paid to buy ya."

Betsy raised her chin. "But there's a new law."

"That law don't mean shit," Ashley chimed in with force. "We haven't lost this war yet, have we? Have we?"

"No, sir," Betsy stammered.

Coco hustled to the hospital that day, leaving before Marianne or the others even knew she was gone. A month passed as she went through the rows of men, bandaging them, feeding them, and helping them get up to use the toilets.

"You're still here," Mrs. Hughes said one day when she noticed Coco staying well after her normal departure.

"Yeah," she said airily and with hardly a smile.

"Everything okay?"

"I feel like I need to do more."

"We all feel that way."

"No, I mean like, away from here...in the battlefield." She paused. "I listened to the men talking today about the battles and the fallen and the prisoner-of-war camps. I want to do more. I feel like I can do more."

"I don't think you understand just exactly what war is, or you wouldn't want to be in the middle of it."

"I see it here every day, just like you."

"No. I've seen it up close," Mrs. Hughes said. Coco stopped folding sheets and looked at her. "Take a walk with me. You are a Southern-born woman—a free black woman," Mrs. Hughes began as they walked out of the hospital and onto St. Louis Street. "How serious are you about doing more?" She stopped walking and turned to face Coco, who pulled her shawl more securely around her shoulders against the cold wind.

"I wouldn't have said anything if I weren't serious."

The woman looked around before continuing. "I know of a job for you. It's dangerous—very dangerous—but if you want to do more, this is it."

"Well, tell me," Coco said eagerly.

"You know the cathedral on Jackson Square?"

"Yes."

"Meet me there tonight at midnight."

"How am I to meet you there with the martial law in place?"

"Figure it out...and make sure you aren't followed." Mrs. Hughes pressed her lips together and raised her eyebrows. "I will see you later, Ms. Toussaint," she said as she turned and walked back toward the hospital.

Coco pondered Mrs. Hughes's words as she walked home through the biting wind. That night, she went to her room early and extinguished her lamp. Instead of lying down, though, she quietly paced the room until she was certain the family had gone to bed. After waiting for the clock to hit 11:00 p.m., she cracked the door and peered out. Softly, she walked through the halls and made her way down the staircases, until she stopped at the sound of Ashley moving around in his chair on the main level. Coco held her breath as she hid behind the walls and made her way through the house to the front door. As quietly as she could, she made her way outside and cut through the yard instead of going out to the main street. Little did she know, a set of bitter eyes watched her from a window in the house.

The cold, damp night made Coco all the more vigilant as she moved through the shadows of the city, skirting the attentive militia manning the streets. When finally she made it to the looming, gothic structure, a cold came to her bones that chilled her more than the wind. She stood with her back to the large stone pillar leading to the front of the cathedral as she looked around herself. There, in the shadows, a tall, lean figure of a man with a top hat and coat walked the paved street toward her, seemingly unbothered by whether the militia would catch him.

"Who goes there?" Coco called out. The man didn't respond but continued his steady stride. She sunk down and took her pistol out of her boot, gripping it firmly. "I say, who goes there?" she called out again as he approached her. She raised the pistol and pointed it at the man. "Come another step closer and I will fire this gun."

The man stopped in his tracks with no apparent alarm. His skin was pale and the beard lining his strong jaw was dark. He was finely dressed in a plum shirt that was pinned with a gold bar at the base of the neck. His long coat fit neatly and was buttoned at the waist.

"What is your purpose?" Coco demanded.

No sooner had she inquired than Mrs. Hughes appeared, walking in their direction. When she approached, she took a deep breath. "Ah," she said, her words making a puff of white in front of her face, "I see you have already met Mr. Kutz. Shall we go in, or do you want the money out of his purse first?"

Coco slowly lowered her gun as Mrs. Hughes walked past her. She glared at Mr. Kutz before following them into the building. As they walked down the hall, she began to hear the low hum of voices and the glow of light spilling from a room with a dozen men and a few women.

Mrs. Hughes took hold of Coco's arm before they went inside. "What is said and done in this room stays in this room. Do you understand?"

Coco's dark eyes reflected the red glow of the lighted room. "Yes," she responded as her heart raced.

"Now, this is a group of very powerful and informed people. If you don't want to be part of something greater like you said earlier today, then you should leave now, before you enter the room. Once you're in, you're in, and eyes and ears will be on you at all times." Mrs. Hughes's stare bore through Coco.

"I'm ready," was all she could think of saying.

"All right." A glint crossed her eyes. "Stay with me and don't say anything, just listen. Most of it will be Greek to you anyway, until you learn our way."

Coco followed her into the room. A few took note of her, but the conversations didn't stop when she entered. Mrs. Hughes was right: she had a hard time understanding the topic of discussion, and in fact some of the words being used made no sense whatsoever to her. After the group seemed to settle in agreement, the conversation broke off into smaller discussions amongst them. Mrs. Hughes motioned for Coco to follow her to where a few gentlemen spoke.

"Mr. Kutz."

The man turned to face them and smiled. "Mrs. Hughes, always a pleasure."

"Though you two have offhandedly met, allow me to make a proper introduction. This is Ms. Toussaint, a lady and Southern loyalist. She is the daughter of one of Louisiana's most prominent plantation owners." Coco wondered how the woman knew information about her father's plantation when she had never made mention of it. Mrs. Hughes looked at her with a flashing gleam. "This is Mr. Kutz, who has most recently joined us from Chicago. He is a Pinkerton detective."

"Have you heard of the Pinkertons?" Mr. Kutz questioned Coco.

"I have heard the name, but I know little about them," she responded. The corner of his mouth rose as he took a drink from his glass. "My apologies from earlier," she continued.

"No apology necessary. One can't be too careful these days."

"Ms. Toussaint wishes to do more," Mrs. Hughes said pointedly.

"I see," he responded. "Do you understand what it means to do more?"

"I would like to say yes, but by the tone of your voice, I assume I do not. Therefore, I am obligated to ask you to educate me."

Mr. Kutz let out an airy laugh. "On behalf of the Pinkerton's and the North, I am heading a team of three people, including myself, into the heart of the enemy. These two individuals have been highly trained to travel undercover to collect valuable information. I myself will be heading to northern Mississippi in three days and would be willing to train you to accompany me."

"Why?" she asked bluntly. "What good would I be to you?"

"I am going undercover as a Confederate general and, for lack of a better way to say this, your color would help provide me with more of a cover."

Coco's head raised as she processed what he was saying. "You...want me to accompany you as your slave."

"Yes, but I would train you to understand our codes and encrypted messages, so you could receive and transmit valuable information."

"I see."

"You need to understand just how dangerous this journey will be. You would be considered a spy for the Federal Army. Death by hanging is the punishment for espionage during this time of war, and you would be subject to execution without trial should they find you out." Coco's heart began to race, but her expression didn't change. "You couldn't tell anyone where you were or who you were with. It would be of utmost importance that you keep this information to yourself. You mustn't tell your friends or family—not even your father. You must...disappear." She pursed her lips before drawing in the bottom one to bite. "I'll give you tonight to think about it, but I need an answer tomorrow," Mr. Kutz continued. "There is no time to waste in educating you on our system and the plan for the journey." He said nothing more but gave her a nod before excusing himself.

Mrs. Hughes didn't even say much to her after Mr. Kutz left; she only looked at Coco with both determination and sorrow, as if she were encouraging and apologizing at the same time. Coco walked home nearly subconsciously, her mind reeling with the choice in front of her. When she made it back into her room safely, she lay on her bed and stared up at the ceiling. She couldn't settle the restlessness in her stomach, though, and finally decided to write her father a letter.

Dear Father,

As you will hear soon enough, I have left without reason and without word. It is not my intent to hurt anyone. I cannot tell you where I am going or why, only that I will take your love with me and answer all your questions when I return. I hope you find comfort in knowing my actions are principled and I am doing what my heart tells me is the right thing to do. It will be hard for me to get word to you of my well-being while I am away, but I will be sure to take care of myself, as I can hear your beloved voice in my heart prompting me to do. Send prayers up for me, Father—prayers for my courage above my safety. I wish I could share more, but I have shared too much as it is. I love you dearly. Please take care of yourself, my sweet father.

Your loving and devoted daughter,
Coco

The next day, she left for the hospital as usual with the plan of telling Mrs. Hughes she would accept the offer from Mr. Kutz. Before she could do so, however, she was met in the street by an unfamiliar face who forcefully urged her into a carriage. The carriage took her to a restaurant in the French Quarter, where the stranger instructed her to have a seat in the courtyard. She sat with nervous anticipation until a familiar face joined her at the table.

"Mr. Kutz, I should have expected as much," she said sharply as he pulled out a chair.

"Ms. Toussaint. Have you an answer for me?"

"I don't appreciate being forced into a carriage by one your people."

"You'd better get used to it if you want to work with me. Sometimes that is the only way to transport information and people safely. Plans change at a moment's notice, and you'd have to be ready for that."

"How can one be certain it is a friendly gesture?"

"We have a list of terms we use—you will need to memorize them—and they are constantly changing."

The waiter appeared at the table to offer them a beverage, and Coco responded, "Water please."

"Order wine. I insist," Mr. Kutz said.

"This early in the day?"

"You'll understand," he responded as he raised his hand to the waiter with the instruction to bring out two glasses of Zinfandel. "Are you a wine drinker, Ms. Toussaint?"

"Only on holiday or special occasions."

"I find that dull," he said flatly as the waiter set two glasses in front of them and made the pour before offering a menu. Mr. Kutz raised a hand toward her; she gave him a slight shake of the head, and he waved the waiter away.

Mr. Kutz swirled his glass vigorously before raising it to his nose to inhale its notes. After taking a drink, he set the glass back down and looked Coco in the eyes. His powerful gaze pinned her, but she refused to be the first to look away.

"Well?" he finally asked.

"I want to help you."

"Very good," he said with more enthusiasm than before. "You will spend the remaining day with me then. We have a lot to go over and only three days to do it. You haven't spoken with anyone about this, have you?"

"No."

He nodded. "Nor shall you," he added bluntly as he raised his glass again. "I may seem rough to you, but I need you to understand how dangerous this is and how important it is that we do not fail. A lot is at stake here, including our lives. There is no room for error."

Coco raised her glass to her lips and took a slow, long drink. She did spend the rest of the day with Mr. Kutz in his private hotel room. He could tell by the apprehensive look on her face that she was uncomfortable entering his room, but he reassured her that it was strictly professional and that she would have to get used to being in close quarters with him. His use of the word colleague relaxed her tension, as well as his mention of a payment of fifty dollars to her for each mission. Soon she was at ease, asking him questions and learning everything she could about undercover work and the campaign.

"My father used to tell me how important the Mississippi River was in the war. He said the battles that would determine the outcome of the war would be fought in our backyard."

"And he is right. The Mississippi is like the lifeline of this country—like the trunk of a great tree." His hands spread wide in the air. "It is the economic lifeblood. As we speak, the northern population, people you think would be untouched by this war, namely farmers, have been suffering these last two years and unable to get their crops to market because of the Confederate control over the river. The governors of the bordering states will soon be facing war among their own divided people as they begin to throw their hands up and vote with the Democrats. If that happens, they will secede along with the rebelling states, just so they can survive."

His voice became passionate as he continued, "If that happens, we lose the war! All will be lost! The president knows this... We must gain control of the Mississippi Valley! Measures to reopen the river must be taken now with no time to spare. This is the purpose of our campaign and why we must be successful in our intelligence operation."

The next day, Mr. Kutz handed Coco some old clothes and ordered her to put them on. She frowned at him. "What is your name?" he asked.

She hesitated. The day before, he had drilled her with the history of her new identity and instructed her that she was only to refer to herself as such. "Mary...Calvert," she responded.

"And what do you do, Mary?"

"I've been serving General Dodson for the past three years."

"Slaves do not wear as fine of clothes as you have, so put this on. And, from now on, you will not be wearing your own clothes anymore." When she came out of the dressing room, Mr. Kutz sighed heavily. "You're still too fine looking," he chided. "Do not keep your hair so well, and stop using oils in it." He turned away, frustrated, which brought a smirk to her face.

"Yas, masta," she mocked.

His head snapped around and he gave her a fiery glance. Her lips were pulled back into a cheeky grin and parted slightly. He made note of the way her brown eyes narrowed and danced with amusement on the platform of her high cheekbones. His lips twitched.

The following day, the two worked tirelessly into the night. Before he sent her away, he gave her instructions to meet him at the train station by 4:00 a.m. as Mary Calvert. Coco didn't sleep that night; her heart beat with wild anticipation. Before she walked out of the house, she left a single note on her pillow with the words, "I will return," and nothing more.

She dressed in the slave garb Mr. Kutz had given her and kept her hair in a loose bun on top of her head. Her dark tresses, however, were soft from years of delicate care, despite her attempt at making them look rough. After carefully securing her birthright in her boot opposite from the pistol her father had given her, she stood straight, took a deep breath, and looked at herself in the mirror. Carefully and quietly, Coco hurried out onto the cool street at 3:00 a.m. The ragged shawl she was given was of little use to keep her warm as she pulled it tightly around her shoulders, and the cold air cut through it and chilled her. Finally, she reached the train station with a sigh of relief as she opened the door and stepped out of the frigid morning. Mr. Kutz had not yet arrived, but then it was not yet four either. Coco nervously sat down.

"Darks wait outside!" a male voice called from behind the counter. Coco didn't realize he was talking to her until he spoke louder and waved his hand toward the door. "Hey, ya waiting on someone?"

She blinked and nodded. "Yes," she said, startled.

"Slaves wait outside!" he repeated with more authority.

Coco's eyes shifted as she stood, made her way to the door, and stepped back out into the cold. Her heart fumed in frustration as she sat on the bench in front of the station house. As the minutes passed, she clung to her shawl and rocked back and forth to try to build warmth. She mumbled her grievances to herself when she was certain it was well past four o'clock. A carriage finally approached, and Mr. Kutz stepped out. The driver unlatched his trunk and a carpetbag from the carriage and placed them on the porch.

"It's after four and I've been sitting out here, freezing, waiting on you! They wouldn't let me sit inside," she scolded him quietly as she stood to meet him on the steps.

He looked at her without expression, his face stone cold. "I'm going in to get our tickets," he said sternly. "See to the bags…and Mary." Inclining his head toward her, he added, "Do not speak to me like that again."

Coco's chest began heaving as she bit her tongue in anger and watched him enter the station. She thought about walking off the porch and heading straight back to Marianne's, and her eyes narrowed as she stood next to his luggage. An hour passed before Mr. Kutz stepped back out onto the porch. The steam and gears of the train could be heard at the back of the station as the onboard service personnel began their calls. Mr. Kutz looked at Coco and gave her a nod to pick up the trunk as he reached for the carpetbag. Reluctantly, she did so, and then, struggling to carry the heavy and cumbersome trunk, she followed his lead onto the train and to his sleeping cabin.

"That will be all," he said once she set the trunk down.

"That will be all?" she snapped.

He glanced up and caught a passing woman's eyes, offering her a snarling smile before his glare pinned Coco. The hue of green she had never noticed in his hazel eyes, flashed. He moved to the doorway and looked down both directions of the car. After grabbing Coco firmly by the arms, he jerked her into his cabin and pushed her back against the wall.

"What are you doing?" he growled, gripping her harder until she flinched. "If you blow our cover, we will be fucked! Right now, it may not seem that big of a deal to you because this is a non-military line, but the next time we get off this train, we will be surrounded by Confederate soldiers. A mistake from you and we will both lose our lives!" His face was close to hers and his voice low but severe. Coco clenched her teeth as he let go of her with a push. His nostrils flared while he regained his composure. "Now," he said more calmly, "I said yes to you joining me because I believed you could do this. If you can't, then get off this train and don't get back on it... I'm not going to let this mission crumble because of you, and I'm certainly not going to die because of you."

Coco suddenly felt sorry for her behavior. Mr. Kutz reached into his vest and took out a ticket. "Here is yours," he said, handing it to her. "The slaves have a different car, if you choose to stay. But you decide. And decide carefully."

She slowly took the ticket from him before he turned his back. As she watched him sit on his small bed, Coco wished to say something but was lost for words. Turning on her heel, she walked away with a decisive step.

CHAPTER TWENTY-FOUR

THE TRAIN ENGINE screeched to a halt and the stack let out a great sigh of steam like the breath from a bear's jowls in winter. Mr. Kutz, dressed in a Confederate general's uniform, stepped from the train and into the bustling station of Vicksburg, Mississippi. The massive transport station housed several trains moving both east and west of the great river, and the noise echoed from the steel beasts as voices and loading bells rumbled like thunder through a stormy sky. Confederate troops in gray uniforms were common in the crowd. Mr. Kutz looked around himself as he surveyed the station when he saw Coco making her way through the people toward his cart.

"Where's the trunk?" she asked when she reached him.

"I paid a man to bring it for me."

"Let me take this," she offered, reaching for the carpetbag, and he gave her a nod.

They left the station to hail a carriage. As they rode, they watched troops busying themselves in organized brigades and divisions, throwing up entrenchment, and making every prepara-tion against attack, which, judging by what was passing before them, seemed not far off. The cry of the city, *"Defend at all costs,"* seemed to indoctrinate the streets, casting tall shadows across every man, woman, and child. Coco's heart sped as the quick-moving carriage jolted her over the cobblestone streets. Confederates surrounded her now like the swamps surrounded the city.

"We're going to drop off the luggage and then proceed to the Warren County Court House," Mr. Kutz said, interrupting her thoughts.

Coco nodded but continued the remaining trip in mindful silence. The courthouse was a looming structure set upon a hilltop. The two-story brick walls were faced with smooth stucco, and fluted columns surrounding the building, giving it the ambiance of imposing dignity. Coco stared up in awe at the large tower shooting up from the roof as she walked two steps behind Mr. Kutz.

"You must be Brigadier General Dodson," a finely dressed man said, extending his hand toward him at the entrance to the courthouse.

"And you are, sir?"

"Mayor Flaggs. It's a pleasure to meet you, sir. Lieutenant General Pemberton will be joining us in a few hours. Please come; let me show you around the courthouse."

"Is there someplace she may…" he began, motioning toward Coco.

"Oh, yes, of course. The slaves typically gather at the lower right water house down the hill there."

Coco watched as the two disappeared into the building before she made her way slowly down the hill. The view of the city was spectacular, and soon she forgot her frustration at being sent away as more black slaves waiting on their masters gathered at the water house.

Hours passed, and it was dusk before she noticed the tall figure of Mr. Kutz emerge from the building. She rushed to him and offered her assistance. At his command that they would be leaving, Coco called the carriage driver around and then waited for her colleague to step in before she followed him.

"The carriage will take you to your boarding house," he said as it pulled to a stop in front of his hotel. "Be back here early in the morning."

"Yes, sir. My, but the weather was fine today," she said quickly, before he had a chance to get out of the carriage. He stopped with one foot out the door and looked at her.

"Come in a minute," he said.

"Sir?"

He gave her a nod, and she followed him out of the carriage. When they entered his room, he closed the door and latched it. "What do you have?" he asked.

"Won't me being in here raise suspicions if someone is watching?"

"No," Mr. Kutz said, taking off his coat. "They would only presume I brought you in to service me." Coco raised her eyebrows as she turned away from him with a blush. "What information do you have?"

"General Grant has been trying for months to get to Vicksburg. He will never succeed—not through the swamps and bayous—and it's madness to keep trying. He's becoming a laughing stock."

"And you know this from…the slaves?" He seemed skeptical.

"Yes," she said matter-of-factly. "Don't underestimate what they know. They are the hidden eyes and ears of everything said and done behind closed doors."

"I understand your point. Can't they be a bit dramatic in their storytelling, though?"

"Maybe for their entertainment, but you know the facts are right. Who more than the enslaved people will the outcome of this war effect? Of course they are going to be listening, paying attention, and sharing the facts."

"Do they know who you are?"

Coco frowned slightly. "No, of course not." There was a pause before she spoke again with annoyance. "You have nothing to say to that?"

"What would you say to that?"

"Well, I would send word to the General Grant that he needs to stop wasting his energy."

"And then what? How else do we take the city?"

Coco began pacing the room as her voice grew fervent. "I don't know. How else do people get into the city?"

"By river and train."

"Well, there you go," she said, letting her raised hand slap down against her side.

"It's impossible to get the ironclad through that part of the river. With Vicksburg on a steep bluff, it gives them the advantage to fire on the ships, not to mention the river there is like the curve of a hairpin. It has been tried, and it failed miserably."

"The railroad then."

"The only railway coming from the east is Jackson, also a Confederate city. The Union would first have to lay siege on that city before heading west, but before that, they would have to lay claim to every other Confederate stronghold between them and Jackson. Seems a bit implausible, don't you think?"

"Well, no. Not if that's what needs to be done. If they want Vicksburg, that's the only way they're going to get it."

"You are audacious, I'll give you that," he said, and Coco stopped pacing and glanced out the window in careful thought. He studied her physique.

Over the next few weeks, Mr. Kutz attended meetings with the Confederate authorities of the city to ensure careful planning for increasing the strongholds of the battlements surrounding the city. Word had been received that General Grant had given up the endeavor to conquer the bayous and headed north, where he was said to have crossed the Mississippi. Coco continued catching word about the latest conquest of gunships, as well as how, along narrow rivers, the rebels used slaves to cut down trees and haul them into the river as blockades to prevent Union advances. The gunships had eventually retreated and made their way back to the Yazoo River. Word also spread among the slaves that rebel officers had been ordered to burn the cotton fields to keep the Union from confiscating them.

As the beginning of April came, Coco felt that their work of espionage was of little value to the campaign. She hardly had time to converse with Mr. Kutz, and he seemed to take little interest in what she told him. One evening, he had spoken quietly for her to go to his room that night. When she arrived, he was short of breath.

"What is it?" she asked.

"Were you followed?"

"No, I don't believe so. What's wrong?"

"We are planning to send a fleet of ironclads through the hairpin. We need to get into the battlement overlooking the river and get an exact count of the cannon and artillery weapons on that bluff. Grant is already on the dry side of the Mississippi, marching his men south, and will be transported by the fleet back across the river. It is our job to get that fleet through Vicksburg's clutches."

"Okay. What needs to be done?"

"I'll be sending you in to gather the intel we need. I feel I am under a scrutinizing eye of late and will not be allowed within a hundred feet of that bluff. But you... They don't know your face, and you can pass for any average slave."

A sound came from down the hall, prompting him to raise his hand over his mouth in a pausing gesture. His eyes shifted before a heavy knock sounded at the door, and he jumped to stand in front of Coco. "Quick, take down your dress!" he ordered.

"What?"

"Just..." He took hold of the front of it and gave it a solid rip, pulling the fabric off her shoulders before he tore off his own shirt and threw it across the room.

Another heavy knock sounded. He shoved Coco onto the bed before proceeding to the door and slowly opening it. The man standing there surveyed him suspiciously.

"Can I help you?" Mr. Kutz asked.

"General Dodson. May I come in?"

Mr. Kutz scowled. "I'm busy right now."

"It will only take a minute."

Letting out a sigh of irritation, he stepped aside and opened the door enough to let the man he knew to be Mr. Winschel, a confederate supporter, into the room. He was a short and bald man with a commandingly large mustache. When he stepped inside and saw Coco on the bed, holding up the top of her dress, he hardly gave her a second glance.

"Your maid needs to go. What I have to say to you needs to be said in private."

Mr. Kutz looked at Coco. She scampered off the bed, holding her dress to cover her chest, and kept her head down as she made her way past the men and out of the room. Mr. Kutz grabbed her by the arm. "I'm not done with you, so don't go far," he said, placing a forceful kiss on her lips before guiding her with a strong hand out the door.

Coco waited in the hall of the hotel, unnoticed. She couldn't tell how much time had passed; she was too preoccupied with the mission Mr. Kutz said he was going to send her on. Her heartbeat quickened as she imagined different scenarios of the coming events.

The door suddenly opened, and the short Mr. Winschel left the room. Mr. Kutz stepped into the hallway and motioned for Coco to come to him. "Mary," he said. She went into the room and waited for him to close and lock the door.

He turned to face her. "I'm sorry," he said as he moved to pick up his shirt. His chest was strong, with dark hair on his pectorals and circling his belly button. Coco's eyes shifted as she tried not to watch him put the shirt on, leaving it undone in the front. "You understand that was necessary," he added before continuing with fresh hatred. "Mr. Winschel is scum, confederate sludge. I despise the worm."

"And I suppose," she said, still gripping her dress, "you have another shirt and trousers that I can put on?"

"Oh no," he said with a blank expression as he observed her. "Sorry. I didn't even... Did I ruin the dress?"

Coco pressed her lips together and raised her brows mockingly. "Yes, you did."

He moved to his chest and began digging around in it. "You have another dress, right?"

"I do, but I'm not going to walk back to my room in a torn dress that will fall if I dare move my hands."

"No, of course not," he said, pulling out a shirt.

"What did that man have to say?" Coco asked as he pulled out trousers as well. "You seem calmer than before."

"Not calmer; I just have more information to process. Here." He handed her the clothes.

Coco went into the washroom to put them on. "So, what is the plan?" she asked from the other room.

"We get the information we need from the bluff, and then we get out of this city."

"You make it sound like it will be easy."

"It won't be easy, but we must be quick. The admiral is sending his gunboats downriver on the night of the new moon to slip by the fortress under cover of darkness. That doesn't give us much time." He looked up at her as she returned wearing his clothes. "So, we have to get you in there." His voice lowered as his approving glance traveled up and down her form. Her eyes glinted. "I'll find out what supplies they may have need of and send you in with that list. Take note of how many men, cannons, muskets, and where they are positioned."

Coco nodded. "I'm ready," she said with confidence.

Mr. Kutz's eyes narrowed at her sure words. "Get back and

302 | JENNIFER SPURGEON

rest. I'll see you in the morning, and we'll get a sure plan together tomorrow." He paused after he stood up. His hand ran through his dark, smooth hair. "You doing okay?" he asked finally as he walked to the door.

She looked him in the eye. "Yes, I'm fine." With that, he gave her a nod and opened the door to let her out.

The next day, Mr. Kutz posted Coco at the entrance to the west battlement, where she watched uniformed men enter and exit. After hours of sitting and observing, she finally moved closer and took a seat in the dirt to chew on hardtack. One man in particular caught her eye as he made his third trip in, and she cast him a smile.

"Need help carryin' that?" she jested as he approached, arms full of firewood. He was in his early twenties and could hardly grow the mustache darkening his upper lip. His gray eyes were slightly slanted, giving him a sleepy look, and lined with thick, dark lashes.

"You been sitting out here half the day... What are you doing?" he asked.

"Oh, my massa told me to sit here like a good girl and wait on him, but I'm itchin' real bad to do something... I done got bored now." She stood and sauntered up to him. "Let me help ya." She gave him a coy smile. "I've often wondered what it was like to look ova the edge of the bluff, or to stand close to those big, strong cannons."

The soldier snorted with amusement and intrigue at the flirtatious, beautiful dark girl. He grinned at her before continuing forward with his load. Once he had passed, Coco rolled her eyes and stomped back to where she'd been sitting. She leaned back against a wall and shut her eyes, and a few minutes passed before a whistle made her open her eyes. It was the soldier, motioning with his head as he continued walking. Coco jumped up and jogged to catch up with him.

"You can help me carry a load in," he said.

Coco grinned, and the soldier loaded her arms full before filling his own. Together, they headed back to the fortress. She held her breath as they crossed the entrance, and her heart raced when she found herself surrounded by the gray-uniformed soldiers. He led her to where they stored the wood for bonfires throughout the camp.

"Can ya show me the edge? I hears it's high up," she said as he emptied her arms.

He chuckled. "I can show you the edge."

As he walked her through the camp, Coco's breath caught in her chest at the sight of cannon after cannon aligned along the bluff and pointed in various directions, including toward the river. There were also multiple gun pits with forts and trenches.

"My gawd," she said with an airy breath. "This is unlike anything I've ever seen. How far does it go?"

"Six and a half miles," he said, looking down the bluff almost as if in a trance.

"I've heard the word 'fortress' used to describe the city, but I had no idea…" She trailed off as her heart sank to a deplorable low.

"Not even Satan himself could scale these trenches or sail this river without us blasting him back to Hell."

Coco looked at the profile of the young soldier, and even lower her heart sank. She knew the likelihood of the young man surviving the war was slim. "Ya and what army?" she teased.

"Me and two hundred of these cannons," he bantered back with a flip of his hand and a pert grin. He was enjoying the conversation with Coco despite the social taboo.

"Ya from this city?"

"No," he said, quickly losing the smile. "I come from Alabama."

"Ya know, once in a while, my massa will let me sketch…and I come pretty good at it. I can sketch a picture of ya, and ya could send it to ya family." The young man looked at her with bewilderment. "It'll give me somethin' to do while I wait on my massa, and ya got a right handsome face—I wouldn't mind sketchin' it."

"Yeah, all right," he said, hesitant. "I don't see how it could hurt. Stay here. I'll go get a pad and pencil."

"I'll stand right here. I won't move a muscle," she smiled and watched him walk away.

Then, after looking around herself, she carefully reached up and removed a short pencil and rolled piece of paper tucked into her hair. She hid herself around the corner of the bluff and quickly began sketching the layout of the fortress. Her lines were quick and short as her anxious hand shook. After flipping the paper over, she wrote an encrypted message describing what she saw. A few minutes later, she rolled the paper tight and pushed it through the thick curls on top of her head, followed by the pencil, and then she fretfully fluffed her hair.

"There you are."

She jerked around with a forced smile, her heart pounding like a heavy rain. "Here I am," she repeated, jittery.

"I talked an officer out of page from his journal." The soldier held up the paper.

"Well, all right then," Coco said as she moved from where she'd been hiding. "Let's see here." She took the page and pencil from him. "Just try and stay in the same pose ya want me to draw ya in." She filled her cheeks with a deep, loud puff of air before she began. As Coco looked at the young man, she noticed her scrutinizing eyes made him twitch with nervousness. She grinned. "Just hold still now. This won't take me long."

She eased into a relaxed state as her hand skillfully sketched the lines of his young face. After rubbing her fingers over the lead, she smeared the lines to create shadows before again darkening the paper with lines.

"You finished?" he asked after some time.

"Patience," she reprimanded him, biting her lip as her hand

moved quickly and effortlessly. After a few minutes, she said, "There."

The soldier moved from his position and took the paper Coco held out. No words were said as his eyes shifted up to look at her face and then back down at the drawing. "Wow," was all he said.

"Send that back home. I'm sure your family will appreciate it."

"I'm sure they will." He reached up and wiped his eye. "This is very good," he said as his brow furrowed with emotion.

"I better get back out to where my massa left me!" Coco blurted out, cutting through the mood. "Thank ya, sir," she said as she started walking toward the entrance.

"Well, wait!" he said, catching up to her. "Why don't ya meet me out here tonight?"

"My massa wouldn't like that none," she said without slowing her pace.

"Just for a little bit of time."

"My massa is real strict."

He grabbed her by the arm. "I said come back out tonight."

She looked at his hand on her before her gaze shifted to his face. "Wait for me at the gate around midnight," she said. "If I can sneak away unnoticed, I'll be here."

The soldier gave her a side grin and a nod as he released her arm. Coco hurried out of the fortress and down the street, her feet nearly moving in a jog as she made her way through the busy city.

CHAPTER TWENTY-FIVE

"MY GOD," Mr. Kutz said as he surveyed the rolled paper.

A grin pressed at the corner of Coco's mouth. "Did I do good?"

"Are you kidding me?" he asked, looking up at her and then back down at the paper with a shake of his head. "This is valuable information. When you didn't meet me this morning, I knew you were up to something, but by God, I didn't think it would be this!" He chortled.

"So here," she said, pointing to the sketch, "the bluff is higher. I wrote down what I thought the approximate height was. I didn't walk the entirety of the stretch, but it's mostly the same in both directions. The rumors have never been truer. It is a fortress!"

"Yes," Mr. Kutz mumbled, studying the page again. "No gunboat has been successful in passing it."

"I don't know how they're going to do it."

"Well, wait…" His brow furrowed. "You say you're pretty sure about the height of the bluff?"

"Yes. I mean, fairly accurate."

"And the river is how wide…and deep?" he asked himself as he moved to retrieve a geographical book he had brought with him. His thumbs moved quickly through the pages, as he mumbled to himself, until he found the information he was looking for. Suddenly, he went silent, his mind racing through new plans faster than his mouth could begin to explain them, an avalanche of ideas triggered by this one, vital, missing piece of information. "Good God," was all that escaped.

"What?" She questioned. "What is it? Tell me!"

"...Now cannons can only pitch down so far." He moved his hands as his eyes glazed over with realization. "If the ships hug the bank of the river near the bluff, they may just be lucky enough to be out of range of the cannon fire." His eyes widened with mischievous delight. "They could slip by...literally right under their noses. I'm going to get this information as quickly as I can to the admiral. We will leave immediately after."

"Won't there be more we can do here?"

He shook his head. "No, it's too dangerous."

"It just seems like leaving now is premature."

"Our job is not to battle but to ensure the victory by carefully playing the prelude, so the battles can be orchestrated just right. We slip in, gather the intel we need, and we slip out long before even one round ball whistles by our heads. We will not see the fruit of our labor, but if we do our jobs right, we will read about it in the newspaper." He grinned at her as he tenderly gripped her shoulders. "You, my dear, may have very well secured the capture of Vicksburg." Coco smiled as a rush, like a great tide, washed over her and filled her soul with power.

Mr. Kutz bought passage for them to leave Vicksburg on April 13th. They traveled by train to Jackson but only stayed a couple of weeks as they heard news that General Grant was marching northeast with more than thirty thousand men. At the reassurance from Coco that she was still willing to take more missions with him, Mr. Kutz booked them transport to the heart of the Deep South, Alabama. Still traveling under the pretense of master and slave, they worked side by side in coding any information that may aid the North.

Weeks passed as they found their way through Alabama and into the industrial capital of the confederacy. It was summer; the days were now long amid bright sunshine and elevating heat. Nature seemed unimpressed by the ongoing war and economic tragedy claiming every household like a plague. The women of Alabama no longer had a hold on the status claim as prominent wealthy, or the unfortunate and poor—the two had become one and the same. Money had become scarce and bread scarcer, as there were no men to aid in harvesting crops or moving goods to the market to sell. What little the women could harvest alone was used to feed their children, which was becoming increasingly harder and, at times, impossible. The situation rapidly deteriorated as armies continued moving forward into battle.

The city and streets had become a common place of unrest as the women took to picketing and protesting what they perceived as rising economic injustices. Coco followed Mr. Kutz as they made their way down rioting streets to a bakery to purchase bread. She waited outside while he went in to make the purchase. Soon he was back, cursing under his breath.

"What is it?" Coco asked quietly.

"The price has gone up again, even since last week. It's ten times higher than it should be. This is all I could afford to buy us right now." He opened the brown paper to reveal a small loaf.

"That's it?" she said in shock, her stomach growling at the sight of the small morsel.

"That's it," he repeated as he wrapped it back up. "Let's take it back. These streets… I'm afraid we may get mugged for it."

Coco looked around at the filled streets of angry and distraught women. "Can you imagine trying to feed a family right now?" She asked as her eyes studied their sunken faces.

"No, I can't."

Hundreds of women raised axes and fists as they chanted, "Bread or Blood! Bread or Blood!"

"Stay close," Mr. Kutz whispered to Coco, taking her hand before just as quickly releasing it.

"I don't think they mean to harm me." Mr. Kutz rolled his eyes at her innocent ignorance. "Just stay near me," he said as he began his way down the street.

The women became more and more fierce as they vocalized their miseries. "Who are ya that ya not on the battlefield?" one of them yelled at Mr. Kutz. "Ya a fit looking man—ya should be fightin' like the rest of them!"

"My husband and sons have all died!" another yelled. "Why are ya still walking these streets? Ya no better a man than they were!" Spit hit him in the face. His jaw clenched as he reached up and wiped it off.

The harassment was relentless as the two struggled through the mob of angry mothers and housewives, who came to believe Mr. Kutz was a wealthy trader and a reason for their oppression. Coco became separated from him in the chaos as the women pulled and pushed at him, demanding relief from their repression. Mr. Kutz jerked around in an attempt to locate Coco, and when he saw her some feet from him, being pushed around, he reached a hand over the women, toward her. Stretching her arm, Coco just touched his fingers when she was knocked away. Another angry woman grabbed her by the hair.

"That's enough!" she heard him yell in a deep, angry voice, but the women would not be swayed and only became angrier. Growing more aggressive, Mr. Kutz pushed his way back to Coco and took her with a firm grip by the arm, shoving her aggressor away. Her eyes met his with a glint of relief. He began leading her again when he was struck over the head with a hard object, dropping him to his knees.

Coco knelt and grabbed hold of him. "Oh my God," she said breathlessly as she held his head in her hands, blood streaming from where the strike had left a gash. The force of the crowd around them pushed her off balance.

She clenched her jaw as her eyes flashed. Coco reached into her boot and took out her revolver. After standing back up, she raised it straight up in the air and sent off two shots. The women close by hushed and stepped away from the two. Coco pointed the gun in front of herself and looked around at the crowd of angry women. They were worn, beaten down by exhaustion and hunger. Reaching out with her free hand, she helped Mr. Kutz to his feet. Blood covered his hand that held the wound. He looked at her, shocked.

"Ya should hang for pointing a gun at us!" a woman yelled out.

"Let's go," Mr. Kutz said as he held her arm for support and led them from the crowd. Coco didn't put the gun away until the mob was well behind them. "I wasn't aware you carried a gun," he stated in a questioning tone.

"Do you not remember our first meeting?" She posed, tucking it away before directing him to sit on a bench.

"You'll probably get in some serious trouble for that, you know."

"Well, we'd be in serious trouble if I hadn't. Be still and let me take a look at this," she said, standing over him. "It needs a couple of stitches, but my, it is causing more of a fuss than it deserves."

"Head wounds bleed a lot. Can you stitch it?"

"You forget I was working at a hospital when you met me," she said with a smirk.

"I have some supplies in my room."

Coco helped him to his room a few blocks away and proceeded to clean and stitch his wound. "We're going to have to leave," he said as she carefully worked. "Maybe we should lay low for a little while—go to some friendly turf."

"All because of a little scuffle?" she teased as she gently washed with a damp cloth where the blood had spilled down the side of his face. She guided his chin upward with her forefinger before tilting his head to the side. After dipping the rag in the bowl of water, she rinsed it and wrung it out again.

"Little scuffle?" He scoffed. "You pulled a gun on a group of protesting white women."

"Who attacked you!" she said defensively.

"Attacked or not, you are a slave and pulled a gun on free women."

"But I'm not a slave," she said confidently as she continued cleaning around his ear.

He took hold of her at the wrist and looked up. "I know, but we must maintain that you are."

Coco was the first to break the stare, and he released his hold. "What do you think will happen?"

"They'll investigate." He paused. "I won't let anything happen to you." She dropped the rag in the water bowl and carried it to the bureau. Mr. Kutz stood and walked over to her. "I won't let anything happen to you," he repeated.

She smirked. "What a strange world we live in when the one defending themselves from their attackers is the one getting tried." Coco looked up at him standing close to her and offered him a troubled smile. With tenderness, he reached up and ran the back of his fingers down her cheek.

A heavy knock came at the door. Coco's wide eyes shifted toward the sound and then back to his eyes. "Give me your gun. We'll say you took it out of my belt." Her hand trembled as she took the gun from her boot and handed it to him. He tucked it in his pants and walked to the door, Coco watching nervously.

When he opened the door, there stood the hotel manager, along with two militiamen. "I assume ya already know why we're here," one of the officers said.

"I do."

"Is that the negress?" he asked with a nod as he looked past Mr. Kutz.

"She did nothing wrong."

"She threatened civilians with a gun."

"Look at what those *civilians* did to me," he said, tipping his head and revealing the stitched wound. "Those women attacked me! My slave did the only thing she knew to do to protect me from that violent mob."

"All the same, we have to take her with us. You can tell it all to the major."

He turned and looked at Coco standing there, her mouth slightly agape. After giving her a nod, she stepped forward, closing her lips and swallowing hard.

"She'll be kept in a cell at the jailhouse," the man offered.

She looked up at Mr. Kutz as she stepped past him. "I expect she will be treated kindly until I see to it that she be released," he said.

"I run a jailhouse, sir, not a boarding house," the man derided with a look of distain. Coco followed them down the hall. "He takes quite the fancying to ya, don't he?" he stated as they walked.

The jailhouse had five cells, each with a single pallet and a bucket in which to do one's business. It was a two-story building with offices occupying the second level. The opening of the main level was a single room with a desk facing the cells. The building sat in an open space with no trees around it to offer any kind of shade, leaving the brick to absorb every ray the sun poured down upon it. There were two windows on opposite sides of the first floor, both of which were open to allow in what little wind could possibly blow. The air was heated before it even reached the windows, though, offering no relief. The jailer opened a cell gate for Coco, locking it behind her when she entered. She sat on the sleeping pallet, staring straight ahead without moving, for how long she couldn't tell. Drops of sweat ran down her head, and her dress was soon wet with perspiration.

Eight days passed. By the ninth, Coco was losing hope of ever seeing Mr. Kutz. She stood on the side of her cell closest to the window, holding on to the bars and looking toward the light. The jailer had already brought her meal for the day: a couple scoops of corn and some dry bread. The sound of men's voices coaxed her to turn her head in the direction of the desk, and her heart leapt at the sight of Mr. Kutz. He stood rigid and strict as the jailer read the letter he'd presented to him. The man folded the paper and, with a stoic look, handed it back to Mr. Kutz before he fumbled in the desk drawer and retrieved the keys to the cell.

"Looks like he didn't forget ya after all," he said, opening Coco's cell door. She looked at him, dazed, as if she were seeing a ghost. "Well, come on." She slowly walked out, her eyes staying on Mr. Kutz. She clenched her jaw when it started quivering and reached up to quickly rub at her eyes. Mr. Kutz didn't say a word; he simply signed a paper and walked out, followed by Coco.

Once they were well away from the jailhouse, he stopped and turned to her. "Let's get you back so you can clean up." She nodded, her emotions almost completely overtaking her. "You got skinny. They feed you in there?" he asked bluntly with a frown.

"Just a scoop of corn and some bread once a day."

"Water?"

"Two cups a day."

He pressed his lips together and turned away, frustration evident on his face. "I'll get you a proper meal," he said as he began walking again with a heavy step.

Coco followed him to his room and, at his encouragement, cleaned herself up and then lay on his bed to rest while he fetched her something to eat. When she opened her eyes, he was sitting on the edge of the bed, watching her.

"How long have I been asleep?"

"All day," he replied.

She began to get up, but he motioned for her to stay put. "Please, relax. I have you a little food." He got up and retrieved a plate that held potatoes, beans, collard greens, and a few strips of bacon. "It's not much really," he said, handing it to her, "but there's not much to be found."

Coco took it eagerly. "No, no," she said, taking fork in hand, "this is wonderful!" She took a few bites. "I'm so hungry," she added as she raised the bacon to her mouth. "By the time the sun was setting on the fourth day, I had lost hope that you were going to come get me."

Mr. Kutz's hand rose to his face and wiped down it, catching on his chin and lingering there. "We're partners. I wouldn't have left you." There were a few minutes of silence as Coco continued eating before Mr. Kutz spoke again. "We need to take a break." She watched him without saying anything. "We've been doing this for nearly nine months now. We need to lay low for a little while—catch our breath."

"Take a break?" Coco asked with an edge in her voice. "The men fighting this war aren't taking a break. No!" she said with a frown and a shake of her head. "Why would we?"

"We are exhausted, and when one is tired, they make mistakes. Mistakes cost lives."

"Are you saying I made a mistake?"

"No," he said, breaking eye contact with her.

"Are you?" she asked again.

"Okay, yes, I am. You compromised us when you pulled the gun on those women."

Coco turned away from him as blood rushed to her cheeks and let out a cynical huff. "I can't believe you," she mumbled under her breath.

"You brought eyes on us—unnecessary eyes—and those eyes start asking questions."

"I was protecting you!" she snapped.

"From what?"

"Those women struck you nearly unconscious! Look at the stitches in your head."

"They were women—they would've done no more harm to me than what they had already done. It didn't merit blowing our cover." Coco's mouth opened in disbelief as she turned away from him again and shook her head. "I am not ungrateful to you," he finally said. "You have proven your dedication and partnership—

under wrong circumstances and bad timing, but proven none-theless.

"Please, learn from this. Do not protect me or yourself at all costs; protect the *mission* at all costs." Mr. Kutz sat on the edge of the bed again and took a deep breath. "Listen, we will take some time off and collect ourselves. It will do us some good as we think about and plan out the next campaign."

Slowly, he reached into his vest pocket and pulled out train tickets. "I bought two tickets—" Her head snapped up and she glared at him with disappointment. His gaze seemed to penetrate through her, commanding emotions, but she refused to turn away again. "To Chicago," he added after a pause. "You are more than welcome to switch your ticket for New Orleans, if you'd rather." He stopped abruptly, his voice dipping oddly as if more should have been said. His eyes dropped to look at the bed.

"Chicago?" she asked, surprised.

"It's a bit farther removed from the war. Not economically, of course, but you know what I mean. Again, I took the liberty, but you can—you don't have to..."

CHAPTER TWENTY-SIX

THE TRAIN KICKED as the front engine pulled, sending a wave of compression between the car's couplings. The whistle sent steam screaming into the air as the train pulled forward, making a clacking sound as it chugged toward its destination. Coco sat, looking out her sleeping car window, as the train rushed through the countryside. A wave of relief rushed through her at the thought of leaving Alabama behind her. She had remained angry with Mr. Kutz, but now the thought of some normality felt refreshing, like a cool drink on a hot, dry day.

Slowly, she opened the brown package on her lap that Mr. Kutz had given her. She beamed as she lifted a peach colored dress with tassels on its cap sleeves and a silk sash hugging the waist. Her breath caught in her chest as she turned it around in her hands and surveyed its intricate design. Coco squealed and undressed from the flannel slave attire before slipping into a more familiar style that reminded her of who she really was.

She sat for a while, looking out the window at the landscape as it rushed by her and realizing just how mentally exhausted she was from their months of espionage. After resting her head against the red velvet seat, she let the train rock her to a sleep so deep and peaceful it was as if ripples of water, moving just enough to tickle her skin, were carrying her. She fell like an innocent child into slumber.

Coco could not tell just how long she had been asleep when the knock on her car door jolted her. Blinking rapidly, she looked around, struggling to remember where she was. She rubbed her temples with both hands before she stood and slowly opened the car door.

"Ma'am, a message," the man said as he handed her a folded letter.

"Thank you," she replied. After sliding the car door closed, she carefully broke the seal and read the contents of the letter. Her lips twitched as she read before she drew her lower lip between her teeth with a smile. She folded the letter back up and placed it in her sack.

It was a couple of days before the train pulled into its destination. Though she had been able to move around freely during the trip, she was thankful the long days of travel had ended. Coco lingered a few minutes before she exited her car and made her way to the depot. She didn't have anything more than her small travel bag containing her few possessions, so her disembarkment was quick.

Coco's gaze moved through the many faces as she stepped off the train. She looked around with bewilderment until her eyes rested on a familiar face. Their gazes locked as he made his way to her.

"Ms. Toussaint," he said, tipping his hat.

"Mr. Kutz," she replied with a tantalizing look.

He motioned for her to follow him and they made their way to the streets. During the last two days of travel, Coco had taken nearly every meal with Mr. Kutz. Their conversations had soon become personal, something they had not done in the eight months prior. Topics had varied from the shallows of their current life to questions that explored the deep waters of the past.

Coco discovered he had a way of redirecting her inquires of him and turning them to herself. It frustrated her, not because he asked hard questions but because she found herself wanting to answer them. It would set her heart racing the way he looked at her when she began opening up, with unwavering eyes and shoulders leaning forward as he listened without judgment or opinion… Coco had shared most but not all of her secrets. She learned that his loving mother had died when he was a teenager, and his father, a doctor who was already absent most of the time, was then hardly ever seen as he buried himself in his work. Mr. Kutz supposed it had been his way to cope with the pain.

She looked at his profile as he followed her into the carriage and began giving the driver directions to where he was to take them. Her gaze lingered around his hairline and the dark hair combed around his perfect ear. She was jolted from her trance as the horse pulled the carriage forward, and she spent the ride taking in the sights. Chicago was a booming city with towering structures and busy streets, reminding Coco a lot of New Orleans.

"We'll rest this afternoon before dinner. I'll make a reservation," Mr. Kutz said, facing forward. The carriage ride lacked conversation, but she didn't mind as she absorbed the beautiful architecture and people around them. The structures soon turned from large brick businesses to tall, slender, and colorful homes-built side by side with hardly any room for lawn. "My sister and her family live here. Her husband is Mr. O'Neill—his family immigrated to the States from Ireland when he was a boy. He works for the Chicago Board of Trade and does very well. He takes good care of my sister and is quite the family man." He leaned toward her. "He's very warm and welcoming. You will like him."

Coco smiled warmly as the carriage pulled to a stop in front of a light blue house with white trim. She allowed Mr. Kutz to help her step out and waited for him as he paid the driver before following him up the walkway. When they entered the house and their arrival was announced, Coco could hear a woman squeal from another room.

"Could it be?" she cried out as she rushed into the foyer. She laughed with delight as she rushed into Mr. Kutz's arms. "Oh, you have made it safely back home! I'm so relieved to see you!" His sister was in her mid-twenties and tall and slender. Her hair matched her brother's in darkness and was pinned smooth behind her ears, contrasting against her fair skin. The two exchanged adored greetings before she looked at Coco with a smile. "And you must be Ms. Toussaint." She extended a hand in greeting. "My, these curls around your face... Very attractive!" She turned and looked over her brow at her brother in a teasing fashion. "Attractive indeed.

"You know, when Steven wrote to me about you, he said you were colored. I didn't know what to expect," she continued in gay full chatter. "We don't have many black folks in Chicago. But you're lighter than I expected. Your skin tone is just lovely, my dear," she said with a smile as she lightly touched Coco's cheek.

"Margaret," Mr. Kutz interrupted with an annoyed tilt of his head.

She looked at him with a raise of her brow. "What? She is... she's lovely. Come now," she continued without a pause for breath, taking Coco by the hand. "Come in and rest. I'll call in some tea to help you relax, and you can nap before dinner."

Margaret led them through a large archway and presented the sitting room. The windows were tall with heavy cream draperies stitched with gold designs. A large Persian rug graced the hardwood floor, nicely accenting the mahogany furniture and the pianoforte near the windows. Coco's breath hitched in her chest as she entered the luxurious room.

"How exhausted you both must be," Margaret continued after she rang a bell and ordered her maid to bring in tea.

"It's nice to be back in society to say the least," Coco said.

"Oh," she sighed, "you are much braver than I am, Ms. Toussaint. Steven told me about your bravery at Vicksburg." Coco's eyes shifted to look up at Mr. Kutz with a warm, curious gaze. "I can't even fathom. How fearful I would've been," Margaret continued. "It was the information you gathered that held vital in the success of those warships getting past the cannon fire."

The maid brought in the tea and served them all a cup. Margaret raised hers. "Here is to you and your bravery, Ms. Toussaint, and to the safe return of my brother. May we see the end of this wretched war soon." Coco and Mr. Kutz raised their cups to Margaret's toast and then drank.

The three continued in conversation for some time, with Mr. Kutz remaining mostly silent as he watched Coco and his sister eventually fall into easy chat. Margaret's two young boys, who were eager to climb on their uncle's knees and spend their time chattering away with him in childish excitement, soon joined them. Coco watched as a new playful side of Mr. Kutz revealed itself.

"He acts all tough," Margaret said, noting Coco's admiring stare, "but he has a soft side few are lucky enough to see." She showed Coco to her guest room after some time and under the encouragement of Steven to let her rest. "I hope you find it comfortable here. If you need anything, let the maids know—it's what they're paid for," she said with a charming grin. "Did Steven bring your bags in?"

"I don't have any. All of my things were left in Louisiana," she answered.

Margaret gasped. "What? Nothing? You took nothing with you?"

"Mr. Kutz had me undercover as a slave… I was in flannel for the last nine months. He bought this for me when we left Alabama," Coco said, lifting the skirt of her dress.

"He could've afforded to let you take one dress with you," Margaret huffed in disbelief. "That brother of mine… I'm going to have a hard talk with him. Well," she continued, raising her brows in defiance, "you can wear one of my dresses for dinner. It may be a little long on you, but it will do for now. Tomorrow, we shall go shopping...and use my brother's purse!" Her defiance turned into a mischievous glint, and Coco beamed at her playful spirit.

She felt very welcomed by Mr. Kutz's sister and brother-in-law. Dinner was lively, full of laughter and easy spirits, as she was introduced to a side of Mr. Kutz that she hadn't yet experienced. As drinks were poured, his eyes lingered more and more on Coco's face and smiling lips. Once the carriage returned to the O'Neill home and the four got out, Margaret invited her brother in for a nightcap of fine port.

"Not tonight," he said, giving her a kiss.

"Very well," she replied as they moved slowly up the walk.

"It's a fine night," Mr. Kutz said, turning to Coco. "Will you take a walk with me?"

"Sure."

"The door will be unlocked, Caroline!" Margaret called over her shoulder. That evening, the two had decided they should be on a first name basis. "I expect you to behave like a gentleman, Steven," she added, snickering.

He shook his head and chuckled at her behavior. "She has always been like this."

Coco smiled. "I like her," she said as she watched Margaret and her husband walk up the steps and enter the house. Mr. Kutz gently took her hand and folded her arm through his, and they slowly strolled down the sidewalk. "It is a lovely night," she said after a few minutes. "Did I understand correctly that you are not staying at Margaret's?"

"No, I have my own apartment here. I'll go home for the night."

"So, it's just me staying with her?" Coco asked brazenly.

"It's more appropriate for a young, attractive woman to stay with a family than to stay with a bachelor." The corners of her lips pulled up as she looked down at the path. "Believe me," he continued, "I would love nothing more than to take you home with me."

Coco's heart raced at his cool words. He took hold of her arm and stopped her, turning her to face him. Her eyes widened at his unexpected gentle direction.

"What?" she heard herself ask.

"Surely you've come to realize that I care for you."

"And how would I realize that? You've always been so cold and businesslike."

Abruptly, and nearly cutting off her words, he leaned forward and pressed his lips against hers. He held her face as his lips parted hers and he began to kiss her more passionately. Coco's heart jumped in her chest as his soft, warm tongue caressed her mouth in a tantalizing way. He stopped and pulled away just enough that she could feel his breath on her lips.

"I'm sorry... You've bewitched me," he said in a low voice as he pressed forward for another kiss.

Coco found herself kissing him back as a rush of desire filled her wine-warmed body. She reached around the small of his back, gently pulling him toward her. Her response only furthered his passion as he wrapped one arm around her shoulders and cupped the back of her head with his other hand, willing her into his embrace.

A sudden clearing of the throat from a person nearby stopped the two mid-kiss as they looked up to see an approaching couple. Coco hung her head close to his chest in embarrassment as Mr. Kutz pressed his lips and nodded to the couple as they walked by, his arm draped around Coco's shoulder and softly rubbing it, as if to sooth a child. He looked down at her as she snickered at the awkwardness of being caught.

"I should probably go back," she said.

He nodded as he tried to capture, once again, her shifting gaze. "Is this the wine?" he asked.

Coco looked steadily at him. "I don't think so," she whispered, luring him with her eyes while tilting her head upward. As he kissed her, both hands cupped the sides of her face before he pulled away. Her eyes captured his, and she smiled.

"I have to take you back," he said, returning the grin.

"I wish you didn't."

"Don't tempt me," he responded with a smirk, his thumb lightly brushing her cheek. He dropped his hand and took hold of her arm, and they walked until they reached Margaret's house. He took her to the door and watched her linger with her hand on the knob. "Goodnight," he said quietly with a deep intake of breath.

She offered him a smile that disappeared just as quickly. "Goodnight." After turning the handle, she stepped into the house and quietly made her way to her room.

She dreamed of Mr. Kutz that night—dreamed of him touching and kissing her in ways she had never experienced. His body was on top of hers, pressing down and moving, sending warmth through her body and suddenly jolting her from her sleep. Coco woke with a strange but pleasurable throbbing between her legs that she had never before felt. She reached down and took hold of herself, letting out a moan as she remembered the passion she'd awoken from. Rolling over to her side, she pressed her thighs together as she took a deep breath. She longed to feel that energy again as she closed her eyes, trying desperately to bring him back.

The next day, Margaret took Coco shopping. She said Steven had come by the house early that morning and charged her with entertaining Ms. Toussaint, as he had business to attend to and would likely be at the office all day. Coco's cheeks flushed as images of him in her dream came flooding back to her mind. That evening, he joined the family for dinner at the house. He seemed to avoid direct conversation with her as they sat at the table, which troubled her. He caught her staring at him as the others conversed, but she quickly averted her gaze and reached for her wine.

324 | JENNIFER SPURGEON

After dinner, Mr. Kutz caught her in the hallway. "Can I have a word with you?" he asked.

"Of course." Her heart pounded, but she kept her voice steady and unamused. They stepped into the sitting room.

"I have this for you," he said, holding an envelope.

"What is it?"

"Your pay for the missions."

Coco slowly broke the seal and looked inside at the check. "This is more than we agreed on," she said, shocked.

"Vicksburg warrants it. That was very dangerous, and the information you retrieved was invaluable." She was speechless as she looked at him, confused. "I would do nothing less for anyone else," he continued.

Coco looked down and licked her lips as she closed the envelope. "Thank you for that," she said flatly. "I do really appreciate it."

"What's wrong?"

"Nothing." She looked up at him with firm eyes.

"Maybe I should apologize for last night. I had too much to drink and should have never been that forward with you."

She ran her tongue over her teeth before she swallowed hard. "And I apologize to you as well."

"Are you upset?" His brow furrowed in question.

"No," she said. "You are apologizing, so I thought it was only right that I also apologize."

His right eye narrowed as he turned his head. "You seem upset."

His tone irritated Coco. "Are you upset?" She cross-questioned with a heavy exhale.

"No."

"Well, you've hardly spoken or even looked at me."

"I'm looking at you now," he said in near mockery.

"What have we in here?" Mr. O'Neill asked good-naturedly as he walked into the room with a brandy. "A lover's spat?"

Coco huffed as her gaze went from Mr. O'Neill to Mr. Kutz. "Not at all," she corrected firmly. "Business. Excuse me." She exited quickly and walked to her room on the second floor, where she went straight to the bed post and gripped hold of it, taking a deep breath. She felt dizzy, and she wondered why she was so frustrated at her encounter with Mr. Kutz.

Suddenly, he stepped into the doorway. "Ms. Toussaint," he said, surprising her. She snapped around to look at him. "What's wrong?" he asked, taking a step farther into the room.

All she could do was shake her head in her own confusion. "Nothing. I...I don't know. I must just be tired from these past few months." Coco wouldn't look at him as she spoke, her voice shaky. "And being here has just..." He moved toward her until he was directly in front of her. "I'm sorry," she finally said. "I've just not been myself today." She looked up at him, her eyes shifting back and forth as she looked into his eyes. A rush of heat came over her as her body craved to feel him like it had in her dream.

Mr. Kutz's lips parted as if he were about to say something. "Don't," Coco whispered with a soft shake of her head. Her eyes lingered on his finely shaped lips, and she instinctively rested her hand on his chest. She felt its rise and fall intensify as he slowly inched his head forward. After raising her chin up toward him, her body followed.

"There you are!" Margaret's voice broke through their passion, stiffening both of them. "Steven, don't you seduce her," she teased. "Come on now, we're going to play Blind Man's Bluff."

Coco looked up at Mr. Kutz and gave a bashful smile. The tender grip of her fingers on his shirt didn't go unnoticed before she lowered her hand and walked toward the outstretched arm of Margaret.

As the next few weeks passed, Mr. Kutz worked at the office, coming by at least once a day to spend time with his sister and Coco. It was a Tuesday when Margaret approached Coco with a letter from Louisiana. She had written to her father and was eagerly waiting for a letter back. When she took it from Margaret with a beaming smile, her face suddenly fell sober. The penmanship wasn't her father's but looked more like that of her sister's.

"Everything all right?" Margaret asked, noticing the change in Coco's countenance.

She looked up and offered a smile. "Yes, I'm sure. Excuse me while I read this in private." Coco walked to her room and closed the door before she eagerly opened the letter. As she read, she sank onto her bed, tears filling her eyes and running down her cheeks.

After sitting in her room for a few minutes to compose herself, Coco finally reached for the door handle and made her way back to where she left Margaret. Mr. O'Neill and Mr. Kutz had come in since Coco had gotten the letter and were having drinks while they chatted with her. Coco stepped into the room, her eyes glazed over with concern. Mr. Kutz was the first to notice.

"What is it?" he asked as Mr. O'Neill was mid-sentence.

Coco could only hold up the letter. Words wouldn't come out of her open mouth.

"What is it, dear?" Margaret asked.

"My father..." she stammered. "My father has been very ill... for months now. They didn't know how to reach me until they received the letter I just sent." She broke down in tears as Mr. Kutz rushed to her side and took her by the arms to help steady her. He guided her to a chair to sit.

"They didn't know how to reach me. He could be dying," she continued saying to herself, "and I'm not there."

"It'll be okay," Mr. Kutz said. "We're going to get you home... right away." He looked up at Mr. O'Neill, who had already stood and was headed out the door, on his way to purchase tickets by train to Louisiana. Coco looked at him, her eyes helpless and sad. "I'll get you home," he comforted her as he stroked her shoulder. Margaret brought her a cup of water and handed it to her, and Coco nodded at Mr. Kutz's reassuring words.

The next day, she was at the station, waiting to board her train. She had said her goodbyes to the O'Neill family at the house and expressed her dearest thanks for making her feel welcome. Mr. Kutz had accompanied her to the station. The train whistle blew, announcing the final call for boarding.

"Thank you," Coco said as she stood, ready to board.

"Write to me when you get there." She gave him a nod as the whistle blew again. "I hope your father gets well."

"Thank you," she said with tears in her eyes.

He leaned forward and gave Coco a quick kiss on the cheek. As he pulled away, the tears spilled over, but she quickly reached up and brushed them away. His lips found hers as he planted a passionate but tender kiss on her. The last call for all passengers to board felt like an ending chapter as he let her go and watched her disappear onto the train.

Coco's travel seemed never ending as she anxiously waited to arrive in New Orleans, where it would be another journey by carriage before she could reach her beloved father.

CHAPTER TWENTY-SEVEN

THE HOUSE SEEMED dark and unnatural, like the pale hand of death had already clenched its fist, laying claim to a struggling soul. Coco slowly entered the house with her bag. There was no air circulation, leaving a stuffiness that suffocated the lungs. The drapes were pulled over the windows, allowing little light to fill the lower level. It was obvious the house hadn't seen life moving around in it for some time. The ghostly feeling sent chills down Coco's spine.

"Hello," she said softly as she set her bag on the floor. After walking to the staircase, she made her way up to her father's room. Her steps were light and reserved, as if walking on eggshells.

Albert's room was as dark as the rest of the house. Coco stood in the doorway and looked at her father lying motionless on the bed and Marianne sitting in a chair next to him, her head resting on the bed near his knee.

"Marianne," she said softly. She stepped farther into the room and lightly touched her shoulder. "Marianne."

Upon waking, her sister looked up at her and gasped. "Coco!" Quickly but quietly, she stood and hugged her. Then she motioned for them to step out of the room, and the two sat in the kitchen as Marianne prepared coffee and poured two cups.

"How long has he been ill?" Coco asked.

"Since mid-June. The doctor thought it was the fever at first, until last month. He said there has been word of another wave of the cholera pandemic spreading through Europe and Africa. Since father has been working with trade cargo from Europe, the doctor is fearful he may have contracted the disease and has said to prepare for the worst."

Coco lowered her head and wiped the tears from her eyes. "I should've been here."

"He was fretful when he received your letter back in January... Though that was more than I got," she said saucily.

"I'm sorry," Coco responded. "I couldn't disclose where I was going... It was for the war effort—to help end this."

"Well, as you were playing hero, trying to save the world, your own father has been dying."

"That's not fair."

"It is, though." Marianne's lips were tight as she struggled to hold back her emotions. "Every trip he made down to New Orleans after you left, he'd ask eagerly if I had heard anything. His face would fall when I'd say no. But then he would always take your side and say that, whatever it was that you had decided to do, you would come out of it successful, because you were a smart girl—damn smarter than any man he's met—and twice as pretty as any girl!" Her voice broke.

Coco didn't bother to wipe the tears streaming down her face; she just let them fall.

"What could have possibly been so important? Did you really believe that some little thing you did could possibly make a difference in this war? The South has lost all her men, and the North... God only knows. But here comes little Caroline Toussaint, the Joan of Arc, half-colored and half-white, bringing America back to its United States."

"Please stop being mean," Coco said through her tears. "You know I love him."

"But have you stopped to think about how much he loved you?" Marianne stopped for a minute as she took a towel and dried her face before handing Coco one as well. "I informed the others when he fell ill, but the doctor recommended no one come because of its contagious state. They have all written to him— even Albert Jr.! I don't even know when they last spoke." She sniffed her running nose and wiped at her eyes again before taking a drink of her creamed and sugared coffee. "Of course Rose, the gentlest spirit out of all of us—nothing would suit her but to be at his bedside. She was here for a few months, but the doctor sent her back when he discovered she was carrying."

A small smile creased Coco's lips. "I miss Rose," she said to herself quietly. "Is Father conscious?"

"He is, however he sleeps most of the day."

A squeak from the back door could be heard as it opened and closed again. Coco shot a look at Marianne.

"It's probably Foy."

"Foy…" Coco's eyes widened. His name was hardly off her lips with airy surprise as he stepped into the kitchen.

When he saw her, the old man grabbed his chest. "Coco, is that you? Is it really you?"

"Foy!" She smiled as she stood to embrace her old friend.

His face glowed with joy as he held her by the shoulders. "Let me just take a look at ya! My old eyes are gettin' dim on me and I can't nearly trust them anymore." He laughed heartily. "By Gawd, Coco, it is ya! Ya father seen ya yet?"

She shook her head. "I just got here."

"He's goin' to be so happy to see ya. Matter of fact, it may be what he needs to get well."

Her soft smile turned sad. "I'm sorry I wasn't here sooner."

"Stop that now. Ya here now, ain't ya?" He paused. His calm

eyes looking at her peacefully. "He's goin' to be really happy to see ya."

The side of Coco's mouth pulled up in a tight, crooked grin. She insisted that Marianne take a break to rest and maybe enjoy a long stroll outside to refresh her. Coco sat at her father's bedside, holding his hand and watching him sleep, until he opened his eyes. They narrowed in confusion as he looked at her before he closed them again.

"Father," she said, leaning forward eagerly and resting her free hand on the top of his head. His eyes opened again. "Father, it's Coco." A faint smile spread across his mouth as he said her name. "Yes, it's me," she said, raising his hand to her lips. "I'm here and I'm not going anywhere."

Coco stayed at her father's side day and night, refusing to sleep in her own room and only leaving when nature demanded it. On nice days, she drew back the curtains and opened the windows to allow a fresh breeze into the room. As Albert began improving, Marianne insisted Coco begin taking some time to step away for her own health. She listened to her sister's advice and busied herself with cleaning for a few hours a day, one room at a time.

She began cleaning Albert's office on a sunny afternoon. There was a crisp bite in the air, the reminder that fall would eventually cease and winter would have her day. As Coco's fingers traced the familiar setting of her father's desk, she reminisced about her younger years, when the family was still together. She picked up his tobacco pouch, still with some old, dried strands in it. Her nostrils widened as she took a deep inhale, and her heart swelled with affection at the familiar smell. Then, looking around, she became determined to bring some order and cleanliness to the room. Minutes turned into an hour when she found a book she had never seen before.

"*Two Years Before the Mast*," she mumbled the title as she turned it over in her hands. "Hmm."

She sat next to the window and started thumbing through the pages until the weight of an envelope stopped the turning. She picked it up to see it was sealed with the governor's stamp and addressed to her father. Curious, she withdrew the contents and read the letter.

My Dear Toussaint,

Yours of the 23rd was received by me just yesterday, and I have at my earliest leisure respectfully replied to it. I will retort to your request the only way I see proper, and that is to turn your appeal over to Mr. Hardy, the clerk of the court of the county, the Casa Curial. Per your request concerning the civil freedoms of your Negro woman slave, Dinah as you call her, aged twenty-six years, and acknowledging upon the receipt of one-thousand four-hundred and fifty dollars as a full consideration therefore and guarantee of the freedom of the said Dinah has been delivered to be recorded and certified. I have further ordered that the said clerk shall give to the said Dinah a certificate of her freedom, in manner prescribed by the law, which is hereby done accordingly.

In testimony whereof I have hereunto set my hand and seal of said county this authentication on the 11th day of November 1848.

Respectfully, Isaac Johnson

Coco's breath was pinched in her chest, and she felt as if her body had lost all ability to move, like an anvil was boring its crushing weight on top of her. She didn't know how long she sat there, motionless, unable to think or feel. She read the letter again before she got up and went to where she knew her father kept the book of sale with all the purchases of every slave he ever owned. It was a leather-bound book held closed with a leather strap. She sat at his desk and opened it near the center. There, in fine penmanship, were the dates and names of purchased slaves and their descriptions, the prices that were paid, and from whom they were purchased. It also held her father's plantation notes of profits and losses over the years—notes of good days and bad days. It was nearly a personal diary. She found herself reading some of the notes out loud as she turned the pages.

Thumbing her way closer to the front of the book, she

searched during the year 1848 and earlier for the name Dinah. She stopped suddenly at the sight of her name. Heart pounding, Coco read the paragraph stating Albert's decision to move Dinah from the fields to the mill. A couple pages prior, he had written his decision to use Dinah as a maid in the morning and about how she followed him to the fields for the harvest after breakfast, expanding a little on their "agreeable conversations." Coco touched the ink on the page, as if it would take her back to that moment in time. It was a glimpse into who her mother was. She turned the pages farther back until she stopped.

19th August 1843; Female Negro named Dinah; no known last name; 21 or 22 years of age; 5'6"; Griffe: half Chitimacha tribe, half Negro; Attractive woman, almond shaped eyes, full lips, high cheek bones, tall and well formed; $1000; New Orleans, St. Louis Hotel

Tears leisurely made their way down Coco's cheeks as her eyes rested on the only known facts she had of her mother. Franny and Nan had often told her stories when she was growing up, but to read Dinah's description on paper, as a formal document, meant something different to Coco. She took out the governor's letter and spread it beside her mother's description, her gaze moving back and forth between the two as she read what was written. After some time, she carefully folded up the letter and put it back in its place between the pages of the book before closing the book of sales. Taking the two in arm as gently as one would hold a child, Coco carried them to her room and placed them in her nightstand drawer.

When she finally decided to approach Albert about her findings, it was a day she believed he was feeling stronger. After carrying in a tray of lunch for him, she set it over his lap.

"You are looking better every day," she said with a smile.

"It's your presence. You give me reason for life."

"The doctor gave us a good report on his last visit—said you are out of danger. You just need to get your strength back up," she said, light natured, as she tucked a napkin in his nightshirt. "And

334 | JENNIFER SPURGEON

you do that by eating." Albert smiled faintly as he reached for his spoon. "May I read to you while you eat?" she asked, her heartbeat quickening.

"Of course. I love it when ya read."

She pressed her lips tightly, rubbing them together, before she swallowed hard and withdrew the book. *"Two Years Before the Mast,"* she said softly. Albert turned to where she sat close to his bedside, holding the book. He briefly stopped breathing and blinked rapidly, his stare lingering on the book before he glanced up to Coco's face.

"Your mother's book..." He paused to catch his breath. "I gifted that to her. She was fond of the written word...a lot like you." A sad smile pulled at his lips.

"I found it while cleaning your office...and the letter inside it." She pulled the letter slowly out of its pages. Albert was lost for words. He took a deep breath through his nose as he vacantly stared forward. "It says, uh," she continued with a gentle voice, "you were purchasing her freedom. What happened?"

He reached up and wiped with his thumb at the tears he forced himself to swallow. "I bought Dinah in New Orleans the summer of 1843," he began, staring down in a daze at the tray in front on him. "I had her working in the house with Franny and Nan. She was educated from her last owner. I was attracted to her, which was strange to me. Something like that had never happened to me before. We had good conversations at times, and I found myself wanting to see more of her...hear her thoughts-just breathe the same air as her for a little while."

Coco watched him as he paused, his expression changing, as if he could hear her again. He blinked again and looked at his daughter. "Justine became very jealous—angry that I had fallen out of love with her and in love with Dinah—and rightfully so. But she became cruel to her. Unbearably cruel. It was after you were born that I built the cabin for ya and ya mother, so she could raise ya peacefully. I gave her what she needed, and I would spend

days and afternoons with ya on my lap and with her in the cabin."
He smiled wearily. "Ya were my loves…" Tears wet his cheeks as
he looked at her.

He cleared his throat, his voice becoming husky. "The fall after
ya turned three, Foy and I were in New Orleans, securing trades. I
had been away for two weeks or so. When I returned, I rode to ya
mother's cabin straightaway, excited to share the good news with
her. It was cold, though… She wasn't there." His breathing quickened like the wind gusts before a storm, and he clenched his jaw
under the blanket of hair on his face. "Justine had sold her four
days before I returned. I looked for her, for years, but couldn't
find her. I always have dreams that I can get her back… Or is she
lost to me forever?" His voice was distant, as if Coco wasn't even
there. "I should have protected her better. Secretly, I hope for the
North to win this war. Maybe then, if she is out there, she would
come back to me. If not for me, I know she'd come back for you."
He looked at Coco with compassionate eyes. She hadn't been
emotional until now, and she broke down and cried.

"The letter ya found in her book," he continued when she
quieted down, "came to me just weeks after she was gone. I had
applied and written a letter to the governor, requesting her
freedom papers to be granted. I was willing to pay any price, to
show her I loved her. I didn't tell her, in case it would be denied. I
didn't want her disappointed, and I wanted it to be a surprise—to
see the look on her face when I told her."

Coco whipped her gaze to meet his. "You really did love her."

"I did. I still do. I want ya to know I looked for her. Over the
years, I found a trail that led to the man who originally took her,
and I found who he sold her to. But after that, I couldn't find
anything. It was like she disappeared." His voice trailed off.

As the days passed, Coco found herself imagining scenarios of
her mother around the house, or walking outside in the cool of
the day when she and Foy tended the garden. As Albert began
getting better, Coco encouraged Marianne to go home to her own

family in New Orleans with the promise that she would stay home and see to their father's full recovery. Winter came with brutal winds and cold rains. Coco hadn't received correspondence from Mr. Kutz for nearly two months now, which troubled her. She'd had correspondence with Liza, though, who seemed to be on the desperate side.

In her last letter, she had begged Coco to allow her to visit and stay a spell, as her situation was one of the most perplexed state and she had nowhere else to turn. Coco had, in her previous letter, explained her father's situation and her regret that it wasn't a good time for company, but at the persistence of what Liza called her life or death situation, Coco conferred with her father, and he was insistent on helping the young lady.

It was after Christmas, and a bitterly cold night, when Liza arrived, shivering, at the front door. Foy, who was staying in the Toussaint house, answered the door and took her to the sitting room, where they were all huddled close to the fire. Coco jumped up to greet her friend.

"I used nearly all I have left to make the carriage fare, but I had just enough to buy this cinnamon loaf." Liza extended her hand and the loaf to Coco, stopping her advance to give her a hug. "It's not much, but it's a sort of a belated Christmas treat." She smiled in her timid way. Coco had forgotten just how bashful Liza was.

"Please come warm yourself by the fire," she insisted, leading her by the hand to stand by the hearth.

"Mr. Toussaint, how are you feeling?"

"I'm doing better. Thank you, Liza."

"I apologize, but I am ever so grateful that you let me come stay with you at this time. This war has just ruined everything."

"Ya welcome here."

"Let me take your cape," Coco said, reaching out toward her, and Liza looked at her hesitantly. "What?" she asked with a furrowed brow and a smile. Her friend didn't say anything but slowly unbuttoned her cape and took it off, revealing the slightly protruding stomach. "Oh my God, Liza!" Coco blurted out, unable to hide her shock. "You're pregnant!"

"Yes," Liza said with sheepish eyes.

"How?" Coco asked.

Her friend chuckled. "Do I really need to explain it to you?"

"Well, no… But why didn't you write it in your letters to me?"

Liza's gaze moved from Coco's to the other two faces in the room, whose stares were just as perplexed and inquiring. "Well, I might as well just tell you all. No sense in keeping secrets. To hell with modesty, right?" She gave a nervous laugh. No one in the room responded; no sound was made but the crackling of the burning wood and the howl of the wind in the chimney flue. "May I have a drink? Maybe whiskey or something?" Her voice quivered with desperation.

"I'll pour ya a glass," Foy said, getting up from his seat. "Sounds as if ya may need a shot of it." He poured a tumbler and handed it to her.

"Well there's nothing to be nervous about, Liza," Coco began, confused. "I apologize about my reaction. It just surprised me is all. You can stay with us until this war is over and your husband makes it home. Is he doing well?"

Liza took a drink and nodded. "Mr. Cott is well, yes. Thank you." There was an awkward silence. "I have not seen my husband in over a year," she finally said. Coco's mouth involuntarily gaped open.

"Well nah there's a problem," Foy said, the sway in his voice matching the dramatic movement of his shoulders. It would have been comical had the news been laugh worthy.

"I know you will all think of me as a horrible person, and how could I impose and bring my shame into your house? But I am desperate and afraid."

"Ya can stay while ya figure out what needs to be done," Albert said. "We don't think poorly of ya."

"It's a slave man's child," she continued bluntly.

Foy raised his hands. "Lawd can take me now. I've done seen and heard it all." Albert couldn't help but chuckle under pressed lips at his outlandish reaction. "Just sit down and relax," he continued, motioning to the young woman. "By the end of this war, the black man may be all that's left. White men going out there, killin' each other until they'll all be dead, leavin' their women behind. What they expect to happen? Women get lonely— they have needs too. And ya be forgettin'... This young woman here, her mother's black and her daddy white. So, what ya worried 'bout?" Foy tipped his own glass of whiskey up to his lips. "Mr. Cott probably die in the war anyhow," he said into the golden-brown liquid as it moved toward his lips. Liza's face flushed red.

"Well, I need a drink myself after that," Coco said. "Pour me some whiskey, Foy, and don't pour sparingly," she jested.

The four sat together until the men fell asleep. Foy passed out in the chair, a soft whistling confirming his deep slumber, with his feet extended on a stool. Coco spread a blanket over him before tucking in the one covering her father and giving him a soft kiss on the forehead. Putting more wood in the hearth, she stoked it back to a blazing flame. She squatted next to it, where her friend sat awkwardly on the floor, leaning back on her arms.

The fire threw a dancing, red glow across their faces. "I'm thankful your father didn't cast me out," Liza said, looking at the couch where the man had fallen asleep.

"So, tell me what happened."

"The bakery where I've always bought my bread...the owner, Mr. Jackson, has a slave who makes the sweet breads. He's always just a kind man."

"Jackson's Bakery on Adelle St?" Coco asked, and Liza nodded. "We went there together a few times," she continued in a hushed voice. A bewildered look overtook her face as she thought back. "Are you saying it was Mr. Adams?" Liza slowly nodded as she pressed her lips together. "Mr. Adams," Coco said again with a crinkled nose. "The older man? How?"

"He was comforting...kind. I invited him over for some tea, and he brought a sweet roll." Liza reminisced fondly. "I enjoyed our small encounters, and an actual evening of normal conversations sounded refreshing. Every time I saw him, he treated me with consideration... He was so caring, and that night was no different. Not even my husband had treated me like that before. It's like, when I'm with him, he actually sees me and is eager to hear what I have to say."

She looked up at Coco's impassive face. "I wouldn't expect you to understand what that feels like," she continued with a sheepish quiver of the lips. "You have a commanding presence about you. I don't. I am often overlooked and not taken seriously. But Mr. Adams... He made me feel like I was the world. And we made love. I didn't know it was supposed to feel like that." She giggled and looked up with a glint in her eye. Coco couldn't help but return the girlish smile. "Mr. Cott could be harsh. I didn't like it. He was always just quick and unemotional. Though he would always kiss me on the forehead after he was finished and express his love, I always felt just..." Her expression twisted into a sour and confused one. "Cold and...alone.

"When I wed him, after our first time, and then the first week and every time after, I often thought we women are cursed if this is all there is for us. We are sent to refinement schools to learn how to become proper wives and women of society—someone who will be respected for her poise and grace. We are to make our husbands proud and be amiable queens of our house, and by doing so, the man would in turn treat us that way." She laughed cynically and looked into the flames. "But what if he doesn't? We aren't allowed to find out who men are behind the closed door. We give ourselves entirely over to one person without even knowing who they really are, and by the time the mask comes off, we are their prisoner for life."

"I had no idea you were so miserable," Coco said, reaching forward and placing a hand on her bent knee. "Why didn't you write me?"

"And say what? What could've been done?" The flames crunched at the wood hungrily as both women watched it feed.

"Tell me more about Mr. Adams," Coco finally said, breaking the silence and the dark mood that was settling in the room.

Liza's face lightened. "Like I said, I didn't know it was supposed to feel that way. He, um..." Her head dropped as she giggled before looking back up at Coco's smiling face. "He made me feel like a woman. I felt empowered. It sounds crazy, I'm sure."

"Not at all," Coco reassured her.

"After the first night, I continued having him over to the house. It grew to where I couldn't stand being away from that feeling for more than a day or two. When I discovered I was pregnant, though, I turned him away. I'll never forget the look on his face as he stood on the front steps and I told him I didn't want to see him anymore. He asked why, and if he could come in to talk. I said no and refused him any answers. His expression will always haunt me."

"So he doesn't know his child is in you?"

"No. How could I tell him? What could he do? I still don't know what I'm going to do." She paused in frustrated thought. "Maybe give the child away," she mumbled.

"You can't do that! What if I had been given away?"

"That's different, Coco. With men it's expected that they have concubines, but for a lady to have a slave's baby... Come on, be realistic, Coco! I am doomed. If anyone finds out I have a child that is not my husband's, I will be cast out with a red letter sewn to my chest! That's why I came here... For privacy when I give birth."

Coco breathed in as the weight of her friend's troubles pressed heavily upon her. "Well, you are in a safe place here, Liza, among friends. No hasty decision needs to be made tonight."

CHAPTER TWENTY-EIGHT

THE WIND BLEW, bowing the tree branches to one side and revealing the light underside of the leaves. It was a cool June afternoon with the promise of heavy rain.

"You barely made it back before this storm hits!" Coco called out to Foy as he rode up with what little they could afford in supplies. She took hold of the horse's bridle as he dismounted.

"Seems to be comin' in real fast. Got sprinkled on some a ways back. It's headed straight for us to be sure."

"Let me take the supplies so you can get him unsaddled." Coco reached for the bags he pulled down from the back of the horse. "Did you remember to stop by the postal house?"

"I did. Ya got a letter there in the bag."

Coco's eyes flashed. "Thank you," she said as she hastily lifted the goods and went inside.

She hadn't heard from Mr. Kutz since November and had given up on ever hearing from him again. Still held her breath every time they received postal letters, though. This one was from Mrs. Hughes. A thin frown creased Coco's brow as she twitched her lips. It was an unexpected surprise to hear from an old acquaintance. She opened it and read the letter quietly. Her breathing quickened, commanding her chest to heave like the trees bending to the stormy winds. Without hesitation, she crumpled the letter in her fist and made her way to her room to start packing her trunk. She left the next day, begging her father's forgiveness for leaving without an explanation, only saying it was too urgent a situation to overlook. With the promise to return, she kissed her father and Foy and mounted her horse for New Orleans.

She rode up to the St. Louis union hospital, still serving as a Federal hospital. The leather squeaked as she dismounted quickly and made her way in. The hospital was full. Wounded men not only lay on cots but also covered the floor with nothing but a blanket to lie on. The scent of the suffering filled her nose, an odor she recognized and would never forget from when she had volunteered—the all familiar smell of blood. She looked around with pity at the men as she carefully made her way between them. When she spotted Mrs. Hughes across the room, she called out to her and headed toward her.

"You received my letter, I see," she said as she continued stitching a man's wounds. "Can we have a word?"

"Sure," she replied evenly, never averting her attention from her work as she pulled the needle outward and pressed it back into the flesh. "Let me drop this needle and let it hang from where I just cut out a round-ball lodged in this man's shoulder. I'm sure he won't mind sitting here in pain while we have our little chat over a cup of tea."

"I'm sorry... I didn't mean right this second," Coco apologized.

"You must have headed straight here after reading my letter."

"Yes, I did."

"To what end, Ms. Toussaint? There is nothing that can be done for them there, but there is something you can do for these men right here, suffering in front of you at this moment."

"I need to talk to you about that letter!" she said forcefully.

"It will have to wait, Ms. Toussaint. This conversation is to be had behind closed doors." Coco didn't budge. She stood still while Mrs. Hughes finished sewing the man's wound closed. "You are stubborn," the woman said as she wiped her hands on her bloody apron and stood. She began walking away with Coco trailing close behind.

"That I am, Mrs. Hughes, and I will stand over you the rest of today and every other day until we can privately talk."

Mrs. Hughes took a deep breath and looked at her. She motioned with her head, and Coco followed her to the back of the building and into a private office, where the woman closed the door. She walked over to a basin to pour water over her hands and wash them in the bowl.

"He was on an assignment in Georgia when they captured him," she said as she watched the blood turn the water rusty.

"Why didn't he tell me about it?"

"Why should he have?"

"We are partners!"

"Partners..." Mrs. Hughes looked at Coco with raised brows. She remained silent. "This was a very dangerous assignment. He did not want you to know about it. He would chide me now if he knew I wrote to you about his imprisonment at Camp Sumter."

"How long has he been in there?"

"A month...maybe two. I don't know for sure. I don't even know if he is still alive."

"I can't leave him in there!" Coco said, pacing the floor as her eyes became shifty.

"He may be dead by now, Ms. Toussaint."

"Well, I have to find out. I have to go to him."

"And what do you plan on doing once you get there? Just walk right up to the gate and demand they release him?"

"I don't know yet, but I'll figure it out. I'm going to go get him," Coco said matter-of-factly. "I will get him out."

"I was hoping you'd say that." Mrs. Hughes smirked.

Over the next four days, she went over the intelligence she had gathered about Camp Sumter. Coco was attentive and pored over the notes relentlessly, keeping herself awake with cups of coffee and splashes of cold water on the face to ensure no minute was lost. The day came when Coco boarded the slave car on the train bound for Georgia. They had darkened her face with makeup to disguise her soft, feminine features, adding extra shade around the chin, and dressed her in men's clothes. She pulled a wide-brimmed hat low on her brow and walked with her head down to avoid eye contact.

Mrs. Hughes stood at a distance in the crowd to make sure there was no problem with her boarding. "God speed," she whispered to herself as she watched the manly figure disappear into the car.

It was arranged for Coco to travel by train to Columbus, Georgia, where she was met by a man posing as her owner who was to take her by wagon south into the heart of Georgia, where stood the Sumter Prison in Andersonville. Coco hardly spoke the entirety of her journey. She found it easier to stay silent, only giving short responses when the situation demanded it and just a nod when possible. Her companion, known as Peter Winslow, a man in his mid-forties, warned her of what to expect once they got there, but no warning could prepare her for what she was to see. The day they rode up to the gate of the prison, a hot June afternoon, the wafting smell of decay hung on the humid air, intensified by the cooking sun. Coco sat still with her head lowered while she listened to Peter address the man at the gate.

"Well, I don't know what the Goddamn hell. Y'alls already using five of my Negros. Alls I know is Wirz order me bring another to work on that extension y'alls so horny about getting done." He spoke with harsh irritation to the guard in question. "Did I waste my time riding him over here? Treating me like I ain't got another Goddamn thing to do. Ya want him or not?" he yelled.

Coco heard the guard reluctantly agree to take the slave for work before Peter walked back over to the wagon where she sat. She raised her eyes to him under the large hat.

"Get on down now," he ordered her. "I'll be back for ya right at sundown. I don't want to have to wait on ya, ya hear?"

Her lips pressed tightly together as she gave a swift nod, and the guard led Coco through the gate on the west side of the prison. The hum of men's voices increased as they crossed the ground and entered through the gate of a fifteen-foot stockade wall surrounding the prison. There was a pile of dead men stacked one on top the other, their eyes glazed over in their sunken, smoky, grime-smudged faces. Their long, tangled tresses were covered with flies, and the smell was horrific. Coco, following behind the guard, raised her hand to cover her nose and mouth.

Standing skeletons with starving eyes and hungry mouths watched as the two made their way toward the north ground. The prisoners stood about twenty feet away from them, forming a line like a wall, but never taking a step closer. She wondered in despair how she would ever find Mr. Kutz in the sea of dying faces. Suddenly, the smell and heat overcame her senses, and she bent over next to the wall and vomited all that was in her stomach.

"The smell will get ya, but ya will get used to it," the guard said as he stood away from her, waiting for her to finish.

She stood and wiped her mouth with her sleeve. "What keeps them from coming any closer?" she asked.

"The dead line."

"What's the dead line?"

"They take one step closer to the stockade, and them guards up there in them pigeon roosts will shoot them dead," he answered.

They continued walking until they reached the north end of the sixteen-acre prison. There, a line of mostly prisoners working on the new addition of the blockade and guarded by armed soldiers were hunkered down, shoveling at the earth. Their spines protruding upward like spikes from the ground. Coco was given a shovel and put to work with the rest of them. As she worked, she studied each of the prisoners working around her, none of which she could make out to be Mr. Kutz.

She worked steadily along with the others, no words spoken among them, until the sun began to set, when she made her way back down the dead line to the gate. Peter picked her up and took her back to the cabin, where he fed her and gave her a place to sleep. Coco lay in bed, eyes wide and staring up at the ceiling, as tears rolled down her temples and filled her ears. The next day was the same, as was the rest of the week, with the exception of new faces of prisoners working beside her. By the end of the week, despair had overcome her. She sat with Peter at the table as he dished her up some beans and bread.

"Ya haven't said much the last couple of days," he said as he handed her the plate.

"I feel so discouraged, and I'm tired. Every day I wake, thinking this could be the day that they bring him to work on the extension."

"Ya do realize there are more than twenty-seven thousand men in that prison, right? And he could very well have already been hung," he said with a sympathetic huff.

"I don't want to believe that it's impossible to find him... I look at the faces of these skeletal men, just trying so hard to make one of them look anything like him. But then I wonder if I would even recognize him if he were standing right in front of me." Involuntary tears filled her eyes. She reached up with the back of her hand and wiped at them.

"Let me see ya hands," Peter ordered. She paused before extending one of them to him. "Ya going to get an infection in that if ya not careful! Let me see the other one." He shook his head as he examined the blistered and torn flesh. "I'll put some iodine on that after ya eat and wrap it for ya."

"Thank you," Coco replied hoarsely.

She kept the wrap on her hands every day when she went back

to the prison. Another week passed, and Coco was still no closer to finding Mr. Kutz. The prison had another influx of prisoners, and by her third week undercover there, had claimed over thirty-three thousand men. She watched as they packed them tighter into the already cramped area, where the men had not even room to sit down on the swampy, black mud covered with vermin.

One hot afternoon, a bell rang out on the prison wall—a brawl had broken out among the prisoners. All the guards moved toward the fight, leaving the workers to move closer to the prison dead line to get the gossip or, better yet, a view of the fight. Coco joined them as they watched. She had been warned by Mrs. Hughes that even prisoners could be informants to gain favors from the guards, and she withheld her urge to use this as an opportunity to ask them if they knew of Mr. Kutz. Her eyes shifted frantically through the faces of the men, pinched with pain and hunger, as she moved along the line, looking for any trace of him. Suddenly, her eyes widened, unsure if her mind was playing tricks on her. The man was severely thin, like all the other prisoners, but something in his profile set Coco's heart to racing. He was some fifty men deep into the crowd, across the dead line.

"Kutz," she desperately called out in a deep tone. "Kutz," she called again, trying to project her voice over the noise of the crowd. He was getting farther and farther away from her. Frantic, she called out in her own voice as loud as she could.

Unnoticed by her, a set of eyes rested on her with a narrow glare. She called out again, this time noting the man in the crowd slowly turn his head with a frown on his face. Her heart raced and her breath caught in her chest. If she crossed the line, she could very well be shot or not be able to get back across it. Coco's feet sunk in the dark mud as she took a step forward and began pushing through the men, her eyes steadfast on the one she thought to be Mr. Kutz. She was one man separated from him when she said his name again.

His head snapped around with fiery eyes, looking over his

shoulder. She stood with shoulders square and chin upright, her hat still pulled down low over her brow. Abruptly, his eye finally settled on hers, his frowning brow a crashing wave that settled into a gentle tide. Coco's lips pressed into a tight line as she realized he recognized her before they parted to inhale a quivering breath. He took a firm step toward her and then jerked her around to face away from him, the force nearly making her lose balance. He stood close to her back, his hand still firmly gripping her bicep.

He bowed his head toward her ear. "What are you doing here?"

"Getting you out."

His grip tightened around her arm. "Are you a fool? There's no getting out. I need you to leave and not come back."

She turned her head to the side. "I'm not leaving without you. I needed to know you were still alive," she growled between gritted teeth. "Partners..." His hand left her arm, and he turned to look around them before he touched her waist. He gave it a gentle tug toward himself; she pressed back into him. In a sudden snap, she turned and looked into his worn face. "Find a way to work the line. It's where I'm at. I'm not going without you." She lightly touched his fingers as she quickly moved past him and made it back across the line.

At the line, a hand stopped her. "You cross that line, you die. They will shoot you dead!" She jerked away from the strange man, but he grabbed hold of her again. "Listen," he said, taking her with both hands. "You will die. I saw you cross over. If you try and cross back, you won't make it. You want to help your friend, you've got to be alive to do it."

Mr. Kutz was quickly on him, pushing his hands off of her and cursing. "He'll die," the man continued, not realizing Coco was a woman. "Try and get back across, he'll die." He put his hands up in the air. "They shoot first, ask questions later. But do what you want." The alarm sounded, pulling their gazes to the wall. "Go ahead," the man said with a nonchalant air.

Coco looked at Mr. Kutz. "I don't belong in here—they can't keep me in here!"

"Sure they can." The man scoffed. "What I want to know is who this guy is to you that you would come into a prison where they hate you as much as they hate us?"

"You don't have to answer him," Mr. Kutz said.

"You don't have to," the man repeated, "but if what you want is a way out, I know of one."

"You don't know shit. If you did, you'd be out yourself."

"I won't be in here long. Suit yourself, though."

Mr. Kutz took Coco by the arm and led her away from the man. He leaned in. "I wish you wouldn't have crossed the line."

"I needed to know it was you."

"I hardly recognized you," he said after a pause. "You look like a man."

"Good," she jeered.

"But I recognized your eyes," he continued, not letting her response interrupt his thoughts. "It's all I can do not to take you in my arms and weep like a babe right now." His eyes burned through her, pinning her motionless.

"What have they done to you?" she finally asked, her eyes filling with tears that she blinked away. "How long have you been in here? And how?"

"What month is this?" he asked with a scowl.

"July now."

He shook his head as he lowered it. "They captured us in May."

"How did you survive them?"

"In the battle, there was a young soldier who got shot down," he said, taking a deep breath. "He was shot down next to me and died. I knew we were about to be taken, so out of fear, I took the young soldier's coat and hat. He had no use for them—he was dead, and I was not. I thought being a prisoner of war would be better than the torture about to befall me and the end of the rope awaiting me as an informant. I was wrong."

Coco's eyes turned downward before she looked around herself, realizing she was not going back to Peter's. She began to tremble. Mr. Kutz noticed and reached up to rest his hand on her shoulder, pressing strongly with his thumb and giving a comforting stroke.

The sky darkened as the sun cast its final ribbons of gold over the horizon. Peter sat in the wagon, chewing on his tobacco with eyes fixed for that familiar figure walking toward him. A brown stream of juice left his mouth, leaving a trail on his chin hair. "Shit," he mumbled to himself.

CHAPTER TWENTY-NINE

"I NEED TO RELIEVE MYSELF," Coco said quietly as the sun was setting.

"It's across the creek. It's—it's..." Mr. Kutz couldn't even finish his thoughts but shook his head with a disgusted expression.

She didn't understand until they crossed the creek and came upon where the filth was emptied. She was horror-stricken at the regular buzz of insects in the air and the large white maggots on the ground, moving like it was alive.

"I'm to go just out here, in front of everyone?" She nearly gagged at the overbearing smell.

"Your shirt's long—just squat down. They'll think you're taking a shit and no one will bother examining otherwise." Coco lowered her head and squeezed her eyes tight and she tried to take a clean breath in. "Let's go. The sooner you do, the sooner we can get away from this."

"I can't," she choked out.

"Come on," he urged. "I'll go too."

She followed him forward. When she could stand no closer to the latrine, she quickly turned around, pulled her pants down, and squatted close to the ground. She looked at the maggots at her feet, starting to climb up over her boot. She tightly closed her eyes again, a whimper sounding in her throat as she held her vomit down. After she finished, she moved away from the latrine as quickly as she could.

Mr. Kutz took her by the arm. "Let's get to the creek. You can splash water on your face."

When they reached the water, Coco quickly lowered herself to it and raised a handful of the cool liquid to her forehead and neck. Mr. Kutz lowered himself next to her.

"My God. How have you survived this?" she asked quietly.

"Hundreds of these men die every day. If sickness or starvation doesn't get him, then that will." He motioned with his head toward the east. Coco turned her head to see three dead men hanging by their necks.

Hers eyes flashed back toward Mr. Kutz as her lips started to quiver. "How am I going to get you out of here? Can this be Hell?"

"It may very well be," he said, his sunken dark eyes looking at her with pity. "I wish you wouldn't have come…" he added, over-come, as he reached up and wiped at his eyes. "Let's find a spot to lie down before there's no spot left and we're forced to sleep standing." She looked at him hopelessly. "The northwest area is the best," he continued, a crooked smile crossing his face. He reached up and rubbed his thumb over her left eyebrow with force before bringing it down again and looking at the dark paint on his thumb. She pulled her hat lower on her brow.

"To make me look more masculine," she said as she got to her feet.

He chuckled to himself, and the two crossed the creek to find a spot for the night. "The men have no choice but to lie close," he said in her ear as they sat on the ground, "but come the witching hour, when the temperature drops, you'll be glad for a close body to offer what warmth it can." He gave her a nod. "Go ahead and lie down—put that hat over your face. I'm going to sit up for a minute, but I swear I'll stay close by you."

Coco lay down on her right side, her head resting on the bend of her arm. She cocked her hat, the brim of it down over her ear and shading half her face. She listened to the men around her talk, not closing her eyes until she was certain Mr. Kutz had lay down next to her.

The night was dark with a new moon. Coco reached up and lifted the brim of her hat from her eyes. The sleeping men around her sounded like a den of bears breathing heavily. She looked at Mr. Kutz lying on his side, facing her. Shifting her weight, she inched a little closer to him before resting her cheek on her left hand.

Coco licked her bottom lip. "Steven," she whispered in a slow, soft tone. "Steven."

His eyes slowly opened and, after adjusting to the darkness, looked at her. His finger went over his mouth, and she moved the hand from under her cheek and rested it on the ground between their faces. He slipped his fingers under hers and gently brought her hand to his lips, where he pressed it to his mouth and held it there. Coco could feel the rhythm of his breath quicken from his nose against the back of her hand. The hair on his face caused her nerves to heighten in sensitivity as he brushed his mouth back and forth, like a cub rooting its mother. She felt his lips press once again before they formed words she couldn't hear. Her eyes closed as he squeezed hold of it. When she opened them again, she saw her hand on the ground in front of her but no Mr. Kutz. She jerked up anxiously to find him sitting on the ground next to her.

"Here," he said, handing her a scrap of hard tack.

"Is that what they give you for food?"

"It was two days ago."

Coco's eyes narrowed. "Two days ago?"

"They don't feed all these men every day. You're lucky to get something every week."

"I'm not taking your bread," she snapped.

"Please."

She licked her lips but shook her head, determined to win the discussion. "Peter will not leave me in here."

Mr. Kutz looked at her questioningly. "Peter?"

"An ally."

He nodded reluctantly. "I hope so," he said, hopeful.

As the hours passed, Coco's countenance fell at no sign of Peter. A second and third day passed. Her stomach gnawed from pain, like the scraping of flesh across a thorn bush until there is no more flesh to give. She stayed close to Mr. Kutz and was distracted by the stories of the fellow prisoners as the days slowly passed. One day, word began going around that the guards were filtering through, trying to find the black man to return him to his owner. When Mr. Kutz heard this, he rushed Coco to the edge of the dead line near the stockades gate. He waved his hand in the air, trying to get the attention of the guards.

"I don't want to leave you in here," she said, turning to look at him.

"You have to." His fiery look and demanding words, leaving no room for debate, quickened her heart. When he finally got a guard's attention, he yelled, "Here's the slave you're looking for! Right here!" He pointed.

"Please stay alive," she begged, her eyes never leaving his face. "I'm coming back. I'm going to get you out... Just stay alive for me."

His eyes glistened stonily as he looked at her. "Seeing you has given me reason. I will live for you. I will stay alive for you," he repeated.

Guards began making their way toward them. "I'm going to come back to work on the wall—"

"Please don't," he interrupted, but she continued.

"Stand at the dead line every day, so I can see your face. I'll look for you." She suddenly gripped him in a hug but released him just as suddenly. Her lips parted to tell him one more thing, but she withheld from saying anymore. Coco turned to look at the guards now standing in front of them.

"Yeah, he's all right," one guard said to the other. "Go tell Mr. Winslow we think we found him. I'll need him to make a positive identification of his slave." The man did as he was ordered. "You can cross over the line there now, but I want you to stand still."

Coco crossed over and did as she was told with her head down. She could hear Peter cursing as he made his way across the yard until he was standing directly before her.

"Ya look at me," he ordered in a sharp tone. Coco raised her head, the brimmed hat still shading her eyes. "Yeah, that's my nigga, and it's about time ya found him. I've been without him for near four days now, so don't expect to get him back before four days, if I even bring him back to work at all!"

"Sir, the slave wandered off," the guard began defensively.

"Wandered off? How the hell does one just wander off when ya guarding a whole damn prison? If this is the pathetic way ya guard ya prison—"

"It's my fault, Massa," Coco interrupted in a deep tone.

"How so?"

"They be hangin' men here, and I wandered to get a closer look."

Peter didn't seem amused. "Nonetheless, I'm blaming the guards," he said before pointing at the men around him. "And I will be talking to Commander Wirz about this! This curious nigga ain't ever seen a white man hang, but I'm blaming ya for losing track of him and for four goddamn days!

"Come on," he commanded Coco. "Let's get out of this filthy, inhumane, piece of shit of a prison..." He continued spatting out curses as he walked away from the guards and toward the wagon with Coco hot on his heels. Neither said a word to each other until they reached his house, where Peter made her a meal while she cleaned herself up.

"Ya need to eat. I know ya have to be hungry," he said when she hardly touched her plate.

"I'm very hungry. I'm just finding it hard to eat when those men in there are suffering from hunger, among other unparalleled tortures."

"What those men are going through is unchristian and a festering shame to the South. It is a violation of the laws of war." There was a pause as they sat silently at the table. "War corrupts," he said, quietly fidgeting with a piece of wood he had been carving, into what he did not know.

Coco rested the next three days, but her eyes refused her sleep, as if the sun had taken hold of the night. After telling Peter about finding Mr. Kutz and her determination to continue working on the additional stockade wall, she insisted she go back, and the two calculated how they might free him. After hours of debate and deliberation, they still could not find a flaw in the prison walls or security. Despair took hold of Coco as she faltered with what hope she had left. A shifty plan was finally set in place. Peter knew it was their only shot at getting Mr. Kutz out, but he was worrisome at the likelihood of its success. The next week was used to monitor the guards and their shifts, and Coco sketched the layout of the prison, paying close attention to the watchtowers.

The day was from the furnace of Hell without so much as a cloud to soften the blazing rays of the sun. Coco entered through the gate in the wall. She had been working every day, each time finding the watchful eyes of Mr. Kutz. Today, her gaze went straight to the line and the faces of the prisoners, searching face by face for him without success. She moved a few feet away and walked with the guard to where prisoners and slaves were finishing up the wall addition. The day was getting long as Coco worked without any sign of him, and she had nearly given up as she walked toward the gate for the evening. Some of the prisoners had taken to yelling out at those arriving from outside the prison walls, and there he was, leaning on a rail near the end.

"How's the wall coming along?" Mr. Kutz called out.

"Nearly done!" she responded, holding back tears of joy. "The days are fair, but I hear it will be harsh weather on Saturday. A storm's coming." She was pushed by the guard near her to quicken her steps.

Peter waited in his usual spot when she climbed into the wagon. With a flick of the rein, they started their way back. Coco began to cry.

"Stop that," he chided. "Hold it together."

Her chin quivered as she pressed her lips tightly together. Peter was a man of few words, always speaking to the direct and literal. Coco didn't know anything of his personal life, nor did she feel the need to. It was part of the job—nothing personal, just the mission. He had a commanding sense about him and seemed well versed in warfare. As he sat at the table, his hooded eyes would glaze over in a distant glare, narrowing under his strong brow. She had caught him leaving the house at three in the morning one day when she couldn't sleep and ventured to get a glass of water. He had positioned his round brimmed hat on his head, wisps of oiled hair dancing around his ears.

"What are you doing?" she had asked. "Why aren't you asleep?"

"We never sleep," he replied, as if it were a pledge of honor and sworn oath, before pulling his hat down and walking out the door. Coco was curious about his behavior, but his authority demanded trust and soothed what fears beleaguered her.

Saturday came. The black ground was muddy, sinking a man's step and covering it with sludge. When Coco saw Mr. Kutz, she moved near him.

"Make a distraction in the south quarters late in the day," she said quickly as he trailed along the line. Her boots sunk deep in the earth and she fell forward into the mud on the line, her arms flung forward. He knelt quickly beside her, as if to help her up, and her eyes pinned his like a moth to the wall. "Make it big, then meet me at the line."

"Get back!" the guard yelled at the prisoner as he made his way to where the slave fell. "All right, get up, and start picking your damn feet up! Where'd you learn to walk?"

Mr. Kutz quickly noticed a shiny piece of steel lying in the dark mud. He stepped on it with his boot and pressed it into the mud as he stood with his hands raised. "Don't want any trouble," he said to the guard with his head lowered.

Coco got up and continued walking. "Lawd," she belted out in a deep octave, "meet me high on the east side, where I'll be workin'. Lawd, high on the east side…"

The corner of Mr. Kutz's lips pulled up into a smirk. He waited a few minutes before sitting down in the mud next to where his foot had pressed the blade into it. He felt around in the sludge until his fingers found the hard blade. After pulling it up, he held it hidden in his hand.

Mr. Kutz went south of Sweetwater Creek, where he knew he'd find six of the most notorious of the Raiders. The Raiders, as the prisoners of Camp Sumter called them, was a gang of criminal soldiers known for stealing and making random acts of bodily violence within the prison. They fueled fear among the men in the camp and thrived on their vicious acts, which they made even in broad daylight.

As the day became evening, he made his way to the man they called Burns. The men cursed at Mr. Kutz as they stared him down, threatening to kill him, but he held to his claim of having information from the guards about a group of men who were going to bring justice for the Raiders' crimes. Burns told the other men to let him move forward. Mr. Kutz told him he could point out the Regulators who were hunting and arresting them, as well as the man responsible for the seventy-five men arrested and being held outside the stockade wall, awaiting their trials.

"You know your men will be hanged, right?"

Burns's face was sunken from starvation, giving his mad eyes a similar look to those of a demon rising from Hell. "Why should

I believe what you tell me?" he asked, spittle flying from his mouth.

"What do I have to gain by telling you?" Mr. Kutz snuffed.

"What do you want?"

"Justice," he replied as he looked around himself before opening his hand, revealing the small knife.

After Mr. Kutz pointed out some of the men, he left the knife with the Raiders and started making his way toward the east side of the prison. It wasn't long before there was a disturbance behind him. His pace quickened to a near jog until he reached the dead line. The watchtower sounded the alarm as chaos was unleashed in the prison and the guards rushed to action. The prisoners and slaves working on the wall stopped, and some moved along the line to get closer to the disorder to get the gossip as others sat next to the wall.

There, shining like his lighthouse, was Coco, darkened and dirty, making her way toward him. She slid across the line, her adrenaline pushing her into precise action. Together, they hunkered to the ground in the crowd, out of view from any guard. She pulled out the black paint and popped the top on it.

"What is this?" he asked nervously.

She began rubbing his face with it, making his skin look dark. "Put it on your hands," she ordered.

"You're kidding me. This is the plan?"

She grabbed him by the shirt and gave it a jerk. "It's all we've got. Now shut up and start making yourself black."

Mr. Kutz rubbed the paint over his hands and neck. Coco pulled a crumpled hat and bandana out from her pants. She hastily tied the bandana on his head, tucking strands of hair under it, before slapping the brimmed hat on his head and pulling it low on his brow. After unbuttoning her shirt, underneath which was a second one, she handed it to him.

"Put this on," Coco ordered as she also withdrew a rolled set of suspenders from her pocket. "No one in prison has suspenders."

He buttoned the shirt and took them from her. "Peter is coming to get you after the sun sets, after the guards switch. Your ears!" She grabbed the paint and rubbed it on them. "Make sure you are on the west line, so he can find you easily."

"How is this going to work?"

"His slave has been lost in here once. Who's to say it didn't happen again? And the night guards won't know the difference between you and I from the first time."

"What of you?"

"I'll be picked up by Peter like usual. The guards switch a half hour after sundown; they won't know he already picked me up. He's going to come in angry and looking for you."

"If this doesn't work, we'll be dead tonight."

"It will work. Just keep your head down." She looked at him earnestly and saw the anxiety in his eyes. "I have to cross back over." Coco glanced over both shoulders and then back at him. "I'll see you tonight." Staying low, and looking up at the wall before moving, she cleared the line to the other side.

Mr. Kutz's heart raced as he stood, head down, and started making his way across the muddy ground. The pop of gunfire sounded in the air, making the men hunker down and look around themselves in fright. Coco jerked, startled, and looked across the line, but Mr. Kutz was no longer where she had left him. After taking a deep inhale, she moved to the stockade wall and sat down until the guard returned and got them back to work.

The sun lowered on the horizon, and Coco made her way out of the prison with the rest of the workers. There, Peter waited. She rushed to him and climbed into the wagon, giving him a confirming nod just as he moved the horses into a fast trot.

"He's ready," she said after they reached the house.

"All right, calm down," Peter instructed as he watched her pace the floor. "Ya work is done and ya did a great job. Now we will see if it works." Coco looked at him with grave eyes. "Sit down," he commanded. "I don't need that kind of nervous energy. Here…"

He poured her some whiskey. "Sip on this." She drank it in one shot. "Or shoot it," he jested, tipping his head to the side before pouring more for her and one for himself.

Peter instructed her to clean up, recline in the sitting room, and try to relax. An hour after sundown, he took hold of his hat, took another shot of whiskey, and made his way back to the prison. He pulled the wagon up to the stockade gate and waited for the guard to approach him.

"What's your business, sir?" the guard asked.

"Business? I'm here to pick up my slave!" Peter boomed.

"Slave?"

"Yes, goddamn it! I bring my slave here every day to work on that new wall of yours," he said impatiently with a wave of his hand. "Now bring him to me!"

"I don't know where your slave is, sir. There ain't no one but the prisoners."

Peter climbed down from the wagon with a threatening manner. His shoulders squared and his chest filled with air as he walked up to the guard. "Ya done lost him before and it took four days to get him back! Are you telling me ya gone and lost him again?" His lips were tight as he spoke between gritted teeth, his eyes sparking with fury.

"I don't know where ya slave is, sir. He's not here waiting on ya is all I know."

"Well, is he still through that gate?"

"I don't know, sir, but if he is, ya going to have to wait until tomorrow."

"Like hell I am! Either we both go in there together and get my property, or I'll pull Commander Wirz from his chamber to come down, and ya two can look together! I don't think he would be too pleased with that option, though."

The guard shifted on his feet. "Ya can take a look, but there ain't no guards going through the prison tonight."

"Let me in the gate," Peter growled.

The man took up his lantern and led him inside after calling out their intentions to the guard on the gate watchtower. As they walked up the dead line, the sound of squishing mud and low voices in the dark gave off an eerie sense.

"Can't see shit out here. Don't ya have some more lanterns?" Peter walked toward where men's ghastly, hollow faces were lit from the distant flickering light, like things from nightmares. He squinted as he let out a long breath and shook his head. "Any ya men see a nigga slave in there?" he called out, hoping for a response. A hum of voices with inaudible words lingered in the distance. "I'll say again, any one of ya men seen a nigga among ya?"

Peter waited a few minutes before turning toward the guard with a frown. "Ya won't get any of ya guards to get in there and find my slave?"

"Sir, there was a prison riot today, leaving five men dead, and seven more imprisoned outside this wall. I don't suspect there to be any tolerance left in our guards to go looking for ya slave."

"A riot, huh?" Peter licked and bit his lower lip. "Damn nigga is curious and has a hunger for violence. The last time he crossed the line was to see the men hang a few weeks back."

"Sounds to me like another night or two in the prison would do him good."

Peter raised his brows with a smirk as he agreed with the guard. "Well, I guess one night won't hurt nothing," he said, sucking air through his front teeth.

"Massa, Massa, is that you?" Peter's eyes lit up, and he turned around faster than he meant to. "Massa," the low voice sounded again from the darkness.

"Bring ya light over here," he requested of the guard as he leaned in and walked toward the line. The guard raised his lantern. "Yeah, that's him all right. Get on over to this side," he ordered the slave. Mr. Kutz made his way to the two men and stopped in front of them, keeping his head lowered. "Skin so black

I can't even see ya in the dark. Expect a good caning when we get back! Come on. Ya wasted enough of this guard's time."

The guard raised the lantern to the black man. Standing a few feet away from him, he surveyed him curiously before growling, "Happens again and he will become prisoner of the Confederacy, no exceptions."

"Understood. I appreciate ya letting me in the gate."

Peter and Mr. Kutz climbed into the wagon, both holding their breath until they were well down the road toward the house. Mr. Kutz looked behind them. "Holy shit," he said, letting out nervous laughter before turning back around. "I'll be damned… It worked!"

Coco paced the floor, clean and wearing a simple plaid dress. Peter had left her instructions of what to do if he did not return. It had been nearly two hours since he'd left, and her heart raced with dread. She tried sitting, but her knees bounced with nervous anticipation. When the door lock turned, she jumped to her feet, holding her breath. Peter stepped through the door, followed closely by Mr. Kutz.

She gasped. "It worked!" Mr. Kutz looked at her after he closed the door, and Coco rushed to him and embraced him. Her heart beat against his chest. "It worked!" she repeated in peals of laughter as she released him and held him at arm's length. Then turning, she embraced Peter.

He smiled at her joy. "All right, calm down. It's not over just yet. We have to be very careful over the next few days until we can get out of here. Why don't ya draw Mr. Kutz a bath while I make him a plate of food?"

Coco agreed and went to do so. Mr. Kutz ate very little, encouraged by Peter not to gorge himself and become ill. He went into the washroom and undid his shirt as Coco walked in with towels.

"I'm sorry," she apologized, startled. "I didn't know you were already in here. I brought you some towels." She observed his torso and the ribs sticking out from his chest. She hadn't realized how weak he was under his clothes.

"I must look hideous," he said, taking note of her gaze and fallen countenance.

"No." Her eyes found his again as she offered a smile. "No." She walked over and set the towels on a chair next to the tub. "A couple of good meals and we'll get you fattened right back up."

Gently, she exited the room and closed the door. After pressing her back against the wall, she tilted her face up and exhaled, tears running down the sides of her face. Coco took several deep breaths as she listened to the water in the tub as he lowered himself in. She stood for several minutes before going to the kitchen and heating more water. Once it boiled, she carried the kettle to the washroom, where she entered and stood near the door. Mr. Kutz, startled, lowered his hands to cover himself.

"I brought more hot water," she said, raising the kettle. "I figured yours had cooled off a little by now." He shifted in the tub as Coco walked up and sat on the stool beside him. She dipped her fingers in the water to check the temperature, her eyes surveying his neglected figure. Her gaze snapped back up playfully to catch his. "It's still warm."

He didn't smile. His face was gaunt and weary, and his eyes seemed sorrowful. "Am I dreaming? Or am I dead?" Mr. Kutz finally asked.

Coco's smile faded. "No," she said, gently reaching up and touching the side of his face with her palm. She then took the soap and rubbed it against the sponge and began tenderly washing his chest and shoulders. The water tinkled like bells as she dipped the sponge and raised it again to his skin. "Let me wash your back," she whispered.

Mr. Kutz sat up as she repositioned herself behind him. She sponged his shoulders with care, and then, as if another force commanded her, she traced his glistening shoulders with her fingertips. Coco leaned forward and touched her lips to his wet skin, pressing them there before moving them and kissing again. She wrapped her arms around him suddenly, pressing her cheek to his shoulder with a lamenting moan. Mr. Kutz gripped her hand to his chest, his heart beating rapidly. He jerked around, slipping and splashing water all over her, and then he grabbed her in his arms and kissed her passionately. With one arm behind her neck and the other around her waist, he pulled her tightly to himself. Coco whimpered under his kiss, overcome with emotion. After pulling away, he buried his face in her neck, and they embraced each other like the ocean does the shore.

CHAPTER THIRTY

As THE DAYS PASSED SLOWLY, Mr. Kutz rested and began healing under the close care and attention of Coco. She remained under the pretense of Peter Winslow's female slave as the two kept their cover until transportation out of Georgia could be secured. Already, the two major railways, the Western and Atlantic, and the Georgia Railroad were no longer running out of Atlanta, and word had spread that Sherman had marched his men south toward Jonesboro and was sure to destroy the Atlanta and West Point rail leaving them no choice but to travel South on horseback.

The August day was one hundred degrees with not so much as a cooling breeze. Coco stood outside on the front porch of the house, sweeping the dusty floorboards. She had little to keep herself occupied and took to enjoying what chores she could find. When she looked up, a streamline of prisoners marched not thirty feet away, under the watchful eyes of Confederate guards. Her heart raced as she gripped the broom handle. She watched the weary men trudge along, once stalwart men now wasted away to nothing but walking bones and hollow eyes. The sounds of commanding voices and iron chains rang out as they marched in silence. Coco's head dropped; she could not look at the dread. Turning on her heels, she burst in through the front door of the house, dropping the broom. She stood and took in deep breaths, her hands folded over her stomach.

"You okay?" a concerned voice asked from the across the room. She looked at Steven and rushed to where he sat. After casting herself over him, she gripped his head in her hands and kissed him fervently. "What is it?" he asked with a chuckle between her kisses, pulling her onto his lap.

"Prisoners from Camp Sumter are marching by," she said, and his countenance fell at the reminder of the prison. "I cannot bear the thought that you were part of that, and that you could very well still be."

"But I'm not," he said, shaking himself from the terror. "Thanks to you."

A moment of silence filled the room as Coco struggled to speak. "I feel wretched for those men…and their families. The war is murder and nothing else." Tears streamed down her face, as she turned her gaze down, away from him.

He reached up with his thumb and dried her cheeks. "I'll take you to a better land where there is no more war," he said, comforting her. Coco looked wantonly at him, and he leaned forward and kissed her gently. "You beguile me," he whispered against her lips.

After forcing her off his lap, he got to his feet and took her by the hand. He led her into the next room and closed the door behind them. Coco stood, nearly weak, as she watched him move toward her. He took her cheek in his hand and drew her into a passionate kiss. After a moment, he pulled away, both breathless as their foreheads remained touching. Steven began unbuttoning her dress as she shook with anticipation. Her heart raced, and she instinctively stiffened as her dress fell in a heap to her ankles. He took in her smooth, dark skin and full, round, young breast. Coco shivered, not from cold but from being exposed to a lustful eye.

Steven lifted her chin with his forefinger toward his face, and her eyes rested on his.

"You are...so beautiful," his deep voice said softly.

Her lips parted as her breath quickened and desire heightened. In a reserved manner, she reached up and started unbuttoning his shirt, exposing his chest, still not fully restored from his months in Camp Sumter. She pulled it back off of his shoulders, letting it fall to the ground. He stared steadily down on her as he reached around and traced her back with his fingertips. She stepped forward, her nipples barely touching his chest and hardening them to a point. It sent a thrill through her body as her loins began craving to feel him. She looked up into his intense gaze and pressed her breast against him as her arms brought him into a kiss.

Feeling him aroused against her heightened Coco's desire as her body yearned with unquenchable thirst, like fire. As the kiss turned passionate, she fumbled with the latch on his pants; Steven was quick to help her. After stepping out of them, he lifted her in his arms, her legs wrapping around his waist, and carried her to the bed, where he gently laid her down. Nervous hesitation overcame her for a moment as she realized what was about to happen.

Steven hovered over her, held up by his arms. Coco looked at him timidly before he lowered himself to kiss her neck and explore the tenderness of her breast. As she looked down at his hair, raven black and shiny like onyx, her fingers wove themselves through its thickness. He enjoyed the pleasures of her body, and she forgot her anxiety as her own pleasure under his leading touch guided her into ecstasy. Coco's hips began to move on their own, grinding up toward him as natural instinct took her over. He pushed back up to hover over her again, his hand lowering to touch her between the legs. Moaning at the new sensation, she gripped his biceps. His eyes, glinting brilliantly like diamonds, looked at her in a way she had never seen before. After moving his hand, he tenderly guided himself into her. Coco gripped him and pulled him toward her, humming in her throat at the weight of his body pressing on her.

His breathing quickened as his passion increased and he moved rhythmically into her. "Oh my god, Steven," she groaned. She pressed her heels into the mattress as she raised her hips to meet him. The pleasure mounted as her buttocks and stomach tightened, and suddenly a feeling she had never experienced, like a thousand lightning bolts all at once, shot through her body, leaving her weak and with the uncontrollable pulsing of her womanhood. He thrust himself harder into her, driven mad by her pleasure, as she lay limp, enjoying the heightened pleasure after her orgasm.

Steven finished and laid limply on top of her. His torso was sweaty as he breathed heavily. Coco's arms came around him, and she brushed his dark hair away from his forehead. He swallowed hard as he turned his head and set gentle kisses to the side of her face. She turned to face him, and they looked into each other's eyes. He looked at her tenderly and she felt an unusual comfort and safety in his loving gaze. Words were not needed. She ran her fingers along his temple as his breathing slowed to normal and his eyelids began to flutter closed.

Coco woke alone in bed, still naked but covered with a blanket. The door to the room was shut. She hadn't realized she had fallen asleep. She remembered Steven moving off of her but still embracing her as they lay there. She never woke when he got up. After rising and putting her dress back on, she opened the bedroom door. She heard Steven and Peter talking from the kitchen.

"So, it's best we leave as soon as possible," Peter was saying. "Will Ms. Toussaint be traveling back to New Orleans?"

"Yes," Steven replied.

"And you?"

"Chicago." Coco stood in the hall, listening, her heartbeat

caught in her chest and strangling her breath. "Where are you headed?" Steven asked.

"Virginia, until the president tells me otherwise."

There were some moments of quiet during which Coco thought she'd walk into the room, but she waited with dismay.

"I can't believe you found me," Steven said with nervous laughter, shaking his head as he sought out the words he wanted to say. "I am forever indebted to you, a debt I would be honored to pay with my life."

"And that young woman?" Peter asked. Coco's hand went up to her chest.

"Yes," Steven said, "her too."

"She is something else. Reminds me some of my sweet Joan. You know, Joan and I, we married in secret."

"Oh yeah?" Steven chuckled, and Peter nodded with a placid smile. "She's too young to get married...and I'm too old for her," Steven continued.

The other man huffed through his nose. "You didn't think she was too young a few hours ago. She's got grit, Steven. She would lay down her life for yours. A woman like that is hard to find. Remember that when you go back to your obligations."

Mr. Kutz looked down at the table. "I do love her," he offered bluntly.

Peter set his glass down hard on the table and leaned over it. "Then don't let a goddamn thing stop you. If you do, you're a damn fool and deserve to lose her."

Coco's hands were over her mouth, wetted from the tears streaming down her face. She quietly went back to her room; afraid they could hear the beat of her heart like the pounding hooves of a thousand galloping horses. She closed herself in the room and sat on the bed for a while, thinking and giggling to herself. Then she walked to the window and looked out, her heart full, until she began thinking about him returning to Chicago. Later, the door to the room slowly opened, and Steven peered in.

"You're awake," he stated, shocked.

"Yes. Just needed a little time to myself before I came out," she said as he moved to stand by her at the window.

"You okay?" He took her by the arm, and she nodded with a smile. He leaned forward and kissed her lips. "Peter is back. He has us three horses. The war is moving south, and we are in a dangerous position here. It's time for us to go." Coco nodded, but she couldn't help the tears that filled her eyes.

The three began their way South through the forsaken farm-lands of Georgia and into the wilderness of Florida before turning their course westward. It would take them weeks before they reached union-controlled Pensacola. They rested in the city a few days before Peter obtained tickets from a federal rail operation that could provide Steven and Coco a roundabout and uncertain route into Baton Rouge.

It was their last night in Pensacola and Coco knocked on Steven's door. "Come in," he said closing the door behind her. "We need to be in the lobby by…"

Coco pressed her lips against his mouth with a passionate kiss. Her sudden forwardness and the way she pressed her body against his aroused him. Eagerly leading her to the bed, he undressed her before undressing himself. Coco clung to him with longing as he pressed into her. Unable to contain her mounting passion, she moved him to lay on his back and she straddled him. Looking into his face, she pressed her hands down on his chest. Her hips rolled in a steady motion. She gripped a handful of his dark hair as she leaned forward. Steven's hands rested on her hips, encouraging her movement. "Kiss me," she breathed heavily. He leaned his head up and found her mouth, pressing his tongue deep inside it. She moaned, and forcefully kissed him back. Grabbing her around the waste, he rolled on top of her and thrust into her. He growled as he orgasmed. His chest heaving as he hovered over her. Then kissing her tenderly, he laid down next to her.

She laid with her head resting on his shoulder. Their fingers interlaced near his head. "So, I will be traveling back to New Orleans and you...back to Chicago." She drew her bottom lip between her teeth.

"Yes." His response was hardly audible.

A slight frown creased her brow as she blinked rapidly. "Will I ever see you again?"

The arm that was under her head pulled her to his chest and held her. She returned the tight embrace. "Heaven or Hell couldn't keep me from it," he said. After leaning forward, he parted her mouth with his own and slipped his tongue behind her teeth. Coco stayed the night in his room, and the next morning they made love again.

The next day the three found themselves at a train depot, ready to board. Peter reached out a hand to Coco.

"Ms. Toussaint, it has indeed been a true pleasure."

"I can't thank you enough...for everything."

"There is no time for tears, my lady," he said, noting the misty look in her eyes. "I hope to see you again, under better circumstances."

Coco shot him a cheeky grin. "No more southern accent, Mr. Winslow?"

"Oh, it comes and goes," he responded with a wink. He moved to Mr. Kutz and shook his hand. "Steven." He gave him a stern nod.

"Allan."

Then the man slapped Steven good-naturedly on the arm and turned to leave the station. Coco looked at Steven curiously. He looked at her with only a smile. The two boarded the northern-controlled train heading west. Steven let her sit next to the window, and he sat next to her. There were hardly any travelers aboard. Coco's heart skipped when he took her hand in his and held it on his lap. Their journey was quiet with neither saying much. A heavy cloud settled over them with the weight of their separate courses.

When the train finally pulled into the depot at Baton Rouge, Louisiana, the two stepped off and looked at each other. Here was where they boarded separate trains—where they said goodbye. Steven walked her to her train to ensure she boarded safely, as hers left before his. Coco could hardly look him in the eye as she became jittery.

"Thank you, Caroline. You saved my life." He cleared his throat.

"I don't want to say goodbye," she said, looking him in the eyes. The whistle blew. "Will you write me?"

"Yes."

"All aboard!" the trainman called.

"I'm afraid I'm going to lose you, like this is the last time I'm ever going to see you," she said breathlessly. The whistle blew again.

"You have to board the train," he said, taking her by the arm and walking her to the car.

Her eyes shifted back and forth. "Steven."

He looked over both shoulders, and then, grabbing her around the waist, he bent her backward in his arms and kissed her. "Get on the train," he said, releasing her.

Coco mounted the step and turned to look down at him as the whistle blew its final call. "Steven," she said again as she leaned forward, where he met her for one last kiss.

The gears clicked as the stack hissed out a cloud of steam. She ascended the steps and bustled to a window seat near where he stood outside the train. Swallowing hard, she pressed her hand against the glass and gave him a smile. His hand came up in a wave. The train kicked forward and began moving down the tracks, it's clanking sending a lonely cry down the track. Coco sat back and wiped at her wet cheeks.

As she approached the Toussaint plantation, the longing for home and seeing her father's face seized her. The lands of Louisiana looked different. Field after field was desolate, overgrown from years of being forsaken. It was the first of November when she arrived. Albert and Foy were walking through the yard toward the house, a rifle kicked over Albert's shoulder and a dead rabbit in his hand. The carriage came to a stop, and Coco got out and thanked the driver, who then pulled away. Albert frowned at the distant sight of someone coming to his house, but as he got closer and realized it was his daughter, he dropped the rifle and rabbit and rushed toward her.

Coco ran to her father and jumped up into his arms, both crying. She was pleased later to learn that Liza had stayed at the plantation with her son, Asa. That evening was a feast of rabbit, cornbread, and grits as the four laughed and enjoyed each other's company. Coco's countenance fell only once, when Liza asked about what she had done and where she had gone while she was away. Coco wouldn't talk about it, and Foy was quick to change the subject when he noticed her anxiety and sorrow. He was always good for making a lighthearted conversation in his old age, and soon the room was laughing again.

A few weeks later, she found an outdated newspaper in her father's office and read about how Atlanta had fallen to the Union, and how the Federal troops marched south, pillaging abandoned homes and the land as they went. Her heart raced as she realized how timely their exit from Georgia had been. She put down the paper and never picked up another until the war ended.

Coco maintained correspondence with Steven. The letters were only monthly or so but held dear and kept in a wooden box lined with velvet. After the war ended in April 1865, she opened a letter from Steven, addressed from Pinkerton National Detective Agency. It was a formal letter holding no sentiment but expressing the thanks and value of her assistance in aiding with missions that helped secure the victory of the Union. Inserted in the letter was a check from the agency, written out to Caroline Toussaint, in the amount of seven thousand dollars.

Her mouth dropped open as her hand covered it. Once the

reality set in after she read the letter a second time, she let out a squeal and jumped up and down. She looked in disbelief at the check again: Caroline Toussaint, $7000, signed Allan J. Pinkerton. She pressed her lips together as she hugged the letter and looked up at the sky. It began sprinkling rain, but Coco welcomed the cool drops.

June 6, 1865

My Darling Steven,

I hope my last letter found you well. I hold close every word you send me and imagine the day I can see you again. I understand you have a pressing issue that is keeping you in Chicago, far from the bayous of Louisiana and far from me. I urge you to settle your matters quickly, for I am sick for you. Can you not share with me the business that has you so grave? It is very concerning to me that you have not yet responded to my last letter. Share with me, if you will, my love, so my treacherous imagination stops toying with me.

In matters of my world, I have decided to buy a house and am using much of what I was paid by Mr. Pinkerton as a deposit. I found one in New Orleans; it is a riverfront property on Saint Charles Street. It is a darling house, though not large nor grander than Mrs. O'Neill's (give your dear sister my loving regards), but it is quaint and suits me. It is the soft, golden colors of daisy with white-trimmed windows, just like the flower. It is three stories with a perfect back yard for my garden oasis. I will be happy there. It is large enough, in time, to house my father as well, if he does indeed go through with selling the plantation.

I miss you, Steven. I'm afraid, if this letter is intercepted, I will be embarrassed to death, as I know I will write you the innermost longings of my heart. I dream often, of the feeling of you on me or the taste of your sweet kiss, and I wake craving you. When I hear your voice in my head or imagine I see your face in a crowd, my body responds to the longing that leaps from my heart. I blush to tell you that, but you would not notice, as it seems rose is the color of my cheeks every day now. Please tell me I have not lost you, as was my fear when I kissed you goodbye. Where are you? Come back to me. My heart is yours and ever always will be.

Yours truly,

Coco

~New Orleans, 1917~

The streets were hot on the July summer day, sending the smell of hot rubber into the air. Car horns beeped along with the sound of trumpets lofting through the old streets, like the fire of romance in the eyes of old lovers. The city was alive.

Mr. Long, dressed in a gray suit with a pocket hanky that matched his tie, darted across the busy street. His hair was parted in the middle and greased down on the side, and he carried a cross-body leather pouch that held his paper pad and extra pencils. He pushed up his round spectacles as he stepped through the doors and into the lobby of one of New Orleans's most popular nightclubs. The bell on the door rang, and an attractive young woman walked into the lobby from a closed room. Her dress was red like her lips, pairing well with her raven-black hair that shined like onyx.

"Hello," she greeted him. "The club doesn't open until six. Is there something I can help you with?"

Mr. Long's eyebrows twitched. "I'm here for the interview."

"Oh, you must be Mr. Long!" she said with a high-pitched, welcoming tone. "Yes, she is expecting you. Follow me. I'll show you to her."

He thanked her with a nod and followed her through the inner club doors. The room was large with grand chandeliers hanging from high ceilings. Round tables with white tablecloths were strategically placed with two red roses adorning each table as a centerpiece. Toward the center of the room, round couches of red velvet curved around one side of the tables. Toward the stage was an empty, well-polished hardwood floor that allowed for the club attendees to dance if so desired.

"Here she is," the young woman said. "This is Mr. Long. He is here for the interview."

"Hello," the old woman said with a smile. She was seated on the cushioned side of the table, and she raised her hand to gesture across from her. "Mr. Long, please sit down."

"Thank you, Mrs.—uh," he said, taking a seat.

"Please call me Coco. Everybody else does."

"Ms. Coco." He nodded with a smile, and then he opened his leather bag and pulled out his pad and pencil. After dabbing the tip of the lead against his tongue, he adjusted his suit coat and extended his arms to give himself more room in his sleeves. The old woman watched him with an amused smile. "This is a splendid club."

"Thank you."

"I personally have never attended but have friends who come here often. They all sing your praise," he said.

She pressed her lips into a smile. "Oh now," she said, flattered.

"This is the twenty-fifth year you've been open! It's a big year for your club!"

"Yes. Yes, it is. Though I try to stay humble, I must admit I am quite proud right now." Her old eyes sparkled.

"Indeed, as you should be," he said, returning her smile. "Tell me a little about when you first opened the club." He readied himself to take notes.

"I opened the club in 1892, and you know, I don't even remember what caused that harebrained idea." She gave a throaty laugh behind closed lips. "I was young and had experienced so much life by that time. I just remember the joy I had when I signed the paper—what fun I had remodeling and decorating the inside!" She extended her arms before her and fanned them around. "It's been remodeled since, but I'll never forget those first feelings. It was like falling in love for the first time.

"I had a few shows here and there—some new acts that would entertain my guests. But it was the spring of 1895, when I first met Buddy Bolden, that I said to myself, 'Now there's a sound I can get behind.' I gave him his first gig! He and the other boys in the band were eager and would play here every week. People loved him! I've had other artists like Jelly Roll Morton come in and make the crowds go wild, but it was Buddy that changed the course of the tune in the music for my club here." She laughed with a smile. "And now people love those tunes! They got a whole new name for that style now—jazz, they call it... Yeah, isn't that something? So now," she said, widening her glistening eyes, "I'm called a jazz club." She giggled, causing Mr. Long to grin.

"That's great," he said, writing down the names on his pad. "I'm told you are having a great jazz weekend event that you're selling tickets for."

"Yes, that's right," she interrupted kindly, "and we're sold out!"

Mr. Long's eyes widened. "Oh! Already sold out!" His pencil scratched on the pad. "It's a charitable event, I'm told, to support our men going into the war."

"Uh huh," she hummed in her throat, "that's right. Every penny. And we're having some special auctions those nights too."

"Wow."

"Yes." She repeatedly nodded her head. "War is cruel. Every penny to our men headed overseas, and to the nurses too! Those women...they give of themselves as much as our boys do, and few people thank them for it. It's hard. I should know."

"And how's that?" he asked, looking up from his writing.

"Why, don't you know?" she asked, and Mr. Long's shook his head. "Well, I served in the Civil War."

"Is that a fact?" His eyes lit up, as if he'd found the cherry on the sundae. She nodded. "How do you feel about this war? Since you've seen what war is."

"Well, this one is farther from home... But the world is getting smaller."

"Some people say it's not our war."

"We have a duty, not just as Americans but also as humans, to uphold the rights and sovereignty of human life and justice. And when called upon to help, what kind of race would we be to turn our back on injustices upon the poor, the weak, or just anybody?" Her head tipped as her hand raised in the air.

"So, you are in favor of the war?"

"It is not something to be in favor of! You never wish for it! But you don't shrink away from it, neither. War is not romantic. It is not glorious, nor fanciful. War does something to a man. You see things that really violate all sense of decency—moments that haunt men for the rest of their lives." She paused, reflecting.

"Well, it's a wonderful thing you are doing for the troops! Just wonderful," he repeated. "I know it is greatly appreciated."

"If only there was more I could do." She raised her brows and cast him a cheeky grin. "But I'm no longer young, and my days of doing more is near over. But I do what I can and am happy to do so."

"Could you tell me more about your life? Where you were born and raised? More about the war of the states perhaps?"

Coco laughed, but when she saw Mr. Long's face and, under his persistent urging, her eyes narrowed in distant thought. She heard Franny's lighthearted laughter ring out and Nan's song coming from the kitchen. Nathan's smile shone through her reflections, and Foy, sweet ol' Foy was there, walking through the fields, rifle cocked on his shoulder. Feeling the sticky heat of long past summers, her hand reached up and gently touched the locket around her neck. Coco inhaled deeply, finding again the sweet mixture of tobacco and the tangy smell of the earth that was her father. Her heart began to race.

"Well, Mr. Long," she said, "it's not an easy tale full of happy endings. If I share with you, and I will share with you, I'll have to take you back to the beginning...to the very beginning." Her eyes glinted with joy, the kind of joy mixed with tears one would have at a wedding. Hours passed, with Mr. Long forgetting his pencil under the lively characters and scenes she painted for him. He sat, lost in her words.

"Grandma." The voice of the young woman who had met him at the door broke through his trance. "I'm sorry to interrupt. It's time for us to go to dinner." She took Coco by the arm and helped her out of the booth.

Mr. Long apologized. "Oh, of course. I got caught up and so enthralled, Ms. Coco, that I lost track of time."

"Oh, it's all right. I enjoy reminiscing once in a while." The young woman kept hold of Coco's arm as they slowly walked out of the room.

"I thank you for your time, and I'm eager to find out how well your auction goes! Please, make sure to pick up this Sunday's paper. I will make sure you are on the front cover," he said flirtatiously, making Coco laugh.

"Thank you," the young woman said. "You know your way out, Mr. Long?"

"Yes, yes, I'm fine." He watched them go but added at the last moment, "Ms. Coco..." They stopped and she turned to look at him. "Did you get back with Steven Kutz?"

Coco smiled. "Mr. Long, I'll save that for our next time together." With that, she turned and walked away.

He lingered a moment, looking around before he tapped his paper pad on the back of the chair and grinned. As Mr. Long left the club with a keen step, he looked up at the sign above the entrance. "*Coco's.*" He smiled. He had his story.

THE END

ACKNOWLEDGMENTS

A very special thanks to a person who brought me comfort and encouragement during the very difficult journey of writing this book. Jerry Jacob, thank you! You believed in me from nearly the beginning and was the force behind me, pushing me when I felt as if I couldn't go any farther. Even though you were miles aways from me, you were right there with me every step of the way sending me funny GIF's or supportive meme's, or just your own words filling me with courage and strength of purpose. You made this journey very special with all your witty "Coco" gifts, cards, and adventures. This book is as much yours as it is mine. Thank you for being a part of my journey, and for making me feel greater than what I am. You mean the world to me! xx

To Dan Cobb...where do I even begin! The first time we met and you learned that I was a writer, you supported me. Any time I need honest feed back, you are always there and ready to pour into me a different perspective, thoughts of wisdom, and multiple glasses of the best wine! You never make me feel like I'm intruding upon your time, which I know is very valuable. You spent hours proofing my first edit, and you held nothing back. Thank you! Your friendship is very dear to me!

To my family. Thank you for believing in my dreams. To Mama: I love how you get so enthralled in the adventure when I read you tidbits from my stories, and you look at me with tears in your eyes and say 'Oh honey, that's good. I feel like I'm in it'. Thank you for being mine. I just love you so much! To Colleen: When we were young, you always came down into the study and sat on my lap to read what I was writing. You've always believed in me. I will never forget that little unicorn plaque you gave me, "Climb high, climb far, your goal the sky, your aim the stars".

To all my friends and coworkers, thank you for listening to me ramble on and on about my trials and victories as a writer. Thank you for being a part of my 'getting there': Robyn, Cami, Cameron, Jessica, Emily, J Teaver thank you for always telling me I'm going to be famous one day. Alex Patsioukov, thank you for being excited with me at every dance lesson and getting goose bumps when we talk about my plans! Michelle, Sarah, Lacy and Ryan, Yelana, Brad, Barth and Vanover, and all my other dear friends that I love! To Bobby, for telling me that I needed to visit New Orleans. For saying, "It's seedy, but perfect for imaginative people like you." You were right, and it inspired me. ...next New York City, since you think it, too, would suite me. Thanks, friends, for always encouraging me, believing in me, and just loving me.

ABOUT THE AUTHOR

Visit Jennifer online
www.jenniferspurgeon.com
Jennifer@jenniferspurgeon.com

Made in the USA
Columbia, SC
25 June 2021